# STORMS FROM A CLEAR SKY

DENISE FRISINO

BH
bookhouse
PUBLISHING

bookhouse
PUBLISHING

2950 Newmarket St., Suite 101-358 | Bellingham, WA 98226
Ph: 206.226.3588 | www.bookhouserules.com

Details by Denise
Copyright © 2020 by Denise Frisino

10 9 8 7 6 5 4 3 2 1

Printed in the United States of America

Library of Congress Control Number: 2020914049

ISBN: 978-1-7349282-0-4 (Paperback)
ISBN: 978-1-7349282-1-1 (eBook)

*Editor: Lori Hinton*
*Cover designer: Laura Zugzda*
*Book designers: Melissa Vail Coffman and Julie Mattern*

*For my husband, Steve, who through the writing of my books, has been my rock. Thank you for reading the research along with me, for stepping over my stacks of files, piles of books and photos to bring me refreshments and encouragement, sometimes in the form of a sweet kiss.*

# ACKNOWLEDGMENTS

I N 2012, MY JOURNEY BEGAN WITH one interview: that of Captain Richard B. McNees, Sr., US Navy, RT. After our many riveting conversations, there was no turning back.

Since that time, I have chased down men and women wearing WWII caps in grocery stores, on ferries, at American Legion Posts, in nursing homes, virtually anywhere I might find these remarkable champions of our freedom. The dye for my story continues to be cast from the memories of those who lived through WWII. Some braved everything to return home from the European or Pacific theaters. Others supported our troops Stateside in any manner they could. Yet all whom I had the honor of speaking with, colored my characters with their private moments.

Sadly, McNees, along with so many of those I mention below, are no longer with us. Yet their stories must continue to be told and their contributions honored. The most remarkable aspect they all exhibited was their humbleness, brushing aside the scars from bullets and battles, claiming their efforts as their duty.

Along with those I mentioned in my preceding book, *Orchids of War*, I need to mention the next round of heroes who shared their hearts and experiences with me.

A special thanks to Dwight Stevens, who I leaned on several times for his incredible memory of his 33 sorties as he piloted his B-17 over France, Germany and Russia. And to Bob Harman, who not only served with Patton during the Battle of the Bulge, but is admired by many as

Professor of History, Emeritus, Seattle University. Hats off to Bob, who gave me several hours of his precious time.

Thank you to Lieutenant Cornel Albert Barron, US Army, RT, one of the first at Dachau; John Burbank, US Navy Seabee on Okinawa; Barbara Bradshaw; Catherine "Sis" Burke and her brother Mike Hobie; Amos Chapman, US Navy, RT, who served in the Pacific; Evelyn Choen, US Coast Guard SPAR, RT; Tom Cope, US Army, RT, who served mostly in the Philippines; Jack Hare, MP in Europe; Harry Faust, US Army, RT, who was shot twice in Europe; Alice Finch, child POW in the Philippines; George Forbes, Merchant Marine delivering goods to the shores of Europe; Jack Hare, MP, 14th Armored Division; Jack Holder, who served as Flight Captain on PBYs in both theaters; Keith Johnson, 9th Army Air Corps, radar technician in Europe; Patsy Love; James Lumsden, US Army Signal Corps in Alaska; Charles Lewis, a B-25 pilot who flew 42 missions in the Pacific; the remarkable Barney McCallum, US Navy, RT who landed on Okinawa; the incomparable Joe Mehelich, "Artillery Joe" to those who served with him in Africa and Europe; Jim Merich, 2nd Lieutenant, flight engineer on B-29's in the Pacific; Mike Meshii, who in the 7th grade began his military training for the Imperial Japanese Army; Chuck McGuire, US Army, RT, who served as a demolition specialist with the "Bastard Battalion," the 187th Engineers; the gracious Yaeko Nakano; Goro Niishimura, US Army, RT, who served in Europe with the 442nd Infantry; George Park, US Navy, RT, Quartermaster, who survived the kamikaze bombing on the *USS Bunker Hill*; Dave Phillips, a weatherman in the US Navy; J.W. Roundhill, who shared a pot of tea as he told of his experiences as a gunner out of England; Merlin Staatz, who served with the 43rd Infantry in the Pacific; "Wild Man" 1st Lieutenant Ray Swalley, US Marines, a pilot who flew with the "Blue Devils" and also survived the kamikaze attacked on his ship the *USS Bunker Hill*; Edward Shepard, US Navy, who survived the sinking of the *USS Helena* and lived to be 101 years old.

A salute to Lieutenant Commander Phil Johnson USCG, Retired, for his consultation and additional editing.

Thank you to my beloved God Mother, First Lieutenant Mary Russel, US Army, who nursed many wounded in tents across Europe.

Patton always promised her a hospital, but she never got one, even in the freezing winter of the Battle of the Bulge. Rest in Peace.

Thank you to Gerald (Jerry) Robinson, founder of Robinson Newspapers, for an enlightening afternoon in the warm sun while he reminisced about Seattle and the impact of WWII.

# PROLOGUE

HE IS GONE. JACK HUNTINGTON, the sinister man with the patch over one eye, who, for months, openly shadowed Billi O'Shaughnessy's every move, intimidating her to help him, dragging her into danger, forcing her to depend on secret hiding places and alternate identities for survival, is gone.

That arrogant bastard just walked out the door. But not before taking her willingly to his bed, and then to the altar.

Just before heading down the concrete steps, Jack glanced back at her. The mist from his warm breath hitting the cold December air did not conceal his steely look of hatred. Billi likened his intensity to a raging, fire breathing dragon bent on revenge. A chill spiraled down her spine with the clear knowledge that the next time Jack Huntington encountered Akio Sumiyoshi of the Imperial Japanese Navy, one of them would die.

# ONE

BILLI O'SHAUGHNESSY HUNTINGTON STOOD LIMPLY LOOKING out
the tall window of her mother's home at the empty street of 30th
Ave South. It was just after 1 p.m. Piles of melting snow still lined the
road. On the other side of the street, a snowman, built by the neighbor's
children, glistened in the cool sun. The hat perched on their frozen
creation slumped down hiding one large black button eye. The other
button seemed to glare back at her, reminding her of her new husband,
Jack Huntington, the elusive FBI agent with one good eye. How startling to look out this very window and not see his dark car occupying
the accustomed spot under the oak tree. For months he had made an
obvious point of parking there in order to watch her, at first to convince
her to help him with his scheme then, ultimately, to protect her.

She felt the weight of Jack's black onyx ring with the diamond in
the middle slip to one side of her wedding ring finger. The new object
carried with it their promise to love and cherish each other, words spoken boldly that morning in St. Mary's Church before a small gathering.
Her divorced parents had held hands as her mother shed a tear. Her best
friend, Eileen Nakamura, was accompanied by her father and brother,
Kenny. They sat with the other two most important people in Billi's
life, the Gunner siblings, Danny and Dahlia. She had noticed Danny
protectively put his arm around his sister Dahlia, whose sad, misty eyes
spoke of her continued love for the unfaithful Eddy and the wedding
she would never experience.

The thought of her only brother, Edward O'Shaughnessy, made her stomach flip. The startling news of Pearl Harbor erupted during their wedding celebration brunch. Their beautiful new beginning had crumbled before them with the devastating news she and Jack had worked so hard to forestall. As promised, the very words she had overheard Akio announce to his men in the Forbidden City Night Club in San Francisco had come to pass. "Christmas will bring these shores unimaginable presents." Indeed, the Japanese present, the bombing of Pearl Harbor, triggered terror around the world.

Billi jumped at the sound of a loud bang. Turning back toward the living room she watched Danny pound on the top of the tall mahogany radio, his anger and dread spilling into the room. At the teenager's outburst Pepper, her courageous guard dog, began circling at the foot her mother's large chair before lying down in confusion. His long Dachshund ears flopping as he looked around the room at the remaining celebrants who sat listening intently with mounting dread.

"Goddamn the Japs," Danny shouted above the voices on the radio.

The occupants in the room all looked startled at the vehemence of the youth's words.

Mrs. O'Shaughnessy sat upright in her large rocker prominently placed next to the fireplace. "Danny, don't take the Lord's name in vain. Especially on a Sunday."

"Sorry, Mrs. O." He forced a semi-apologetic smile her way.

In response, the older woman's shoulders raised and lowered in what Billi recognized as her mother's non-verbal expression of confusion. The earth shaking events of the last few hours must be hard for her mother to grasp. Just this morning Billi had announced, no insisted, she would immediately marry Jack. Then, hours after the rushed wedding came the blaring news of war, with the attack on the Pacific Island of Oahu, where Eddy's squadron stationed at Kane'ohe, were directly in the line of battle.

Aware the Japanese plot to conquer the Pacific and spread their control into the United States crept into motion almost one year earlier, Billi's heart ached not only for her parents but those parents whose sons perished in the early morning hours defending America. She hated the dark, frightening secrets she had come to know from her time spent working with Jack. Posing as "Ginger the Vamp," had only unlocked doors to the horror and greed dragging the world into an unwanted war.

She crossed the room, scooped up her beloved pup, putting one hand on Danny's young shoulder. She could feel his tension and anxiety as she watched tears stream down his face. He had so wanted to follow her brother Eddy into service. Yet, as a senior at Garfield High School, and a member of the Army National Guard, his duties lay elsewhere.

Mrs. O turned and looked up at her daughter with unmasked strain. "Have they said anything yet about Kane'ohe Naval Base?"

Billi worked the lump in her throat to create a passageway for her answer. "I haven't heard anything, Mom. But Eddy is fine." She wished she believed her own words.

Her father inched closer to his estranged wife and knelt, grasping her hand. "Now Gertie, darlin', Edward will be killin' those Japs like nobody else." His Irish brogue strengthened with determination as he repeated the promise he and Eddy exchanged at the train station so many months ago. "Head down an' heart up. That's how you'll survive." He patted her hand as if the mere action solidified a pact with God. "He'll come home safe to us."

The numbers of those killed that early Sunday morning of December 7th, 1941, continued to mount as the radio announcers scratched together the events unfolding in the beautiful islands of Hawaii.

Dahlia covered her eyes as she bent forward, her blond curls bouncing with the heaving of her shoulders. It was evident to all that Eddy remained the love of her life, a life that had been spent in each other's company since childhood. Even though Eddy had recently professed his love for someone named Lani, an exotic island beauty where he now lived, color still rose to Dahlia's cheeks at the sound of his name.

"Don't worry, Sis. Nobody stands a chance against the likes of Eddy. Those . . ." Danny shifted under Mrs. O's glare before continuing, "They don't stand a chance."

Billi watched the group wondering at their future. Since the beginning of last June, so much change had bumped into their lives. They had called themselves the 'Gang of Five': Billi, Raymond, Eddy, Dahlia and young Danny, their tag-along chaperone. But when Raymond

Richardson, her fiancée, unexpectedly died testing a new plane for the Army Air Corps, the security of their beautiful world shattered. Then Jack stepped through the cracks into their lives bringing with him suspicion, fear and hatred. Until today. It all seemed so impossible.

"And now we take you to Honolulu." The announcer's voice caught the attention of those in the room as they waited, their eyes now riveted on the old Lexington Superheterodyne. They were lucky to still have the large polished radio. It remained the only good piece of furniture that had lasted through her father's many business ventures. Her mother took the radio, along with the children, when they parted ways so many years ago.

Billi focused on the emblem, "Made in the United States of America" just below the round speaker portal hoping one of the old tubes did not blow before the excited voice hurriedly let loose the latest updates.

"Hello NBC. This is KGU in Honolulu, Hawaii. I am speaking from the roof of the Advertising Publishing Company building. We have witnessed this morning the distant view of the battle of Pearl Harbor and the severe bombing of Pearl Harbor by enemy planes, undoubtedly, Japanese. The city of Honolulu has also been attacked and considerable damage done. This battle has been going on for nearly three hours. This is no joke. This is real war. We cannot estimate yet how much damage has been done but it has been a very severe attack. The Navy and Army appear now to have the air and the sea under control . . ."

A woman's voice broke into the announcement, "Just a minute, may I interrupt for a second please. This is the telephone company. This is the operator."

"Yes," The man's voice remained calm.

"We're trying to get through on an emergency call."

"But we're talking to New York, ma'am." The flabbergasted reporter responded.

The air waves emitted static before a different announcer's voice took control of the situation, "Just a moment please."

"They've lost contact with Hawaii." Dahlia whispered.

Billi watched as her mother's grasp tightened on her father's hand, their bond strengthening with the disaster now facing every American with servicemen in Hawaii. She felt her knees buckle at the weight of this reality. Letting a wiggling Pepper free, she sank down on the couch next to the sobbing Dahlia.

The pounding at the door startled them out of their trance and Pepper, with his piercing bark, charged out of the room toward the foyer.

Billi hurried behind her fierce little beast, adjusting her blue chiffon wedding dress. Jack must have left something. She felt her heart lighten, remembering the warmth of his touch and all he had taught her about lovemaking the night before their marriage.

As she passed through the large wooden pocket door toward the entry, she tried not to show her disappointment at the small figure that banged heavily, rattling the glass.

She hurried to open the door before his determination took its toll. "Hello, Victor."

"Hey, Billi." The puffs of his breath as he spoke signified the chill in the air. "Mom wants to know where Pearl Harbor is. She's real upset. Won't stop crying. She said you would know."

"Come in." Billi held the door wide, then waited as the youngster stomped in then respectfully removed his heavy snow boots.

Victor meekly followed Billi into the living room to wait for Mrs. O'Shaughnessy to answer his mother's question. Mrs. O, the block captain, knew everything, or at least that assumption spread through the neighborhood. Sometimes, that "everything" evolved into more than the neighbors wanted her to know.

"Come with me," Billi instructed the youngster when her mother seemed unable to comprehend the question. Of course, Billi realized, many people would not know where to find Pearl Harbor in the vast outside world. Until today, it was of no consequence, unless you knew someone stationed in paradise.

She lifted the multi-colored world globe from its stand and put it on the dining room table. This ball of a map emerged as a vital part of their existence when first Raymond, then Eddy, had enlisted.

She noticed Victor's eyes rest beyond the globe on a stack of untouched schnecken, her mother's famous sticky cinnamon buns encrusted with walnuts. "Go ahead," she encouraged him, "help yourself."

Someone should be enjoying their partially consumed wedding feast. Billi regarded the table where the half-drunk crystal glasses of champagne, recently raised in toasts of good fortune, remained a testament to the startling impact of the news of Japan's attack.

She spun the globe waiting for Victor to choose a delicacy.

"We are here." Her finger marked Seattle, Washington, on the green landmass of North America. Then her finger moved across the blue representing the Pacific Ocean to land on a speck of a green island that sat among four other islands surrounded by lots of little dots. "This is the island of Oahu, where the Navy base of Pearl Harbor is located."

"That's far away." His statement sounded reasonable, even though a bit muffled as he swallowed the gooey dough. "Why is everyone so upset? How would the Japanese find us here?"

Billi almost dropped the globe, remembering the conversations between the Japanese spies she had overheard in the Forbidden City Night Club in San Francisco. She saw the image of the fan with the three Watatsumi, the Dragon Sea Gods, hiding the details of a new Japanese weapon. She began to tremble, the large orb shimmying with her fear.

"Hey." Victor's voice finally broke into her thoughts. "Isn't Eileen a Jap and her brother Kenny?"

She looked into his young eyes squinting with hatred for the enemy who had just plunged American into a war it never wanted. How could she explain something she herself did not understand? The Japanese Imperial Governments Special Envoy Kurusu arrived in Washington D.C. on November 15th, bringing renewed hope to the US. Across the country the isolationist believed that along with Ambassador Admiral Nomura, the two Japanese diplomats could convince the Land of the Rising Sun to build a compromise with America. Through the efforts of United States Secretary of State, Cordell Hull, a meeting had been arranged with President Roosevelt to garner such a deal for peace. Then on Wednesday, November 26th, 1941, Hull conveyed President Roosevelt's demands to the Emperor's ambassadors to relay back to Japan. Americans clung to this exchange as an opening for peace.

She could not imagine how to explain the Nippon lies and deceit. Over the last eleven days Emperor Hirohito and Prime Minister Tōjō Hideki had stalled for time so they could send their ships from Japan across the vast ocean for this early morning attack on Pearl Harbor.

"No. Eileen and Kenny are American, just like you and me," Billi spoke her words with conviction as if not only answering Victor but shoring up her own misgivings.

Victor popped the remaining piece of his delicacy into his mouth then eyed her suspiciously as he chewed. She realized at that instant that those who did not already hold the American Japanese as friends would now view them only as the dangerous enemy. Furthermore, they made an easy target as few had strayed from what was known as Japantown, just a few blocks away. And, compounding the situation, there were those who refused to learn or speak English, depending on the younger generation to be their interpreters as they moved through their lives in this new country.

She encountered these facts personally while overcoming the language barrier and immersing herself in the Japanese way. Her gift for the Nippon language and culture recently plummeted her into danger, binding her to Jack.

As she lifted the globe back into its stand, she paused to observe how peaceful the world looked in the blues and greens of the sphere she held.

She turned to face Victor smiling at the dusting of sugar glaze clinging to his upper lip. Danny strode past the younger child, giving him a playful swat on the shoulder, before reaching for his deserted cup of coffee. Their friendly interchange continued when suddenly Billi felt her stomach lurch. Such youth, such beauty. How would this war affect these two young men?

Her gut-wrenching sensation mirrored her reaction from a few months ago. On October 27th, 1941, General Tōjō Hideki surprised the world by adding the title of Prime Minister of Japan to his role as leader of the Imperial Rule Assistance Association. At that moment Billi knew the world had changed for the worse. Tōjō's propaganda to expand the Greater East Asia Co-Prosperity Sphere, extending their empire beyond China throughout the Indian Ocean toward Australia, projected a tone for success through ultra-nationalist militant ways. There was no room for the human spirit, only the strict obedience to the wishes of their emperor, Hirohito, seen as their God. An emperor secreted away in his castles, far removed for his subjects, whose view of the world arrived on the lips of treacherous individuals such as Tōjō.

Her mind flicked to the dark alley in San Francisco when, posing undercover as the wayward Ginger, her identity and ability to understand Japanese became apparent to Akio, the spy. Her knees weakened at the memory of the look in his black eyes, lust mixed with rage. He would show her no mercy, as the Nippon soldiers would show no mercy to any captive.

She fought back her tears and began to pray. She prayed for those who had lost their lives this morning, hoping her brother was not among them. She prayed for Jack and those she knew would rally to fight for the United States. She pleaded with God that this new conflict would end quickly so that the youth of America, like the two young boys who innocently stood before her, would not have to endure the horrors of battle at the hands of the military machines like Akio.

Straightening, Billi mustered up a smile for Victor and Danny. She could not sit back and wait. She would find a way to utilize her unique abilities with the Japanese language and knowledge of their culture to help halt the spreading war that she and Jack could not expose in time to prevent this morning's surprise attack. Filled with the vigor of the call to duty she hurried past the two young men. No one could know of her intent, especially her new husband.

THE FREEZING WIND SWEPT across Jack's face, bringing with it an icy rain that struck his bare flesh with stinging force. He blinked at the slight thud of a frozen pellet bouncing off the patch over his right eye. Most of the snow had melted away. Only the crests of the hills held the reminder of the white storm which camouflaged Akio's escape as his small boat slipped beneath the twirling crystal flakes on Dyes Inlet two days ago. The sound of the small motor retreating under the cover of the white blanket still buzzed through Jack's mind, reverberating defeat. He hoped Akio had bled to death from the knife driven deeper into his assailants' shoulder as they struggled, tumbling down the slick slope to the water's edge. Jack now understood the path of Akio's escape. His blood ran cold with the knowledge that Mr. O'Shaughnessy's home on Erlands Point lay on the other side of a small jetty of land, easily accessible by boat from this very spot on Bainbridge Island.

Jack leaned back under the cover of the long veranda that wrapped around the elegant house on the crest of the hill off Crystal Springs Drive. He had seen enough. This side of the island provided perfect viewing for all ship traffic passing to and from Bremerton Naval Base. Furthermore, the extremely convenient short distance by water to Dyes Inlet gnawed at his growing frustration.

A rap on the window from his assistant, Niles Duckworth, drew his attention. The look on Duckworth's face through the glass expressed the importance of his discovery. Jack stepped across the wide porch and inside. From almost every point in the deep-hued wood paneled living room, the view of the driving rain hitting the water provided a constant reminder of the ease with which the spies watched their prey. On a clear day, the view would be limitless.

"The closets showed little sign of anyone living here." Duckworth kept his voice low, controlled. "They must have known we'd come here fast."

Jack nodded then walked further into the room. The brick fireplace sat across from the windows. It would have been so easy to stand here in this dim room, with the dark wood floor to ceiling, and not be seen. If the large, wrap-around covered veranda offered too much exposure, then simply stand at any window to observe the sloping hill down to the beach and Sinclair Inlet. Across the Inlet, Illahee Dock protruded into the waters providing mooring for large US Navy ships. Also convenient, this inlet flowed directly to the Bremerton Naval Base to the north, the Pacific Coast Torpedo Station to the south, and just around the corner to Rich Passage at the foot of Fort Ward before continuing into Puget Sound beyond. The main thoroughfare for naval traffic sat in clear view. To examine any ship and its cargo from this vantage point became mere child's play. This home on the hill presented the perfect observation point as it posed as the summer home of the Japanese Consulate.

He knelt to check the thick pile of ashes in the fireplace. Very un-Japanese to leave behind these telltale clues. Some of the clumps of embers resembled books as they still clung together in one black heap. With his gloved hand he fished out the remains of a long, twisted article, possibly of clothing. As he held it higher for inspection it snapped in two. Then his one good eye saw it and he rocked back on his heels with relief. Tucked on the outside of the fireplace, caught in the groove of the brick, was a button from a shirt. The opalescence of the pearl barely twinkled in the dim light of the late afternoon.

Akio had been sloppy in his retreat. True this summer residence of the Japanese Consul afforded the perfect placement for espionage. But more importantly it served as a refuge and safe harbor for the badly bleeding and injured Lieutenant Commander Akio Sumiyoshi.

Jack stood and headed for the kitchen with Duckworth following silently behind. The tall ceilings and high cupboards reminded him of the O'Shaughnessy home and his new wife he had left behind in pursuit of the one man he was bent on sending to his grave. The white walls and ceiling created a glaring contrast to the rest of the house. The light lingering aroma of cooked fish, garlic and onion reminded him of the streets in Japantown. He opened the stove, but the racks were bare and impeccably cleaned of any information. The cupboards held intricately designed Japanese plates, teacups and serving dishes. The embossed gold dragon swirling around the cups reminded Jack of the fan displaying three dragons spiraling out of the water. The fan presented to Billi as a gift by Professor Fujihara, which held the hidden valuable clue of the intent of the enemy.

Duckworth opened the last cupboard nearest the door. As Jack moved closer, he smiled. The bottle was in an image of a stout fisherman holding a large carp under his arm. The porcelain image sat on what looked like water, his black hair was pulled back, his small goatee and arched eyebrows enhanced his expression of humble richness. Jack lifted the sake bottle then shook it, only a splash of liquid remained. He flipped it over, noting the name, recognizing the origin and quality.

Kamotsuru Sake. Akio kept a supply of this brand in the room they shared at Toyon Hall while attending Stanford. Jack's anger mounted as he recalled the traitor's voice bragging about visiting the ancient Kamotsuru brewery, just outside of Hiroshima, during one of his many privileged excursions with his famous grandfather, Count Kawamuro Sumiyoshi. The Count was later bestowed with the rank of Admiral. On many occasions, as the sake surged through Akio's veins, his hatred and disdain for all things not Japanese seeped forth as he raged against the lazy and worthless Americans.

Over the last few months, Jack spent hours trying to reconstruct some of those scenes and to recall Akio's scraps of doodlings that he had protected with a vengeance. Those very abstract drawings represented more than mere idle folly. Suspicion bloomed with the realization those scribbles provided the blueprints for the development of advanced war machinery. However, how that new design would impact the war, still remained unsolved. Hopefully, the fan with the spiraling water dragons, now in Billi's possession, would lead them to more answers.

"The stairs are over here." Duckworth took the lead down the narrow hall to the lackluster steps to the upper floor.

As Jack stood in the middle of the one large room which created the second floor, the view again grabbed at him. He felt his heart pound in anger. Even with the pelting rain he could clearly observe a Black Ball Ferry slide out of Rich Passage and head toward Bremerton. From this vantage point the naked eye had several minutes to observe the cargo, but with the use of binoculars or any form of telescope, the details would be remarkable.

"Christ." He stood and took a deep breath. "Why the hell does the consul from Japan need a summer home, and why here?"

The rhetorical questions hung in the air. He did not expect Duckworth, who possessed many obscure facts, to answer.

Turning his attention to the stripped bed, Jack noted a rust colored blotch that spread against the white of the mattress only to trail off like a thin river. Blood. His excitement surged to anger when more of the life-giving fluid could not be found.

He examined the closet to find it matched Duckworth's description, only a few items hung sparingly from the rod. He checked each pocket then pounded on the walls looking for hidden drawers. The fact that very little dust lingered spoke volumes. The house was kept in impeccable shape. Someone had been living there year-round.

The sight of the small amount of blood disturbed him. Jack raced back down the stairs to the kitchen, jerking open every drawer to scan the contents.

Duckworth stood waiting in the archway to the living room when Jack faced him.

"It's not here," Jack growled.

"What?" Duckworth moved closer to look at the open drawers.

"The knife Billi stuck in Akio's back." Jack ran his gloved hand through his hair. "It was still embedded just below his shoulder when he escaped with Hatsuro. He has it and plans to return the favor. He will make it his mission to kill my wife using the very blade she planted in his back. Her father's kitchen knife."

He slammed the drawer shut then brushed past his assistant toward the front door. Together they walked under the protected ceiling of the porch and out into the sleet. Heading down the hill toward the beach, they passed the distinctive arches that created the base for the veranda. Jack ducked underneath the elegant arch on the north side only to emerge from one of the other four identical curved structures that graced the front. There was no trace of a small boat in the recesses under the decking.

The rocks slid under his foot and he heard Duckworth crunch behind him as they made their way down the shore. A small boathouse stood empty. All traces of footprints, or a boat being dragged ashore, now washed away with the receding tide. The telltale line of dried seaweed, bits of sun-bleached sticks tossed with specks of reddish crab shells, ribboned undisturbed down the shore. They climbed up to stand on the rooftop deck of the concrete boathouse. In silence they watched the blustering wind pushing white-tipped waves over gray water. A masterful view in any season.

"What the hell were we thinking." Jack pulled his hat down lower adjusting his coat for the climb up the hill.

"The summer home of the Japanese Consulate was off limits until now." Duckworth's attempt to raise his bosses' spirits missed its mark.

"We need to keep a watch out on 304 30th South for a bit longer. He's probably out to sea by now. But that doesn't mean he hasn't sent someone else for his prize."

He watched Duckworth's expression as the stout man translated the meaning. Very little escaped his quick-witted assistant, and for that reason Jack trusted him to watch over Billi.

Duckworth blew out a deep breath as he regarded Jack, then nodded.

Both men understood that the "prize" Akio would be willing to pay anything for was Jack's bride, Billi.

# TWO

Eddy used his dirty sleeve to wipe the black soot and grime from his face as he worked through the twisted steel, gouged earth and carnage to the make-shift hospital tent where the injured and dying awaited their fate. Shouting echoed from every corner of the Navy base at Kane'ohe as the stunned men attempted to put out fires, dig through the wreckage for those injured, and assemble foxholes with weapons in the event of another attack by air. Or perhaps, even more frightening, by sea. With few PBY planes, patrol flying boats, left operating to scout the surrounding waters, Japanese ships, loaded with troops, could be on the horizon.

Yet, for now, Eddy had only one purpose, to check on Sam, the seventeen-year-old kid from Missouri. When they first met on the ship over from the mainland, Eddy instantly took a liking to the naive farm boy, privately pledging to protect the hardworking youngster. A pledge twisting his gut with the reality of today's attack.

"Where is he?" Eddy's voice reached a frantic pitch as he stood in the very spot he had left the injured Sam. The image of the blonde kid's trembling hand holding his stomach as blood dripped from his shirt burned at Eddy's eyes like the black smoke of death. Before he had rushed back into battle as the second round of Japanese dive bombers continued their assault from the heavens, Eddy instructed a medic to stay with Sam. That happened less than an hour ago.

Whimpers came from two beds away. Eddy turned to follow the blood splattered across the floor trailing to the line of maimed sailors which continued out into the harsh sunlight marred with drifts of smoke.

As Eddy hurriedly searched among the wounded soldiers, the chaplain moved in his direction, mirroring his pace.

"Who?" The chaplain spoke softly.

"Sam. The blonde kid from Missouri."

The chaplain reached for Eddy's arm, but he spun away grabbing at a medic carrying a tray of supplies. "Where's Sam?"

"He didn't make it." The medic looked devastated by the mounting death toll around them.

"What?" Eddy wheeled around starting further into the makeshift hospital desperately yelling, "Sam, hey Missouri."

The chaplain caught Eddy in a firm grip.

"Where is he?" Tears, mixed with fear, streamed down Eddy's face as he stood broken with grief. Mounting anger welled up and he spit his rage at the man of God. "Sam was just a kid. He'd never even been with a girl."

"This way, son." The chaplain relaxed his grip on Eddy's arm as he guided him past the wounded to another area where the line of sailors lay in peace. The peace only the dead can know, despite their mangled bodies.

Eddy removed the fabric coving Sam's boyish face. Even in death, his lips seemed to form that famous half-smile. Eddy's heels snapped as he saluted his fallen friend.

"Was anyone with him?" He whispered afraid of the answer.

"I was." The chaplain helped straighten the cloth of the departed as Eddy's hands shook fiercely with the final task. "He talked about you, Eddy, and wanted to be there at your wedding to Lani, something about hula skirts."

"Ain't that somethin'." Eddy attempted the homegrown Missouri twang, only one of Sam's endearing traits.

When the chaplain looked at Eddy questioningly, he said it again, adding, "It was the kid's answer to everything. In fact, 'ain't that something' should be on his goddamn gravestone."

The chaplain nodded, seemingly ignoring the ill use of God's name. Forceful cries of profanity had filled the air in the past few hours as they do in all battles.

"Thanks for being with Sam." Eddy nodded at the man of the cloth whose lined, haggard face was in keeping with his unkempt graying hair. "And God bless Billy Mitchell for having the guts to write his book about the battles in the sky and the Japanese attacking us here in Hawaii. They should have listened to Mitchell, not court martialed him. This might not have happened."

"I read *Winged Defense*." The chaplain smirked. "Mitchell was only half correct when he published his report in 1925. You ever heard of Rear Admiral Yarnell and his victory attacking Pearl Harbor in a staged military exercise in 1927?"

Eddy shifted, leaning into the conversation. "You have my attention."

"Fleet Problem No. 13." The chaplain brushed some ash from his arm before continuing. "The War Department didn't like the fact that Yarnell had bested them with his witty maneuvers, so they made the umpires change the results. But Yarnell was clearly the winner. He brought his aircraft carriers, the *Saratoga* and the *Lexington*, to the north of Oahu and launched the attack. He had his pilots' strike the airfields first, not a single plane got off the ground for a counterattack. The battleships were splattered with the white flour from bags his planes dropped as mock bombs. Yarnell had them. But Mitchell had already predicted Japan would attack us here."

The chaplain reached inside his pocket then shook a cigarette out of the packet toward Eddy. For the first time Eddy noticed the other man was missing three fingers on his right hand.

"You see any of this?" Eddy tried to keep from shaking as he held the cigarette against the lighter the chaplain calmly offered.

"I've seen more than I care to discuss."

"When did you say this fake attack was?" Eddy waited as he dragged on the cigarette, finding no consolation in the current discussion. He noticed the clamp of anger settle over the preacher.

"Sunday, February 7th, 1927. At dawn."

Eddy felt the air leave his lungs as if he had been kicked in the stomach. "About fourteen years ago. Holy shit."

"That's what I said." The chaplain's eyes held the remorse of his knowledge. "The Army and Navy brass completely ignored Rear Admiral Harry Yarnell for his brilliance and foresight. Claimed he cheated by attacking on a Sunday morning."

"Well, the Japanese sure didn't ignore Mitchell or Yarnell." Eddy stomped out his cigarette. He saluted the chaplain before leaving to process the information heightened by the preventable destruction around him.

No words could describe his confusion and anger. Twice the US had been warned of the vulnerability of these islands by experienced and reputable warriors of the skies. Twice those in charge disregarded the defenselessness of an air attack from the north of the island. First Captain Billy Mitchell, then Rear Admiral Yarnell were proven right today. They had warned the United States decades ago, that the next battle would be fought from the sky and that the Japanese would attack Hawaii. Thousands of men and women paid the price confirming the predication no one wanted to believe. Now, this Sunday morning, the soft brush of the cleansing winds could not alter the future. A future of bloodshed, battles and revenge.

Eddy felt his hatred for the Japanese seep through his veins as he walked past the wounded out into the afternoon sunshine. The sun hit his white skin where tears had cleared away the dust and soot of battle. He stood a moment breathing deeply of the salt and smoke. This was just the beginning. Life had changed forever for him today, and Sam, he realized, marked the first of many friends that would meet a grizzly death in an unwanted war. He straightened and took another deep breath. He looked up at the soft clouds in the blue overhead, where the enemy had so easily descended on them bringing mass destruction.

The sky. He vowed that is where he would be, soaring into the heavens, fighting like hell.

"Hey, Eddy," a voice came from behind him. "Captain Hebert wants you and your old Bantam convertible at headquarters asap. Most of our trucks and jeeps were hit. You must live under a lucky star."

"What?" Eddy chuckled at the concept of a lucky star, and it felt good. "On my way."

As the sun shone on the blue waters off the West Coast a small plane bumped along the rough tarmac at the California Border Air Service Field just north of Tijuana. The jarring movement pulling at the stitches in Akio Sumiyoshi's shoulder. He pushed stale air out through his nostrils, conjuring an image of Billi to subdue his distress. In his mind she contorted with pain as her indignant blue eyes filled with fear. He vowed to live through any battle to seek his revenge.

"I have your things, sir." Tak Nakamura half bowed at his new commander, keeping his eyes lowered.

"We will continue our conversation once we are aboard." He squinted at the young man he brought with him from Seattle. He had requested Tak be assigned to him, not for his abilities, but for his knowledge of Billi.

As he stepped from the aircraft, he felt the pressure of the bandage covering his right foot, where, when fighting with Jack, a bullet ripped through his shoe destroying his big toe. He pushed through the pain to focus on the approaching short man dressed as a fisherman whose rigid step and neatly cropped black hair told of his military training. Akio hoped no one else observed the obvious incongruity of the man's movements and his attire.

"It will be a great day for fishing."

Akio recognized the staccato of Ito's speech and replied tersely, "Only if we catch something. The order Niitaka yama nobore was given to Admiral Nagumo days ago. Is there any news?"

"Yes, the order 'Climb Mount Niitaka' was successfully put into motion by Admiral Nagumo. We attacked Pearl Harbor as planned. We wait for more results. But, as hoped, we caught them off guard. We will prevail." Ito bowed quickly.

They crammed inside a newer Ford truck then headed up State Route 75 to Palm Avenue, curving toward the water's edge. Turning left on Seaside, they jostled toward the Imperial Beach Pier. At the sight of the long structure Akio relaxed, now back in familiar territory. It brought to mind his travels over the years, hustling up and down the Silver Strand to San Diego to obtain information and recruits for his country. Adjusting his arm to ease the cramp in his back, he sighed with relief. Within minutes he would be safely aboard one of the many fishing boats his navy used for their espionage along the shores of California, safe from the long reach of Jack.

The disrepair of the Imperial Beach Pier reflected the recession of recent years. Yet, the site of the dilapidation only inspired Akio to fulfill his dream of rebuilding America under the guidance and strength of the pure Nippon bloodline. They made it halfway down the length of the long pier when, without warning, his right shoe, with the damaged toe, caught on one of the large nails protruding from the weather worn slabs of lumber. He began to fall forward, then felt the hands of the young soldier, Tak, hold him steady. He stood a moment regaining his equilibrium. It was not his beloved sea that twisted his mind, making him dizzy, but his wounds. Sweat dripped at his temples as he took deep breaths of the salt air to calm himself. He could not falter now, success was to be his.

The moment passed and without acknowledging the young man from Seattle, Akio stepped forward. He continued past the few fishermen who eagerly bent with anticipation over the railings of the pier, their eyes trained on their lines, as if willing unsuspecting fish to their hooks.

Akio concentrated on the end of the dock, extending far out beyond the white swells of the surf, and the waiting boat. They worked down the steep ramp then onto the craft rising and falling on the rolling waves. The smell of oil from the many large containers on deck filled his senses and, for the first time in his career, his reaction was one of nausea. He needed rest. He needed to heal, for being sick only demonstrated weakness. Much remained to be done.

The fishing craft skimmed across the surf in the early afternoon sun with the breeze bolstering his strength. Once offshore, Ito headed them due south along the Mexican coastline with no US Navy ship in pursuit. Heading below, Akio relaxed over a cup of strong ginger tea attempting to appease his rioting stomach.

Akio, unaware of when he had drifted into a stupor, snorted to consciousness at the bust of joyous shouts.

"We have more regarding the attacks." Tak beamed with his announcement.

"Speak in the language of your homeland. Not that of the enemy." Akio chastised Tak before the other men.

Standing taller, Tak continued his translation of the radio report in the tongue of the Land of the Rising Sun. Although born in Seattle, the younger sailor appeared proud of his father's wisdom shipping him back to Japan for schooling. This education automatically included the military training of blind submission to the wishes of the emperor and the elite who controlled the armed forces. He was what the Americans call a "kibei," born in the United States but trained in Imperial ways. Tak represented a dangerous tool for the emperor due to his citizenship.

"To the honor Tora, Tora, Tora will bring us. To the complete surprise of the attack," Akio raised his voice above the others. "We salute our brave flying men who will lead us to swift victory. Soon all of Asia will be ours as well as these shores."

The boat drifted on the small waves of the ocean as the jubilant members of the Japanese military joined their voices, thrilled by the onset of the expanding world war.

EDDY GUIDED HIS OLD Bantam convertible up the winding road toward the Pali with Captain J. Hebert seated beside him. His senior officer clutched a satchel that Eddy understood held the reports of the destruction on their base. At Pearl all such reports would be compiled, revealing the truth of the day.

"What a damned way to start a Sunday morning." The captain broke the silence as they hit a bump marking a crater in the damaged road. "Slow down for a moment."

From their vantage point they could see drifts of smoke emitting from the extensive tally of disfigurement at Kane'ohe base. The burnt shell of hangars that housed the PBY patrol planes resembled skeletons protruding from the ground. The blackened airplanes rested at odd angles on the shoreline while little white specks of uniformed men appeared like worker bees buzzing about their precious hive.

"Holy mother from hell." Hebert pushed his cap back removing his sunglasses. "Look at that. VP-11 and 12 Squadrons took a heavy hit. Not one plane on the ground is working. It's damn ironic that the only PBYs left in operation are the three that are on patrol. At least let's hope they're still in the skies. Just pray kid, that at least 3 of the 33 planes we started with this morning are operable. We have a big fight on our hands against those Japs."

As they rounded the corner into the greenery of the Pali it felt surreal to be in such beauty after experiencing such a bloodbath. Eddy slowed as they passed an AT&T headquarters, miraculously unharmed at the crest of the incline.

Hebert's arm went up in command as he pointed at the station. "Quick. Pull in. I need to send a message."

Eddy willingly followed orders. Leaving the engine to cool after the climb, he followed his commander into the station with the large radio tower. The two communications men dripped with sweat, their faces set in disbelief as the tales of horror continued to spew in across the ticking machines. All bases had been hit within minutes. All caught off guard. All raids bringing heavy causalities.

"Tell them to use anything, coffee if they have to, but to dye those damn white uniforms brown. They make great targets in all white." Hebert barked into the phone.

Drawn in by the commotion of the radio station, Eddy watched in awe as the lights on the radios blinked incessantly, streaming the abysmal news.

"O'Shaughnessy," Hebert belted in Eddy's direction.

Eddy snapped to attention. "Yes, sir."

"Better send back home a quick message, son. Your family will be worried. No telling when we'll get those post cards out. Poor families."

"Yes, sir." He hurried toward the men to scribble a brief note below his home address. "Dear Mom. I'm fine, not a scratch. Will write later. Love, Edward." He reflected on his words. The cryptic message was at least not as bland as the post cards Hebert was referring to. Tomorrow, all personnel would be handed the card to check a box, alive or injured, and sign their name. Then the post cards would be mailed home. It would take days, if not weeks, for those parents and loved ones to hear if their child lived, lay suffering with injuries or had died in the battle.

With a sigh of relief, Eddy handed the slip of paper to the dark-haired telegram operator who nodded, then concentrated back on the strips of amassing Teletype before him.

Eddy steered his yellow and green car down the highway toward Honolulu, as they watched thick, dense smoke billowing against the blue sky. The darkness drifted up over the green hills in the direction of the magnificent home where Lani Daniels, his fiancé, lived with her parents. He tried not to think of their spacious dwelling, three floors of large glass windows built into the side of the hill with a sweeping view of Pearl Harbor and beyond. He focused on the memories of the evening he and his buddies, Sam included, had spent at the luau honoring Mrs. Daniels. As he followed the road ahead, he blinked away the image of Lani's beautiful face with its strong influence of her Portuguese and Hawaiian heritage.

He shivered at the memory of the feel of her long, lustrous black hair, an attribute of her grandfather's Japanese bloodline.

It was hard to tell all the destruction from this distance, but those emerging onto the streets, looking frightened and shocked, told the story. A few locals gathered around a bullet-riddled car straddling the road. A man's arm dangled from the shattered window as he slumped lifeless over the steering wheel with blood trickling down his lifeless face, splashing onto his Sunday-best suit.

Eddy drove around the crowd continuing past residents hurrying from one damaged building to the next. A palm tree christened the top of one home, flattening the roof. Further on, glass and splintered wood littered yards. While some homes remained pristine, others bore the scars of the bombs and bullets.

The frenzied chaos of Pearl Harbor prevented easy navigation. An unimaginable tangle of twisted steel and grease-soaked bodies spread before them. They left his car tucked behind some wreckage as Eddy followed his superior to a low, two-story building adjacent to the berths where sinking ships still belched flame and smoke. They mounted the stairs and hurried down the hall toward the office of the Commander in Chief of the US Pacific Fleet. The echoing of their feet on the hard cement blended with the other sailors coming and goings. They entered the outer office but found little room to stand, as men in all stages of dress, hurried in and out of the inner sanctum of Admiral Husband Kimmel's office.

All motion stopped as the Admiral, grief stricken, stepped through the arch of his office door into the waiting room. The case for his glasses bulged in his left breast pocket, where the singed hole from a bullet pierced his uniform shirt.

"You made it. Come in." Kimmel seemed to brighten at the sight of Captain Hebert. "Hope you have some good news."

Hebert straightened, adjusting the satchel he carried. "I'm afraid not, sir."

But by then the Admiral had drifted back into his private office, where one window held the evidence of a hole from the bullet that had struck him.

The commotion in the office started back up again as the captain motioned Eddy forward. He spoke low, "Get some food. One hour."

"Sir," Eddy tried to not to sound as if he were begging, "do I have permission to leave base to check on my fiancé. She lives just above the base in the hills."

"Be here in one hour. We'll head back tonight."

BEFORE EDDY MADE IT OFF the base a figure rushed in front of him, frantically waving. He pulled to the side of the busy road.

"Shit, Joe. Why the hell didn't you see them on your damn radar?" Eddy hollered at his Army friend who scrambled into his car.

"I did. I called and told them there were planes coming in. The truck picking us up at the radar outpost to take us back was late. So, I just kept on training the new guy on the equipment and I saw them at about 7:30. I called Eddy. I swear. But no one would listen. They said they were expecting planes from the mainland. I just want to be sick."

"Those bastards."

"The worst part is we were right." Joe's frustration streamed into a continuous rant. "No one paid attention. No one in the Army or Navy gave a damn about the war warnings that were sent out earlier, the importance of the Japanese burning their records at the consulate, the enemy planes on the radar . . ."

"They got Sam." The words caught in Eddy's throat.

Joe's head went back while his hand covered his face. "Son of a bitch. God help us."

"I'm heading up to check on Lani. I'll try to find you later."

Joe tumbled from the jeep with the heaviness of someone who had seen into a future that no one was willing to believe.

"I hope she's okay. I'll be watching for you."

The convertible lurched forward climbing up the hills past a small group gathered around a blood-stained bed sheet covering two limp bodies. The dead remained in the grass in front of a small house. A man wept openly as he reached for the tiny shoe of the child who lay next to what appeared to be his mother. Civilians, at work and in their homes, had felt the sting of the attack.

He pulled up the Daniels driveway and felt his breath leave him. The large glass windows on the top floor of the three-tiered house were shattered, with large jagged pieces missing.

Eddy rushed up the steps to find the oversized wooden door, engraved with pineapples, ajar. Gingerly, he stepped inside. He could smell the blood before he rounded the corner; it filled his nostrils and burned acid in his gut. He followed the trail of blood toward the kitchen where Mrs. Daniels famous deep voice chanted in ancient Hawaiian.

A large shard of glass, red-tipped, was in a bucket next to Lani. Her eyes were closed as sweat poured down her forehead. Her mother dabbed cool water on her brow while continuing her song. Lani's muu-muu was ripped open and her father bent over the wound just below her navel, where the sharp glass had pierced her soft skin. An open bottle of scotch stood nearby, christened with bloody fingerprints.

Eddy knelt beside Lani as her eyelids slowly opened.

"It hurts, Makuakane." She licked her dry lips as she looked at her father.

"But it will heal." Mr. Daniels remained focused on the few crude stitches he had sewn into her lovely skin to stop the blood.

"You'll be fine." Eddy made certain his voice reflected the strength of her father's words.

Lani turned to face her fiancé. "I knew you would come."

She lifted her hand and Eddy took it in his. Their simple touch flooding him with a mixture of remorse and desire.

"Help me with this," the urgency of Ben Daniel's tone was unmistakable.

Eddy gently lowered Lani's hand to grip one end of the bandage. He watched her father work the long strip of cloth around her small hips attempting to reinforce the crooked threads tentatively holding both sides of the large uneven gash together.

Her mother, the songbird of the islands, let loose her powerful, earthy voice, providing the rhythm for their efforts. She beckoned the healing spirits as the two men lifted the bundled Lani. As one, they carefully made their way out of the house toward Daniel's truck.

"Where are you taking her?" Eddy choked out.

"To our doctor."

"Does your phone work? Can I call?"

The large man nodded his consent as Mrs. Daniels struggled into the truck bed to sit next to the swaddled figure of their child. Her chant had never faltered. Her plea resonated through the lush green hills surrounding them, as she called on Koleamoku, the God of the art of healing, to come to her daughter's side.

Eddy stood alone trying to recapture his fortitude and willingness to return to the marred base below where the somber haze of smoke shielded the dead.

# THREE

T HE EARLY RAYS OF THE MORNING SUN pushed through the cloudy
Seattle sky leaving streaks of red. He hoped it was not an omen. Red
sky in the morning, Sailors take warning. Jack looked out the window of
the 6th floor of the Federal Building at the blue waters of Puget Sound.
With no wind, the surface appeared so calm, unlike the rest of the world
that continued to reverberate with the news. He focused back on the stack
of pages before him, all arranged neatly down the long, high polished table
in chronological sequence. The night passed too quickly leaving him with
a sense of frustration and little accomplished. The pages told the story. He
had missed the timing for the war that exploded across the Pacific.

All the reports gathered originated from "highly reliable sources." Very
few knew the depth of the danger they contained, especially when read in
sequence. These telegrams, some going back years, represented the communiques between Tokyo and their Japanese Consulates on American soil. Luckily,
the United States recently developed their newest, highly secretive weapon to
read them, the decrypting machine they entitled "Magic." Without employ-
ing the use of Magic to break the Japanese "purple code," none of the information complied on the table before him would have been available.

Jack reread the transmissions he had underlined carefully in pencil.
The first one, translated February 7th, 1941, supported the need for his
task force along with the growing suspicion of the Japanese.

From:    Tokyo January 30, 1941
To:       Washington
            Foreign Office Secret

Heretofore, we have placed the emphasis on publicity and propaganda work in the United States . . . we have decided to deemphasize propaganda for the time being, and instead, to strengthen our intelligence work . . .

Please, therefore, reorganize your intelligence set-up and put this new program into effect as soon as possible.

Cable copies of this message, as "Minister's order" to Canada, Mexico (a copy to be relayed from Mexico to Mexicali), San Francisco (copies from San Francisco to Honolulu, Los Angeles, Portland, Seattle, and Vancouver), New York, New Orleans, and Chicago.

Jack found the next message between Tokyo and the consulate to be more specific.

1.  Establish an intelligence organ in the Embassy which will maintain liaison with private and semi-official intelligence organs . . .

2.  The focal point of our investigations shall be the determination of the total strength of the US . . . divided into three general classifications, political, economic and military . . .

The concept of using foreigners, other than Japanese, to infiltrate government agencies, factories and transportation facilities, as well as cooperating with German and Italian intelligence, painted a vivid picture of the vastness of the espionage web. The planning had been so thorough that spies were instructed once war broke out 'the intelligence set-up will be moved to Mexico.'

Jack scanned another highlighted date: February 15th, 1941. Tokyo had asked the consulate in Washington D.C. to supply intelligence involving the US and Canada.

1.  Strengthening or supplementing of military preparations on the Pacific Coast and the Hawaii area: amount and type of stores and supplies; alterations to airports (also carefully note the clipper traffic).

2.  Ship and plane movement (particularly of the large bombers and sea planes).

The Land of the Rising Sun had set its sights on American shores long before 1941. Jack looked at the corkboard where a Japanese map, published in 1934, hung in full display. Small red lines, originating in Tokyo, traced across the vast Pacific Ocean leading to their intended goals for their expansionism. One curved downward slightly to land on the Hawaiian Islands. Another stretched straight across to San Francisco, where his family lived, with a smaller red loop leading to Los Angeles, San Diego, then all the way down the coast of Mexico where it created circles around the Bay of Magdalena before continuing to the Panama Canal. Yet another arched high to land on Seattle, where he now sat in frustration attempting to defend his new bride and her family only a few miles up the hill. Above that dotted line, the Aleutian Islands and other parts of Alaska appeared as targets.

Next to the ominous map, a pin held a copy of the letter sent by the Chancellor of Japan at the Los Angeles Japanese Consulate asking for copies of the "entire water system of this city." The request was dated June 28th, 1934.

Japan's desire to conquer, driven by totalitarianism and their belief their Emperor is their God, had already brought destruction to one of the maps proposed destinations. Which of the red lines would they attack next?

He twirled his pen nervously between his fingers as he leaned over the mass of paperwork before him. Skipping over the next few decoded communiques he settled on the June 10th, 1941 dispatch sent to San Francisco, Los Angeles and Seattle. All three were west coast cities with heavy naval activity.

> ... observations of the movement of the American Navy
> is one of the most important matters, will you observe
> the movements of ships and gather other information
> that may be of interest to our Navy ...

Jack marveled that by June 23rd, a mere thirteen days from the time of the request, Sato, the lead Nippon contact in Seattle, responded with details of Bremerton Naval Base, Seattle Ports, Sand Point Naval Air Station, and Boeing Airplane Company. The spy's swiftness coupled with specific details showed great ingenuity.

He tossed his pen down and worked past the following months to the more recent requests from Tokyo. On November 23rd, 1941 San Francisco had been asked to reply to a new request by December 1st. Seattle reported on the *H.M.S. Warspite* moored for repairs at the Illahee Dock across from the Japanese Consul's summer home. Yet, above all else, the newly decrypted messages between Honolulu and Tokyo now jumped out at him. On November 18th, Honolulu reported back to Japan detailing the warships at anchor in specific areas within Pearl Harbor. "Strictly secret" appeared on some communiques from Tokyo to their spies, including one message instructing Honolulu to report not only on daily ship movement, but also when there was no movement in the harbor.

His head hurt, he should have seen these signs that pointed toward the events of the attack. Jack scratched beneath the black patch that covered his bad right eye. He knew more exchanges had not been translated as yet and that thought froze his heart. He slumped into the tall backed chair to rest his throbbing leg. Yesterday's rummaging around the Japanese Consulate's summer home on the beach, exasperated the deep wound from Akio's blade. He recalled the anxiety and determination in his wife's blue eyes as she seared his bloody incision closed. He let his mind wander with visions of retaliation.

The knock at the door rattled his thoughts. Jack stood to unlock the door allowing Duckworth to slip inside.

"A new message from reliable sources, sir." Duckworth's voice reverberated with a mix of frustration and excitement.

Jack regarded the cable sent from Tokyo to Washington, on December 5th, 1941.

Will you please have Terasaki, Takagi, Ando, Yamamoto,
and others leave by plane within the next couple of days.

"We can check our lists for their names and star them, but I'm certain they're long gone." Jack did not hide his bitterness and let the paper with the late news float toward the table, enabling it to find its own spot, disrupting his methodical order. "Are the men ready?"

"Yes." Duckworth straightened. "They're all a bit nervous and want at those Japs."

"Tell them to be careful. We don't want a war breaking out here. Many are still loyal to the Emperor." Jack shuffled the papers back into his briefcase and locked it.

"Sir." Duckworth waited until he had his boss's full attention. "You did everything you could do. They'll listen now."

"I sure as hell hope so." Jack reached for his coat when there was a tap at the door.

Duckworth opened the door a crack and a young man announced a call on the special line for Jack.

The faithful Duckworth followed his boss down the hall then waited outside the small office while Jack stepped inside to pick up the receiver.

He closed the door behind him. "Huntington here."

"Jack," The stern male voice did not hide his agitation. "Well, here we are. Damn it all. Have your men begin at once and I want you to keep reporting to me separately. I don't want Hoover in on this just yet. Time to make certain all is kept tightly in our loop. How many out there are aware of Magic?"

"Like before, just Duckworth." Jack responded to the force of the accusation. "We're sharing the intelligence as you requested, under the category of 'from reliable sources.'"

"What about the girl?"

"She knows very little, except for helping us locate the spy ring. And, in that situation, she was invaluable." He tried not to sound defensive.

"Are you sure? Can you control her?" The voice had not faltered with its demand, too much was at stake.

Jack stifled a laugh. "Well now, sir. Controlling most women is difficult, but this one in particular is extremely strong headed. But she is completely on our side."

When he did not hear any response from the other end of the phone Jack added, "I've got it covered."

"How, Jack?" The tone was not a threat but of sincere concern, man to man.

"I married her yesterday morning." He felt the lump in his throat as he admitted his actions. Who was he protecting with his rash behavior, Billi or himself?

"Congratulations. Well done. I expect to hear from you soon."

"Yes, sir." Jack held his breath hoping that was all.

"Oh, and Jack." The man on the line barked a laugh. "What a hell of a way to spend your honeymoon."

Jack couldn't agree more.

It was still early Monday morning as Danny adjusted the knobs on the tall wooden radio in the O'Shaughnessy living room where everyone gathered close to listen. Mrs. O held Pepper on her lap, gently swaying in her prized overstuffed rocker, anticipating the President's speech. Mr. O had pulled up a chair next to her to dutifully tend the fire.

Billi watched her parents, grateful to her mother for allowing her estranged husband to stay in their son Eddy's now empty room. Having them facing this new world together seemed appropriate.

"Is Dahlia joining us?" Billi wandered to the window to search the quiet streets, aware that most of America remained inside their homes listening for the President's words. She longed to see Jack's car pull up to park in its usual spot across the street. His lack of communication suddenly stretching her nerves beyond control.

"She's got classes. She said she doesn't want to miss any of them because when she becomes a nurse, she can really help with the war." Danny straightened with pride at his sister's dedication. "Boy, it sure was good to hear from Eddy."

"Yes," Billi answered for her parents who were still grappling with the concept of their son surviving in the midst of the bloody attacks on his base at Kane'ohe. She realized that Danny spoke for his sister too. Everyone in this room thought Eddy and Dahlia would be married long before Billi. How swiftly the world had changed.

"And what about your classes today?" She directed her question to Danny.

"I wanted to be sure I heard the President. Then I'll head in. I'm just missing gym. Here we go." Danny backed away from the radio and stood fidgeting with his jacket.

Billi left her post at the window as the President's voice became clearer across the airwaves.

> Yesterday, Dec. 7<sup>th</sup>, 1941—a date which will live in
> infamy —the United States of America was suddenly
> and deliberately attacked by naval and air forces of the
> Empire of Japan.

Billi felt her knees give way as she lowered onto the couch attempting to memorize every word. The President recounted the situation of betrayal from Japan, how they extended promises of hope to America while secretly planning the attack on Pearl Harbor. She listened with great intent as he mentioned the aftermath and condition of the US bases.

> The attack yesterday on the Hawaiian Islands has
> caused severe damage to American naval and military
> forces. I regret to tell you that very many American
> lives have been lost. In addition, American ships have
> been reported torpedoed on the high seas between San
> Francisco and Honolulu.
> Yesterday, the Japanese government also launched an
> attack against Malaya.
> Last night, Japanese forces attacked Hong Kong.
> Last night, Japanese forces attacked Guam.
> Last night, Japanese forces attacked the Philippine
> Islands.
> Last night, the Japanese attacked Wake Island.
> And this morning, the Japanese attacked Midway Island.
> Japan has, therefore, undertaken a surprise offensive
> extending throughout the Pacific area. The facts of yesterday and today speak for themselves. The people of the
> United States have already formed their opinions and
> well understand the implications to the very life and
> safety of our nation.

The encouraging words drifted by with mounting anger, coupled with applause, from those in congress.

> With confidence in our armed forces—with the
> unbounding determination of our people—we will gain
> the inevitable triumph—so help us God.

I ask that the Congress declare that since the unpro-
voked and dastardly attack by Japan on Sunday, Dec.
7th, 1941 a state of war has existed between the United
States and the Japanese empire.

In less than seven minutes President Roosevelt's speech drew to a close.

War. Billi watched as Danny suddenly stood in the large archway of the two wooden pocket doors holding the world globe. The
same globe she had just held out for their young inquisitive neighbor,
Victor, who asked the same question so many had in the last twenty-four hours—where is Pearl Harbor?

"Dang." Danny spun the globe running his fingers between Hawaii
and Japan. "So, where's Midway? And what were those other places?"

Mr. O's Irish accent reverberated through the tall room. "Guam,
the Philippines, Wake, Midway." He paused waiting for Danny to find
the specks of green amongst the massive blue. "When ya add in Malaya,
and Hong Kong the damn Japs have taken over most of Asia."

Danny's face went white when he finished locating the last of the
list. "Holy damn . . ."

He froze mid-sentence as Mrs. O twitched in her chair. Pepper,
sensing the tension, buried his nose under her arm.

Billi let the driving impact of the President's words slowly take hold.

"The dirty bastards lied ta us." Mr. O began to pace. "They must a
been plannin' this for months. Yet tellin' us they want peace. May they
burn in hell."

No wonder she had not heard from Jack. He had been right all
along. The sub-culture of the Japanese on American soil, still faithful
to their Emperor, had provided not only information but also funds
to support the attack. By now Jack and his men would be scouring
Japantown for those they suspected were involved. And that put Eileen
Nakamura and her family right in the path of the inquisition.

Having spent a restless night trying to figure out how to intervene,
Billi stood. As she headed toward the front foyer, Pepper leapt from her
mother's lap and charged toward the door.

"Not this time, Pepper," she instructed her dog. "I'm heading to
visit Eileen and . . ."

"You mustn't go there anymore," Mrs. O spoke sharply.

Turning back toward the living room, Billi looked at the astonished threesome. "What are you talking about? Eileen hasn't done anything."

Mrs. O raised and lowered her shoulders as if to punctuate her words.

"We are at war with her people." Mr. O took up the argument.

"We are at war with Japan. Eileen is American. I won't be long." Billi disappeared out the door before anyone could dispute the point further.

THE SUN ROSE BRIGHT AND PROMISING in contrast to the half-burnt planes and debris, the grim reality of the massive destruction punctuated by the new day's shining light on the windward side of Oahu.

Eddy carried his shovel to the line forming along the beautiful white sand beach. The salty winds from the Pacific Ocean no longer a soothing breeze, but a reminder that the Japanese had sailed through these very skies, demonstrating their ability to reach far and wide in their quest to secure their country's needed supplies and their desire for dominance. This morning the air tasted bitter, like his heart. His shovel struck the ground with a vengeance while tears that he refused to allow yesterday, flowed onto the finely ground pearl-colored earth. He would dig six feet deep, like the others in the row, and lay to rest the young man who had never been with a woman, let alone lived to see his eighteenth birthday. His family back home, not only suffered from the loss of their only brother, but the funds the young sailor's time in the service provided the struggling family. Death penetrated far and wide with darkness like no other.

He stood on the crest of one of the white sand dunes that formed North Beach at Kone'ohe Naval Air Station and gingerly picked a red petal from his dress whites where it had stuck with the sand and tears. Eighteen holes held new wooden coffins with handmade, white plaques swiftly painted and driven into the earth. A red lei draped over each marker resembling the red blood spilt in defense of America. Eddy lifted the errant petal into the sea-whipped breeze. He watched it float through the shafts of sunlight to settle next to the neat row of names, each adorned with a red, white and blue flag rippling as if in salute.

It was a temporary resting place, the bodies would be sent home or buried permanently elsewhere on the island. But for now, Aviation Machinist's Mate Sam Creasmann would have to wait to return to his beloved mother, sisters, and farm in Missouri.

He felt his stomach tighten as he cringed at the sound of the Marine honor guard rifle volleys split the same skyline where yesterday, the enemy swarmed with their killing machines. He promised those souls that stretched down the beach the only thing he could, payback.

The moody clouds reflected those mourners who slowly ambled up the beach toward their barracks. Suddenly, Eddy turned around, his black dress shoes sunk into the fine sand as he stared back toward Sam's name.

Grateful to be alone, he spoke his impassioned words to his young friend. "Hey, Missouri, I have a favor to ask. You ride my shoulder and watch over me. Okay? Don't let me do anything stupid, because I'm going after those Japs. And then I'm going to go visit your mother and make certain you've made it back home. Now, 'ain't that somethin'?"

The tears came again, and he let them. What the hell was going to happen next? The only thing he could count on; the fact he would bury many more friends before this war was over.

# FOUR

AKIO REPRESSED HIS SMILE AS HE watched sweat drip down Tak Nakamura's forehead. He knew the sensation, that the young man's eyes burnt from the salt produced by his own body. The mere fact this young kibei had not blinked demonstrated his potential.

"How long have you known her?" Akio's finger tapped the photo where Eileen and Billi stood arm in arm. It was the very photo Tak stole from his sister's dresser, giving it to his superior months ago. The one Akio copied then cut out Billi's head. He had the decapitated image placed on her bed in her small apartment on Maiden Lane in San Francisco. A warning Akio looked forward to fulfilling.

He watched Tak's eyes for any flicker of falsehood.

"So long I cannot remember." Tak's voice remained strong with the truth.

"How did she come into your home?"

"She has always been with my sister."

"Your sister's name again?"

The young sailor hesitated. "Eileen."

"There is no Eileen in our Nippon heritage?" Akio demanded, his anger surging at the insolence of the act.

"Meisa," Tak blurted, blinking his eyes.

"Is she?" Akio pressed.

He did not answer.

"Is she cheerful as her name reflects?" Akio's low voice held a threatening tone.

"Only upon occasion." Tak snorted.

"Would she be cheerful in bed?"

"What woman would not be cheerful in your bed?" He bowed.

Akio considered the youth's clever response coupled with the quick bow, forcing their eye contact to be severed. He would have to watch this one, for Tak's loyalty might falter.

He stood, towering over the sweating young man who held secrets to Billi. "How do you like being on a submarine?"

"It is an honor to be on any ship that will destroy the enemy," Tak demurred.

Akio drew in a large breath of the stale air. He could feel his own body temperature rising as the flesh around his wound burned. "Did the fishermen bring us more fuel?"

"There is much whispering of this. It is said we will meet with others again tonight when we are clear to surface at Magdalena Bay."

Akio slid his finger down the photo of the two young women, following the curve of Eileen's hips. "Meisa. I look forward to tasting her fruit." He flipped his other hand in dismissal, as Tak stomped out the door.

EILEEN'S BENT HEAD DID NOT shield her red, watery eyes. "What will happen to us?"

Billi sat down next to her on the small single bed in the very room where they had spent much of their childhood. Today, the room echoed with the memories of the two dressing in exquisite traditional Japanese attire, securing each other's obi, fitting on Auntie Katsuko's wigs, and perfecting their makeup in preparation for one of the many performances they would appear in together, side by side, as always.

She answered her friend in Japanese, "I do not know. But you had nothing to do with this, do not fear."

"You must not speak in Japanese anymore to me." Eileen snapped. "We are American and will speak English."

The lump in Billi's throat made it impossible to respond. Her head bobbed with their new reality.

"Father has insisted that we all speak only English." Eileen twisted and untwisted her handkerchief around her graceful left hand.

"I saw his new signs in the windows. They're very nice." Billi hoped that Mr. Nakamura's large, freshly painted, signs he had hung in his store-front windows, would sooth the anger spilling into the streets. "We are American" the bold letters proclaim. Unfortunately, the devastating news coming across the radios, reflecting the headlining of the special edition papers, only hammered home tales of the horrific attack and the mounting number of Americans dead and dying.

Silence pushed in around them. The wedge of the war had struck, planting itself between loved ones. Billi gasped for breath. This was the home of her mentors, where she had learned so much of the culture she had come to love. She felt torn by the last few months, her involvement with Jack and the dangers that lurked around his edges.

Unexpectedly, the image of Akio twisting and thrashing in the bloody snow with Jack as they ruthlessly fought, gripped at her heart. She sprang from the bed beginning to sweat.

"I know you cannot stay," Eileen spoke with a hush. "Go. We can meet again later."

"It's not that. It's . . . sorry. I got distracted."

"Yes, that seems to be happening a lot lately." Eileen's smile was a gift. "You have a husband now."

She had not heard from Jack in over twenty-four hours. Not one word since he had rushed out the door leaving behind their wedding party. The feel of his kiss a blissful memory that now floated like a dream beyond reach.

"Have you seen that young man you liked again?" Billi heard the swift beating of her pounding heart as she posed the question.

"You mean Sanzo?" She blushed slightly at his name.

"The friend of Tak's who wears the dark hat with the light band?"

"Yes, the one you got so upset about when I mentioned he wanted to talk with you. Did you want to meet with him?"

Billi checked herself before responding, merely shaking her head "no." More than likely, the young man Eileen had set her heart on, Sanzo, had already been gathered up with the others being questioned by Jack or some of his FBI men. She remembered first speaking with Sanzo at a bookstore in Japantown in San Francisco. Then he appeared in Seattle chatting like old friends with Eileen's brother, Tak. This connection only solidified Sanzo and Tak's involvement with the West Coast Japanese intelligence.

Attempting to deflect the topic she asked, "How is Kenny taking all of this?"

"Oh, he's at school. Luckily, Garfield High has so many different cultures and so many Japanese students that, hopefully, he won't get hurt."

"No one is going to hurt him. He's Kenny, star of the football team."

Eileen only nodded, then her face took on a dark expression. "Tak has not been home. Father is very worried about him but believes that since his black trunk is still here, Tak will return." She let out a small gasp. "Oh, I hate this. I'm so frightened."

"Don't be. You are an American, you were born here. Nothing will happen to you."

"I hate my parents' homeland right now. Why did the Emperor do this?" She patted her eyes with her handkerchief. "I am so glad I did not go back to Japan with Tak. I don't want to ever go there."

"I do." Billi sat down again. "Well, not right now. But when all of this is over. I want to go see the temples, the country, the people. We can go together."

"You are married. Do you think your husband will let you go there?"

Billi rolled the notion around for a moment. It was clearly not a coincidence that Jack had prevented her from winning the competition and the coveted trip to Japan last summer offered through the University of Washington. Thank heavens he had. She quivered slightly at the thought of being from the United States in enemy territory. The terrifying image of Akio beheading David in that dark San Francisco alley nearly rocked her off the bed.

"Are you okay?" Eileen leaned in toward Billi.

"Yes." She caught her breath. "Yes, I can make my husband let me go." She forced a smile that did not match the twisting of her stomach. She could never visit the Land of the Rising Sun if Akio remained alive.

"LOOKIN' GOOD, EDDY." Scooter tossed him a bottle of pop.

Eddy caught it midair, downing a sip before removing his gloves and flight gear. "The damn thing whistles from all the bullet holes but it still flies."

The two young men regarded the battered PBY. The ground crews had pieced together a few planes for training and scouting. Every minute spent in the air became a minute closer to revenge.

"Any updates?" Eddy handed Scooter the empty bottle with a smile.

"We're getting a new ninety-day wonder as navigator."

"Christ," Eddy almost spit out his pop. "Three months of training and he's going to be responsible for saving our asses in a tight spot."

"Don't snap your cap. We're going to have plenty of time to figure him out."

"He got a name?"

"Fletcher something or other."

"Carlyle."

They turned in the direction of the voice.

"Fletcher Carlyle, the ninety-day wonder from Idaho."

"Idaho." Eddy eyed him. "Why navigation?"

"That's where I was born. My dad was a traveling salesman, of sorts, and we saw a lot of the country. I was his navigator at age seven."

Eddy extended his hand, nodding at Fletchers firm grip. "And now you're ours. Glad to know you can read a compass. We'll be depending on you up there to get us home."

"I'm Scooter, who has been tasked with this blowhard. But he's good to have when it comes to meeting Janes."

"Rule number one. Never listen to this guy." Eddy's smile solidified Scooter's observation. That winning grin definitely appealed to the ladies. "We're going to get some chow and then head out on our second rounds this afternoon. So, we'll see you then Fletch."

Walking shoulder to shoulder past the burnt skeleton of Hanger 3 Scooter pushed his sunglasses further up on his nose. "You didn't give him any clues on where to meet us."

"He's a navigator, he'll find us."

As usual, Eddy tapped the bullet hole in the exterior wall of the mess hall. It remained a stark reminder of just how close that deadly slug whizzed past his head the early Sunday morning of December

7$^{th}$. It quickly became his ritual to tap the wall, an act of defiance and good luck.

It was cool inside; the hall and the windows were shut against the promise of rain. The billowing dark clouds had picked up speed across the horizon, cutting the day into night.

They loaded their tray with chow then made their way to the front table where other pilots and crew hunched over their plates.

"Just met our new navigator," Eddy spoke to the men gathered at the table. "He's not bad."

"Couldn't be as bad as the news." Charlie one of their wing gunners mumbled.

Eddy froze, noticing Scooter do the same, their gaze fixed on the other gunner.

Allen, the other wing man, put his coffee cup down. "Cap just left. He wants us in the briefing at 1400, probably to talk about the losses on the Enterprise."

Scooter dropped his fork. "Figured this lecture was coming."

"How bad?" Eddy held his breath.

Hank, their radio man, gave his report. "Rumor has it ten men, ten planes. Including the three that were shot down by friendly fire trying to land at Ford Island that first night . . ."

"Shit is going to happen." Scooter broke in.

"Yeah, but it was our own goddamn men those damn trigger-happy fools shot down," Charlie grumbled.

"Anyone could have done the same." Eddy tried to calm the bubbling tempers. "It was a horrible night for everyone."

"We had two planes land here that night and we didn't shoot our own pilots." Allen, no stranger to guns being raised in Arkansas, bit into his eggs, chomping on his food in frustration.

Eddy calmly eyed his wing gunners. "And when we're up there, it's you two we're depending on to make every bullet count. Riddle the Japs and the Jerries, not our boys."

Friendly fire, as it was so erroneously labeled, had claimed more victims. There was nothing that could be added that would erase the horror and heartbreak of friendly fire.

In the silence that now hovered over the table, Eddy choked down his food. What if the briefing was about orders? Orders to leave the island—leave Lani?

It seemed that every office on the 6th floor of The Federal Building in Seattle held exhausted agents and frightened Japanese. Those being questioned, ranged from professors, fishermen, doctors, grocery store owners, lawyers, journalists, priests, seemingly all walks of life.

Jack closed and locked the door to the conference room then slumped into his tall-backed chair. He removed his black patch, massaging his right eye, letting the air cool the skin around the damaged orb.

He snorted at how the fates had played one hell of a trick, years ago, when he and Akio became roommates in Toyon Hall while both attending Stanford University. He could still see the look of hatred in Akio's eyes the day he viciously sliced Jacks cheek and eye with his rapier style sword while they parried in preparation for a fencing competition. And now his hatred for Akio took on a whole new meaning.

His head throbbed while frustration burned his gut. If he had killed Akio that snowy day at Dyes Inlet, at least he would feel some satisfaction for the predicament he found himself in. With fierce recognition of the amount of work still ahead, he stood and regarded the battered black trunk that occupied part of the polished conference table. He switched on the light, as the day had long ago faded into darkness, then focused on the trunk with the promise it held.

The hardest part of his day had been watching his new wife leave the apartment, where the Nakamuras lived on the second floor, and not taking her in his arms. Her determined stride, her long legs, the rhythm of her hips, had stirred his memory of their one night together and he wanted more. Yet, dutifully, he had remained out of sight.

Jack arrived alone at the Nakamura's home to collect Tak, the oldest son, a kibei, known to still be active in the Japanese military. Tak, however, nowhere to be found, had long since disappeared.

The kind Mr. Nakamura, having just attended their wedding, did not look surprised to see Jack. The white-haired Issei sat and spoke softly in his broken English of the change in his eldest son. How this promising young man returned from studying in Japan bitter and filled with hate for America. Tak's transformation broke his father's heart as his training left him defiant, wild, uncontrollable and violent. When questioned, the elder Nakamura listed the places his son frequented: the Star Pool Hall, the Stacy Street Tavern, the Golden Donut Café and others. Jack recognized the names as businesses being used as centers for intelligence gatherings, where spies exchanged information to be sent back to Tokyo and which his men were already scouring.

Finally, Mr. Nakamura had led Jack down the hall to Tak's bedroom. As the door swung wide, the story unfolded. Tak had left in a hurry. A few items of clothing were on the floor, others hung from drawers not completely shut. Mr. Nakamura had stepped around the mess to the far side of the bed. With a flourish he pulled away a white sheet hastily draped over a black trunk. Tears filled his eyes as he nodded toward Jack.

Out of respect, Jack had brought the trunk here, to his makeshift office away from prying eyes. Now it sat before him like a harbinger of evil. Dreading the truths it held, Jack put his patch back on, then called for Duckworth. He ran his hand along the top of the black object, waiting.

"Thought you might want this." Duckworth handed Jack a long wood handled screwdriver as he entered the room.

Jack slapped the metal of the tool against his hand, testing it, before he put it into the loop that held the lock. With one quick jerk, the hinge splintered from the dry wood. Jack lifted the lid and the smell of musty clothes floated into the air.

Carefully, as if handling precious china, Jack removed the objects one at a time. A black kimono with a dragon embroidered with gold thread swirling up the back left little doubt as to what else would be inside. A photo of Tak, his face blank, devoid of expression as he stood in his white Imperial Japanese Navy uniform rested on top of the long cold steel sword of a warrior.

Jack's brow furrowed, where was the gun? He tapped the bottom and listened for the hollow sound before moving his hands along the lower edge.

"Just as I thought." Jack pushed on the bottom left corner feeling the wood move. He gently slid the one-inch thick drawer from its hiding place then set it on the table. Both men leaned over their new-found treasure. There, neatly folded was a yellowed sheet of paper with the exacting kenji script flowing from right to left. A map of Seattle and outlying areas was delineated by pencil hash marks, cutting it into sections.

"Christ, is that what I think it is?" Duckworth could not control his concern.

Inscribed above a large, shaded area of the Seattle waterfront were the words "Kaigun-chūi T. Nakamura." To confirm his understanding Jack would have Billi translate. However, he was certain it marked the area Tak Nakamura would command in the event of a Japanese uprising.

# FIVE

Jack held Billi's elbow guiding her down Pike Street toward the Coliseum Theater. The elaborate terra cotta exterior appeared to spill inside, providing the interior with the ornate opulence of a bygone era.

"Is this a date?" Billi teased, excited to be with her husband after so many days apart.

"Can't a man enjoy and evening with his wife?" He removed his hat and smiled.

"Of course, but I find your choice of the movie remarkable."

"I thought you liked Cary Grant?"

"I do. I like him in comedies. And Joan Fontaine is rather easy on the eyes."

"Did you know she was born in Tokyo?" He still held her elbow as he chose seats toward the back of the theater. "She actually attended the Tokyo School for Foreign Children."

"You are full of surprises." She sat on his left side, then turned toward him. "Is that why you chose *Suspicion* for our first movie together?"

Jake didn't comment, he couldn't admit to the real purpose for their surprise outing.

Billi continued in a whisper. "Did you read the book, *Before the Fact*? It was quite thrilling."

"It's always interesting to compare the two, book and movie." Jack quietly acknowledged as the lights dimmed.

The newsreel began with a hush. Prepared before the Japanese attack on Pearl Harbor, it showed footage of Boeing's new Flying Fortress on a "Hop to Hawaii" taking thirteen hours and fifty-nine minutes to land on the calm Island at Hickman Field. The beauty of the images now cut cruelly into their hearts. Someone in front of them sniffed, obviously stifling tears.

Jack felt Billi take his hand and he clasped his fingers around hers. The simple act brought him a sense of peace, a normal moment between husband and wife in a world exploding around them.

The short newsreel ended as it began, in silence. Jack waited. He released Billi's hand in the event she could sense the tension streaming through his veins. Then he watched what he had come for. Three men and two women, all seated in different areas of the theater, stood and began to leave.

As the RKO emblem flashed onto the screen in preparation for the main feature, the five movie goers headed down the aisles toward the exit signs.

Jack whispered before standing, "I'll be right back. Nature calling."

He hurried in the footsteps of two of the men through the bright lobby and out into the fading afternoon light.

"We got five," Duckworth announced.

"That was all that left this time?" Jack walked toward the small group of Japanese who had paid good money just to watch the newsreel. They stood silent, surrounded by local police.

"Take them in for questioning and get me a copy of that newsreel. I'll call L.A. later to let them know what I find. But messages are still going out. Thanks."

Jack turned back toward the Coliseum Theater's front door.

"Enjoy the movie." Duckworth's voice held a bit of laughter.

Jack paused to regard his faithful accomplice. "*Suspicion*."

"Yeah. It's everywhere." Duckworth nodded then turned back toward the group of potential spies.

Jack sat in the dark smoke-filled office in the Seattle Federal Building. He gripped his cigar between clenched teeth as he pushed the button to rewind the movie projector once again. The thought of how long this form of espionage had existed gave him a headache. It was so simple, yet it spread the message across the country to movie houses everywhere.

He heard the door open, then close, and could smell the light scent of his wife's perfume as she sat down on his left side. Duckworth took the seat to his right.

"What is this, Jack?" Billi's voice was quiet with wonder.

"Do you recognize it?"

"Yes, we saw it yesterday at the movies."

"Do you remember what happened next?" He needed to know that in these dangerous times she remained vigilant of her surroundings.

"You excused yourself." She sounded perplexed.

"What else?"

"A few others needed to use the restroom too and got up."

"Billi, did you see them come back?" He watched her, trying not to sound frustrated.

"No." Her head went down. "I saw. They were all Japanese. Did you arrest them?"

He ignored her question. He pushed the "on" button and the projector began to spin. "Tell me what you see. What doesn't fit with the newsreel?"

She leaned forward intensely. When the short film concluded she spoke. "Again."

Jack obeyed replaying the ten minutes of news and topics of interest.

"Oh my God. There." Billi's hand shot up as she pointed at the upper right-hand corner of the screen before the words disappeared. She sat back in astonishment. "How and what does it mean?"

"One Hideyoshi Yamatoda, boss of the Tokyo Club in Los Angeles, established the Nichibei Kogyo Kaisha Film Exchange, a movie theater. He also owned a movie distribution company and a small, well equipped, production company. Before delivering the newsreels, he inserts the code. Have you ever seen anything like this before?"

She looked directly at her husband. "No. Have they arrested him too?"

"No," Jack spat the word in disgust. "There was a turf war over the many Japanese clubs along the West Coast from Alaska to Mexico. A lot of money flowed from the whore houses, gambling joints, selling drugs, pay offs, and who knows what. There was also much vital information exchanged through these sources. Being the boss made you

STORMS FROM A CLEAR SKY | 47

rich, powerful, feared and vulnerable. So, his rivals kidnapped him and packed him down to Mexico. He escaped, returned to L.A., pressing charges against his rivals. However, he was up for a murder trial, so he snuck back to Japan last April before we could get to him."

Billi did not respond to the images of the dark side of the culture she had innocently become immersed in.

Duckworth leaned forward attempting to draw Billi back to the images on the screen. "We think they're dates and places."

"To Off Joshler, by large snow." Billi repeated the odd words. "Who is Off Joshler?"

"No one we can find. We tried Officer, all kinds of names. Nothing." Duckworth looked up at the frozen image.

Billi squinted in concentration. "Well, they couldn't communicate in their language, far too recognizable. Why is 'by large snow' on the second line? The spelling of Tōjō is included. What letters does that leave?"

Jack handed her a piece of paper then left her alone. He had already tried that combination but drew blanks. He hoped someone with knowledge of the Japanese language could formulate some other meaning.

He sat back and watched the embers from his cigar fall into the ashtray while observing his stunning wife. Not only her physical appearance but her quick mind pulled at his heart while her intense eyes sent waves of desire through him. He could not risk losing her. He would not allow her to become a statistic of conflict, no matter his orders from the highest ranks.

"Wait," Billi broke her own silence. "There has to be an easy formula. They would not send out a message of importance across the country that is overly complex."

Duckworth's enthusiasm matched Billi's. "What if you take the two lines separately?"

"Yes, To Off Joshler." She scribbled on one line and then wrote "by large snow" on the second.

The men waited, when suddenly her expression changed.

She looked at Jack with tears in her eyes. "Large snow is one of the twenty-four Sekki. It is the ancient method of dividing the change of seasons in a calendar year."

They looked at her encouragingly.

"Taisetsu, if I remember correctly, it's the twenty-first season of the Sekki."

Jack wanted more. "Is there a specific day associated with Taisetsu?"

"December 7th." Billi's whisper shot lightning through his veins.

"Christ." Jack bolted from his seat. "What does 'To Our Joshler' mean?"

Billi shook her head "no."

Duckworth moved to the edge of his seat, leaning closer. "Okay, the second line is straight forward, and it is a date. A date on which we know what happened. All hell broke loose and thousands died. So that line needed to be very clear to people watching, especially since this movie was released in November and took some time to reach theaters across the country."

"Right," Jack agreed. "So maybe this second date hasn't happened. We need to figure this out now."

"Is there coffee?" Billi bent over her writing with renewed interest.

Jack nodded toward Duckworth. "How about some sandwiches to get us through the night?"

When they were alone Jack put his hand on Billi's shoulders then kissed her forehead. "Thank you."

She didn't respond but kept her focus on her task.

He picked up his cigar, moving closer to the large screen. The slippery bastards. He couldn't show the panic this trickery instilled in his psyche. They had unearthed a whole new level of espionage, one that had been baffling the FBI for months. Reports surfaced of sighting of the same activity. In various cities across the country, some of the suspected Japanese they shadowed, would leave the theater after the newsreels. At first, the FBI thought the content, the reporting of the Empire of Japan's brutality, their aggressiveness in China and other Asian countries, had upset the moviegoers causing them to leave in disgust. But, suspicion of other activities had piqued Jack's interest.

Suspicion. The word made him smile. In the movie, the Hitchcock climax held hope, with a twisted happy ending. Jack prayed that in real life, the twist of this ugly combat would hurry to an ending. As for happiness, that was made in Hollywood, just as these covert deadly messages had been.

He turned toward Billi as she concentrated on her work. His conscience ripped him in two. He couldn't let her get more involved. If anyone associated with Akio found her . . . he fought back the haunting images of slow torture. No. After tonight he would not let her close to his work. The more she knew, the more vulnerable she became. The gloominess of the room reflected his mood. He moved to the projector to snap it off then bumped into a chair on his way to the light switch.

Billi blinked at the brightness. "Yes, that helps. It would also help if you would sit down."

Jack huffed over to a chair and sat. The anticipation of discovering the next date made the air crackle with tension. He jumped when Duckworth entered with a brown bag and coffee. The aroma of the stimulating brew seemed to lift everyone's spirits as they briefly indulged in cold ham and cheese sandwiches.

The clock on the wall ticked just past 2 a.m. Several sheets of paper formed a fan across the desk where the projector once sat. Others were crushed into balls of aggravation on the floor.

"Oh, what am I missing?" Billi moaned. "Like I said, it should not be that difficult."

"If you know the pattern." Duckworth sounded just as forlorn. "We've tried removing the capitalized letters, TOJ, with the small o next to it—Tōjō. But that's not a date. We've tried every combination with the lower case . . ."

"Wait, is that an 'l' as in level or capital 'I' as in I am?" Billi pointed to Joshler. "It would make it too obvious if the message appeared all in caps, so one letter is hidden. Oh, maybe I'm just crazy."

"What would that spell? Tōji?" Jack leaned over the words with renewed interest. "Does that represent a date?"

"Damn," Billi cursed. "How stupid of me. It is that simple. And it's another season of Sekki: Tōji, Winter Solstice, the darkest day of the year."

"December 21st." Jack agreed.

"Yes," Duckworth chimed in. "Look. To Off Joshler. T, move two letters over and add TO, then go three letters to make it TOJ, then four letters makes it Tōji."

Billi quickly pointed out, "That follows Akio's threat of a gift for Christmas eve."

"An attack on the mainland, somewhere." Jack paced now, following the same pattern he had most of the night.

Duckworth shot up clutching a white sheet with lines of doodles. "If you remove those letters, look what falls into place. Combining the first two words you get 'off.' The last word is a scramble."

As he read out the letters Jack wrote them down. It only took him a second before he looked straight at Billi. "Shore."

"What is coming?" Billi's voice trembled.

Jack didn't hesitate with his conviction. "Submarines."

# SIX

THOSE IN HAWAII ANXIOUSLY ANTICIPATED ANOTHER attack by air and by sea as false rumors of enemy sightings poured in from all corners of the islands. Sleep became a dream, as everyone remained on duty and constant watch.

Eddy slipped from his post to look across at the blue green waters toward the beach where he and Lani had pledged their love. It was odd that the tranquil sands of their day of joy and love existed so close to the base where so much death and destruction had occurred. In keeping with his new ritual, he stepped closer to the marker of his fallen friend and let the wind take his words toward his grave.

"Hey, Missouri, it's not looking good out there. The Japs are kicking our ass. Look out for Lani, would you? Not sure when I'm going, but I'm leaving her for you to watch over." For the first time in the last few days Eddy smiled. "Now ain't that somethin'? Me leaving my girl for you to watch over. The world is upside down."

"Hey, Eddy," a voice came from over the dunes.

Eddy started toward the man calling his name. "Yeah?"

"They want you in the office. Maybe it's your car again." The sailor sounded hopeful that the request to report did not bear ill news.

"At least I'm good for something." Eddy shook his head hurrying his step.

They started off silently, in matching stride, passing men bent in labor over pieces of PBYs. Others filled in the chuckholes where bombs left scars in the tarmac and the white sands.

"Good luck." The sailor waved as he diverted toward the mess hall.

Eddy continued across the lawn to the low building which housed the main headquarters. The coolness inside did little to relieve the fever pitch of activity.

"Flyboy, you've been grounded for a while it seems." Captain Hebert's voice held no malice with the announcement.

"What, sir?" Eddy stood rigid. He had big plans for this fight, and they all were in the sky.

"They requested you at Pearl. Seems all that book reading and testing you were doing is going to pay off. You have a security level that they need for now, until replacements make it here."

Eddy felt the tension leave his body. "Yes, sir."

"You'll be back here soon. Don't get too comfortable on that side of the island." Hebert eyed Eddy. "Put you closer to that girl for now too. But, don't get distracted. We need you, son."

"Yes, sir," he half shouted.

Papers in hand, his duffel bulging, Eddy took a last look at Kane'ohe before he started over the Pali.

Puffs of black smoldering smoke still lingered over Pearl Harbor when Eddy arrived. Men wore their black, oil and soot-stained clothes like badges of honor. Like Kane'ohe, men had spent their nights in dug outs manning guns, eating cold baloney sandwiches, watching the horizon. The last few long nights did not pass without mounting tragedy.

Eddy sat in an office with a stack of papers before him. His year as an intern at the law office, coupled with the stack of reading he had consumed during down time, both while training at Camp Luce and on the journey over from San Francisco, were now coming into play. Whether his level of security clearance or that nosy Jack that had put him at this new desk didn't matter. From what he scanned in the stack of reports, this job offered valuable information. Hopefully, something he could use when back in the air.

"Hey, how long do you plan on working tonight?"

"Sir?" Eddy stood.

"It's late, sailor." His superior tossed more sealed envelopes on the desk. "Didn't I see you at that football game on Saturday night?"

"Yes, sir. A friend of mine was playing for Oregon."

"Too bad they lost." He watched Eddy for a moment. "Do your friend a favor. They have the team up at Punahou. Swing by and cheer him up. Football players might think they're tough, but this is different."

THE SOUND OF GRAVEL SHIFTING under Eddy's shoe bounced off the stone buildings on the Punahou campus filling the otherwise silent night. A small cloud moved over the stars and the waning gibbous moon, but not before he recognized the barrel of a gun pointed at him.

"Hey, Truck, it's me. Put the gun down." Eddy's voice was calm but firm.

"Christ, Eddy. You scared the shit out of me." Truck lowered the gun, smiling. "How the hell did you find me?"

"I smelled you." Eddy chuckled, slapping the back of the enormous football star. "Why are you alone?" He silently cursed Coach Spec Keene for volunteering the Willamette Football team to guard the school grounds that housed the ammunitions for this war.

"Andy nearly vomited every time they put a gun in his hand. He can tackle a man so hard it hurts, but he can't hold a gun. They're going to send someone else out soon. But I sure am glad to see you."

Eddy noticed Truck held the gun with an ease of familiarity. For him, like many raised in rural areas, hunting became a sport, a hobby, a passion. Yet, tonight posed a very different situation. The possible target being human made the perspiration drip into the big guy's eyes as the young athlete stood alone at the entrance to Punahou School in the darkness of the imposed black out.

"I can't stay, just wanted to check with you before I head back to base. When are you heading home?" Eddy held a cigarette in Truck's direction.

"Why the hell not?" Truck snatched up the smoke as if accustomed to the bad habit, only to cough roughly on his first puff. "We don't know yet. They can't find us room on a boat. Hell, I'm not certain we won't be blown out of the water when we do start for home."

"You'll be fine. Just write me when you get there."

Truck's eyes shifted to Eddy's newly dyed uniform, the brown splotches from the coffee thicker in some spots. "What about you?"

"I'm in it till the end." The words floated between them, as a sense of urgency had swept over their lives.

"Well, we'll get those damn Japs soon enough." The smoke ringed the football player's head in frantic puffs of uncertainty.

Eddy heard the plural reference of Truck's words. He realized that, for his friend, the prospect of joining the service was reflected by the easy manner with which he held the weight of the gun: dangerous, yet powerfully enticing.

"It's a hell of a mess right now." Eddy's statement echoed his emotions more than the world situation.

"Sure as hell is." The larger fellow nodded.

They smoked in silence as overhead small fluffy clouds floated past bright stars. The warm wind off the ocean calmed their senses with the tantalizing wisps of blooming flowers. The sounds of the night filled their ears as the two young men struggled with their own immediate concerns.

"What happened to that girl you were with?" Truck looked sideways at his friend standing half in the shadows.

"She's injured, a shard of glass cut into her." He could speak no further of the image of Lani, her damp hair circled her strained face, as her pain took hold of her body.

"Sorry." The scene, far too familiar, need not be described. "Shirley McKay, you met her, she came over with her dad to watch us play in the Shrine Bowl. Damn, I wish so many of us hadn't been so seasick, we would have given those Hawaiian's a better game. Anyway," he shifted his cigarette to emphasize the shift of his thoughts before continuing. "Shirley's working down at the hospital helping as a nurse's aide. She can barely talk when she gets back to the hotel. It's horrible what she's seeing."

"It's good of you all to help."

"Hell, they enlisted us. They had us string barbed wire along Waikiki beach. One minute we were swimming, the next we were digging foxholes and handed these old rifles. They're moving us up here on campus to sleep in the dorms so we can watch the place. Do you think the water towers have been poisoned?"

"No." Eddy stomped out his cigarette. "Don't believe everything you hear but stay alert."

"Eddy," Truck's voice lowered as he struggled for the words. "They say there were about twenty-four thousand people at the game. How many of those who watched us play died? It's just such . . . I'm mad as hell and scared."

"We all are, Truck. We all are."

A car approached from down the road. "There they are." Truck's voice sounded relieved.

"My cue to leave." Eddy turned to his old friend extending his hand. "Stay well and write."

Truck gripped Eddy's hand. "She's Japanese, isn't she?"

"Lani?" Eddy lied. "Hawaiian and Portuguese."

"Take care of yourself. And I hope she gets better. It's a hell of a mess right now."

"Don't shoot anyone on our side." Eddy threw him his pack of cigarettes. "I'll be waiting for your letter from Oregon."

As Eddy passed the other young football player joining Truck on the night watch, he saluted the young man. The call of duty ricocheted across oceans and mountains, rippling through all ages as America stood tall, cinching her belt, readying for the unspeakable.

BILLI WRAPPED HER LIGHT BLUE chenille bathrobe closer as she started down the spiral stairs, wondering where her husband had spent the night. How quickly she had become accustomed to his touch. She blushed at her own longing as she let Pepper out the front door and stood a moment in the dark regarding the empty street. It had rained the night before creating a few shimmering puddles on the black road. She felt a sudden chill and drew her robe closer, the unrest of the world carried on the wind. Her pup sniffed the air, snorted, and looked back at her. She motioned for him to return. Obediently, he swept past, barely touching her robe, to lead the way into the living room. The big dark house felt exceptionally cold this December 11th morning as she bent to make certain the damper in the fireplace was drawn tightly shut.

The home seemed empty since her father returned to his small cabin on Dyes Inlet. Good news came in the form of the increased demand for food supplies at the Navy shipyard at Bremerton, meaning more work for Mr. O'Shaughnessy. The thought of her father delivering fresh meat to the men at the base made his manual job all the more important. She smiled at how he adjusted from riches to rags and back again, always with a plan, always with his sparkling Irish ways. A crafty survivor who had taught his children the valuable lesson of bouncing back.

She stood to snap on the lamp that sat on top of the radio, then turned the dial to adjust the volume. A man's voice spread into the room with the daily news, a constant in their lives, as music now seemed a luxury. Billi headed through the dining room, her slippers padding underfoot as she reached the kitchen. She flipped the switch allowing the lights that hung from the tall ceilings to brighten the gloomy room. The sun not expected to show itself for another hour, might not appear at all through the heavy Seattle clouds.

Pepper sat in front of his empty bowl whimpering.

"Yes, I see you." She reached for the can of Folgers Coffee, to prepare her morning brew and then for the sack of Gaines dog food. Pepper spun in circles in excitement. "Okay." She held the bag higher, teasing. When he stopped, he lowered onto the floor, tail still wagging, with eyes fixed on her. "Good boy. You are my little hero." With a flourish she filled his bowl.

The coffee began emitting its rhythmic belch of black liquid. In the unusual quiet moment, her thoughts turned to Jack. She began pouring herself a cup when, hearing her mother scream, she jumped. A bit of the scolding liquid splashed onto her hand. She wiped it on her robe as she and Pepper raced into the living room.

Mrs. O collapsed into her rocker her eyes wild as she gripped the folds of her dark robe.

"Die Welt untergert, die Welt untergeht," she repeated near hysteria.

"Mother, English." Billi knelt beside her, taking her plump hand. "What is it?"

A man's voice barked incredulously from the radio, "Germany and Italy have declared war on the United States of America. At precisely 3:30 Berlin time, the German Chargé d'Affaires in Washington handed American Secretary of State Cordell Hull a copy of the declaration of war . . ."

Billi plopped onto the floor, letting the message pierce her startled mind. Germany declared war on America? Joining the Axis with Italy and Japan meant the spread of combat and fatalities. American blood would be spilt around the globe.

"The world is going under." Her mother's chest heaved as she translating her German words, the language spoken by her Bavarian immigrant parents.

"No, we mustn't believe that." Billi got on her knees before her mother, her voice raising. "We cannot believe that, mother. We will win. We will fight the Japanese, Italian and Germans and whoever it takes. But we will win."

Her mother's big brown eyes fixed on her. "Yes. Many will be massacred. What is the point?"

Billi stood. "We have to get to work. I'll get you some coffee." She stopped in the door frame looking back at the slumped figure of her mother. "And no more German. We only speak English." The urgency of her own words startled her. Words that Eileen had spoken just days ago when her father had insisted that they only speak English in their Japanese household. Would that help? Would merely speaking one common language create the solution? Invisible borders were being defined within America at a time when success demanded unity. It would take more than a common language to win this war. But at least, Billi realized, it was a beginning.

AKIO SAT IN HIS BUNK and wiped the sweat from his forehead. His soaked body felt as if his fever had broken. He slid to the floor then buttoned his shirt before leaning out into the cabin way. The heavy smell of the diesel from the subs engine mixed with the body odors of the crew and the cooking oil from the galley. He needed air. He grabbed at the wall, waiting, listening, then realized the boat was not moving. Stepping back inside his berth he caught his reflection in the small mirror. He squinted back at his own image observing the darkness under his eyes and how the loss of blood paled his skin. He breathed deeply and almost fainted. Yet, neither rest nor weakness were options.

He forced himself to relax with the knowledge that the gods favored him. He nodded, silently thanking the heavenly spirits for intertwining his private battle and need for retaliation, with the glory his new concepts for warfare would bring him. With the aid of his advanced designs for attack weaponry, the Land of the Rising Sun would emerge the conqueror. The Emperor himself would acknowledge Akio's superior contributions to maintaining Japan's superiority. Of this he remained certain. Soon, he told himself.

Moving down the tight passage, he stopped short of the control room to observe. The crew appeared efficient but sluggish, he planned to make certain they did not continue in this fashion.

Tak straightened before him to give his report. "We are awaiting the signal from the fishing boats and are preparing to surface."

Akio stepped toward Tak, unleashing his hand across the younger man's face. "You were to wake me before we arrived." He smiled, watching Tak's rage turn both of his cheeks red.

A shout broke the tension filling the room. "The signal, sir."

Akio observed the hatred build in Tak's expression as they listened to the sound of the captain climbing the steps to take the periscope. The captain gave his commands immediately, "Surface. Prepare to bring the fuel on board and set to recharge."

As the submarine lingered on the surface, the glistening of the phosphoresce in the night waters magically played in the light of the moon as a fishing boat approached. Luckily, the encircling protrusions of land which created Magdalena Bay, off of Baja California, offered incredible protection from prying eyes. The bay created a perfect setting for refueling and collecting intelligence.

When the boat came alongside, the crew set about transferring the priceless cargo. Akio observed as men moved with precision at a hurried pace. Before long he noticed a stout newcomer watching him. A thick woven poncho covered the stranger's expansive belly.

He lit a cigarette then moved further up the deck of the sub. Through the half-light he glared back at poncho-man. Snorting out a puff of smoke he approached the insolent fellow but halted as the captain appeared, quietly taking up his post next to the visitor.

"We will not take him ashore. He does not need to recuperate. His attitude is dangerous." Pancho-man spoke gruffly while continuing to glare at Akio. "Take him up north as instructed. He knows that shoreline well and will serve us better there."

The captain grunted his acknowledgement of Akio's fate, then addressed him directly. "You will take Nakamura with you. I will write your orders."

Without another word, the captain turned to follow the man in the poncho below deck.

Akio stood stunned by this new development. Obviously, the captain and this strange man did not appreciate his standing in the Imperial Japanese Navy, nor did they appear to know of his ties directly to the Emperor. He threw the remains of his cigarette into the black sea. That did not matter now. Being tethered to Tak Nakamura could have its rewards, he planned to exploit the younger man to his benefit. Furthermore, he would be fighting along the American coast within reach of his intimate enemy and the woman he dreamed of splitting open.

Once again, he thanked the gods for their kindness.

# SEVEN

PEPPER STARTED BARKING AT 3:00 A.M. He charged the door as Billi slipped from her bed. Grabbing her old light-blue chenille robe she listened for any noise.

"Shush," she reprimanded her dog. "You'll wake the whole house."

When she opened the door, her faithful dachshund bolted down the hall on his short legs, disappearing down the steps. She heard his growling stop as her pulse began to beat faster. She crept to the top of the spiral staircase amazed by the echo of heavy snoring bouncing along the hall from her mother's bedroom. Gingerly she descended into the dark foyer. Clinging to the handrail, she lowered herself over the fifth step from the bottom, avoiding its loud creak.

She tested the handle on the front door, but it did not give, the lock still held tightly. Everything appeared as it should, the blackout curtains remained pulled all the way with no movement disturbing the room. She felt her heart race when she saw no sign of Pepper.

Cautiously she moved into the pitch-black living room, then past the tall wooden pocket doors into the dining room, where the scent of their pot roast dinner lingered like old perfume. A noise from the kitchen made her stiffen. She eased open the top drawer of her mother's sideboard to feel for the handle of the long carving knife, the one her father had just sharpened. Gripping the handle made her think of Akio and the stout steak knife she had driven into his shoulder. She wished it had been his heart. She began to shake, unable to swallow, as perspiration formed on her brow.

A dish clinked breaking her stupor. She put the knife behind her as she pushed into the kitchen. She smelled him first and stood motionless. It was his own scent, a mixture brewed of cigars, whiskey, hard work and fear, that made her tingle inside.

She reached for the light switch, but his hand covered hers. "Not yet. I just want to hold you in the dark for a while."

Jack worked his hand up her arm to her face. She felt the heat of his touch travel down her neck to the opening of her robe and her flannel nightgown. She let him continue, her breath escaping in short gasps.

"I. . ." She leaned back to catch her breath. "I have a knife."

"I wouldn't expect less." Jack pulled her against him to kiss her.

A whimpering brought them back to their surroundings. Jack snapped the light on to discover Pepper sat waiting for more treats next to the plate he had placed on the floor to quiet the pup's growls.

"I see you're spoiling my dog." Billi challenged her new husband with a steely look.

"Our dog," Jack corrected. "In a marriage, all possessions go with the deal."

Billi pulled the sharp blade out from behind her back, smiling coyly. "The knife is mother's."

Jack took the cutting instrument then put it on the counter. "You won't need it."

They regarded each other as the knife had cut through their jesting to the heart of their situation.

"I hope not." Billi stepped closer leading Jack to the kitchen chair. "Sit. You look hungry."

"You always this bossy?"

She let the personification of Ginger answer. "You ain't heard nothin' yet."

She removed his patch putting it next to the drink she poured for him. The tall glass of dark amber liquor glowed under the kitchen light. He nodded his thanks, took a sip and loosened his tie.

She watched him run his fingers through his thick hair, recognizing the gesture as one that meant trouble. Anxious, she headed for the refrigerator jerking it open.

"How long do we have?" Billi had her back to him when she posed the question.

"I leave at 6:00 a.m. for San Francisco."

"Will you give my love to your family?"

"Our family. I'll make a point of it."

She knew he watched her and attempted not to show the apprehension settling around her. "Hot or cold?"

"If you're talking about wanting you . . ."

"Your pot roast. Do you want me to heat it up for you?" She turned now holding a large pan.

His smile was devilish. "The answer to both is hot."

She put the pot on the burner, turned it on low then faced her husband. "Listen buster, this is gunna take a while. What do ya say we make the best of our time?"

As she moved toward him, her hips swayed with each step, as if she were wearing a hula skirt, like the one she wore when she posed as Ginger.

"Ginger? Is that you? I thought I was talking to my wife." He leaned back into the chair to watch her move.

"Not tonight, buster. Tonight you're all mine."

LANI LAY IN HER BED with her thick black hair clinging to the dampness at her temples. Her mother pushed a few wayward strands from her distinctive dark almond shaped eyes, both attributes of her beauty, gifts from her Japanese grandfather. Her fever, now broken, left small beads of sweat clinging to her moist nightgown.

Eddy stood looking down on her small frame. She had never appeared so frail or so Japanese. He swallowed the words of the pledge he had recently made to his dead friend, Sam, then bent to kiss her forehead.

"Hi darling," he whispered.

Her lips curled into a soft smile.

"You get better and I'll be back soon." Eddy set his small gift, a sweet-smelling gardenia, on her pillow squeezing her hand in comfort. When he felt the faint pulse of her fingers tightened in response against his shaking hand, he smiled.

"Ko'u Aloha," her lips barely moved with her words.

Mr. Daniels followed Eddy out into the hallway, escorting him toward the front door.

"The cut was deep. She is lucky to be alive. The vet hopes she will . . ."

"The vet?" Eddy halted, stunned.

"There were no doctors available. I took her to the best man I know." The strength seemed to have drained from him as he clamped his large hand on Eddy's shoulder. "She may not walk."

Eddy faltered as Mr. Daniels' grasp tightened, holding him upright with the shock.

"Come," the command was spoken quietly. "Pray with me."

Mr. Daniels suddenly turned leading the way toward a small chapel out beyond the main garden set back amongst the beautiful deep purple bougainvillea and lush greens. Inside, candles burned below an ornate Portuguese hand-carved crucifix. Six rows of benches sat on the tiled floor with the sheen of their wood lit by the glow from the afternoon sun streaking through the cut glass windows.

The cool inside added to the comforting surroundings as Eddy knelt next to Lani's weeping father, praying for her recovery in the very chapel they had hoped to exchange their wedding vows. She must walk again. He bent his head, bargaining with the gods of all religions. She promised to be the mother of his sons. She must walk again.

BILLI HURRIED DOWN SOUTH JACKSON STREET into Nihonmachi, past several new signs above stores and restaurants declaring the inhabitants of Japantown to be proud Americans. She turned up 7th then entered the door that lead to the apartments above the Nakamura's store. The familiar stairway, filled with the various scents of cooking, had not changed in appearance. But now, a ripple of dread seemed to secrete from the silent walls. No laughter permeated through the plaster, radios were silent, while the hush of the unknown smothered every step as she approached her friend's door. She paused to observe the kenji for peace proudly nailed just to the left of the entrance.

Peace. Could such a thing ever be accomplished again?

She knocked gently and waited.

Eileen smiled, warm and inviting, bowing slightly to her friend who risked being seen entering their building. "Please." She motioned her friend inside. "Father is in his room."

They sat on the couch across from the simple wooden Butsudan altar in honor of her deceased mother, nestled between the Geisha dolls brought from her homeland and her father's white orchid. The elegant plant's tubular vine, the aerial root, reaching for new soil in an attempt to spread life while the last bloom clung defiantly to the tall stem.

"It is amazing the beauty that still exists after all this time." Eileen's words reflecting Billi's thoughts.

"I have never grown an orchid before."

"They mirror the soul," Mr. Nakamura's soft voice came from behind the two young women who, as one, turned toward him. "Ah, it is so refreshing to have such beauty in our house."

Billi shot a quick glance at her friend, not understanding the intent of the elder man's comment.

"He is speaking of his beloved flower." Eileen whispered.

"Perhaps." Her father smiled at them. "Are we having tea?"

The couch quickly emptied as the young women scurried into the kitchen to prepare. Eileen took out her mother's beautiful teacups with the hand-painted elegant cranes circling the outside. When held to the light, the lithopone image embedded in the bottom of the fine translucent china appeared as the head of a geisha. With great remorse Billi realized the danger of her desire to dress in Auntie Katsuko's beautiful kimonos and wigs, as was their custom for the tea ceremony, or to dance at Bon Odori.

Eileen's voice broke through Billi's thoughts as she boiled the water. "Have you heard anything, Billi? Has your husband been able to tell you anything about what they are planning for . . ."

"No. Don't think of that now. Let's have some tea and speak of happiness. Like the old days. I'm just as frightened as you are. But we can't control what has happened. Okay?"

"Has being married made you this wise?" Eileen smirked.

They hugged, binding their sisterhood, their years together.

"For today there is nothing but what is inside these walls." Billi hoped her words sounded convincing. More importantly, that she could abide by her own ruling. She had never lied to Eileen before. Yet now, she felt her involvement in the underworld of war created prickly armor, letting nothing near her, even her best friend.

"Good." Eileen wiggled free then opened a small box filled with sumptuous wagashi treats. She neatly placed three of the special confections on a small china plate. She handed Billi the heavy kama kettle before gathering the green powder and other items needed to make tea properly. "It's your turn to pour."

When they returned to the living room carrying their implements, they found Mr. Nakamura sitting at the low table, his shoulders stooped. Billi noticed the worried look controlling his face. Since Tak had not returned, the FBI had questioned this humble, elderly man more than once, but had not held him overnight, like some of the others.

She lowered across from him then bowed, beginning the ancient art of the tea ritual. The intricacy of the tea ceremony represented one of the aspects of the Japanese culture which had lured her into the maze of fog surrounding her life.

She struggled with the meaning of the words he had spoken to her a few weeks ago as they stood watching the snow begin to fall. His words, propelling her to the Nippon Kan Theatre to observe the kendo competition, had been few but potent.

Mr. Nakamura had mumbled as if not speaking the words himself but those that had been channeled through him. "The professor asks for you. You are to bring him gifts that were given once for the winter."

Billi had found her University of Washington Professor Fujihara at the theater that evening. She shivered at the memory of being secreted backstage into a small dark room. The professor sat dressed as a competitor in traditional attire, his kind face concealed behind a mask. His words were interrupted by a loud crash from outside the door, forcing her to flee, before she understood his request.

It remained a clue needing an answer. Her heart broke at the thought of Professor Fujihara being involved with the deeply rooted spy network sending vital information back to Tokyo. The object he was searching for must be of value. However, over time, he had bestowed her with many small gifts. The words "something for the winter," did not help clarify what the professor desired.

In the dizzying last few days she had not thought to question Jack about the professor. She made a note to inquire the next time they spoke. The memory of the sensation of his touch in the early morning hours as they satisfied their lust made her blush. At the thought of her husband the kama in her hand wavered a bit as she poured the steaming water into the green mixture.

At the slight, Mr. Nakamura looked up, slowly smiling. "Your husband has chosen wisely."

Her blush deepened, and she could not keep the smile from her face at his compliment.

"Did you ever think that you would be a bride before Christmas?" Eileen teased.

"No." The word caught in Billi's throat at the reminder that Christmas, and the threat, drew nearer. If Akio had spoken the truth about Japan planning more attacks on American soil, then massive amounts of work lay ahead. She blinked, forcing the image away to focus on the ritual before her. For this brief moment, these familiar walls of her youth provided only the beauty of friendship, banishing the hellish skirmishes around world.

AKIO LISTENED TO THE BARK of the seals as they slipped through the night toward the docked boats of the fishing fleet at Terminal Island. Their oars remained soundless, even with the heavy pull of their weight. They could not afford to draw attention from either the US submarine base at San Pedro, or the Naval Air Base. How fortunate that this jetty of mostly man-made land, just south of Los Angeles, had attracted the largest number of tuna canning warehouses. Starkist, Chicken of the Sea and nine other companies had structures that loomed above the small Japanese village erected to accommodate the workers the tuna industry attracted from abroad. Japanese men, women and children established the company town here on Fish Island. The fact that these sons of Nippon occupied the area conveniently wedged between easily observable military bases Akio found most cunning.

He climbed on board the trawler, controlling his repulsion at the stench of fish guts and diesel fuel. Tak stepped behind him as an older fisherman spoke his greeting in the villages local kii-shu ben dialect. Akio turned to Tak for interpretation, but the younger officer remained silent.

Nodding, they followed the man's ancient limp off Fish Harbor wharf to Tuna Street then ducked into a dark building. They passed from the front of the Tokiwa Low restaurant toward the kitchen, steeped with the aroma of traditional Japanese food.

A man in a tailored suit stood out among the pots and pans. "It is good to see you again, Lieutenant Sumiyoshi."

Akio blinked in recognition of Mr. Nakuche. It had been many years and clearly the stress of his assignment as lead communicator from Los Angeles to Tokyo had changed the man before him.

"I am honored you have come yourself." He bowed at the man in the impeccable suit. "This is Tak, who has worked with Sato in Seattle."

Nakuche grunted in Tak's direction, scrutinizing the newcomer. "Your visit must be short." He moved to a small table where three individual trays awaited laden with delights from the sea. He motioned Akio and Tak toward empty chairs. "The FBI have removed many of our men from this island for questioning. These are very uncertain times."

A slight woman, her hair pulled back from her broad cheekbones, approached them carrying a bottle of warmed sake. At the sight of her round figure Akio felt his appetite for other pleasures aroused. He pulled his concentration back to the agent.

"The ship is only receiving intermitted radio messages. Have my orders changed?" Akio knew he rushed the conversation, but his sudden urges made him anxious for business to be completed, allowing pleasure to begin.

"All consulates are closed, and they continue to search homes. But now that Germany has joined us, it will only be a matter of time." Nakuche poised his chopstick waiting, obviously not wanting to be hurried with the deliverance of his news.

Akio lifted the lid to the special lacquerware jubako box to find one of his favorite delicacies, unagi no kabayaki. He nodded again at the preparation of the unaju, and lifted a piece of the fish from the steaming rice. The special tare, a well-guarded recipe for the sweet soy sauce, reminded him of home as he crunched into the rich, fatty eel. His pleasure apparent, the others began, sampling from the variety on their trays. Raw tuna was beautifully placed with the deep green of the seaweed. It was a feast in these times, not only for the eyes, but invigoration to a sailor who knows the importance of his superior culture.

The woman poured more sake, the appearance of her wedding ring held no meaning for Akio. His needs grew stronger with the warmth of the alcohol and her nearness.

"It has been determined that you will meet the I-17 off Mendocino soon. Our fishermen have carefully surveyed the depths and landscapes of the coast shorelines there and beyond." Nakuche spoke between bites. "The submarine has left Honolulu and should be here shortly."

Akio was relieved, things were improving. He would be aboard a long-range B-1 submarine cruiser, a far superior craft, in his opinion, than the one he recently left. He raised his sake to his lips, allowing the bold flavored liquid to slide down, comforting, inspiring. His eyes leveled on Tak. The sudden desire to make this insolent young man know the true meaning of respect grew deeper.

"The Emperor will be pleased when we hand him the much needed resources this country has to offer." The agent smiled wryly.

"Ah, but the Emperor will be greatly pleased when we hand him this spy." Akio dug out the photo of Eileen and Billi, sliding it across the table.

Nakuche studied the picture before speaking. "She seems nothing special."

"I am referring to the Caucasian with the blue eyes. She is a slippery eel. You must notify me personally if you see her. More importantly, she must be kept alive." He sat back in his chair with confidence. "She is a great prize."

The agent handed the photo back. "Who is her accomplice?"

"She is worthless." Akio snorted.

Tak shifted in his seat, his anger apparent.

Nakuche turned his gaze on the young man. "Is she a trifle of yours?"

Akio watched Tak's lips tighten. Prudently, the young sailor did not answer. He turned his attention back to the women pouring more of the clear, warm liquor.

"Yes. The Emperor will be pleased with those who have shown him how worthy they are to receive so much as a blink from his imperial eyes. To Emperor Hirohito." Akio raised his delicate sake cup as the others quickly imitated his action.

Their meal finished, the man in the suit seemed satisfied with the extent of their exchange departed. Tak was left to guard the front door, instructed to fetch Akio only if he saw any questionable movement.

The effect of the strong sake lightened Akio's step as he followed the woman down the small paved walkway leading to the fronts of several homes. The one-story structures were identical, long, barracks like, and owned by the canneries.

"My husband will be honored to know that I was able to provide you the comfort of the ofuro," the woman spoke softly as she guided him down a sand path alongside the length of one structure. "He is part owner of a boat and is able to provide quite well. We have a Victrola and several records from Japan. I will play you something soothing if you wish."

Akio found her broken Japanese distasteful.

She stepped up onto the wooden walkway that ran along the backs of the houses then bowed toward the bathhouse structure on her back porch.

"Fresh water has been prepared for your visit." She remained low in her bow as he passed.

Inside the small hut-like structure, Akio removed his clothing then stood on the slated floor, letting the hot soapy water drip onto the sand below before stepping into the deep, pot-shaped, cast iron ofuro tub. At first, his right foot throbbed at the stub of his missing big toe. Then the pulse of his heart as he sank into the steaming water. A whiff of the smoke from the fire burning underneath the tub rose around him.

"Come," he commanded.

As the woman shuffled into sight, he noticed her hesitancy.

"Tell me how does the wound on my back heal?"

Her eyes widened as she approached. "It is very angry."

"You will put some medicine on it and a proper bandage."

"Yes." She bowed again. "I will go and prepare them for you."

He watched her go frustrated by the gibberish of her words, as this fishing village had concocted its own speech, part Japanese, part English, no longer the masterful language of their race. He splashed at the water deciding he will not allow her to speak as he finds comfort with her.

She had left the back door open for him. In the darkness he glanced briefly about before being drawn inside by the sound of a lone female voice singing a famous Japanese song, *Sendo Kawaiya*. Akio snorted at the meaning of the song, "cute girl standing at the prow" as he examined his surroundings. This girl who prepared his bandage could not be considered "cute" by his tastes, but her home was well kept. The walls of the two-room structure displayed cheerful photos of Japanese gardens with brightly blooming trees.

"We are lucky that there are only two families that occupy this building. Some have four." She bent over the table, cutting the bandage as she spoke.

Akio did not know if she spoke her words as a warning. He snorted again. Words would not stop him. He moved through the arch to the back room where a bed took up one corner. That will do, he grunted. More to his liking, there was no child to hamper his entertainment.

"Your husband will be home soon?" He thought it wise to know his timetable.

She turned with a poultice and bandage in her hands but did not meet his eyes. "Only when the authorities release him with the others. I am uncertain of his crime. He is a good man."

He hated her voice, her speech, it irritated him. He settled in one of the two chairs near the table waiting. Her touch felt gentle and soft, stirring his longing for it to travel elsewhere on his body. He sighed with the resolve that, as a warrior and a true loyalist of the emperor, it was his right to take what he needed to fortify his soul. The music swirled in his head. It was only when he realized the warmth of her fingers no longer pressed against the fresh bandage, that she had stepped away from him.

Head low, she held his shirt out in his direction.

Suddenly, he stood, grabbing her outstretched arm, drawing her close to him. His lips were on hers before she could resist. When she attempted to pull away, he clutched her tighter, fully aroused.

"Do not make a sound," his whispered warning reverberated his lust.

He ripped at her blouse, ignoring her look of terror and disdain. Again, she pushed back, when his open hand left a red mark across her face. He watched her eyes, like a caged animal she looked for an exit. She would find none.

She grabbed at the pair of scissors on the table then held the point out toward him. His laugh filled the room as he easily pried the projectile from her grasp. He held it now, fingering the point, admiring the steel and the sharpness. He determined she must be taught a lesson. His hand went over her mouth as he pushed her back onto the table, the sight of her blood sending a thrill down his spine.

THE LOOK OF SURPRISE on Tak's face did not alter Akio's movements. He stood at the sink patting cool water on his blood splattered shirt. It had been a mistake to cut her so deeply, she had become weak and limp. He pitied her husband as he found her to be unimaginative in sex.

He turned back toward the inquisitive young sailor. "We must go. Has anyone gone past?" Akio recognized the disgust in Tak's eyes, he did not approve.

"No. It is quiet." Tak turned back toward the front door jerking it open to step outside, leaving Akio in the semi-darkness of the restaurant.

Akio followed as they hurried down the wharf, watching Tak's slumped shoulders. How dare this impudent young man condemn his superior's action? He controlled his urge to hit the contemptuous fool over the head then slip his body into the water. His restraint, due the nearness of the military bases and the reaction to finding a Japanese corpse floating in these waters, made breathing difficult. He would wait. Tak would meet his death. He would see to it.

# EIGHT

M RS. HUNTINGTON AMBLED TO HER FAVORITE rose-covered chair, yet remained standing, breathing deeply. Sighing, she took in the splendor of her home in Hillsborough, admiring the light from the tall stained-glass windows. Her eyes fell on the forlorn Christmas tree holding the place of honor next to the massive hearth. She shrugged, forcing her nagging depression aside. It had been fourteen years since her husband abruptly took his life, his statement regarding his perceived financial failure during the stock market crash. Had he believed in himself, in his dealings, he would have realized the outcome would turn to profit again. She missed him, their extravagant life of travel and entertaining, but now she must make room for the living. In a few months' time, the arrival of her daughter's baby would restore joy to this grand house. For now, she must make the best of what the world lay at her feet, holding on to the hope the war, and its misery, would end swiftly. She bent her head in a quick prayer for her son, Jack, whose whereabouts kept the entire household in suspense.

At the sound of footsteps Mrs. Huntington looked up to watch Bella, her lifelong maid, struggle an oversized box into the living room. She smiled at Bella, the woman who raised Jack and Lilly with love, sternness and wisdom. Over the years their lives had intertwined with dependency and understanding.

"This is the rest of the decorations." Bella placed the large box before the spotless hearth. Using a small towel to wipe the dust from the lid, she examined her handiwork. As she stood, her black skin glistened with exertion.

"Are we too old for this, Bella?" Mrs. Huntington rested her hand on her high back chair.

"No, ma'am." Bella's southern upbringing clung to her words in a soothing manner. "It's been too long since we've done up this house right at Christmas."

"Oh, are we decorating?" Lilly shuffled in, the mound of her belly beginning to protrude on her small frame.

"Yes," the two older women agreed in unison.

"What fun." Lilly hurried to open the box.

"Fun? What has overcome the house of Huntington?" Jack's growl was pure joy to the ladies.

"Oh." Lilly dropped the lid, dashing to her brother. "And here I thought the fun would be all mine."

"Ah, that's more like it, Frilly my dear."

Lilly stood on tip toe to peck at his cheek, then stood back holding her belly for him to admire.

"Where's your bride, Jack?" His mother's voice did not hold the prickling sound of disapproval, but one of acceptance.

"I'll bring her down soon. But this is a short business trip." He took his mother's hand then brushed a kiss on her cheek, inhaling her ever present scent of roses.

"Bella." He regarded her smile. "Are you keeping the women of this house in good shape?"

She feigned a scowl. "And what else would I be doin'?"

The mere sound of Bell's southern way of speech sent a sense of relief though Jack. He was home. If even for a brief moment his spirits improved.

"Well, I see all is in order here." Jack turned toward the tree. "And that there is a bit of work to do."

Lilly rushed back to the box extracting two taciturn stockings. "Look at these." Her excitement spreading to the others. "We'll have to make two new ones, or is that three?" She looked coyly at her brother.

The air seemed to be sucked out of the room as Jack stood, not comprehending the anticipation on the three faces before him.

"Christ," Jack blurted when the intimation of Lilly's statement came to him. "Listen Frrillly," he dragged out his pet name for her, "there's a war . . ."

"Have a seat Jack," his mother interrupted.

Jack sat, hating his words. "Sorry."

His sister nodded then continued her search through the box.

He was at a loss for words. Lieutenant Todd Archers, Lilly's husband, had died on the *USS Reuben James*, just days after their marriage. The aggressive act by the German submarine on October 31st, 1941, should have drawn the United States into war back then. The Navy claimed the Reuben James, acting as part of an escort envoy out of Newfoundland, knew the position of the wolf pack and had deliberately placed herself between the pack of submarines and the American ammunition ship carrying much-needed supplies to Great Britain. Todd was just one of the one hundred souls lost that day.

Lilly sat on the couch next to her brother holding out an old, hand carved Santa. "Here, you decide where he should go this year."

He kissed her forehead accepting the peace offering. It was a game they had played since childhood, moving Santa around the house.

"Just not in my stove again," Bella interjected.

"You promise, Jack?" His mother had not joined in the merriment. "You promise to bring her soon?"

He met his mother's stare. "Yes. Billi sends her love. I hope you will find room for another Mrs. Huntington in this house?"

The wrinkles in her cheeks rose with her smile. "I look forward to it."

Jack nodded; a bit uncertain at the wicked look his mother gave him. What had he done not telling his mother before they were married?

At the knock from the inside of the kitchen door, Jack hurried toward the sound. Standing to the side, he pushed it open quickly, ready to intercept the intruder.

"Sorry, Mr. Huntington." Howard stepped back, hands held up in defense. "I didn't want to interrupt but was looking for my mother."

Bella's ample bulk almost knocked Jack off balance. "That you, Howard?"

The tall man scooped her up in his arms. There cheeks pressed together, matching dark hues, son resembling mother, against the white walls of the kitchen. Their laughter resounded the joy of the moment.

"I am so happy to see my baby. Sit"

Howard did as told.

Jack watched the display of love with a tinge of envy. He forced aside the fact that overt affection was something his own mother had never afforded him, something he himself sought in Bella. He approached the table where he had spent many a time with Bella, extending his hand. Howard stood, accepting the welcoming handshake.

"Nice to see you again, Howard. Will you be staying long?"

Howard bit his lip. Jack regretted the question, seeing the look of concern cross Bella's face.

"Of course, he will." Lilly smiled at them from the archway of the kitchen door.

Jack stood back for a moment watching the scene as the three sat at the table chatting. He took in the aromas of Bella's labors, the covered wooden bowl where the yeast of her rich bread began its magic, the ever-present scent of coffee, all that reminded him of comfort, gnawed at his senses. He longed to stay, to fill his day with uncomplicated tasks.

"Well, I have to be off." Jack nodded before disappearing.

Lilly followed him into the foyer. "Jack is there something . . ."

"Just work," he cut her concern short. "I expect to see this house fully decorated when I return."

"Yes." Mrs. Huntington eyed her son, adding a rare smile. "A lot remains to be done."

Jack studied his mother, her wisdom and ability to cut straight to the heart of a matter defined her strength. She had never been more astute. Indeed, a lot remained to be done.

BILLI STUFFED THE COLLECTED ITEMS for emergency use into the designated boxes then waited. Mrs. O, perched in her big chair, dutifully noted the supplies on her mounting stacks of paper, as she nodded for her daughter to continue. Being a block watch captain had taken on a whole new meaning.

"I'm going to contact the War Department about hanging a blue star banner in our window for Eddy." Her mother hesitated, pen poised above her paper, before continuing. "And, of course, request a gold star for Mrs. Thompson."

Billi followed her mother's gaze past her sleeping puppy to the over-flowing box of donations set to one side for delivery to Mrs. Thompson at the end of the block. Chuck Thompson turned nineteen last August. A photo of his young smiling face in his white Navy uniform sat on the Thompson mantel. A constant flame of a candle glowed between his photo and an old flute since the news arrived that Chuck, along with all his fellow band members, went down with the *USS Arizona*. His latest letter arriving after the declaration of his death.

His exacting handwriting claimed he, along with twenty others in the Navy Band Unit, had qualified for the finals of the Navy's annual Battle of Music. They were slated to compete at Pearl on December 20. Chuck went on to promise his mother that he and his beloved flute would be safe.

This joy was not to be. Preparing for the daily morning activity of raising the flag, the band sat on the deck when the attack began. They hurried to their battle stations below the gun turret. The sad consola-tion for the loss of the entire band—unanimously the other Navy bands declared those lost souls on the *Arizona* as the winner of The Battle of Music for 1941.

Billi sighed heavily at the image. Death had entered their neighbor-hood. A death that would be marked by the color gold.

"Yes, Mother. I'm certain she would appreciate the effort and the gold star." Her thoughts drifted to Raymond Richardson. She could see the three of them sitting in the big cedar tree out back. She had claimed the branch in the middle flanked by Eddy and Ray, their initials carved into the rough bark in everlasting entitlement to their perches. As far back as she could remember, to the very first time Eddy brought Ray home, the three were thick as thieves.

She twisted the black onyx ring with the small diamond in the middle her husband slid on her finger just ten days ago. It felt much lighter than the ostentatious ring Ray presented her with. The three large diamonds, steeped in family history that ruthlessly entwined her husband with her deceased fiancée, left a heavy weight on her heart. Ray, the brave pilot, who tested a plane not ready for battle, spiraled to his death creating the twists of fate which brought her Jack.

The sudden urge to speak with her husband brought her to her feet. She ran to the phone in the hall, fingers shaking, as she placed a call to the house on San Ramundo Road, in Hillsborough, California.

She waited, impatient with her uncontrollable need. The operator had not come back on when she heard a click. Nosy neighbors made her blood boil.

"If there is anyone else listening in, hang up now or I will report you." Her words were like fire running through the party line her mother shared with a few neighbors.

"No, it's just me." Excited, Bella continued in her matter of fact fashion, "You lookin' to talk with Jack, you're out a luck. He's gone."

"Oh, Bella it is so nice to hear your voice." Hearing Bella's rich manner of speech made Billi realize how deeply she missed Jack and his family. "Is he coming back soon?"

"Only the Lord knows that." Bella's tone softened. "Are you comin' down like he says you are?"

Billi felt her heart flip at the invitation. "Yes." She nearly fumbled her words as she worked her fib. "Yes, but Bella I want to surprise Jack. He's not expecting me for a few more days, but I plan on leaving tomorrow. Will you help me."

"Yes, misses. I won't tell him nothin'. You just get here."

Billi rushed into the living room, startling her dog and Mrs. O. "Mother, I'm heading to California to see my husband." She held her breath, waiting for the back lash.

Mrs. O raised and lowered her shoulders. "I figured you would. Papa gave me some money toward your ticket."

Stunned, Billi stood a moment realizing her parent's full acceptance of Jack. "I'll be back soon. I promise." She went to her mother helping her up. The two women entwined in a show of love that bound mother and daughter with understanding and acknowledgement.

As Billi pulled away, she looked in her mother's big brown eyes recognizing her admirable resilience. "I'll make sure Danny and Dahlia are on hand. But I have to go."

"Of course, you do." Mrs. O held her head high. "You're a wife with duties."

Billi kissed her cheek, then like a whirlwind, darted from the room. At the sound of her shoes hitting the wooden stairs Pepper jumped from the couch to follow his mistress up the spiral staircase.

EDDY MADE ROOM ON HIS bunk for Scooter, it felt good to be back at Kane'ohe, if only for a brief while. His top-secret clearance and desk job at Pearl, while interesting and closer to Lani, was clearly not where he intended to remain.

"That was some ride." Scooter shook his head.

"Got to love a wingspan that lets us float just above the water for that long. Would have been a long swim back to base." Eddy let out a deep sigh, rubbing the ache in his forearms. The joke remained you could always tell a PBY pilot by the size of his forearms. The lack of hydraulics in the steering meant maneuvering the large boat of a plane with sheer manual strength.

Beauregard Applewich, their newly assigned flight captain, stuck his head in the door. "Thanks, fellas, for a great introduction today. I'm off to see why the engine sputtered like that and make sure it's corrected. Had me going there for a minute the way you just rode the wind home."

"You're with the best crew, you know," Scooter teased.

Eddy not to be outdone added, "Don't ever listen to his BS or your eyes will turn brown like his."

Beau presented a cheshire smile as he nodded. "See you in the morning then."

They heard Beau's footstep from further down the hallway.

"What are you thinking?" Scooter toyed with the unlit cigarette in his hand.

Eddy shook his head at his predicament. He only wanted to punch holes in the sky fighting the enemy. Like the others, he wanted payback. He deflected the conversation away from his true thoughts.

"I hope Truck and the Willamette football team make it back state-side safely."

"You go and see them off?" Scooter sounded genuinely interested.

"The team just left on the *Lahaina* in exchange for helping with the wounded aboard, most dying from burns. He said he hoped he didn't spend the whole time vomiting from the smell of the burnt flesh. I don't envy them, zig zagging through waters infested with Japanese submarines. They might be home for Christmas."

Scooter snorted. "Christmas. The only gift I want is those damn Nips dead."

"We all do." Eddy stood uncomfortable and edgy.

The casualties in the Islands continued, with the tally of deceased markedly in favor of the Japanese. He walked to the map one of the men had plastered on the wall, pins stuck out where the local attacks had occurred since December 7th. One pin, about 800 miles off Hawaii, was marked Dec 11 – *Lahaina*, a freighter carrying molasses and scrap iron had been hit, four dead that day, two at their own hands. A pin labeled Dec 14 – *Høegh Merchent* protruded near Kauai, where a Norwegian motorship had gone down with the crew scrambling for their lives. Dec 17 – *Manini* and today a new pin floated proclaiming more destruction, Dec 19 – *Prusa*.

Scooter came up beside him. "They sure have balls." He pointed to the different colored flags stuck in the harbor at Kahului, Maui, dated December 15. "That took balls. Surfacing and firing into the harbor. At least this time their aim was off. That pineapple cannery could have been you or me."

"Are you trying to cheer me up?" Eddy turned to his friend and co-pilot. Restlessness with a mounting sense of doom lurked in the halls, seeping into the men, who with each announcement of another loss, felt the prick of the defeat. Like the map on the wall, the men carried every unanswered attack like markers on their souls.

"What are you learning when you are called to Pearl?" Scooter's question came across as demanding.

Eddy didn't answer, his status with security prohibiting discussion. Besides, for the most part, his duties were merely as a delivery boy, able to carry important sealed messages between commanders.

He turned back to the display of local attacks in the last few days. The maps on the walls at headquarters for the Pacific Fleet looked like a pin the tail on the donkey gone wrong. The Nippon flags spread across China, Borneo, Formosa, Malaya, Luzon, recently pushing further into the Philippines. They reflected the fingerprints of a greedy nation seeking supremacy, not only in the Asian Pacific, but now slithered across the oceans to Australia and the United States.

"Okay, I know you'll tell me if it's important." Scooter started toward the door. "Let's get to mess before the others for once." He waited by the door until Eddy caught up with him.

Eddy stopped before his friend, eyeing him defiantly. "No, I have not seen Lani in the last three days. She has shut me out. Is that what you're after?"

"Look, when we're up there, I need you with me. I need to be sure you're all mine in the sky, not some . . . some . . ."

Eddy began a halfhearted swing, but Scooter stepped back. They breathed heavily at each other like professional boxers deciding who would deliver the first blow.

"You're my co-pilot, my first concern when under fire, and hopefully my best man when I marry Lani." Eddy snorted.

"Do I have to wear a hula skirt again?" Scooter demanded.

"Only if you want to, you son of a bitch."

"Okay. That's more like it."

They shook their anger away in unison as they attempted to push through the opening as one.

# NINE

As Billi moved further into the train bound for San Francisco she scrunched between the young soldiers, scanning their proud faces. Such innocence. She noted that, for some, the hair on their chins barely sprouted. While their eyes filled with a mix of determination and trepidation, their words, as if scripted, boasted of valor and bravery. The sight of the young soldiers, sporting their new uniforms as a sign of their manhood, clawed at Billi's heart.

When she stepped from the train, the Southern Pacific Depot presented a mass of movement. Young girl's tears mingled with those of mothers as the tan or white clad uniformed boys disembarked or loaded. The steam from the train only heightened the mystery of the mighty at work as to who among the valiant soldiers would return. She prayed for each and every one of them.

"Billi." A voice emerged from the crowd. She looked around, her suitcase swinging with her efforts.

"Billi."

She saw a scarf waving above bobbing heads then started in its direction.

Lilly had her arms wide and inviting. As they hugged Billi felt the ever-growing bump of new life. "You look fantastic."

"As do you, Mrs. Huntington." Lilly laughed. "You will have to tell me how my brother proposed and, well, everything."

"Does he know I'm here?" Billi could not keep her anxiety regarding Jack's response from her question.

"Not yet. But we made him promise to have dinner with us tonight." Lilly led the way through the long wooden benches cramped with soldiers. They skirted behind the occupied tall stools at the counter where the neon sign announced, "Fountain Lunch," continuing past another such sign, "Drink Coca Cola," then out under the massive Spanish style arches. Lilly had parked her mother's old car just outside the depot at the corner of 3rd and Townsend. The 1928 La Salle's elongated lines and golden and tan paint stood out amongst the modern black sedans.

Lilly constantly chattered the entire drive to Hillsborough while Billi's nervousness allowed her only a few brief responses. Neither the rain splashing against the large windshield nor the moisture from the bay, with its lingering scent of the saltwater, impacted her concern. The thought that Jack would not accept her on his turf crept through her like slow molten lava.

They pulled into the garage next to the massive brick Tudor home then stepped out into the chill of the dark enclosure. The rain dripped off her coat as they scurried across the expansive driveway then into the arched wooden front door.

As they entered, Bella rushed out of the kitchen then stopped, eyeing Billi suspiciously. "Come with me," Bella demanded. "You need a bath and to fix your hair before dinner."

Lilly giggled, shrugging. "I'm taking a nap." But instead of heading up the stairs just before the grand archway leading to the living room, she marched into the kitchen.

Bella hesitated, clearly torn between her two young charges. Should she protect her baking from a ravenous pregnant woman or make sure Billi emerged presentable for Jack's return?

"Don't be cuttin' into my pie. Sugar and butter are harder to get these days. There's milk, and biscuits, and jam." She grabbed Billi's arm with determination heading her toward the stairs. "Hmmph, you sure did create a commotion around here."

At the top landing Billi stood a moment at the wrought iron railing that overlooked the living room admiring the spattering of Christmas cheer artfully adorning the fireplace, piano and tree. Her mother would approve of this scene. For a moment her heart went out to her mother, childless for the Holidays for the first time in over twenty-two years.

"Ah, it is you."

A voice form behind Billi broke her spell. She turned to face her new mother-in-law, scolding herself for not hurrying along behind Bella to avoid this encounter until she appeared less disheveled.

"Yes, hello." Billi shifted her suitcase uncomfortably, as the older woman seemed to appraise her appearance with some distain.

"Welcome, Mrs. Huntington." The older woman smiled and the lines around her eyes deepened with the act. "I see Bella is getting you settled in."

"Yes, I am thrilled to be here. Thank you." Billi almost curtsied in the awkward silence that followed.

"I am certain my son will be pleased to see you."

Billi noted the slight teasing in her tone. She swallowed hard before speaking. "It's a surprise."

"I am sure it will be quite the surprise." Her smiled disappeared. "Run along."

As she moved back into her large bedroom, Billi heaved a sigh before continuing down the hall where Bella stood anxiously waiting.

"Thank the Lord that's over with."

Bella shook her head while throwing open the door to the room Jack now occupied. When Billi saw the double bed, neatly made, she suddenly became nervous. She smelled him as she entered, then paused, not certain where to put her suitcase.

Bella took the case from her. "Here, lemme help you."

Billi awkwardly watched as the large woman hefted the case onto the dark bedspread snapping it open. Then, removing the top layer of clothing, Bella moved toward the closet to hang Billi's blue silk dress.

Tucked in with her clothing Billi spotted a green gift box with the distinctive *Fredrick & Nelson* scrolled in cream across the top. Excited, she reached for the surprise. "It's from my mother." She briefly read the tag then corrected herself. "And my father."

"Well, open that box." Bella sat on the bed waiting.

Billi removed the lid and blushed. "Oh, it's beautiful." She gently took hold of the thick lace lifting the white satin night gown from the box. She held it up against her body, the lace plunged low in the front and even lower in the back, almost to her waist. The rich material gleamed in the light.

Bella slid from the bed marching into the adjoining bathroom. "Hummph, we better get you cleaned up. My, oh my."

The hint of Bella's hum, barely audible above the running tub water, made Billi hopeful. She tucked the nightgown back in the box then lowered onto the bed, praying that her husband would indeed respond with joy at her sudden appearance.

SHIRLEY CHOW CRAB WALKED to her usual hand carved wooden chair, lowering herself with disgust. Her long-painted fingernails tapped the head of one of the dragons holding a large ball at the end of the armrest. Her traditional brown gown, not in keeping with her stature in the community or her accumulated wealth, concealing her badly crippled legs. As she leaned toward Jack, one of the elaborate, etched bone hair combs that held her tightly coiffed bun in place shone in the light. Only the slightest beat of the cabaret music floated down the hallway, penetrating the wall of this back room in The Forbidden City Night Club.

"Will you visit Terminal Island?" Her strong voice poised the direct question.

"How long ago did your sources say this happened?" Jack picked up his scotch focusing on her eyes to see if she changed her story.

"Three days ago. The old man said they came by boat and where there for about two hours. Akio is swift with a knife."

The scotch did its magic as it slid down his throat. He wanted to scream. Akio was close, offshore somewhere along the coast. In three days he could have made it back to Seattle. He would alert Duckworth to step up his surveillance on 304 30th Ave South.

Luckily, a curfew had been put into place after the riot in Seattle on December 8th. That night panic streamed through the streets as about one thousand agitated men and women congregated downtown. The crowd raged out of control breaking windows throughout the city in order to knock out the business lights shining brightly during a blackout. Now patrols canvased the streets. Yet, he knew even that would not keep his hard-headed wife inside.

Before he could answer, the door opened as Charlie Low, owner and proprietor of the club, walked inside. Shirley gave a slight nod in Charlie's direction as he sat next to her facing Jack.

Jack swirled the remainder of the brown liquid in his glass. "It's good to see that the war has brought even more prosperity to your establishment."

Charlie lit a cigarette, speaking between puffs. "Yes, the soldiers have priority at the front tables, and we are considering adding another show. My girls are doing all they can for the war effort." He smiled before adding, "How is Ginger?"

Jack snorted, leaning back. "She's doing fine."

"It seems trouble follows her." Charlie shifted to Chinese speaking in a low tone to the powerful woman next to him.

Jack watched Cheryl's one eyebrow raise.

"Will you take Ginger with you to verify the story at the fishing village?" Shirley's question held a hint of urgency.

Jack felt his jaw tighten. Something was afoot. He masked his concern amazed at how she always seemed to be one step ahead, empowered by her vast stream of informants. "I leave tomorrow and will keep you informed, as I know you will me."

The dragon lady smiled. "Enjoy your evening."

Jack grabbed his hat before leaving. He stood in the hallway for a moment as the girls in their skimpy costumes, bustling in preparation for the next number, brushed past him. What secrets surrounded the exchange between Shirley and Charlie? The fact that the matron of San Francisco's China Town quickly dismissed him without sharing the new information put him on edge. Yet her involvement with locating Akio remained priceless. Her ulterior motive, buried deep in the shadows of this section of the city, worried him the most. She held her cards extremely close making her one to watch.

Hurrying down the length of the steep stairs leading up to the nightclub, he continued past the line of waiting patrons extending out past the cover of the canopy, down the block. He pulled the collar of his overcoat up against the rain as he passed the eager faces of the young men in uniform. Such youth.

His pace down Sutter Street intensified with the guilt of his situation. Due to his eye injury he could not join the military to fight alongside the brave men. His feet pounded the pavement with frustration and hatred for Akio. Jack let loose a deep breath reminding himself the gloves of restraint no longer existed. Nothing stood in the way of killing the enemy, specifically Akio.

Jack entered the side door of the Sir Francis Drake Hotel then took out the key to his secret office on the mezzanine floor. He waited for the second, empty elevator. Working the lock behind the curtain he stepped inside the cement room with the one light bulb, a table and two chairs. He bent over the brass peek hole on the floor that overlooked the portion of the lobby between the elevators before tossing his hat on the table. In just over two weeks' time everything in his world had changed.

He slumped down resisting the temptation of the scotch bottle he kept stashed on the shelf. The irony of this cement room, once the clandestine storage for liquor during prohibition, transforming into his private headquarters, seemed to echo his hardened feelings of failure.

He reached for the phone, the only other object in these sterile surroundings, then used his secured line to call Seattle.

Duckworth's voice lifted his dreary spirits.

"Any good news?" Jack barked into the phone.

"Then you've heard?" Duckworth voice sounded tired.

"Fill me in."

"Like you instructed, we've only had one man outside Mrs. O's house at night. We haven't seen Billi coming or going for a few days. Have you talked with her?"

Jack realized Duckworth's concern. Billi, a known escape artist, had done it again. He ran his hand through his thick, black hair. He had tried the house at 304, but the party line constantly buzzed, blocking his call. He should have been more persistent.

"I'll try again and let you know. Anything else?" As if that wasn't enough.

"The submarine attacks seem to be ramping up along our coast as you know. But here's a good one. The Army heard some Japanese going out loud and clear from Grays Harbor along the Washington coast. Thought it was someone sending radio signals to the subs. When they tracked it down, it turned out to be a white kid playing a Japanese record dressed in a kimono. The kid was scared to death. Told the police he found the kimono and records in a deserted house and was just messing around."

"Well the Japanese subs are out there, and someone is sending them signals." Jack removed his patch from his right eye, rested his elbow on the table putting the weight of his aching head into the cup of his hand. "Get some rest. I'm heading to L.A. in the morning to confirm a situation. I'll call you after I talk with Billi."

He massaged around his bad eye as he listened dejectedly when the operator came back on the line explaining there was no answer at the O'Shaughnessy home. Jack decided he would have Duckworth install a private line at 304, he reasoned the safety of his wife was still connected to that of the nation. Akio would not give up his need to avenge his loss of face until he had breathed his last breath.

# TEN

JACK SMELLED THE ROAST AS HE walked through the front door and allowed the sensation to work its calming magic. He had outlined his plans for tomorrow on the long drive home, deciding to leave for Los Angeles before dawn. The description of the attack on the woman at Terminal Island, plus the man seen near the area, fit Akio top to bottom. His stomach continued to boil with acid at the realization his enemy lurked within reach. As he reached the archway into the grand living room, he stopped stunned, silently taking in the scene.

Billi stood before the fire, her blue dress shimmering in the light, while his sister sat with her feet up on the coffee table and his mother rested in her accustomed chair. They were laughing, a sound that had not filled the room in years, and it lightened his heart.

Jack removed his hat descending the two polished wooden steps. "Am I interrupting? It appears you started the party without me?"

"Never, dear brother," Lilly giggled, holding a glass of champagne out in salute. "You are the party."

Again, all three women laughed, causing him to halt, frozen in their midst.

"Give your bride a kiss, Jack." His mother instructed.

He noticed his mother's half full glass accompanied by the rosy color in her cheeks. He looked at his wife sensing her tension. Before he could move Bella came down the steps carrying a tray.

"We've been waitin'." Her smile beamed as broadly as possible. She placed the tray on the table then stood back proud of her pre-meal offerings of cheese, crackers and stuffed celery.

"To the bride and groom." Lilly's glass shot up into the air again.

Jack's hand shook a little as he poured himself a glass of cheer before starting toward Billi. His confusion gave way as his spirits soared at the sight of her. He stood awkwardly next to his new wife then took her hand. He had never kissed a woman in front of his mother, not the way he wanted to kiss his wife right now.

"Well," his mother demanded.

He kissed Billi's cheek as her soft scent of lilac water made him want to ravage her on the spot.

He looked around the room. Bella had her hands on her hips, which meant he was about to get a talking to, his sister had a devilish twinkle in her eye, and his mother regarded him with that look that meant she expected more from her only son.

"Oh, good heavens," his mother groaned.

Billi bumped Jack with her hip and he raised his glass. "To all of the beautiful women who make this gracious home one a man wants to return to. And, especially to the addition of my amazing wife, Mrs. Billi Huntington."

"Not Ginger?" Lilly pouted.

"Oh, Ginger still exists." Jack smiled at them.

BILLI RESTED HER HEAD on Jack's shoulder as they sat in silence in his father's study. The pine walls warmed by the firelight cast a mellow mood over the young couple.

"Thank you for coming." He kissed her forehead.

"I wasn't sure, but I want to help, Jack. Let me go with you tomorrow." She toyed with his patch that rested on her lap, giving him time to weigh the situation.

"I need to show you something." He pushed from the couch leaving the depression from his weight in the soft leather. Helping his wife to her feet he led her to the far side of the fireplace. Pressing his hand against the mantel on the far corner, a drawer slowly eased out. Jack reached inside extracting a hidden handgun.

"You need to learn how to use this."

Billi took the weight of the gun in her right hand, looked for the safety lock then snapped the cartridge holder open. "I'll need bullets first."

Jack shook his head while handing her the box of bullets. "I should have known."

"You can thank your brother-in-law, Eddy, and your late relative, dear Raymond, for my talents."

"Speaking of Raymond, you left something here." He pulled out the top drawer of the heavy desk as his hand covered a small ring box. He held it out to her. "From both of us. Only to be worn when you're ready."

Billi instantly recognized the engagement ring Raymond had given to her. The three large diamonds that had draped on her finger in an uncomfortable fashion, appeared different to her now. Oddly, Raymond's mother, being a part of this old San Francisco family, had purchased this very ring from Mrs. Huntington after the stock market crash and Jack's father committed suicide. The ring belonged with this house, and now, in twists of fate, so did she.

"Thank you." She held back the tears of Raymond's memory as she regarded her husband. She gently put the gun back in the hidden drawer. "Not quite yet." She smiled. "Rings and guns. You are full of surprises."

"Ah, but the pièce de résistance." Jack walked to the wall behind the desk and put pressure on the center panel. "Note that it doesn't squeak? It was one of the many wise instructions from my father. I was to keep this secret from mother."

Billi leaned into the dark smelling the faint whiffs of smoke. Jack put her hand on the switch and together they flipped on a soft golden light. Before them carpeted stairs made for a soundless descent. She wondered in what manner his father had used this passageway.

He started her down the stairs whispering, "It comes out in the living room, to the left of the fireplace. No one knows of this. It is only for emergencies."

At the bottom, soundlessly the door opened into the large living room. Billi slipped into the darkness, recognizing their position, listening to the rain hit against the tall stained-glass windows. A draft seeped in on the bustling wind pushing against the two sets of French doors facing each other across the deep oriental rug.

They stood a moment, their bodies pressed together giving off their own heat, his breath warm against her ear.

"I have a gift from Mother and Dad for you," she whispered.

He stood back, uncertain of the offering.

The voice of Ginger continued, "Oh, I think you'll like it." Swaying, she took his hand leading him back up the hidden passage.

BILLI ADMIRED HER REFLECTION in the bathroom mirror. The white satin negligee with the neckline of heavy lace made her feel elegant and daring. She fluffed her hair once more, swishing toward the door leading directly to Jack's, now their, bedroom. As she reached for the doorknob, she heard a knock on the door to the hallway. She opened the bathroom door a crack peeking into the bedroom.

Bella stood just inside the hallway doorframe, her old bathrobe secured over her nightie and ample bosom. Jack watched her with apparent intensity.

"There's a lady at the door askin' for you." Her agitated voice addressed Jack as her hands found her hips. "This better be business. You got one wife up here. Now there's another filly askin' for you in the middle of the night. What in the name of the good Lord have you been up to?"

Jack edged Bella out into the hall shutting the door behind him. Quietly, Billi slipped from the bathroom pressing her ear against the wood, holding her breath to listen.

"Shh, calm down," her husband whispered from the hallway. "Did she say who she was?"

Bella's attempt at a whisper could be heard in New York city. "She told me she isn't talkin' to nobody but you."

"Tell her I'll be right down."

"This better be business." Bella boomed.

Billi's heart pounded as she rushed back to the bathroom, closing the door.

When Jack knocked, she innocently opened it. She noted the impact of her new nightgown cross his face as he fumbled to button up his shirt.

"I don't know how much of that you heard?" He eyed her suspiciously. When she didn't answer he continued. "I have to take a meeting. Stay put. I'll be right back." He kissed her briefly before turning to leave.

Billi waited for the sound of his footsteps to die down, then grabbed Jack's thick robe from the bedpost. As she wrapped it around her, she inhaled his scent, strong, masculine, which only set her further into motion. She needed to find out what this strange woman, who came calling in the dark of night, meant to Jack. She thought of his father's study and slipped down the hall. Quietly closing the door behind her, she felt her way beyond the desk to the paneled wall. Imitating Jack's movements for earlier that evening, she pressed against the panel, nothing happened. She repeated the motion on another panel, still nothing. Returning to the first, she pushed harder. The door gave way and she scurried down the carpeted stairs in her bare feet.

She had to be careful not to lean too heavily against the secret door leading into the living room for fear it might open. When she clearly heard the woman's voice, she sighed with relief.

"We traveled first to La Palma. Our contact there updated us on the Japanese activity along the coast of Mexico. He gave us a map of where the Japanese ships were entering the estuaries. It was suspected they were storing fuel there for their subs. He gave us the name of more contacts and we were on our way. When we neared the ocean, we met another contact, who provided us with a small boat. At night we headed through the estuaries toward the ocean. We were lucky to locate the Japanese operation."

"How long were you there?" Jack's question held the tone of an inquisition.

"We camped across the waterway for one week. Their docking station was rudimentary but efficient and well hidden by the jungle." The female voice was smooth and silky.

"And you're sure no one saw you."

"We would be dead if they had."

Jack's voice came from further in the room. He had moved. "How many submarines did you see?"

There was a pause before the well enunciated voice continued. "Two in the week we were there. The dock was very active. It appeared to be built with a concrete mixture of shells and sand that projected into the inlet, quite resourceful. There were several oil drums with long hoses in constant motion. The subs were guided up the estuary by manned dugouts tethered to the bow. One sub had a large fishing vessel follow-ing, possibly to conceal the activity. The perfect refueling station hidden by the thick brush."

Billi realized Jack had moved again when the stranger purred, "Thank you, Jack."

Billi felt her body stiffen.

"What did you observe in Guaymas?" He continued to lead the interview with precision.

"We just passed through as tourists but were able to witness sev-eral Japanese stores, empty of clientele. The Japanese owners were very watchful, and they all had brand new cameras and trucks. It seems that there was one particular Japanese man who bottled Coca Cola. Every new arrival from any Nippon ship, went directly to his store first. Jack," the voice intensified, "our contacts told us the same was happening in Panama. Japanese owned stores sat empty, no patients at the dentist's offices, farmers with new trucks but no crops, fishermen without fish on board. And there are several groups of Germans. But the most concern-ing detail we heard was that the crews on the fishing vessels change. One group left on a boat and a different crew returned on the same boat. They were changing crews offshore."

Billi heard her husband pacing in front of the wooden panel she stood behind.

"Were you recognized?"

"I hardly think the name Rochelle Hudson is that well known in the jungles of Mexico. I'm not that big of a star." Her laugh sounded rehearsed. "Van Zandt advised us to leave shortly before the war broke out."

"How is Rufus?"

"Still crazy as hell. Come here."

Billi nearly fell through the door. The image of the striking beauty Rochelle Hudson luring her husband closer got her blood boiling. She held her breath waiting but heard nothing from the other side. She could not barge through the door now. She hurried up the secret pas-sage, gently closing the panel then bumped into the desk. She tip-toed down the silent hallway toward the balcony above the living room. If discovered here it would be better than in the passageway she rea-soned. From her perch above, she saw the movie star and her husband side by side, a drink in their hands, hovering over something on the coffee table.

"Thomas took all of these as I posed," she pointed to one. "This last one is the storefront of the Coca Cola building in Guaymas." She slipped the photo's back inside a manila envelope then sat back against the couch.

"This is a beautiful home, Jack. You need the right woman to fill it with children."

The impact of her perfect smile on Jack was not lost from Billi's observation point.

"What about you?" Jack leaned back next to her sipping his drink. "Any plans along that line?"

Billi gulped in disbelief. Her husband clearly just made a pass at this star of the screen.

"I have enough on my plate. But maybe someday." She kissed him briefly on the cheek then stood. "I'd better get back. Thomas is due in tonight. He's been sharing our findings with his commander at the Navy. Being an officer has many duties." She set her empty drink on the coffee table. "If the Japanese or the Germans had discovered we were not just some tourists in Mexico, they would have tortured him."

Jack stood. "Thank you for all you have done." He kissed her forehead. "And tell that lucky bastard of a husband I said hello."

His arm went around Rochelle as they disappeared under the balcony. Billi felt her knees give way. She leaned back again the wall for support. Her husband had not told the beautiful movie star he was married.

# ELEVEN

THE JAPANESE ON TERMINAL ISLAND REGARDED them suspiciously. Jack knew the effect his black eye patch and slight scar had on those who encountered him for the first time. He had perfected a look which usually brought apprehension and cooperation to those he addressed. He glanced around noticing Billi remained off to one side next to a group of female factory workers, where she could readily listen to the ladies hushed conversations.

He regarded the small group of men. One, his legs bowed with age, ambled forward and gave a slight bow. "I Mr. Tanaki."

Jack looked down at him, noting his gnarled hands from years of labor, his scent of fish mingled with the sea, and unflinching eyes.

"Are you the one who took the stranger to a meeting?"

His white head barely nodded.

"He was an Imperial Japanese Navy officer." Jack watched the reaction in the older man's eyes. It became apparent the man before him had not known Akio or anything about him. Hearing the group of women mutter amongst themselves he glanced around, thankful for the presence of his wife.

One woman clad in her work attire broke free of the group stepping forward with determination. "You bring back husband?" she demanded. "We need fish."

A young girl tugged at the woman's arm, but the older woman did not budge. The resemblance told Jack they were mother and daughter.

"We need—" the older woman looked at the child then spoke in Japanese.

"Protection," the girl translated.

"Por-tek-son," the mother repeated, waving her finger at Jack.

Jack turned to Mr. Tanaki. "Can you show me where you took him."

Tanaki lead the procession past the tall torri gate, marking the entrance to a Shinto shrine. As they proceeded Jack noted the Los Angeles City school built for these residents looked like no other with its distinctive additions of a Nippon style pond and bridge leading to the expansive school grounds. The small group proceeded off Terminal Way onto Tuna Street then down a few blocks passing many established businesses. The eerie scene of women watching over their pool halls, hardware stores and café's, brought home the point that most of the men of the island had been removed.

Jack quickly looked around to assess the small village. One woman, whose dress indicated she did not work in the factories, caught his eye as she intently watched Billi. With a hint of what appeared to be excitement, this woman suddenly left the group to duck inside a doorway.

When the old man stopped in front of the Tokiwa Low, Jack quickly observed its proximity to the wharfs and fishing fleet. He waited a moment watching the heavy boats rock ever so slightly on the salty winds from across the sea. His frustration emerged as he pushed through the door to the restaurant. Akio lingered out there somewhere, and it made Jack's heart race frantically.

The startled woman behind the counter stepped back, fear covering her face. Mr. Tanaki moved from behind Jack hurriedly speaking to her in their local kii-shu ben dialect. The elder's words seemed to calm her a bit.

Jack turned toward Billi at the end of the counter. She stood quietly with the same faraway look that had come over her last night. He did not have time to consider her sudden coolness toward him at the moment.

The Japanese woman shuffled toward the back of her establishment. "Two men come here." She pointed to the last table.

"Do you know the names of the two men?"

"No." The strength of her answer held truth. "No. Two men come. Meet Nakuche here."

The older man scolded the woman in their private language.

Jack pulled out a photo of Akio and the older man fell silent. He nodded once adding, "Young man too."

Jack spread several photos on the table and the gnarled finger pointed at Tak.

"Tak Nakmura?"

The man's eyes squinted, accompanied by a grunt of consent.

Jack smelled his wife's light fragrance as she approached to look at the photos he had spread out across the table. He heard her slight intake of breath as she recognized not only Tak, but his father, Mr. Nakamura, Professor Fujihara, along with other businessmen and leaders from Seattle's Japantown and elsewhere.

Jack did not look at his wife but sensed her anger. Collecting the photos, he put them back in his pocket addressing the Japanese couple before him. "Where is the woman?"

The restaurant proprietor hesitated briefly, then led them out the back door. They approached rows of barracks like housing, differentiated by personal touches, some with small gardens, short fences or colorful curtains. About halfway down one grouping of homes, they stepped onto a wooden boardwalk following it to the back of the structures. They halted before the shut door of a darkened home. The woman signaled for them to wait as she knocked, then entered.

From inside the house they heard only the voice of the woman who had guided them here, her tone sounded pleading, yet reverent. She reappeared shaking her head "no."

Billi pushed past the woman into the darkness. Jack didn't know what to do. He waited. He heard a few incomprehensible mumblings then saw the anger in his wife's steely blue eyes as she motioned him forward.

Jack stood above the bed where a woman lay with bandages running across her face and covering her hands. He saw the agony in her eyes as he squatted next to her. Pulling out a photo of Tak, he turned on the night light next to the bed. The woman nodded.

"Did he do this?" Jack's voice was a whisper.

She shook her head "no" and Jack heard his wife sigh with relief.

He pulled out another photo and the woman propelled herself to the far corner of the bed, pressing up against the wall, her eyes filling with tears. The cry that she emitted was one of a mute. Akio had not only sliced her hands, and face, but had cut off her tongue.

Jack stood, watching bits of blood mix with salvia run down her chin. He shouted, as if this broken woman could not hear as well as not speak. "We will find him. He will pay for this."

All three women regarded him now. He would find him. He had to. The woman before him was yet another warning of what Akio had planned for Billi.

"Thank you." He looked from the woman on the bed to his wife. Billi allowed him to take her elbow. He felt her lean into him, unsteady, as they headed out of the small, dark home.

The light puffy clouds overhead in the blue sky created a stark comparison to how he felt. There was nothing bright about what they had just witnessed. Billi pulled her arm from his grasp and he let her go. He had no idea what had come between them. When he had returned last night to their bedroom, she was fast asleep, the enticing negligee replaced with a long flannel nightgown. She must have overheard some of his conversation. He watched her head for their car, the sway of her hips taking their effect on his senses.

Jack's left eye caught movement and he turned toward it. A car hurried down the street toward Billi. Jack leapt forward as the car slowed next to his wife. When the back door swung open a hand reached for her. A bullet whizzed past Billi's shoulder and into the side of the car just in front of the driver's door. At the sound of gunfire, the car sped off.

Billi scurried backwards turning toward her husband. He held his gun aimed at the departing automobile, ready to fire again.

They regarded each other, both digesting the incident. Akio's tentacles stretched to this Japanese village. Kidnapping Billi, even in daylight, was obviously a risk worth the reward. Not everyone on Terminal Island held allegiance to America.

AKIO COULD FEEL THE HEAT of the chase. They had sighted another US merchantman to attack creating almost uncontrollable excitement. Two days ago, December 18th, 1941, they had reported back to Tokyo that their I-17 sub sunk the freighter *S.S. Samoa*. He had seen the blast of the torpedo, the shattered lifeboat hanging from its davit and the unmistakable list of a badly damaged ship. Now he watched an oil tanker, the *S.S. Emidio*, heading south along the Pacific Coast, right into the portion of the coastline the I-17 was charged with canvasing.

From the moment Akio stepped aboard this submarine, just a few days ago, he had understood the mission. On December 10th, nine submarines left the Hawaiian waters in pursuit of a Lexington-class carrier heading toward San Francisco. Once the submarines reached the mainland, the orders Captain Kozo Nishino of the Japanese's Navy's I-17 received were simple. All nine submarines were to lay off the coast in designated areas from Mexico to Canada to destroy as many American ships and kill as many of the enemy as possible. Cape Mendocino, north of San Francisco, where the I-17 prowled provided a treasure chest of American ships for the taking as they traveled up and down the coast.

Akio noted the time, 1:30 p.m., and smiled as he watched the *Emidio* attempt to escape. Running their sub on the surface at twenty knots made the larger ship easy prey. Conferring with the captain, he gave the order for the deck guns to open fire. One 5.5-inch shell hit the radio antenna, another dismantled a lifeboat from its davits, sending the now useless skiff crashing into the water.

*Emidio* appeared to be slowing when Akio saw the unthinkable. A white flag fluttered in the brisk wind while the crew appeared to be preparing the remaining lifeboats to abandon ship. He could feel his anger above all else. Surrender showed weakness. Unlike the US forces, the Emperor ordered his troops to never surrender, it was a sign of disgrace. The sniveling Americans deserve to die.

"Fire." He raged.

One blast hit its mark just below crewmembers lowering a lifeboat, tumbling three men into the cold, choppy water. Lust for more blood surged through his veins as he watched some of the crew attempt to row away from the burning vessel. Licking his lips in anticipation he scrambled to the machine gun where Tak stood ready at the mount.

"Shoot them." He waited for Tak to take aim. "Now." He yelled in his ear.

The bullets fell wide of their destination, spraying the tips of the waves. "Planes approaching. Clear the deck."

The command broke through his rage as Akio signaled all below. As the sub dove deeper a depth charge rattled their submarine, vibrating fear among the crew. Sweat dripped from him, as the heat in the confined area rose to uncomfortable temperatures. He looked over at Tak noting the young officer averted his gaze. Akio's anger flared. Tak had purposely missed the easy target of the men in the rowboat. He looked away, envisioning his chastisement of the young sailor.

Ten long, silent minutes passed before Akio approached the captain.

"We must risk surfacing to sink that ship." Akio looked directly at his superior, challenging. He was well aware of the orders from Tokyo, he and the captain had discussed the plan at length. Allied battleships, or any other large cargo vessel, were to be sent to a watery grave. All submarines were to continue this pattern until Christmas day. On December 25th, 1941 all nine submarines were to surface, pick a prominent city or oil refinery and fire off their remaining shells, then using their heavy deck guns, blast the beach and beyond. They were to inflict as much devastation and wreckage as possible, striking a blow not only to the shoreline but to the heart and soul of the American psyche. With this tactic the United States would come to realize the prowess of the Emperor and surrender.

The grunt from his captain confirmed more than his acceptance of the plan. It resounded of their conspiratorial desire to kill.

They barely broke the surface when they fired at the drifting *Emidio* from about two-hundred feet. The torpedo's wake sped straight for the ship, just below the tower. The loud blast shot metal, smoke and white water into the air. Yet, another sound persisted, the pesky aircraft bombers returned. As they dove below the surface the depth-charge dropped by the scouting bombers exploded closer this time, knocking out their communication. Hoping the pilots would conclude they had landed a hit on the submarine, they stayed below, waiting for the dark of night to recharge their killing machine.

Akio could feel the adrenaline pump through his veins. They would report the sinking of another ship and several dead. Sinking helpless ships, killing Americans, destroying their cargo brought glory to their ship and the Empire. He spotted Tak as he made his way down the passage and grabbed him from behind. He had his hand digging into the younger man's throat when another officer pulled him away.

"You insulant dog." Akio breathed heavily at Tak. "We are here to massacre these undeserving Americans bastards. Or does that description fit you, kibei?"

Tak was not given an opportunity to answer as Akio's fist found his cheek, knocking him back against the wall. He slumped to the ground where Akio kicked him before stepping away.

He stood beside his commander when the radio man rushed forward. Not only had their connection been reestablished but the news cable held joyous information. Three US battleships, the *USS Missouri*, the *USS New Mexico* and the *USS Idaho* were heading for port in Los Angeles. Their I-17, along with the I–9 and I-25 were to intercept their expected arrival on December 25th, 1941. The Christmas surprise Akio predicted.

JACK SAT AT HEADQUARTERS in the Presidio across from a major he had never met. He put his hat on his knee then leaned in to read the mounting list of assaults by Japanese submarines.

> December 14, the tanker the *St. Clare* – shot at off the mouth of the Columbia River.
>
> December 17, a sub sighted off of San Francisco. Luckily, the American troop ship made it out of port unscathed as they began their journey across the Pacific to an unknown fate.
>
> December 18, the *Samoa* – attacked and damaged.
>
> December 19, a sub reported off of Cape Blanco, Oregon.
>
> December 20, the *Emidio* – hit off of Mendocino; the *Agwiworld* attacked off of California; another sub spotted in Seattle, Washington.
>
> December 22, the *H.M. Storey* – hit by Japanese submarine gunfire again off of Mendocino.
>
> December 23, the *Montebello* – sunk off of Cambria, California; the tanker *Idaho* damaged in the same vicinity; and the *Larry Doheny* attacked further up the California coast.

December 24, the steamer the *Absaroka* – struck off San
Pedro and the *Dorothy Philips* attacked in Monterey Bay.
"How many dead so far?" Jack tossed the report on the desk then sat
back anticipating the answer he already knew.

"Five on the *Emidio*." The major's voice flattened by the devastating
report. "One more on the *Absaroka*. Several injured, not to mention the
loss of supplies. And they are not done yet."

"You can be assured they will attack again tomorrow, Christmas
Day." Jack picked his hat up off his knee then stood. "But now that we
have most of the Terminal Island fishing fleets grounded, their subs will
run out of fuel soon. They will be heading to Mexico to resupply before
heading back is my guess."

The major tossed his pen onto his desk in frustration. "Hell of a
way to spend Christmas Eve, waiting for more enemy subs to sink our
ships off our own coast."

"Better than being aboard one of the ships, or being in the heart of
the battle, say the Philippines, or Africa right about now." Jack crammed
his hat on his head. "Merry Christmas."

As he headed out the gates of the Presidio, he tried to bolster
his spirits, but the totality of the puzzle had not surfaced, and the
missing pieces nagged at him. If the submarine attacks alone were
the reason for claiming a "Christmas present for America" as Akio
had bragged to his men last month, then what made recouping the
fan with the dragon design so important? Why risk so much for the
object if the submarine attacks are the goal? He had dismissed the fan
as inconsequential now realizing his misstep. He would rethink the
part the fan played in all of this and use it to draw Billi out of her
intensifying blue mood.

As he pulled into the large circular driveway, the house on San
Raymundo appeared lifeless. Weeks ago, the ladies of the household
had busied themselves draping the windows with black curtains. He felt
confident that the darkened home posed no danger to the enemy, yet
inside his wife remained the object of much interest. He took a deep
breath; he could not lose her now. He felt the sharp dagger-like pain
as he realized his need for Billi dangled between two worlds, his love

for her and the important part she played in defense of the country. Uncertain which of these held the higher rank, he steeled himself as he stepped from the car.

Jack swung the door wide, lumbering under the last-minute gifts he scrambled to purchase. Modest but practical had been his approach in these unpredictable times. The hallway light sported only one lamp instead of the normal four while the living room was pitch black. He felt his way to the unlit tree then placed his presents under the scrawny limbs. Hearing a burst of laughter, he followed the sound to the kitchen. The white walls gleamed bright against the black curtains that covered every inch of the windows.

"Well, come in and join us," his mother demanded. She sat at the head of the large kitchen table, an apron over her dress, her hands deep inside a pumpkin.

Bella raised her eyebrow in his direction, the warning not missed on him. This was Mrs. Huntington's first attempt at cooking in years, an event that should not be taken lightly.

"Jack be a dear," Lilly cooed, "bring in the sherry. We need to toast."

He noted that Billi had kept her attention on the dough she was rolling, and it made him nervous.

"We're celebrating the first pumpkin pie of many." Lilly's smile brightened. "We're going to make pies and deliver them tomorrow to the social hall in Burlingame. They are sponsoring a dance for all enlisted men in the area. And Billi and I are going to attend."

He did not know why the statement upset him so. He pushed through the door back toward the darkness of the living room. He found the sherry on the sideboard next to the scotch. Pouring himself a stiff double, he tossed it back, hoping it would clear his mind. She had not looked at him. She remained cold and elusive. He poured another considering if he had made a terrible mistake by making her his wife.

He put the top back on the crystal container before he could slosh a third drink into his glass. Snatching the sherry, he headed back where the women contentedly crafted their pies.

The merry making in the kitchen attacked his nerves. He stacked a pile of cold-cuts and cheese on his plate excusing himself. In the darkness of the large room he grabbed the bottle of scotch, plopping on the couch to eat his bleak fare not knowing how to approach his wife.

Jack jerked awake. The coldness of the room in contrast to the warm touch of Billi's hand on his forehead. He wasn't aware of when he passed out or how he managed to finish most of the scotch. He sat up slowly making room for her next to him.

"Merry Christmas." He coughed to clear his throat.

"Yes." She remained at a distance as she sat.

"What have I done, Billi?"

"Not exactly how we pictured it, is it?"

"The day isn't over. We can make it what we want." He spoke softly, hopeful.

She picked up his eye patch from the floor where it had fallen, placing it on the coffee table.

He reached for her left hand where his father's ring slumped to one side. The black oynx with the one diamond set in gold too large and definitely too manly for her slim finger.

"You have something of mine, and I think it's time I had it back." He tapped the ring he had placed there on their wedding day.

As she turned to face him, he saw the anger flashing in her eyes. She pulled her hand free as she began to remove the ring.

"Is that why you didn't tell that woman you were married?" Billi's voice echoed the frustration he had watched building. "You had no intention of remaining married to me?"

"What?" He calmly reached inside his pocket then pulled out a small box. "What woman?"

"The movie star." She stood. "The one who said you should get married and fill this house with children."

Jack stood, suppressing his relief at finally understanding her coolness. He had been a fool not to have asked earlier, more importantly, not to have realized she would have listened.

"Here." She held the ring out to him. Her voice steady as she continued. "I'll pack my bag and be gone before the others wake up."

He took her open palm that held the ring placing the small box next to it.

With a stunned expression she dropped back down on the couch.

"You're right." He lowered next to her. "I should have told Miss Hudson, who is married to an old friend of mine, that I had entered the blissful life of marriage."

"Hummph." She attempted to sound like Bella.

"And, furthermore, Mrs. Billi Huntington is the only woman I would ever want to fill this house with children."

"Keep going." She straightened.

"You aren't going to make this easy, are you?"

"Depends on what's in this box." She lifted her palm out so that it remained between them, like a protective guard dog.

He whistled. "I'll take my chances."

She set his father's ring on the coffee table, just out of his reach, then made a grand show of opening the box. The genuine smile on her face told the story.

"It's perfect," she whispered. The wedding ring set shown with the simple elegance of one large diamond raised just above the others trailing down the sides.

As she stood, the sun's early morning brightness struggled against the black curtains holding the promise of a bright Christmas day. She snatched the black oynx ring off the coffee table then headed toward the archway and the stairs leading to the upper level.

Jack watched her leave a bit bemused. "Aren't you going to put it on?" When she didn't answer he became concerned, "Should I help you with . . ."

"No." She did not break stride as she continued, "I was hoping you would help me with something else."

"Oh, Ginger. I have missed you." He ran his hand through his hair then followed quickly in her steps.

# TWELVE

Y ES, MOTHER. WHEN I CAN I'LL come and visit." Billi watched the
sparkle of her new ring as she held the phone receiver.

"Tell Jack thank you for my Christmas present. It is so wonderful
to have my own phone line." Mrs. O's voice came through loud and
clear.

Billi wondered at the truth behind her mother's statement. She
knew her mother, enforcing her rights as block captain, would, from
time to time, listen in on conversations of those she shared the par-
ty-line with.

"Will do. And tell Dahlia and Danny hello from us."

She heard her father's voice in the background. "Pepper sends his
love too darlin'."

Billi fought back her tears and loneliness. "It was good that you
heard from Eddy."

"He's working safely in an office." The relief in her mother's voice
evident.

With great trepidation she broached the subject of Eileen and her
family's wellbeing. "Has anyone heard from the Nakamuras?"

An uneasy silence followed. Then her father took the lead. "No.
They are stickin' to their own. It's for the best as there are rumors not to
be discussed on the day of the birth of Christ."

Billi heard the upspoken warning, not only to dismiss the subject
but of the rumblings on the streets against the Japanese, and it made
her shiver.

The fact no new attacks from the Empire along the West Coast came blaring across the radio filled her evening with hope. No more surprises on Christmas Day. The news up until now held horrific stories as the US took a beating. Children wrote Santa asking for war bonds instead of toys.

"Isn't it wonderful Churchill is at the White House with President Roosevelt? They'll get us back on track." Her mother sounded enthusiastic about Churchill's speech. "He claimed we had 'drawn the sword for freedom and cast away the shadow.' So poetic. But do you think it will really take as long as he has predicted? 1943 seems so far away? What does Jack think?"

She kept her voice steady. "Jack believes the tide will turn."

The simple words seemed to have soothed her mother. When the line clicked dead, Billi slowly lowered the receiver. Around the globe, soldiers hunkered down in their respective battlefields, longing for their loved ones and an end to the madness.

"Are you ready?" Lilly swept into the room, holding a pumpkin pie in each hand above her protruding belly.

The sight lifted Billi's spirits. "Remember those are for our soldiers." She warned grabbing her coat.

Lilly ignored her, turning toward the front door and the sound of her mother's approaching car.

As dark settled around them, the entire household waved away the car offering pies and smiles to be shared with the troops. Not only a bit of holiday cheer and comfort for those about to head for the trenches but tucked in each crimp of the pie crust were prayers for their safe return. A reminder everyone shared the responsibility for the security of this great land.

SUNDAY DINNER SAT HEAVY in their bellies as Billi sat across from Jack in the small wood paneled office of their private sanctuary. She extracted the fan the Professor had presented her that day of the competition from its hiding place. The pillow Eileen made her as a parting gift, with its intricate embroidery and secret pocket, had become a symbol of their bond and their deceptions. They belong together, pillow and fan. She held the fan under the desk lamp swirling it in the concentrated glow.

The images of the three fierce dragons, seem to become one rising from the water with her movement. The wings spread in the air from a folded position close to the body to their full extent.

"They fly so majestically," she observed. "What makes them so different and the source of such intrigue?"

"That is your job to figure out." Jack tossed his writing pen on the desk to lean toward her. "What did you call this image?"

"Watasumi, God of the sea. In ancient belief there were three; upper, middle and lower Gods. They rule the waters." She watched her husband rub his right eye, an act of frustration.

She held the fan now in front of her, considering her husband over the top curve. "What flies from under the water that is dangerous?"

"Submarines that can surface and fly a scouting plane already exist." He snapped.

"There is always room for improvement."

"Are you referring to me?"

"Well that too." She fluttered the fan with an innocent look. "How would you improve on that—-plane? And why would you?"

She watched him now, glad to be working together again as a team. The days leading up to Christmas had been lonely. While his family had kept her busy with preparations and volunteering at the local social hall, she had deeply missed the connection she felt when working by his side.

She realized when he didn't answer that more was on his mind than the fan. "What is it Jack?"

"I'd like you to head home for New Years."

His bluntness caught her off guard. "Any particular reason?" The fact he had called Seattle her "home" brought back her old fears. She folded the fan, tucking it into its purple case, then inside the hidden pocket of Eileen's pillow.

"I'm heading to Hawaii and I need to know you're safe." His matter of fact answer held no hidden clues.

Or, she considered, they had both reached the same conclusion. This mansion rested on the crest of a hill, on acreage, surrounded by thick trees making it easy to approach. Furthermore, if Akio's underlings were going to stage a kidnapping, her presence here also put those in this house at risk.

"When?" She leaned back watching him, attempting to memorize every facet of his face, his slight scar, the eye-patch. Hawaii, dangerous territory so far away, beckoned.

"I leave in the morning. I found you a seat on the train." His words came across as unemotional, almost dismissive.

"Does this have anything to do with Eddy?" She suddenly became frightened, recognizing he held something in reserve.

"I'll see him, but no. There was an incident on the small western-most island of Ni'ihau."

"You have my attention." She attempted not to show the acid of alarm bubbling inside.

"It appears the Japanese thought the island of Ni'ihau was uninhabited and instructed their pilots to use the flat fields as emergency landings. My guess is they were told a submarine would pick them up offshore. After the attack at Pearl, one the of Zeros in trouble crashed in the field, as instructed. Luckily, the first person on the island to find him, a Hawaiian, decided to relieve the stunned pilot of his pistol and papers that were on board."

"Quick thinking." She realized the next portion of the story would be disturbing.

"I don't have the full report from Lieutenant Baldwin. In short, there were a handful of Japanese on the island. However, three of them decided to help their homeland pilot, Nishikaichi, get his important papers back. They held some of the Hawaiians as prisoners, threatening them with confiscated guns. One of the islanders escaped and, with others, rowed all night long to Kauai'i for help. Before reinforcements could arrive, there was a scuffle. A sheep herder named Ben Kanahele was shot three times by the Japanese pilot, but this powerful man still managed to pick up his captor and throw him against a wall. His wife, Ella Kanahele, then hit the downed man's head with a heavy rock. Ben slit the pilots throat."

The gruesome images made her flinch. "What does this mean?" She knew the answer before she asked it. It meant even more trouble for those of Japanese descent living in America. The image of her best friend Eileen floated before her.

"You have to go, Billi."

"Yes." She reached for his hand as her heart sank. "I will be safe at home. You won't have to worry."

JACK STOOD AT THE LARGE second floor window in the corner office of the Commander in Chief of the US Pacific Fleet, Admiral Husband E. Kimmel. This vantage point overlooked the twisting metal, and listing battleships left behind at Pearl Harbor. If the United States had wanted to draw Japan into the war by relocating an advance portion of the Naval Pacific Fleet from San Diego to Hawaii, then that chess move had decidedly instigated its intent. Japanese expansionism, especially their aggression in China, had attracted world concern. Therefore, on February 1st, 1941, according to General Order 143, the United States Naval Fleet was divided into Atlantic, Pacific and Asiatic Fleets. The mass destruction outside the window in the harbor provided proof that the Japanese quest for power would be countered only through retaliation and brutal fighting.

He shifted his hat in his hand attempting not to think of the growing numbers of those who lost their lives just outside this window in the harrowing ninety minutes of the surprise attack. Over two-thousand-four-hundred had passed so far and nearly one-thousand-two-hundred wounded. Jack realized the man he waited to finish his phone conversation would take the fall for the unprepared base and the loss of the fleet moored at Battleship Row.

"Yes, we were given 'war warning' on November 27th. But we thought the Philippines were the target and the Japanese got them too, remember? The same damn day if you don't consider the time zone," Kimmel growled into the phone. "And where the hell was the Army? They were supposed to be protecting us." The phone went down with a bang.

Jack heard the creak as Kimmel rolled his wooden chair back, then the sound of shoes as he approached. The two stood for a moment looking out at the scurrying men below near the submarine berths as they removed debris, repaired ships and prepared for battle all in the same fluid movement of worker bees steadfast and united on their mission.

"Damn lucky they missed the subs and the oil tanks. At least that's what Admiral Nimitz pointed out when we toured the damage.

You know, I was standing right where you are watching that morning. See that bullet hole?" Kimmel's Kentucky upbringing slightly influenced his speech.

For the first time Jack took in the appearance of the window, not what lay beyond. There was a small even hole, with snake like cracks ribboning out from the center.

"Bullet hit me right here." The Admiral's hand went to his left chest, over his heart. "Unfortunately, I had my case for my glasses in that pocket and it stopped the bullet. Wish the bullet had killed me and I'd died with my men. War shows no mercy."

The sincerity of Kimmel's hushed tone made Jack pause. He nodded toward the sad face of the man who had witnessed so much death, then turned to look out the corner window. He let his mind imagine what it would have been like to have these two large windows, one facing west, one north, filled with Japanese planes, bombs, and smoke, raining death and destruction over the easy prey on a Sunday morning?

The disgust was evident in the Admiral's frustration when he spoke. "I supposed you know that the atmospheric conditions blocked any radio contact that morning. So instead the War Department in Washington sent me the most important war warning regarding the attack by telegram. I got the telegram after the Japanese arrived. But I suppose the FBI knew more than I did about the attack."

"Perhaps." Jack waited, watching.

"On the 10th the Imperial bombers sank the Brit's battleship *The Prince of Whales*." His voice took on more volume as he continued, "and their cruiser the *Repulse*. Jesus, from land the Japanese sent their airplanes to the South China Sea and sank both ships in one day. This changes everything. If big ships are that vulnerable, we have to rethink the use of our flyboys."

Jack realized the Admiral's ramblings were more venting than conversation. He simply smiled at the man with the dark rings under deep set eyes flanking a long-pronounced nose.

"Actually sir, I'm here on another matter. Have you even seen this man?" Jack pulled a photo of Akio Sumiyoshi from his pocket.

Kimmel briefly leaned over the photo. "No. But ask the dock workers. A lot of Japanese work there. How else can I help you?"

"Your permission to move about the base is greatly appreciated. Thank you, sir." Jack nodded starting for the door. As he pushed it open, he paused under the arch that led to the outer room where a line of uniforms waited their turn to speak with the Commander in Chief who would be replaced by Admiral Chester Nimitz in two short days. "It was an honor, sir."

Jack passed the line of tense looking faces as he headed for the sunshine and the many docks of the harbor where Japanese locals worked side by side with the Navy. He intended to question the workers on the base first, then question the Japanese and Germans rounded up as suspects immediately after the bombing.

THE MORNING PROVED UNFRUITFUL with no one claiming to recognize Akio. Jack dropped his bag and suit jacket on the large inviting bed, then moved toward the bright sunshine coursing through the large window. He opened the two small panels flanking the oversized glass to let the ocean breeze pass over him. The beautiful azure waters with the white tips of the waves crashing into the sand just beyond the palm trees calmed him.

He had always longed to be in this incredible "Pink Palace" where his mother stayed months on end in the good days of their lives. He had never been allowed to her paradise, but left home to work and study. And now, in the midst of terror and strife, he stood in room 380 of the Royal Hawaiian watching a few soldiers work their way through the small opening in the barbed wire at the water's edge.

A sense of relief came over him at the thought his mother would never witness the sight of the lounge chairs stacked to one side replaced by the razor-sharp fence of war. The incongruous image of such beauty jarred by the constant reminder that the enemy forces could breach these shores at any moment tugged at his heart making his mind race.

"Where the hell are you, Akio?" he growled at the expansive sea. He felt so helpless, so far from the woman he loved. The warm breeze stirred thoughts of Billi. He closed his eyes envisioning her strong stroke as she plied these translucent waters.

The solid outer door echoed with a heavy knock. Jack turned in time to see the intruder not wait for his response but stride toward him, fists clenched.

"You son of a bitch." Eddy's emotions carrying his swing well beyond their mark.

Jack ducked, then grabbed Eddy's shirt pulling him close. "If we're going to win the war, you better improve that swing."

"What have you done to my sister?"

"You mean besides making her my wife?"

They breathed heavily into each other's face, not moving but letting their mutual anger bind them into one united creature. Slowly, Jack loosened his grip on his new brother-in-law's uniform.

"We're supposed to be fighting on the same side. Have a seat." He motioned toward the couch that occupied the alcove by the window as he moved toward the door to the hallway. He left the solid outer door open, allowing the daytime breeze to pass through the slats of the louvered inner door.

Jack picked up a bottle of scotch from the sideboard on his return. "You need a drink." He lowered into the overstuffed chair pouring two generous shots. "To my new in-law."

Eddy took the glass, gulping down the warm liquid.

"How's your girl? Lani?"

At the sincerity of Jack's question Eddy appeared to relax. "She's recovering. How's Dad, Mom and Billi?"

"Very well, and very worried about you. Look." Jack leaned forward, his voice dropping a notch, "I requested you as my driver for these few days because I know you have special clearance, how sharp you are, more importantly, you can also keep your mouth shut."

Eddy shifted at the quasi compliment waiting, then broke the silence. "How'd you get that?" Eddy raised his empty glass toward the patch across Jack's eye.

"Never turn you back on untrustworthy friends." His smile was rueful as his one good eye challenged Eddy to pry deeper.

"What kind of friends do you hang out with?"

The rattle from the knock against the louvered door did not break the tension between the two men locked in private combat.

"Open," Jack finally bellowed. As the door swung wide, an MP escorted in a towering Japanese-Hawaiian, who meekly stood, gripping his old hat.

"You John Mikami, the taxi driver?" Jack stood tall gluing his eye on the oversized man before him. He noted the dampness of the fellows loose Hawaiian shirt and the dust on his sandals.

"Yes." Mikami spoke low, as the perspiration dripped down his temples.

Jack nodded at the MP before the soldier left.

The slowness of his words enhanced Jack's threatening tone. "Did you bring a street map?"

The big man's head bent, he appeared to focus on the floor, before nodding "yes."

"Is this the man?" Jack held the photo out. "Mr. Morimura? You drove from the Japanese Consulate around the island?"

When Eddy leaned over the photograph of the Japanese man wearing a suit, Jack noticed a look of shock on his new brother-in-law's face. Eddy recognized Mr. Morimura, the handsome man with the long hair.

Suddenly, Eddy jumped into action. He pulled the round table to the center of the small adjacent room.

"Bring the map here," Eddy commanded, tapping the table. "And it better include all of the island."

Jack observed the lumbering, hesitant steps of the man, smelling his sweat as he shuffled toward Eddy.

From inside his old hat Mikami extracted his brown and green parchment. The folds of the parchment paper showed signs of wear as his thick brown fingers trembled opening the map.

"How many times did you take Tadashi Morimura for drives?" Jack's edginess split the room.

"Many times." The big man's voice remained low with guilt.

"Whose Ford were you using? A '37 wasn't it?" Jack knew who owned the car in question. He also knew that at 9:30 a.m. on December 7th, all members of the Japanese Consulate, a mere seven miles from Pearl Harbor, had been placed under arrest inside their own building. Unfortunately, most of the files and important papers had already been burned by the time of the Americans arrived.

The taxi driver sighed heavily, "Richard Kotoshirodo. He work for da consulate."

Eddy looked stunned but quickly recovered. "Besides Ewa, where else did you go?"

The large finger fumbled toward Kokokahi Road on the east coast of Oahu toward Kane'ohe, Eddy's base, "We go here. He walked for bit, then say go back."

"Could he see the base?" Eddy's anger apparent as he clenched his jaw.

"Yes." The tall figure bent closer to the map. "We go here. Then here." His finger moved near the Army's Schofield Barracks, Hickam Air Force Base, Wheeler Army Airfield, then to the beach at Haleiwa. "Most of time he go here." His large paw moved west of Pearl Harbor. "But he really like to go here." The point of interest was up Makanani Drive, a mere six miles from battleship row.

"What's that?" Jack studied the map, pressing the points of interest into his memory.

"Japanese tea house. He drink much there. Sometimes he spend da night." For the first time the taxi driver looked directly at the other two men.

"Show us." Eddy started for the door, flinging it open, waiting.

Jack grabbed his jacket then followed the scent of the big man's fear out the door.

EDDY GUIDED THE CAR up toward the Alewa Heights. From his rear-view mirror, he had an unobstructed view of the destruction at Hickam Air Force Base and Ford Island beyond. He shifted his eyes briefly observing the strong profile of Jack who kept his watchful eye on the taxi driver in the front seat.

"Go here, up dis drive, Makanani Drive. Lady owner from same island in Japan as Morimura I think, Shikoku Island. She have many geisha here." The sausage finger of Mikami pointed to a driveway leading past a well-kept, Japanese style garden to a simple two-story structure with elongated eaves which curled slightly at their ends. A sign scripted in the language of the brazen new enemy read "Shuncho Ro." Below, the translation in small letters read *Spring Tide Restaurant*.

Jack held the door for their guide as Eddy rounded the front of the car then followed them to the entrance. No one answered their knock.

"Kick it." Jack's head nodded toward the taxi driver.

When the large man did not move Eddy drew his gun. "I think he means for you to kick in the door."

The giant's shoulder drew back then with one solid thrust of his massive leg the latch gave way, leaving a dusty large footprint of Mikami's sandal.

A faint scent of sweet perfume met them as they entered the cool dark room. Eddy threw the shutters open allowing a stream of light to fall across the dropping heads of an old ikebana arrangement. The specific placement of each flower now bent with abandonment, their once brilliant reds and greens, browned and decaying, like the ships in the harbor.

Jack mounted the stairs with Eddy on his heels, breathing in the slight dust of desertion. The ladies had left in a hurry with drawers still hanging open. Very un-Japanese in their flight. Unless the spies had left days before the attack, they could not have gotten very far, maybe the higher regions of the mountains or the North Shore where their tea house and its activities might be unfamiliar.

Of the four rooms upstairs only the one that faced the south held their attention. Eddy waited as Jack slid back the closed shutters over the windows.

"Holy Shit." Eddy squinted into the bright sun, his mouth twitching in anger. "How the hell did this happen?"

When Jack moved toward the closet the stunning view below emerged clear and devastating. Far out to sea the beautiful tropical green waters met the blue sky in one peaceful line. In stark contrast, nearer to shore the USS Oklahoma lay on its side just off Ford Island. On what remained of battleship row, the shiny oil slick from the USS Arizona drifted on the waves, marking the spot where 1,512 sailors lost their lives. Further down the harbor at pier 1010, only the partial hull of the USS Oglala listed above the waters.

Inside the closet Jack worked a compartment half concealed by the wood master's artistry. After a few moments a hidden door slid open and he reached inside. The three tall legs of the telescope widened once removed from the confinement of the small space. Setting the tripod and scope before the window, Jack hunched over, peering through the lenses.

Eddy recognized the mixture of hatred and anger in Jack's good eye as he straightened, his tense body as rigid as one of the legs of the tripod. Eddy stepped forward to bend over the viewfinder. With powerful clarity focused on its prey, he watched the sailors perform their overwhelming duty of removing the rubble and debris to prepare for future battle.

"Goddamn it. I can see the wedding ring on that sailor's hand. This is one hell of a telescope. You can read the name of each boat and their position like nobody's business." Eddy slowly rose to look around the room for more evidence then stopped as the large man shuffled forward, filling the door frame.

"How many times did you say you brought Tadashi Morimura from the Japanese Consulate here?" Jack's voice did not veil his unspoken threat.

"He come here in the evenings for months." Like the perspiration on the man, the mumbled words dripped into the hallow of the room. "I don't go inside. I don't come up here." He added in a hurry, his hands, palms up, lifting with his shoulders begging for understanding. "I take him to sightseeing airplane once with geisha from this tea house."

Jack and Eddy stood shoulder to shoulder in their renewed amazement. The task for any spy to gather valuable information from this spot emerged boundless. How easy to observe the movements of ships, the submarines, their moorings and the times of the PBY patrols. The mechanisms of Pearl Harbor were handed to the enemy on a lacquered tea tray.

"Did he use binoculars at Kane'ohe?" Eddy demanded, remembering the last time he spoke with Sam, visualizing the kids blood soaked pants from the wound in his stomach. He waited but realized the use of binoculars was irrelevant, just driving up the Pali one had a superb view of their field. A good spy, like Morimura, would know where to get his information.

"I don't see any." The big man's half smile and willingness to help at this late date mirrored the image of a pathetic puppy brushed aside for having peed on the best rug.

The sun sat above them as they drove down the hillside toward the harbor. Cognizant the view from the tea house paralleled the same vantage point from Lani Daniels parents' home, Eddy's exasperation got the best of him. He hit the steering wheel with his open palm. The reality hit hard. The dashing Japanese man in his bright Hawaiian shirt he met at the Daniels' party, the one he stood next to as they admired the view of the lights on the sleeping American fleet below, was the very man who would hand over the map of the US ships at port. The maps of Pearl Harbor found among the debris of the downed Japanese planes and mini subs, displaying the painstaking detail of the position of each vessel carefully broken into five segments, materialized as the handiwork of the man who posed as the vice-consul at the Japanese Consulate. Eddy's gut had been right.

They left the taxi driver on a corner watching him scurry down the block.

Eddy turned to regard Jack. "Do you know where Morimura is?"

Jack ignored the question. The FBI had failed. Tadashi Morimura, a handpicked spy, just set sail back to Japan aboard the Swedish exchange ship the *MS Gripsholm*. He could only hope that the man who would arrive in the Land of the Rising Sun as a hero was being swapped for an American who held as much knowledge of the enemies working as Morimura.

Eddy jerked the car into the traffic wishing he had killed the handsome spy when he met him. He prayed this shadow did not somehow implicate Lani's family.

BILLI SAT FOR A MOMENT in the silence of her mother's living room, petting her puppy for comfort. Alone at her mother's house did not fit her vision of how she expected to spend her first New Year's Eve as a married woman. She wondered what Jack planned for tonight, secretly hoping her brother kept a close eye on her husband. The thought made her smile. She closed her eyes attempting to breathe deeply pushing aside her growing disquiet. Even at home things had changed dramatically. Danny, a senior at Garfield High School, a reservist, packed his duffel bag to head off to war. His high school diploma, his sports scholarship, set aside for a gun. As if sensing her hopelessness, Pepper nestled his long nose further on her lap. Billi, in response, smoothed his soft ears as the two dozed in contentment.

At precisely 6:00 p.m., Pepper leapt from his master's side, charging with his loud bark toward the front door. Danny followed his sister Dahlia and the newest addition to the gang, his beloved Susie, as they swarmed into the darkened O'Shaughnessy house.

Mrs. O hurried to adjust the fire in the hearth. Billi recognized her mother's attempt to ward off the anxiety now abiding in every home. The warm flames leapt wildly against the chains of the grate in uncertain restraint, casting flickering shadows against the floral wallpaper.

"How do you like it?" Danny slowly turned so Billi and Mrs. O could admire the khaki pants and matching shirt that draped loosely on his small frame. His red curls now cropped short.

Mrs. O burst into tears plopping into her chair causing Pepper to leap into her lap seeking attention.

"Very nice." Billi's exuberance did not conceal her lie. "Is your mother joining us later?"

"She's not feeling well and had to work late. So, she's sleeping." Dahlia answered for her younger brother.

"We'll send home some of the leftovers. There's plenty." Billi took her friend's coat.

"You have to promise to eat, Danny. You're too thin." Mrs. O interjected, wiping her eyes then forcing a smile across her damp cheeks.

"Oh, there will be plenty of that." He hiked his pants up, his belt having no effect on his slim hips.

"Speaking of eating," Billi began, "we've prepared all of your favorites."

"Swell." Danny put his arm around Susie in an unaccustomed manly gesture. "You'll write me, won't you, honey?"

"Of course, I will." She blushed at his overt attention, then giggled.

"Come here." Mrs. O shifted Pepper to her other side allowing her to fish into the pocket of her apron.

Danny stood above her, the glow from the fire casting his shadow across the room to the long black shade that hid his image to the outside.

"Keep this with you at all times." The black beads of the rosary dangled between her fingers. "It was blessed by Bishop O'Dea years ago." She held her head high with her offering.

"I won't let it out of my sight." The light tinkling of the beads as they cascaded into his hand accentuated the silence that followed. He bent down to kiss her cheek making Pepper whine to be a part of the exchange. "I promise."

"Then help me up," she demanded, shifting toward the front of her chair. Her voice inched an octave higher as she fought more tears in her march toward the kitchen with Dahlia and Susie following behind. "Let's get that stroganoff onto the plates."

Billi watched Danny. He slowly faced each wall as if attempting to imprint the colors of the faded wallpaper, the smell from the kitchen, and the warmth of the blaze into his memory. When he finally faced her, she could sense his tension.

"I have something for you too. Actually, Kenny sent it." She raised her cupped hand toward him. A small package with the distinct fold of ornate paper rested in her palm.

Kenny, his Japanese friend of many years, had sent him a parting gift. Danny lifted the lid of the handmade box extracting the delicately folded paper crane, the gold paper catching the light. Tucked at the bottom of the box lie a handkerchief, the head of a tiger and his initials embroidered with French knots.

"Eileen made that for you," Billi whispered. "Only women born in the year of the tiger are said to be able to embroider those knots for protection. They wanted to be here but felt awkward."

The look on his face told her not to continue. She held back, not explaining further the meaning of Eileen's version of the Senninbari made to protect warriors. Nor did she mention the tiger held a special significance for luck, as the fierce animal could roam far only to return safely home.

"Okay," Danny responded as he stuffed the material and paper bird back into the box. He put his gift on the sideboard behind them, out of sight.

Billi bit her lip, hoping his gesture of indifference did not reflect a growing sore that would fester into a full-blown infection of hatred.

The kitchen door swung open as a procession of platters flowed into the room.

"That looks grand," Danny announced in Susie's direction as she placed the steaming bowl of thick beef stroganoff in front of him.

"Does he mean my meal or that young blonde?" Mrs. O, as usual, spoke to anyone who would answer.

"Both." Dahlia brushed past the older women with another steaming plate.

Mrs. O's shoulders went up and down with her dismay at the reason for this mock celebration. "He's just too skinny," she mumbled again then shooed Pepper under the table.

# THIRTEEN

LANI LOOKED UP AT EDDY IN his coffee-tanned uniform. "So, your sister's husband is on the Island?"

"Yes. He wants to meet you, the most beautiful girl in the world." Eddy's smile held hope.

"No." She pushed herself up higher on the pillows of the bed her father had placed in the soft light of the windows off the kitchen. She straightened her blue muumuu with the white hibiscus flowers carefully over her right leg, where the long scar, traveling from her belly down part of her thigh, slowly healed. "Maybe some other time."

Eddy tried again. "The doctor said you should get out some. Let's go for a ride. We can go . . ."

"No, I don't want to." She turned away from him, her beautiful long hair snarled and flat from lying on it.

He moved to face her. "Okay, but promise me you will come out with me soon." Taking her left hand in his he bent toward her ear to whisper. "I love you. Besides you can't get rid of me that easily. This will pass, you will get better."

She smiled, allowing him to kiss her cheek. "Yes. Now, can you please bring me some juice? And then you must go."

Eddy paused at the kitchen window. Outside Mrs. Daniels cut flowers as she sang an old tune born of the islands, her famous lyrical voice sending shivers through him. Captivated by her spell, he felt the voyeur, as her voice raised to the gods above, her chant became more pronounced. To the earth born rhythm of her song she swayed, flowers in hand, disappearing behind the purple bougainvillea into the small chapel.

"She takes a daily offering for my recovery to the chapel when she prays." Lani's voice sounded flat in comparison to that of her mother's as she leaned against the kitchen counter.

"Then see you have nothing to worry about. You'll be fine soon."

"Eddy the optimist." Her brown eyes searched his face. "You need to go now. Mother will help me back to my bedroom."

Eddy drove wildly down the winding road from Aiea Heights, the breeze off the ocean filling his nostrils, carrying hope. All would be well. It had to be. He sped down King Street to Kalakaua Avenue then toward the Royal Hawaiian. His hope of sharing the New Year's Eve sunset with Lani was not to be. No, tonight he would drink at the Royal Hawaiian with his new brother-in-law until he felt nothing.

He parked the car just off the large turn around in the front of the Pink Palace of the Pacific then dashed up the gracious steps to the expansive corridors of the H shaped hotel. Hurrying toward the veranda, he paused, struck by the Navy men lined up in comfortable chairs under the covered porch overlooking the acres of royal garden. The last of the tourists had left their dream retreat for the journey home. These new Navy men came ashore from submarines for a well-deserved respite before they would return to dive below the surface of dangerous waters protecting Allied shores.

At the far end, half concealed by the high back rattan chair, Eddy recognized a hand sporting a black oynx ring, holding a cigar. Jack sat, extending one leg to its fullest, the one Eddy noticed Jack favored lately. His brother-in-law never mentioned his new limp and that whet Eddy's appetite to needle the arrogant son of a bitch.

He strolled past the other sailors then leaned his back against the thick ornate stone railing in front of Jack.

"I take it she isn't joining us?" Jack's voice held compassion.

"No." He let out a long breath before continuing. "She's still in too much pain."

Jack rose, pressing the stub of his cigar into the tall decorative brass receptacle filled with sand. "Come on. You look like I need a drink."

Eddy fell in behind Jack. "Was that a joke? You do know what a joke is don't you, Jack?"

When they entered the Persian Room, Jack lingered at the top of the few steps leading down to the main dining room where a raised stage sat off to the side. Through the tall windows the rays of the setting sun cast streaks of red across the horizon. He envisioned the photo in his father's office back home in California. The image of an opulent era which faded into oblivion with the onset of the great depression. The picture showed his mother, young and regal, pausing in her shimmering evening gown that came to just below her knees. Her coiffed hair, adorned with a beaded head band, sparkled as bright as her smile as she posed on these very steps. The image captured the custom of those social elite. Upon entering, one waited briefly for recognition before sauntering down the stairs to dine.

"The twists of life," Jack mused. Brushing the image aside he descended, motioning to the table furthest from the stage, nearest the window. The half empty room seemed hallow and bland without the echoes of laughter or the soothing sounds of the Royal Hawaiian Orchestra. The night before the attack on Pearl, Military officers hosted a Christmas party in this very room. The last song conducted by the now famous Harry Owens, drifted out over the sea, more than likely heard by one of the many Japanese submarines surfaced offshore to recharge their batteries in anticipation of their attack. Jack shook his head at the irony as he heard Eddy order drinks before they even sat.

"I love her, Jack." His melancholy mood seemed to pull him down into the plush seat.

"Then stay alive. I head back soon, and your training will intensify. Fly straight and come home in one piece." He took his drink from the waiter's tray holding it skyward in a salute to the young man who would face the danger he could not.

As they slugged down more of the brown liquid Jack's anxiety increased. He had to find Akio, or at least rout out his web of contacts costing American lives. Simply put, Japan needed fuel and materials to survive. As the scotch burned across his tongue and down his throat, he worked the problem for the millionth time. Something about the wings on the dragon encrypted into the fan Billi had received from the Professor held the key. Subs could carry an airplane. Airplanes would win the war. Akio, while studying in the engineering department at Stanford, must have designed a new deadlier weapon.

"Jack, you there?" Eddy broke into his thoughts. "I think you should name your first child after me, Edwards. Edward." He slurred his own name as the hooch outmatched the food. Eddy tried to light another cigarette. "You are going to have children aren't you Jack? Lani and I are going to have several strong sons. She's prom, promised me that."

Jack let his breath out slowly. Understanding the young pilot's demise into the blurred world of booze, he hoped the evening held some degree of healing. After Eddy's third aborted attempt with his lighter, Jack stood taking his arm. "Time to get you upstairs."

As Eddy found his feet, he slammed into the table sending a dessert plate to the ground. The piece of china, with the soft floral print, smashed into several pieces.

"Won't be the last relic around here that will be lost to the war," Jack mumbled. "Hopefully, something of this fine place is left after you sailors are finished with the building."

"I'll glue it back together," Eddy announced to the Japanese waiter who hurried toward the breakage.

Jack escorted Eddy through the door leading to the grass patio where the sound of the ocean swept across them on the floral scented island wind.

Eddy slumped onto the ledge of the stone border, the sand and ocean at his back, and wept. "They killed Sam. 'Ain't that somethin' he would always say. Ain't that somethin'? I hate the Japs and yet Lani's part Jap . . . Japan . . . ese. How the hell's this going to work?"

"I don't know. But look on the bright side. According to the Alien Enemy Act the president . . ."

"Aliens and Sedition, 1798. John Adams." Eddy sat straight to continue his lecture. He waggled his finger at Jack. "Beginning law classes. Remember? When I make it out of this shit hole, I'm going to be an attorney. No. A goddamn great attorney. And I'm going to sue you for marrying my sister."

"Not if she kills me first. There's rumors building of putting all Japanese stateside into relocation camps and I'm going to be the one that breaks it to her."

Eddy found the situation hilarious causing his body to rock with laughter. "I'd rather fly into a horde of Jap Zeros than have to tell that to Billi." His arm swung into the air carrying him backwards into the sand.

Jack stood above Eddy as his limbs tightened into a ball, his laughter morphing into sobs. The moon broke free of a small cloud and shone across the water, lighting the tears that streamed down Eddy's cheek.

"Dahlia." The muted cry came from the curled-up form on the cool sand.

Dahlia. Jack let the name of the young blond back in Seattle roll around in his head. Eddy, in his altered state of loss, laced with booze, had just uttered the name of the woman who still held his heart.

Dahlia.

BILLI SAT ACROSS FROM Duckworth at his desk in the downtown Seattle Federal Office, the very office where she had made the deal with Jack to help unearth the Nippon espionage ring the night of her mother's birthday party. So much had changed in those few months. She waited for her husband, so many miles away, to gather his thoughts before continuing.

"What are you thinking, Jack?"

"Is your mother standing guard over the black outs?'

"There are no lights on our block at night. She told the neighbors if she sees any lights, she will shoot them out herself."

While the image sounded humorous the situation continued as dark as the shades pulled every night to hide the life within.

"What can I do to help?"

"Stay out of sight for a while yet. There is talk of, well—just pray."

As new as their marriage was, his comment set her back. She wanted to reach through the wires of communication to touch him.

"You do the same. I love you." She blushed as Duckworth looked the other way.

Then the line went dead, the long cables reaching her husband now silent.

She fought back tears, then sat taller looking around the room. Her eyes fell on a map on the wall. Duckworth had pins sticking in the world map where the Axis quickly took control. Their sharp points with small flags of the Rising Sun, appearing like butterflies vying for the same space as they expanded from Manchuria, Shanghai, French Indo-China, Thailand, the Philippines, Malaysia and now Singapore possibly the next to fall. A constant reminder of the swiftly spreading threat. Across the water in Europe, pins with swastikas blanketed the land crossing over into Africa.

"Could we have prevented this?" Her words were more of a reflection than a question. She sat back in the chair with a deep sigh.

"No matter what happens, he truly loves you."

Duckworth's words shocked Billi out of her stupor. She adjusted her skirt catching her breath. "Niles." She hesitated, speaking his first name sounded odd as Jack had always only called him by his last. "Niles," she spoke again, "I know you are here in the capacity to watch over me as well as manning this office. That act alone speaks volumes of my husband's concern for my safety. But, if anything happens to Jack, please don't send anyone else to tell me. Please come alone. I couldn't hear the words from anyone else."

Niles' head bobbed once with complete understanding of a task no one would cherish.

At 1:40 a.m. Eddy felt a hand shake his shoulder. He jumped from his bed to face the sailor who roused him.

"You're needed at command. Now." The sailor squinted at Eddy. "You the one with that special clearance?"

"That would be me." Eddy hurried into his uniform.

The man shrugged before leaving. "Make it double time, someone has a bee in his bonnet."

Command had kept Eddy at Pearl for the last few days as things were heating up, creating a demand for more runners with high security clearance. The souls of his feet hitting the concrete echoed as he raced down the empty hall. Inside the office the smoke from a cigarette created a white stream under the lamplight.

"You're needed at the dungeon. Must be something big." The dark circles under the captain's eyes told the story.

Eddy's heartbeat matched his run. The dungeon, the basement of the Naval Administration building which housed the highly confidential Station Hypo. The non-descript office where men worked in total secret with few on the base even realizing they were there. He scrambled down the stairs and took a deep breath before knocking. He had only been here once before but had memorized as much of the layout as possible.

When the door opened, the Marine in charge of security loomed over him.

"Lieutenant O'Shaughnessy reporting." When the big man didn't acknowledge him, Eddy added, "Special rating."

Finally, he stepped to the side. "Rochefort has something for you."

Eddy entered with the excitement of the task. He hurried around the Marine's desk, maneuvering toward the back where Commander Joseph Rochefort, the genius codebreaker, sat hunched over a stack of papers, wearing his bathrobe.

"O'Shaughnessy, isn't it?" He stood, stretching.

"Yes, sir." Eddy answered.

"You have the special rating but aren't you a pilot?"

"Both, sir."

The commander rubbed his deep-set eyes then checked his watch. "To hell with the hour." He picked up a large envelope. "Get this to Admiral Nimitz. Don't let anyone else touch it. Got that?"

"Yes, sir." Eddy felt the weight of the envelope and the mission.

As the slender man slid back into his chair, he regarded Eddy. "Replacements with your security level are arriving soon. You'll be needed back in the air. Best of luck, kid."

Eddy clicked his heels, ignoring the sense of doom that surrounded him in this underground office of secrets, where boxes, files and stacks of confidential messages demanded top security, even from those preparing for battle above.

When he reached the area where jeeps were kept, a guard emerged.

"Need a jeep to deliver a package." Eddy half shielded the envelope.

"Who for?" the man sounded skeptical.

"Nimitz." Eddy stood taller with the name.

The man came at him with his hand extended. "I'll take it for you."

"No deal. I just need the jeep."

In the dark, he hurried toward 37 Makalapa Drive, the residence of the Commander in Chief of the Pacific Fleet, Admiral Chester Nimitz. Eddy made it through the first two sets of MP's, both wanting to be the one to deliver the packet and have the privilege of meeting Nimitz in person, inside his home. He parked across the street, taking a deep breath before heading up the steps leading to the white two-story home.

As he hurried under the canopy, another MP stopped him. "I'll take that." The strong voice was one used to getting his way.

"Orders, sir." Eddy became more determined with his duty. "I am to place this in Admiral Nimitz's hand personally."

The two eyed each other, neither wanting to give an inch.

"Better let me ring that doorbell." Eddy broke the intensity of the standoff. "This is for the Admiral and it's to be delivered now."

The brute moved aside.

It took only a few moments before the door was opened by the Admiral himself. Eddy noticed the flustered maid hurry around the corner only to be waved away.

"Apologies for the hour, sir." Eddy snapped his heels in his best salute. "A package, sir."

"Come on in, son." He smiled as he shut the door. "Good job getting past my guards."

"Thank you, sir."

He followed the camel hair bathrobe of his superior into the living room where a piano sat at the far end. In the adjacent room, a chandelier hung over the dining room table. The surrounding fit the responsibility.

"What's your name?"

Eddy could feel the rush of blood surge to his face as he repeated his name and rank.

"So, what is it you have, Edward?"

"You can call me Eddy, sir." He held the package out. "From Commander Rochefort, from Hypo, ah, the dungeon, sir." He wanted to kick himself for his bumbling answer.

Extending his left hand to collect the valuable classified information, Nimitz nodded toward the envelope Eddy tightly gripped. "You can let go of that now, son."

Eddy did not show any reaction to the fact that part of Nimitz's ring finger was missing. He knew the story. Nimitz's Annapolis ring saved the rest of his finger when he got it jammed in a diesel engine. Somehow, this god of war, appeared so human. His white hair still held the flatness from sleep, yet, even at this hour, those unnerving eyes reflected the alertness of a man who had the weight of the country riding on his shoulders.

Nimitz flipped the envelope over, extracting the pages. He read just a few lines, before regarding Eddy. "Thank you for getting this to me. Good job. Show yourself out."

As he quickly strode out of the room, the Admiral tucked the decrypted information under his arm while pulling at the belt on his bathrobe.

Eddy felt his adrenaline surge as he stepped out into the cool of the night. His mind went wild with the possibilities of what information he had just delivered from the ever-vigilant codebreakers to the Commander in Chief of the Pacific Fleet. He remembered Rochefort's words, "Best of luck, kid."

JACK FELT LIKE AN ASS. He didn't divulge to Billi he'd arrived state-side days ago. He rattled the ice in his drink, vowing to bring her to this spot someday. Louis' Restaurant, built into the cliff above the Sutro Baths, offered a view of the Gulf of the Farallones and Point Bonita Lighthouse like no other. Of all his haunts in the San Francisco Bay Area, this small family-run Greek diner remained one of his favorites.

Tonight, as the clouds gathered around the setting sun, the wind whipped white tips on dark blue waters toward shore. He watched the salty froth spray up over the rocks. The mesmerizing swells gave no clue of what lurked beneath, ready to sink more ships.

He cast a look south at the expansive Playland-at-the-Beach sprawling below the famous Cliff House. The massive playground covered almost three city blocks. What would the Japanese think if they came ashore here among the Ferris wheel, the carousel or the Big Dipper roller coaster? The structures erected for pleasures would amplify the enemy's concept that all Americans were frivolous. The fact that the rides continued to entertain while men strung barbed wire down the beach or installed anti-submarine devices along the same shore made Jack shake his head. He gulped the rest of his scotch.

He nodded to the young Greek owners as he left. Their small boys a reminder of why people had come to America in the first place, for a new beginning. A concept now under attack, along with its people.

As he stepped out into the setting sun on to Point Lobos Avenue, he heard the booming of the guns practicing over in the Marin Highlands at Forts Baker, Berry and Cronkhite, where troops prepared to defend the Golden Gate Bridge and San Francisco Bay. Inland lay Mare Island, the oldest US Navy submarine base. No matter the proximity of the armed forces, the people along the coast remained nervous.

Jack started his car heading back toward the bustling city. He drove down the Great Highway then turned into Golden Gate Park where pitched tents accommodated the overwhelming numbers of young volunteers. Starting on December 8th, 1941 the lines to join any branch of the service transformed the Bay Area, like other major ports, into a citadel city of war. The glow of lanterns inside the large structures nestled among the trees, with their ghostly, luminous appearance, he regarded as beacons of hope, a testament to the brave.

Sliding out the side door of the Sir Francis Drake Hotel, he headed down Powell Street toward the entrance of Chinatown to make his first brief stop. A dense fog wrapped him in dampness. In response he pulled his coat tighter. The absence of lights created an eerie sense of unrest in this vibrant city where soldiers now roamed every street inhaling their last gulps of freedom before battle.

A dim light shone under the canopy that extended past the entrance to the Forbidden City Nightclub. Drawing nearer, Jack snorted at the jubilant vibrations of a party in full swing. He climbed the stairs to the raucous sound of hoots and hollers from the servicemen crammed in around the stage. The maître d' nodded in recognition then lead him down the hallway to the private door.

He smelled the incense as he stepped inside. The stillness of the semi dark room a striking contrast to the frivolity of the floorshow with the reverberating echoes of the enamored audience.

Shirley Chow sat in her usual chair with the hand carved dragons creating the armrest. Jack considered her tight chignon which offset her high cheekbones and suspicious eyes. Shirley embodied the spirit of the fierce mythical creature she surrounded herself with.

The crooning voice of Larry Ching's version of, *I'll Never Smile Again*, a song Frank Sinatra put on the billboards, faded when he closed the door. How apropos he considered as he sat, wondering if the world in general would ever smile again.

"The war has been good for the club, but not for our homeland." Shirley's direct assessment of her situation drew Jack's attention. "My war with Japan started in 1932 with the January 28th incident. The underground never gave up when they declared tentative peace on the streets. Then again Japan began killing hundreds of thousands in 1937. Since the beginning of your war with Japan many of my family have disappeared. We gave money to the Bank of China and Madame Chiang for more airplanes. America has signed an agreement to help. It is said that Chennault attracted 300 Americans to China to fight against our devilish enemy. Have you any further knowledge?"

"The American pilots in China have named themselves the Flying Tigers." Jack presented old information, not willing to divulge more.

Shirley cagily nodded. "That brings hope to our skies and our people. May they bring much destruction to our enemy."

Jack did not need to remind this dragon lady of the swift progress of the Japanese as it appeared America presented little help to her country. Especially disconcerting news gnawed at him when hearing the reported actions of some top brass, such as General MacArthur, who demanded his men keep fighting as he retreated from Luzon. America needed a miracle.

"If the Japanese land on these shores we will escape to a small town in the middle of this vast country. We are prepared." Shirley's voice held the steel of her decision.

"If I can help in any way, please let me know."

"A warning will help." Her tone changed, almost desperate. "Have you located Akio yet?"

He shook his head wondering at her continued interest in the vile man. "Sharing information is always beneficial. If you hear something contact me." He waited.

Finally, she spoke. "Shi. Shi."

Jack stood, scooping up his hat. It was the answer he desired from their brief meeting. Yes, Shirley Chow who possessed her own spies, would share her valuable findings. Their bond held as they continued to depend on each other in their search for the same man. For now, at least.

# FOURTEEN

Jack passed several soldiers carrying heavy boxes as he headed down the hallway of Building 35 inside the compound of the Presidio. Western Defense Command spouted with activity like an overflowing fountain. The gait of every man appeared to be double time.

Removing his hat, he entered the waiting area outside Lieutenant General DeWitt's office. When the office door opened, a young officer motioned him inside. Jack took a deep breath before entering.

"There's a damn war going on out there and I'm stuck here." DeWitt looked up at Jack from behind his desk.

"I heard your talk to the city leaders at the Civil Defense Council meeting was well received." Jack sat, putting his hat on his knee. He did not like the sixty-one-year-old DeWitt for his finger pointing ways and narrow mindedness.

"This city needed to wake up to the fact we are at war. We have proper blackouts, now don't we? And no more enemy planes flying overhead." He removed his wire rimmed glasses to furiously polish them with his immaculate handkerchief. "I'm moving the Rose Bowl game inland, to North Carolina. I'm also relocating some of my records and staff to Salt Lake. The Japs could be here anytime. The sub net is up across Golden Gate. The biggest concern is I don't know what to think of what is going on over in Building 640. Not sure I trust them."

DeWitt referred to the converted hanger next to Crissy Field currently acting as a training area for young Japanese American soldiers who spent their days hunched over textbooks, learning how to translate and decode documents. More importantly, how to interrogate on the battlefield, a tool to be employed when they were shipped to the Pacific Theater on missions that only guaranteed their slow death, if they were captured.

"Any more news from Hawaii?" Jack waited.

"The Emperor can't be trusted. I suppose you've read the report about that one damn Zero pilot on that Ni'ihau Island in Hawaii."

Jack nodded, aware of every detail regarding the incident that appeared to confirm DeWitt's opinions.

"Harada, the Jap who lived on the island and helped the pilot, killed himself. But his Japanese wife, who also aided the pilot, is being brought back to Oahu and we'll throw her in the brig. My point is, given the opportunity these Japanese, American or not, will help their emperor. Hell, any number of them could be sending more messages back home as we speak. Bottom line, Japs can't be trusted."

Jack considered the Lieutenant General, feeling the sting of his words for those who truly embraced America as their home. This Ni'ihau incident, implicating those born on US territory turned traitor, only heightened the concerns of the President. The monumental question remained. How to distinguish the difference between those loyal solely to the United States, versus those sending messages and monies across the Pacific to the Emperor empowering his fight against America? The man charged with contributing toward that determination sat before him.

"Today is the last day for all enemy aliens in the San Francisco area to surrender their radio transmitters, shortwave receivers and precision cameras. Then we'll see what we find. Right?" The General's stern look foretold the path he would insist upon.

"The problem remains we can't search the mixed homes." Jack made his plea. "We can search those of the aliens but not those who are American born. So, if they live together and have contraband, we can't search without a warrant."

"I'll look into that and see what I can do. Remember, you can go in with good cause. But I'll have the judges ready to sign warrants night and day. Just find the bastards that are communicating back to Tōjō important information about our fleet and shorelines." He pointed to a map of the Pacific coastline that sprawled across his wall next to photographs of the US Army's 42nd Division while in France during world War I. In one snapshot, DeWitt stood among the distinguished 42nd alongside MacArthur and Donovan, a reflection of his accomplishments and frustration. "I'm in the process of creating military areas of exclusion along the coast for all aliens. It will be a major project but must be done before the saboteurs can strike our strategic bases. Their continued adoration of the Emperor cannot be broken. At any moment, if the Emperor implored them to act, they would rise up against us. They can't be trusted."

Jack studied the lines created with pins linked together with red string down the coast defining the proposed exclusion map. Seattle was well within the off-limits area. He could feel the rumbling of a hornet's nest brewing.

THE KNOCK ON THE DOOR at 304 30th South was drowned under the response of Pepper's bark. His short legs worked a fast path to the front entrance while he spun in circles, warning of an intruder on the porch.

"Hush, Pepper." Billi wiped her hands on her apron peeking out the window. She flung the door open and smiled. "Ah, my other keeper of the gate. Come in."

Duckworth shook the wet from his hat then stepped into the warmth of the house. "Don't mind if I do. Hi there fellow." He bent to pet the pup.

"What brings you? My husband misbehaving?" Billi attempted to keep a light touch to her voice, not revealing how the ball of twisting nerves cramped her stomach at the sight of her husband's aide. A fear that one day he would bring her the news that would smash her dreams. She thought of Mrs. Fredricks, down the street, who opened her door to strangers only to have them inform her of her sons' valiant death at Ewa Field, just west of Pearl Harbor. Everyone feared these strangers who climbed steps to front doors bringing sorrow to so many families in the neighborhood.

"Coffee?"

Duckworth followed her into the kitchen, where grayness of the dripping rain filled the large windows. "Just a quick cup, if it's made. Then you'll need to come with me."

"Mom is at Church rolling more bandages to be shipped overseas." Billi suddenly laughed. "But you know that."

Duckworth nodded as he accepted the china cup with the rich warm brew. "He's okay." Duckworth cut through her nervous chatter.

She smiled brightly. "Of course, he is."

"He wants to talk with you . . . in private."

"I'll get my coat."

The darkness inside Federal Building reflected the dreary day outside. She stepped lightly so the click of her heels became barely audible on the polished floors. They entered the familiar room and she sat at the desk, her stomach in knots as she waited to hear Jack's voice.

The tension grew as the minutes dragged by until finally Jack's strong voice broke through the receiver. "Hello Duckworth. Were you able to wrangle Billi into the office?"

"Right here, sir." He handed the black receiver to Billi. "I'll be outside."

Her hand trembled a bit as she lifted the phone to her ear. "Hello."

"How is Mrs. Huntington today?" A hint of mischief carried through the line.

"She's fine and so is your mother-in-law and puppy. A package deal, you know."

They exchanged brief sentences wrapped in longing, disguised, in the event those whose job it was to listen to all conversations, somehow broke into this secured line.

"Jack, there's something I need to say. I didn't understand one word. I looked all over for the Professor . . ."

"I know. And please be more careful next time, stay out of Japantown."

"But the word," her voice grew hushed with impatience, "I thought sensuikan was battleship, but it is used for submarine."

"All . . . right." He dragged the word out. "That fits."

She waited as the impact of this new interpretation floated between them. "I just found out yesterday and that's why I asked Duckworth . . ."

"Akio is fully aware of the oil refineries on the coast and the shipping traffic between Los Angeles and Seattle. The Japanese fishermen have been dropping lines measuring the depth of the harbor off

Terminal Island for years." He barely caught his breath before continuing. "They think they have dishonored us by these slight jabs of their sword. Luckily, the waters at Pearl Harbor are shallow. As we speak the boats are being righted and repaired. They missed the massive tanks that store our fuel leaving us enough oil on the island to fuel several battles. Had they gotten those it would have been a different story. Already new planes are under design. Even Admiral Nimitz, after his inspection of all the bases on Oahu, pointed out their failure to annihilate the fleet. They have made a dent, they have dragged us into this conflict, but this is America. Soon we will be better armed and ready to destroy them."

The phone was silent as husband and wife both caught their breath. Billi realized his pep talk held a different message. His last two words, "destroy them." That was the attitude, the goal. There was no hiding the anger, the need to conquer, the need for retaliation.

"What about the Nakamuras? What will happen to those who are American now?"

"They are still seen as Japanese by the Emperor even if they were born in America and are expected to serve the Land of the Rising Sun. Not just to pay homage and send money home for the war effort, but to serve in their armed forces. So, that makes it complex."

The distance between them grew as the words rang in her ears. "Complex? Is that what they are saying? Complex that a child born in America is no longer an American?"

"Listen, Sweetheart. The minute I know more about what is being decided you will be the first to know. But right now, I have to go and make some arrangements. Believe me that I love you. We might have a long way to go with this, Billi. Stay strong."

"Yes," she weakly answered.

"Stay out of Japantown for now. Okay?"

Billi emitted her second "yes" even softer, dreamlike, as the walls to her world began to fall away.

"YOU ARE SO NERVOUS." Eileen whispered to her friend as they sat together in her small bedroom.

"Me. Never." Billi examined Eileen's strong profile, so markedly Asian. "I promised this is the last time, but tell me what the man asked?"

Eileen moved to sit opposite her friend on the small bench in front of her makeup table. "I had never seen him before. He approached me in the store when father was out making a delivery. He said he had heard that you and I danced together at Bon Odori. That everyone still talked about it. He thought it would show great unity if we danced together again and asked where he could find you."

Billi tried not to show her concern, but Eileen must have noticed her cover up as she bent closer to her friend. "No. I did not say where you lived."

"Thank you. What did he look like? Would I recognize him?" She forced a smile.

"He was short and thick, a bit older." She appeared to become intent on recreating his vision. "He spoke with a heavy accent as if he had only been in America a short time."

"Did you notice his hands?" Billi sat perfectly still.

"His hands? He brought a tin of Ronin tea to the counter. I remember he was tapping the top of the tin impatiently. I think I saw a scar on his hand."

Billi could feel her throat grow dry. "Did he buy anything?"

"A bottle of sake and the tea."

The room began to spin as she grasped at the meaning of the appearance of the stranger with a scar on his hand. Could it be Hatsuro, the man who was always at Akio's side, even during the attack on Dyes Inlet?

"How long ago did this happen?"

"Right before all of this happened. I didn't think it was important and when I remembered, well, we haven't seen each other in weeks." Eileen's voice rose with a touch of hysteria as she spoke.

Billi reached across to take her hand. "It's okay. I'm glad you told me. If you see him again. If anyone asks for me, send Kenny right away to tell me. That's all. But please, don't tell them where to find me."

She silently cursed Jack for telling her to stay away, not visit Eileen. This important information would have reached her earlier.

The wind whistled through her coat as Billi walked up Jackson Street toward 30th Avenue South. The chilling breeze awoke her senses, intensifying the mounting fear of her new discovery. The concept

Hatsuro was here in her hometown looking for her sent shivers up her spine. Inadvertently, she looked around behind her into the shadow of the streets. The dark settled in so early these winter days, coupled with the bitter cold made being outside past 4:30 a challenge. The usual busy streets felt deserted, a reflection of the times.

The sound of laughter up the block made her lift her head higher into the wind. A group of playful young Asians approached, their merriment welcome. Kenny had grown taller in his senior year and she recognized him immediately.

"Kenny," she called out. The group fell silent as they neared. "What are you doing out past the curfew?" She half whispered looking at the faces of his friends.

"I'm Chinese." His dark eyes twinkled with mischief as he pointed to the yellow button pinned on his lapel that erroneously made the claim of the origin of his birth as Chinese. "I can be out all night long."

"You rascal." She couldn't help but laugh. She flawlessly switched languages. "You had better hope the night watch don't discover this. I don't want to have to bail you out."

"I'm very careful." He answered in English with his devilish smile. "You sound more like my sister every minute."

"I don't want to know where you got that yellow button."

A head of dark hair behind Kenny suddenly slumped forward in awkward admission, hiding the features of his Chinese face.

"Okay you guys, be careful." She shook her head at the ingenuity of youth as she continued up the hill.

Billi listened to the drifts of their merrymaking as they continued down the road that seemed to create the invisible divide between Chinatown and Japantown. She crossed Empire Way and started up the hill when a dark car pulled up behind her. Duckworth must be at his job again she mused. She turned to look at the car, realizing something amiss. The driver behind the wheel of the dark Buick was taller than Duckworth. She gripped her handbag tighter, quickening her step, when she heard the car door open.

"You spoken for, lady?"

Her purse hit the ground as she leapt into Jack's arms. The warmth of his body relaxing her tense nerves as she slumped against his chest.

"Why didn't you tell me you were coming?"

"And have you tell the neighborhood? Look Mrs. Huntington, spies don't work like that. Now get in the car, please."

He held the door for her as she slid inside the Buick. Jack pulled away from the curb, turning the car in the opposite direction.

"And where are you taking me?" She couldn't take her eyes off his profile as he focused on the sleet pummeling the windshield.

"Spies don't tell that either."

"I suppose you have already spoken with your-mother–in-law?"

"I was grilled by the block watch captain but was eventually given permission. The dog on the other hand was a bit tougher to get away from."

"Our dog."

"Yes, that one. But, tonight no dog, no mother-in-law." His smile spoke of his intentions and Billi felt herself blush.

When they pulled off 4th Avenue onto Seneca, Billi held her breath. Even in the black out, the towering Olympic Hotel cast a shadow. A porter with a dimmed flashlight approached the car as Jack eased from the driver's side to open the trunk. When Jack opened her door, she was not totally surprised to see her new suitcase being carried up the stairs along with a black satchel.

"Well, this should be interesting." Billi nudged her husband as they passed into the grand lobby. The subtle lighting the black outs decreed, etched the signature of America's new existence. The chandeliers gave a warm muted glow to the large panels of American Oak and the wide veranda above the main foyer. Jack veered toward the reception desk as Billi started across the terrazzo flooring toward the Palm Room. She didn't hesitate in her stride. Interesting she thought, how before she would have fumbled at her purse, aware her attire did not suit the grandeur of her surroundings. The discord around the world proved a great equalizer. Now, her old coat, sensible shoes and worn purse symbolized the war-time efforts to provide for those on the front line first.

"A table for two," she announced as the maître d' considered her. "My husband is checking us in." The new word in her dictionary, felt odd. But then, the sensation of her husband's presence, at times, made her nerves rattle a bit. He led her toward the back of the room to a table under the tall glass ceiling. The gaiety in the room in sharp contrast to the darkness outside. Among those who slumped with travel-worn shoulders were young men preparing for battle through the hooch bottles passed freely their way.

When the maître d' turned to find Jack looming over him, he appeared startled. The patch over his eye having its impact in the shadows. The smaller man quickly took another look at Billi before departing.

"One moment." Jack stopped him short. "Two Manhattans."

"Of course." He half bowed as Jack lowered across from Billi.

"Now, where were we?" He placed his hat on the empty chair and ran his fingers through his thick dark hair.

Billi's words tumbled out between them. "I'm scared."

Jack looked concerned, "Why? I already know everything there is to know about you."

"Not that," her voice squeaked a bit. "I was just with——" She froze, aware she had broken his rule.

"Yes." His good eye became stern as his lips tightened.

Billi weighed her words. If she relayed her suspicion about the man asking around for her, Jack would never allow her to leave the house. Besides, that happened weeks ago yet nothing had come of it. No, she would not spoil their evening with her private uncertainties.

"I think we should buy some of these young men a drink." Her words materialized into a concrete idea.

"And which ones would you have me spend my money on?"

Billi sat tall as she scanned the room. Tucked in a corner, a young couple held hands, heads almost touching. His white uniform and polished shoes a reflection of his choice of service. Her simple gold wedding band, unadorned dress and slightly worn shoes a statement of their status.

She nodded in their direction as Jack smiled. "Good choice."

The waiter placed their chilled drinks on the table as the candlelight danced across the amber liquid.

Jack spoke quietly with the waiter before lifting his glass to tap hers. "To my thoughtful and beautiful bride."

They settled back to let the alcohol work their nerves.

"You look a bit tired," Billi spoke softly.

"Is that an invitation to skip the meal?"

"No." She swallowed another sip. "Just an observation."

"They have doubled patrol all up and down the coast. Airplanes are scouring the shores, the Coast Guard is patrolling the beaches on foot and with dogs. Now we wait."

"Well, I'm glad you're waiting with me then." She giggled as the spirits she had downed far too quickly sent a tingling sensation through her.

"I fear you are about to start singing for me." Jack smirked at the recollection of the night Billi, drugged by Akio's men, sang for him for hours on end in the top room of the Sir Francis Drake Hotel. The night she stole his heart.

"You told me I wasn't bad? I thought you enjoyed the show."

The waiter appeared with two more drinks as Jack's smile broadened.

"I see what you're up to." Billi toyed with the stem of her glass. "I'm a married woman now. I have standards to keep."

"Interesting."

"But I do have one thing that is worrying me?" She sloshed another deep sip.

"Yes?

"Who packed my bag?" She blushed as she watched his good eye.

"My mother-in-law." He sounded proud of his choice.

Billi brightened. "Good then I don't have to worry."

"About what?" He looked a bit perplexed.

"Pajamas."

"I told her not to bother. You won't need any."

"You did not?" Billi's voice rose with curious indignation.

"We'll see." He finished his drink while the glint in his eye made Billi not press the matter any further.

# FIFTEEN

J ACK DROVE PAST THE STONE TOWERS that flanked the Montlake Bridge skirting the University of Washington toward Sand Point. He had left Billi before she woke, gently tucking the covers over her naked body. The memory made his head spin, he had never been so torn by duty in his life.

He turned right into Naval Air Station, Seattle, Sand Point, stopping under the expansive brick structure arching over the road containing the guard house. The sentry stationed in the small enclosure at the gate pointed in the direction of Pontic Bay, at the north end of the base. He continued down the road toward the water parking between building 1 and 27. Before him a PBY waited, Aircraft Scouting Force US Navy printed boldly on its side.

Jack scrambled up the eight steps to enter the aircraft. He headed for the glass turret in front, unfolding his map of the region for the hundredth time.

"Morning, sir. I'm you chauffeur for the day. Merrick." The Pilot nodded in the direction of his co-pilot. "And this young man is Kerr."

Jack handed him their itinerary. "Thanks, Merrick, Kerr. Anything else you two think might be of interest I'm all ears. Just attempting to stay ahead of the game and thought a view from your perspective would be invaluable."

"Yes, sir." The pilot quickly scanned the page before handing it to his co-pilot, adjusted his eye goggles, then focused on the gears.

As they headed north over Lake Washington Kerr confirmed their route. "It might be best to keep the coastline up to Canada in view, then turn around to head down over the San Juans. Is that appropriate, sir?"

"Jack. You can call me Jack." He tossed his hat aside to work his binoculars. "That's perfect."

The weather gods smiled on them, as the clouds proved to be light and scattered, providing a fantastic view of the blue and green below.

A few boats plied the waters as Jack zeroed in on them. For the most part fishing trawlers, ferries and the occasional smaller craft moved across the surface. Jack quickly assessed the challenge the Coast Guard and Navy faced managing the numerous bays, inlets, and straits which compose the expansive dots of green islands below. What a haven for nefarious activity. Prohibition must have run amuck in these islands in its heyday.

Jack checked his map as they flew over Whidbey Island. "Any Navy airports up this way for support?" He looked at the long channel of the Salish Sea stretching for miles down the Strait of Juan de Fuca dividing Canada and Washington State.

The two pilots regarded each other.

"To your left is Oak Harbor." Merrick dipped his wing allowing for a better view. "There are plans to build an airport in that vicinity."

"Hope they hurry up. That's one hell of a long stretch down that waterway for subs to make it inside." The view irritated Jack.

Merrick righted the PBY then continued in silence up to the furthermost town of Blaine.

"I'm turning around Jack, unless you need something else?"

"That's fine." He grumbled.

From this vantage point, the easy accessibility by water overshadowed the beauty of the islands. He attempted to breathe through his mounting agitation wishing he'd brought his flask. He checked his map noting they had just passed over Shaw Island traveling between San Juan and Lopez Islands. Again, the expansive blue of the Strait of Juan de Fuca raised his blood level.

"If that is Fort Warden ahead, who's watching the strait?" Jack's nervous tick of running his hands through his hair accompanied his question.

Merrick banked the aircraft west down the strait. "Ahead." He pointed as he continued, "is Ediz Hook at Port Angeles. There's a Coast Guard station there with Captain Mac just itching for a fight."

Kerr laughed. "I flew with him once. MacDiarmid is a wild card who keeps his men on their toes. Staged a fake attack recently and had the whole coast up in arms. Literally."

Somehow the image made Jack breathe a bit easier. If a Navy man willingly complimented a Coastie like Captain Mac, he must be doing something right. The rivalry between the two services protecting American coastlines was put aside in this time of dependency. In fact, most of the Navy ships heading into battle were skippered by the Coast Guard.

They flew over Point Wilson lighthouse bringing into view the "Triangle of Fire" as the three forts defending Admiralty Bay and the entrance to Puget Sound were referred to. Forts Warden, Casey and Flagler remained as old citadels recently reactivated to full capacity in the event their old guns were needed.

"I see you have Bangor on your list, Jack." Merrick sounded quizzical. "We'll head over but they're just getting that up and running."

Merrick spoke the truth as they headed over the expanding supply station at Naval Support Base Bangor.

"That's Dyes Inlet straight ahead." Kerr announced. "Keyport is to your left and we'll be close to Bremerton Naval Base in minutes, but the barrage balloons hide most of it.

Jack focused his binoculars on Illahee Dock then worked his lens across the water to Crystal Springs Drive locating the Summer Home of the Japanese Consulate. From up above the pathway Akio took by boat from Mr. O'Shaughnessy's cabin on Erlands Point, nestled on Dyes Inlet, the short distance around the tip of Manette to Crystal Springs Drive, appeared like child's play. By car the journey would have taken hours. By boat, the trip to safety and escape a matter of minutes. The home used for espionage, so perfectly situated on the bluff, again rose his ire.

"You okay, sir?" Merrick didn't appear to miss much.

"My brother-in-law flies one of these." Jack wasn't certain why he made the claim. A distraction seemed appropriate.

Kerr twisted in his direction. "Where's he based?"

At the word Kane'ohe the pilots fell silent, exchanging a brief nod.

Jack shifted, not intending to appear distraught. "So, will I be able to find Boeing from up here? Rumor has it that art director, John Detlie, has big plans."

"Yes, sir," Kerr, the chatty one, brightened. "They just have the cover over Plant number-2, but I hear they will construct what appears from the sky to be entire city blocks with houses, trees and everything."

Jack had read in a secured report one of the streets would be named "Burlap Boulevard," and for the first time all day he chuckled. Covering the Boeing plant from any enemy eyes was ingenious, and Hollywood had stepped up to do what they do best, create a fake world.

"In fact." Kerr smiled, encouraged by Jack's change in mood. "The first time one of the Boeing test pilots approached he couldn't figure out the entrance, flew right over it."

There were heading east toward the south end of Lake Washington when Merrick spoke, "Anything else, Jack?"

"No. Thank you. Let's head back."

They banked heading north as Jack watched the small white caps on the lake below. The wind was at their tail. He remembered the night he had followed Billi into those chilling waters in the dark. The memory made his heart beat faster. Any of the waterways they flew above today could bring a submarine, especially a mini sub, to take her away from him forever.

Like a cold mistress, the wind-blown surface below gave no hint of what lie below her depths.

As JACK AND BILLI started up the concrete steps to the front door, Mrs. O stood outside directing two men carrying a new mattress up the stairs. Pepper growled at the strangers, guarding the door, making the scene almost comical.

"Go on, right up to the top of the stairs then turn right into the first room." Mrs. O's hand waved toward the stairs with excitement. "Now, Pepper stop barking."

"What is she up to?" Billi felt her breath tighten as she stepped inside watching the men struggle up the spiral stairway.

"Isn't it grand?" Her mother beamed. "I'm bringing in soldiers."

Billi heard her husband grunt behind her and suppressed her own bewilderment.

"They've asked me to house some of the young men who have nowhere to stay." She continued in a whisper, "And I get to make a few extra dollars this way. I'm calling our home Fort Knox of Seattle, it's my little gold mine."

Billi picked up Pepper to calm him then turned to face her husband. She could tell he considered the new arrangements, a house full of men and his new wife, a bit disturbing.

"Maybe you should be wearing the three-diamond dinner ring. The one men can see from one block away." Anger tinted is voice.

"This one will do." She flashed the modest diamond and band in his direction.

"I have six men arriving tomorrow morning." Mrs. O charged up the stairs.

"Six?" Billi tried to calculate where the six would fit.

"Mother, where will I sleep if you have the other rooms full?" she demanded.

Her mother peeked over the top of the beautifully curved railing. "Well, you're never here when Jack is in town, and the rest of the time you can bunk with me."

"With you," she squealed. Her objection came too late, her mother disappeared down the hallway while her husband chuckled from behind her.

Billi stormed into the living room, unceremoniously dropping the dog, to glare at Jack. "This is not funny. She snores."

A knock at the door interrupted their stand off as they headed toward the intruder.

Dahlia stood on the porch hugging her coat.

Pepper emitted his high-pitched welcome as Jack opened the door. "Welcome to Fort Knox."

"Fort Knox?" A cold wind entered with Dahlia.

"One of mother's schemes." Billi helped her off with her damp coat.

"I just wanted to drop off a small gift for your mother." She held up a wrapped box.

"Oh, you shouldn't have." Mrs. O appeared in command at the top of the railing. "Billi get her something to eat, I'll be right down." She waved before she turned back to her upstairs task.

Dahlia sat between Billi and Jack, a pile of food before her as Mrs. O bustled through the large pocket doors separating the living room and dining room to inspect her guest's plate. Satisfied, she nodded and started for the kitchen.

"The Army and Navy have been sending recruiters to high schools." Dahlia announced between bites.

Billi watched as Dahlia's words halted Mrs. O in her path.

"Since I have one more year of nursing school, I have time to choose which service I'll enter. Oh, and Danny sends his love. Have you been getting his letters?"

"Yes, but skinny little Danny shouldn't even be in the Army." Mrs. O's concern swept her into action. She picked up a platter of leftovers, "I'll make a package for your mother. I'm glad she is doing better."

Jack waited until Mrs. O left the room then his head hovered close to Dahlia, his voice almost a whisper. "Eddy is doing well. And he said to say hello."

"Did he, really?" Dahlia barely breathed the words.

"He misses home too," Jack's calm voice held hope.

Billi broke in. "We can give you a lift home. It's too cold and dark to be walking." Glaring at Jack, she started to untie her apron before storming into the kitchen.

JACK EASED inside the warm car next to Billi. They silently watched Dahlia enter, closing the door to the apartment she shared with her ill mother.

Billi gathered her coat closer. "You shouldn't tease Dahlia like that."

"How was I teasing Dahlia?" The rain clung to his coat and hat.

"Eddy. Eddy has called their relationship off because of his new girlfriend over there."

"I don't think that is going to work out." He pulled the car from the curb heading them back toward the luxury of the Olympic Hotel.

She folded her arms in exasperation. "Why? How do you know?"

"Remember, I was in Hawaii and spent time with Eddy."

"What? When you said you spoke with him, you said it was by phone and it was business."

"Not exactly." He kept his eye on the road, not intending to encourage her wrath. "I spent quite a bit of time with your brother. He's a good man."

"I never know where you are anymore. I feel like you are a wind that blows in and then is gone. Something I can't grasp." Her hurt reflecting in her voice.

"Billi, no one in any branch of the service can tell where they are heading or stationed to any member of their family. Those days are over. Locations, any remarks about drills or anything that might be overheard or fall into enemy hands that gives any inkling of the number of troops or their whereabouts, will be cut out or marked out of any letter headed home. Don't forget . . ."

"Loose lips sink ships," they chanted in unison.

They arrived at the hotel in silence, which they maintained until they reached their room.

"But how do you know Eddy and his girlfriend, Lani, won't get married? Did you meet her? What's she like?"

Jack sat her on the edge of the bed to continue their conversation. "Two reasons."

"I'm waiting."

"When he was very drunk one night, he was upset. Remember, Billi, Eddy is a changed man. Seeing death will do that. He began to cry and he called out Dahlia's name. Not Lani's."

"You heard this?"

"I was sitting in the sand next to him."

She looked down at her hands in her lap. "And the second reason?"

"Lani is part Japanese."

She began to straighten. "But that should have nothing to do . . ."

"But now it does."

A long pause hung between them.

"He said she was a Hawaiian beauty, a rare and tropical beauty. What changed?"

"Pearl Harbor."

"I see." Her shoulders slumped. She knew any inter-racial marriage between white and Asian cultures was frowned upon, yet the depth of the divide had widened.

"Is there anything else you have been keeping from me?" She looked at him directly waiting.

"Yes." He rose and with long strides reached the American oak chest of drawers at the foot of their bed. When he returned he held his hand behind his back.

Billi bit her lip as he placed a small box in her hand. She slowly lifted the lid to discover a beautiful broach with one twinkling pearl set just below the words "Remember Pearl Harbor" etched in gold.

"This is gorgeous." She kissed his cheek.

Billi kicked off her shoes as she moved to the side of the bed snapping on the small night light before turning off the wall lamps. With the blackout curtain behind her she slowly unbuttoned her dress and let it fall to the floor. Her slip and undergarments landed around her feet. The pearly white of her skin in sharp contrast against the black backdrop.

"Take off your patch," she whispered. "See me with both eyes."

"That's not all I'm taking off, madam." His voice exhibited his deep desire as he slowly mimicked her movements. Within moments a stack of his clothes circled his tall frame.

Billi noted the red scar on his thigh a reminder of Akio's sword. She had never stood naked before a man before, nor, for that matter had a man stood so comfortably before her. The electricity between them palpitated with desire, yet neither moved. Then Billi lifted her hand, inviting.

That slight movement propelled Jack forward.

# SIXTEEN

AKIO STEPPED FROM THE SUBMARINE ONTO the dock inhaling the scents of home. The Kure Naval District swarmed with men in navy uniforms or those who wore the clothes distinguishing them as shipbuilders. The mass of bodies moved with precision from one chore to the next.

The sudden command to withdraw from America's coastline on Christmas Day met with mixed reactions among the submariners. For him, while it took him from his prey, it brought him closer to the man who could further his career. Admiral Yamamoto. He intended to send a letter to his grandfather's acquaintance, Yamamoto, regarding his design for a new aircraft. His fear grew daily that someone would steal his sketch imbedded within the design on the sensu, now in Billi's possession. He must act swiftly.

His legs wobbled a bit as he hit dry land, so he paused to take in the glory of Japan: efficient, powerful, a sight to behold. He regarded the port where, in 1940, he had witnessed the launching of the largest battleship ever built, the *Yamato*. He nodded in reverence toward the direction of Mount Yasumi, the tip buried in the thick dark clouds heavy with rain. Wrapping his jacket tighter against the cool air he smiled then inhaled the fresh air of his birthplace. The act strengthened his decision. The Admiral would recognize the glory of his design.

Akio noticed Tak, hanging back, seemingly unable to decide what to do with his shore leave. He would have him followed. Better yet, he would arrange for a geisha to ply him with drink then pry into his life in Seattle. Maybe the young fool would divulge what he knew of Billi and the priceless fan. His men continued dutifully to acquire the precious object. He smirked at his other instructions; the long-legged Billi must accompany the fan. He licked his lips in anticipation.

"Tak," he shouted over his shoulder. "Come."

The sound of hurrying feet reassured him the youth obeyed as he led the way to headquarters. Pointing to a chair for Tak just inside the offices of the Admiral Toyoda Soemu, he strutted toward the young ensign at the front desk. He presented a beautifully handwritten note, tucked inside an envelope marked with his family seal, a seal that still raised eyebrows, placing him in the inner workings of court. After all, it was his grandfather, Count Kawamuro Sumiyoshi, who had been entrusted with two young princes to raise as his own grandchildren until his passing. One of those two charges, Prince Michi, now occupied the Tokyo Imperial Palace, bearing the name Emperor Hirohito.

"See that this is presented to Admiral Yamamoto in Tokyo immediately." The young officer at the desk bowed in Akio's direction.

Never before had Akio felt the power of his lineage so strongly. The war against the Allies presented many opportunities for success. However, for now, hunger nagged at his reasoning, not only for the fresh food of his country but for a woman. Having killed the enemy, he deserved unbridled respect. He desired the rewards of a returning war hero, the satisfaction of food and the feel of soft flesh.

With Tak in tow, he hurried toward the hanamachi district where the geishas abound. Halting before his favorite ochaya, he slid inside the gate to the tea house, waiting to be recognized.

Hamako, the proprietor, stepped beneath the open arch greeting him with a deep bow. He had noted the hint of fear in her demeanor but brushed it aside. The stupid girl she sent him last time left him wanting, aggravating him. He displayed his dissatisfaction on the white satin skin of the novice.

"Honorable one, you grace my house." She purred.

"It is my money that you honor, Hamako. However, I am willing to let you make amends for your last indiscretion."

"Your kindness will be well rewarded."

Akio watched as her gaze fell on Tak waiting just inside the courtyard, exuding discomfort.

"His inexperience should not be rewarded with your choicest plum." Akio watched the young man blush and despised him even more. "Wait." He addressed the red-faced youth.

Leading Hamako past the pine tree, he stopped just outside the main hall of her establishment. The pleasing scent of the kitchen within filled his nostrils with the promise of intricate flavors. Hurriedly, he made his demands known. She nodded, quickly returning to a bewildered Tak. Akio watched the two disappear inside the long wood and paper structure of the ochaya. He snorted, wistfully hoping his plot did not exhaust his monies too rapidly.

He did not hear Ine approach until her soft gown brushed against the small stones moving them ever so slightly. She said nothing but turned to lead him inside, past the kitchen to the end room. Sliding the shoji screen wide, she waited to remove his shoes before they entered the washitsu, the last of the tatami rooms on the main floor.

Akio watched Ine float above the tatami mats, her movements as graceful as soft wind, as she set a steaming bowl of rice and eels on the chabudai he sat before. The highly glossed wood table reflected the images of the private garden outside the open screen doors. Again, the thrill of his accomplishments amplified with the anticipation his design for his new killing machine would bring him glory, made his blood run hot. The sake she poured would be the first of many tonight.

"How the hell did this happen?" Eddy slammed his fist into the wall of the officers' club barracks. "What did the report say? Twenty-nine lost? Shit, and just thirty miles off Upolu Point. Why didn't we see the sub on our morning scouting on the 27th? We could have saved those young guys onboard the old *Royal T. Frank*. This is a hell of a way to start the new year."

Scooter didn't answer, he let the weight of the news carry him down onto his bunk.

"I hear most of them, all islanders, just finished their training at Schofield Barracks and were being sent to the big island to be deployed." Eddy continued his rant. "The nine survivors, hidden in a hospital, are calling themselves the 'Torpedo Gang.' The goddamn 'Torpedo Gang.'" Eddy shook his head with the irony. "And the worst part is, I can't tell anyone about it. Top secret. Hell, the captain's wife hasn't been told yet that her husband is dead, and it happened three days ago. The hell with top secret."

Eddy started for the door as Scooter shot to his feet, blocking his passage.

"You want to get thrown in the brig? Lose your security position? Or worse, be stripped of flying?"

Eddy blinked, his rage subsiding. "Hell no. I just don't want them to do that to our families. If I go down, you have to promise to tell my mom. Visit her."

"You need to get up in the air. This desk job is making your nerves rattle. I'm going to visit your mother with you. Remember?"

"Yeah." Eddy swatted at Scooter. "And you better keep your mouth shut on this."

"We need to sink more subs. They're getting on my nerves too."

"We will. We'll get the Jap bastards." Eddy blinked again. Every time he uttered the words of war, he felt his heart harden and the image of Lani drift further away.

THE MEETING ON THE BASE at Pearl Harbor had droned on longer than expected when Eddy got free for a short break. Eddy checked his watch again, almost 3:30. He prayed he had not missed her. He drove down Kalakaua Avenue enjoying the trade winds as they passed through the open windows with their warm sea air. He turned at Kapahulu, again at Leahi, then stopped in front of Waikiki Elementary. Adjusting his shirt, he removed his Kimmel to straighten his hair. His heart lightened as he stepped from the car spying the bright colors of Lani's muumuu. When she moved to the side Eddy saw three children lined up waiting for Lani's attention. The largest of the family attempting to help the other two with their gas masks, which drooped heavily from their small shoulders. He jogged in their direction.

"Here, Kailee, put your gas mask over this arm to carry your books. And do not forget to bring your mask tomorrow." Her voice, while gentle, remained firm.

"I hate dese things, Auntie," the smallest protested.

"I know sweet one. But everyone has to carry them at all times." Lani's injury prevented her from bending all the way down to the small girl.

Eddy knelt before the little girl. "Here." He adjusted the heavy pack of equipment on the back of the small brown body. "Does that help?"

"No." Her little foot stomped, creating a small cloud of red dust which covered her bare feet. "I hate dis." Tears ran down her full cheeks as she pushed Eddy away. "I want Papa."

"He at home. Come. We go now, sister. You a big cry baby." The older boy adjusted his mandatory gas mask then started on the long walk home.

"I hat dis." She dropped the mask and hose attached to the heavy pack.

"Look." Eddy picked up the hideous looking necessity then placed the goggles and breathing device over his head. He rolled his eyes which appeared magnified behind the lens.

The youngest looked up at him with fascination.

"Can you do that?" His muffled voice steamed up the mask.

"I try." She reached her small hand out allowing Eddy to help her put the mask over her face.

"Let me see." He encouraged her.

The tiny child scrunched up her face while crossing her eyes.

Eddy didn't have to pretend, he sat back on the red earth laughing. "That's good."

He heard Lani chuckle as he made faces back at the little girl dwarfed behind the mask. She hunched her back, imitating a monster, then hurried off to catch her older siblings.

Standing close to Lani, he could smell the soft fragrance of the flower in her hair as they watched the three children playfully making their way toward home.

Lani broke the silence. "That was nice of you."

"I have my moments." He touched her arm. "Would you like to go for a swim?"

"No." She turned away, the tips of her long hair slightly lifting in the breeze. "No, I'm not ready yet. For anything," she added.

"How about dinner?"

"I see the doctor again tomorrow. And we should know more soon." Favoring her injured side, she limped away.

He stepped in her path. "Don't you understand? I don't care what the doctor has to say. I know you will get well. And I'm not going anywhere. I will always be here for you. I love you and still plan on marrying you, Lani."

He kissed her lips and she briefly responded. It was not much, but it gave him hope.

JACK HOVERED OVER THE PAPERS covering his desk in the small confines of the secret room in the Sir Francis Drake Hotel. Having barely slept, he had arrived yesterday, February 1st, to meet with Thomas C. Clark, the newly appointed Coordinator of the Alien Enemy Control program within the Western Defense Command.

Today's events brought the registration of all alien Japanese, but more importantly, the organized random searches of homes and businesses. DeWitt had kept his word giving his blessing. The hunt could now begin in earnest.

The papers assembled before him presented the root of mistrust and great alarm among those US decision makers. The Land of the Rising Sun prospectus, recently issued to all Japanese across the US, written by the Sponsor Committee for Heimusha Kai in America, revealed their attitude and blatant intent to their followers.

He re-read the top paper in the stack.

> As far as our patriotism is concerned, the world knows that we are superior to any other nation. However, as long as we are staying on foreign soil, what can we do for our mother country? . . . we, the Japanese in the United States, have been contributing a huge amount of money for war relief funds and numerous comfort bags for our imperial soldiers.
>
> . . . We are proud to say that our daily happy life in America is dependent upon the protective power of Great Japan! We are facing a critical emergency, and we will take strong action as planned. We do hope and beg you all to cooperate with us for our National cause.

In the margin on the next sheet he read the handwritten notation, "established, Los Angeles, April 1940." He circled the date and continued reading.

> With the grace of the Emperor, the ZAIBEI IKUEI KAI is being organized in commemoration of the 2,600th Anniversary of the Founding of the Japanese Empire to Japanize the second and third generations in this country for the accomplishment of establishing a greater Asia in the future . . ."

He couldn't deny their own words. The words of those groups fully supporting the Emperor and his loyal armies. The words of those who organize and demand attendance at Emperor worshiping ceremonies, where they face toward their home country of Japan and bow their heads. He read on.

> . . . ready to respond to the call of the mother country with one mind. Japan is fighting to carry out our program of Greater Asiatic co-prosperity. Our fellow Japanese countrymen must be of one spirit and should endeavor to unite our Japanese societies in this country.

He lit his cigar, focusing on the raid planned for the Hokubei Butoku Kai, the Military Virtue Society of North America, in Alameda County. Since 1931 this establishment had well known links to Tokyo. Sources said branches of this group, across America, were created to instill the military virtues of Bushdio to the young boys through judo, kendo and sumo wrestling. The enrollment in California alone was estimated at 17,800 students, all learning the highly militarized skill used for centuries by the Japanese in battle.

An additional concern, the Kibei Shimin movement, sponsored by the Japanese Association of America, recently encouraged some of the tens of thousands American-born Japanese living in the motherland, to return to the United States.

Why? Jack could only come up with one conclusion, those returning were indoctrinated, their loyalty to the Emperor would support any subversive activity on American soil. In 1941 alone, the association successfully helped over 1,570 find passage, securing them jobs once they entered West Coast ports. Adding to that complexity, over 1,150 additional alien Japanese re-entered the US. There were others, brought across the ocean secretly, posing as fishermen in Alaska, finding their way down the coast as engineers, saboteurs and spies. Coupled with the fact that, over the last few months, FBI agents had unearthed stacks of Japanese war bonds and munitions as they searched homes. Things were not tallying up in favor of the innocent.

Bolstered by the numbers before him, he stubbed out his cigar then grabbed his hat. He could not think of Billi today. He would wear his heartless and threatening look of the FBI agents sweeping through the enemies now living in his beloved hometown to bring them to justice. His dream of dreams would be to find Akio among them.

# SEVENTEEN

JACK LOOKED AT THE CONCERN ON his mother's face as she waved the *Los Angeles Times* in his direction.

"Have you read the column by Walter Lippmann from last Friday, February 13th?" Her voice almost squeaked with excitement.

"The government is taking strides to round up the Japanese aliens." He hoped his words would console her.

"But Walter, who I respect, claims that the West Coast . . ." her head bent as she read aloud, "'is in imminent danger of a combined attack from within and without . . . It may at any moment be a battlefield.'" She lowered the paper and glared at him. "Jack, this is terrifying."

He stared out the stained-glass windows, considering the many colors which created the soothing sensation, knowing that in life, the colors of the skin seemed to only bring fear and agitation.

"Jack," her voice was sharp. "Say something."

"Did you know that my wife's best friend is Japanese?" He turned back toward where she sat in her tall, floral chair. "Eileen is a lovely young woman, born in America. Her father owns a store in Japantown in Seattle. He is well respected but is an alien."

It was her turn to remain speechless.

"You will be fine, mother." He smiled at her. "Just think of any intruder getting through Bella, only to discover our pregnant and cantankerous Lilly. I'll have someone check in on you."

He accepted her half smile as her reply. Kissing her forehead, he scrambled out the door, not wanting any further discussion. His mother's concern reflected the hysteria building along the coast. Dangerous groups let it be known they intended to take the law into their own hands if the aliens continued to freely roam the streets and the waterways, especially close to military bases and facilities.

Arriving at the hidden room of the hotel he sat at his small desk to wait for his private, secured line to ring. His cigar burnt to a stub, his nerves raw, his mind a frenzy of information and questions as time ticked by. Finally, the phone shattered the silence, echoing off the cement walls.

"Yes, sir." Jack swallowed with excitement.

"What did you think of DeWitt?" the voice roared.

Always to the point, Jack mused. "He dislikes the Japanese, but you can't deny the facts. In Monterey alone on the 12$^{th}$, we unearthed over 60,000 rounds of ammunition, shotguns, rifles and maps for a variety of locations. The nightly reports of signals by flashing lights continue to pour in, these signal lamps keep moving, changing locations. We are still intercepting illicit radio communications, again from various locations. Needless to say, there has been an increase of incidents of Japanese being attacked, not only by whites, but also by some Filipinos. Obviously, a reaction to the disturbing news of the atrocities occurring in their homeland since MacArthur declared Manila an 'open city,' as he escaped to Corregidor."

Jack hoped he didn't sound bitter about the bombastic Army general who failed his men when they were first attacked on the 8$^{th}$ of December, representing December 7$^{th}$, the same day as Pearl, with the time difference. Rumor had it McArthur partied well into the wee hours that morning, appearing stunned and disoriented when woken to the news of Pearl Harbor. Yet, prior to the attack on the Philippines, some of his pilots begged to be airborne, suspecting the "war warning" applied to the Philippine Islands. However, McArthur, unable to give any command, allowed terror to sweep over the Philippines before any American planes could take off in defense of the islands. Then the general left behind the damaged city, commanding his few brave forces to fight to the end. Jack hoped to God the overwhelmed soldiers got the hell out of there alive.

"I studied the new maps you sent." The stern voice broke through Jack's disgust at the incompetence of some leaders.

From the sound of the voice, Jack realized a decision had already been made. He looked at a copy of the latest map he had recently submitted, just a sampling of California. Was it simply a coincidence or strategic planning? Several outlined areas indicated airfields, bridges, power lines, oil fields, virtually every utility and important facility throughout the Santa Maria Valley. All specifically populated by Japanese. In stunning comparison, the adjacent fertile agricultural fields remained devoid of those of Asian descent. He studied another page. Again, the pattern presented itself, only this time the markings surrounded the oil fields, Ellwood, Summerland, and El Capitan, separated by miles, yet the Japanese homes clustered around those fields. The Santa Barbara lighthouse, harbor entrance and airport also bore the mark of intense alien habitation. Along the coast to the north a stretch of open beaches, spanning almost twenty miles, almost entirely inhabited by Japanese, presented the perfect landing strip. Other maps from along the coast reflected the same findings. He feared what this selective occupancy implies in those vulnerable sites.

"Yes, tallied with the Imperial navy's submarine attacks of our coast, the incidents in Hawaii, the exploding expansion of the Rising Sun's forces throughout Asia, and MacArthur's departure, — excuse me sir, I realize he is a friend. But, it's pretty lopsided right now."

"I signed Executive Order 9066 today and I expect it to be put into effect immediately." In the brief pause both parties considered the ramifications of the newly imposed existence for so many. So far 1,266 alien Japanese have been rounded up, along with Germans and Italians. But that was about to change.

The voice took a softer tone. "How's married life?"

"More interesting every day." Jack breathed deeply, imagining Billi's response.

"Well, she did a great deed for America. Keep up the good work and if you see anything that I should be apprised of, don't hesitate, call. Your input is valued."

The conversation with the one man shouldering the weight of the crippling situation ended as it began, abruptly. Jake let the receiver dangle in his hand for a moment, reminding him of the world twisting in the winds of turmoil.

AKIO STRIVED TO OVERCOME his deep disappointment at his reprieve being cut short before he received a response from Yamamoto. He had been ordered first to the Kwajalein Atoll, where the other submarines remained nestled among the protective islands, waiting commands. Luck shone on him when command selected the IJN I-17 submarine for a special mission. Now, he stood topside dreaming of glory as she neared the California coast.

He would not be deterred this time as he chose his target with great care, the oil field at Ellwood just west of Santa Barbara. The night of the 23rd proved a bit blustery, but this shoreline he knew well as he selected the only area where they would not be spotted by shore patrol. After conferring with Captain Nishino, he directed the 5.5-inch deck guns toward the Richfield Aviation fuel tank. The shells lobbed through the night skies, destroying a derrick and pump house, nearly missing the local Wheelers Inn.

While the shells stuck the pier and the catwalk, not one American plane flew out to defend their shores.

"Why does the sky remain empty?" Captain Nishino observed.

"Americans are weak. We have shown them they are never safe and will be defeated." His pride in being the first to strike the US mainland apparent. "We have had extreme success. Panic will spread."

He noted the sweat dripping from Tak's forehead wondering at the source. Only two options presented themselves, the exhilarating maneuvers of the big guns or fear for a country he was born in.

Akio's thoughts turned to Billi. He swallowed his frustration at the report she had been spotted less than one-hundred miles away on Terminal Island in Los Angeles but slipped through his network of spies. More disturbing, shortly after that incident, Billi appeared back in Seattle, complicating matters, as she remained surrounded by family and Jack's minions. Her unpredictable movements, amplified by the loss of his supporters now in prisons, added to the risk of capturing her and securing the fan. He would have to wait.

As the I-17 started her descent into the dark cold waters he marveled at the success of their mission. His notes would reflect, they reached their destination at 19:00, took fifteen minutes to ready, fired 16 shells in twenty minutes, then slipped away escaping all damage.

His accomplishment would not go unnoticed. The fame of his actions ensured his request for a meeting with Yamamoto would be granted.

JACK COULD FEEL THE STEAM of his anger surging through his nostrils. He had left in the dark of early morning, his destination the wreckage of the oil fields near Santa Barbara where a Japanese submarine just shelled the shoreline. Yet, before he could complete his findings he climbed back into his car, heading along the coastal highway, over ninety miles south to the City of the Angels. Los Angeles suspected an imminent attack.

Slowed by the black out, with headlights painted halfway up the lamp to provide some visibility on the curving road, he reviewed his findings. While the damage to the oil field appeared mild, the interviews in the Santa Barbara sheriff's office had been frenetic. The Reverend Basham claimed he watched the submarine head south toward L.A. and had clearly seen "signal lights" from the ship to someone on shore. In fact, several people reported observing "signal lights" that dark night. Those calls of alarm imposed a black out for the rest of the evening. The most disturbing part of the report came from the sheriff. He claimed his men reported the incident to the Navy shore patrol, yet no planes responded to defend them in time. Why did it take the US squadron from Bakersfield almost three hours to respond? Calls for help went unanswered until 10:00 p.m., well after the established blackout, after the radio station had gone silent, and after the highway was cleared of all vehicles. He hit the steering wheel in frustration. The airport sat approximately 90 miles away, therefore taking three hours to respond made no sense. With the failure of defense from the military, disparaging families quickly packed up to head inland, fearing another attack.

The audacity of the timing of the attack stunk of Akio. The Japanese shells hit American soil as President Roosevelt began his fireside chat, his poignant message blaring across America:

> The broad oceans which have been heralded in the past as our protection from attack have become endless battlefields on which we are constantly being challenged by our enemies.

It lodged a psychological win for the land of the Rising Sun, even if their gunmen missed the oil field. The first attack on American soil brought with it, not only the success of instilling the jitters along the coast, but numerous predictions of another attack on the larger target, Hollywood. These predictions, not only from Navy intelligence, came from some of the local Japanese, claiming another attack within a twenty-four-hour period.

Jack turned down south Gaffey Street toward the upper reservation of Fort MacArthur, where the Point Fermin Lighthouse, built in 1874, guided ships safely to shore just above Terminal Island. He knew the old, big guns would be ready with anti-aircraft support. Lighting his cigar, he stood a moment observing the dark skies, praying for Billi's safety and for strength when he had to face her.

Jack's exasperation mounted as he scanned the horizon. Akio sat out there on these very waters, just beyond the waves crashing against this very hillside.

"Sir." A voice interrupted his thoughts. Jack turned peering down at the young man, whose blue eyes blinked in response.

"The commander asked me to give you a report. All is calm now, sir, but an alert was called at 19:18 and lifted at 22:23." The pace of his speech increased with his raw nerves as he recounted the story. "The air-raid sirens were blaring, and the air-raid wardens were ready at their posts. Our guns remain at ready and so are the search lights. We'll get 'em sir. If they're Japs out there, we'll get 'em."

"Thank you." The kid reminded Jack of Danny with the echoing lust of the young for revenge.

He snorted. Revenge, the bond that propelled him and Akio toward an unknown future. He remembered the proverb, "When you set out for revenge, dig two graves." He intended to dig one grave pleading with God to make it today, February 25th, 1942. Checking his watch, he read 1:10 a.m.

Not certain when he had fallen asleep, Jack bolted upright at the tap on his car window.

"Radar's picked up an unidentified object about 120 miles west of here." The blue eyes of the youth seemed to bulge with excitement. "Sir, we're on heightened alert with total blackout, we've recalled the air-raid wardens to their posts."

Jack hustled from the car again checking his watch, his cat nap had lasted until 2:15. He sensed the panic vibrating across the cool bracing air, as men stood ready and eager. Stomping his feet against the chilled ground, the weight of his gun bounced against his side, as he waited.

He heard the air-raid sirens just before 3:00 a.m. then fast-tracked it toward command headquarters.

"The colonel is reporting seeing about 25 planes at 12,000 feet." Blue eyes told him as he stepped inside.

"Where?" Jack demanded.

"Over Los Angeles, sir," he squeaked in reply.

Jack stepped back outside, tilting his hat back to examine the star-studded skies. Nothing. He couldn't make out anything in the darkness above or plying the surface of the waters.

And then it happened, seemingly at once, four batteries of anti-aircraft artillery filled the skyline. Search lights quickly sliced the black heavens with shards of light, as the ack-ack boomed from various locations around the city. But where the hell were these planes? The anti-aircraft shells continued to burst above, illuminated by the search lights like the fourth of July. He stood in wonder unable to identify what the big guns were aiming at.

Jack stepped back inside.

"Sir, reports are coming in from all over of aircraft spottings, swarms of enemy aircraft." Blue eyes gulped.

"What is the radar saying?" Jack suspected the frenzy now uncontrollable.

"Nothing reported."

Outside, the blasts became less intense, only to start back up again. He stood sentinel at the shore until the all clear signal finally at 4:14 a.m. For just over one-hour Los Angeles had been under attack, or the show in the heavens was one heck of a mistake.

Jack pulled his coat closer, starting back toward the command post. The situation would not be unraveled for some time and the pit in his stomach told him it wasn't going to be pretty for the military.

The radio exchange caught Jack's attention. The Army Air Corps had decided to keep its pursuit planes on the ground until they determined the whereabouts, number, and direction of the oncoming attackers. For that small miracle he was thankful. With the wild and terrifying reports coming from all directions, the chances of their own men being shot down, would reflect the incident the night after the Pearl Harbor attack when "friendly fire" over Ford Island shot down our own men returning from a mission. A grievous and horrifying mistake easily made by the intensity of not knowing when the enemy would strike again.

He held his breath as the report continued. Men working the night shift at the airfield near Los Angeles, hid under wings of the planes they were building for protection from the chunks of shrapnel from the massive guns as they hurtled back to earth. When these formidable flying objects began piercing the aluminum of the wings they hid under, the workers ran for cover and the safety of the buildings.

Jack feared the night cloaked many disasters. At dawn he slowly cursed the streets of Los Angeles. The exhausted defenders of the sky, the air-raid wardens, or those who had just stepped outside to watch the show, worked their way to their homes. However, not empty handed, as the bullet casings and shrapnel made easy pickings of war time souvenirs for the young or old as the day began. He passed homes and businesses with broken windows from the massive blasts of the anti-aircraft guns. Cars abandoned or wrecked remained in various angles along the streets.

The aftermath unveiled a grim reminder of the city waiting to hear what damage the 1,440 rounds had done to the enemy. There were rumors of a downed enemy airplane in Hollywood, but that had been just that, a rumor. Five causalities were reported, three from auto accidents in the black-out, two others died from heart attacks. Yet, no proof of an enemy invasion. The blasts created a forty-mile arc of entertainment as civilians sat on hills or their roof tops to watch the powerful guns respond to unidentified sightings. The first major incident on the mainland proved to be an undeniable mess. If the enemy roamed the skies over this city, sent from submarines or from hidden fields in Mexico, they had succeeded in delivering a blow to the morale of the country.

Regardless, the events of the last twenty-four hours added fortification to the President's and DeWitt's opinion concerning the need to protect the war zone along the West Coast. Jack knew the clock just reset for those Japanese who remained in their homes in the newly defined area. More significantly, the pace to move them further inland just increased dramatically.

# EIGHTEEN

BILLI SAT NEXT TO EILEEN ON the living room couch at 304 30th South, the strong voice coming over the radio held their full attention. Pepper gave one last bark at the deep voice, then settled at their feet.

Mrs. O hurried through the front door, brushing small specks of snow from her hair and shoulders. "It's the end of February, for heaven's sake. When is this cold going to stop?" She dropped into her high-backed chair, coat and all, in exhaustion.

They listened as Navy Secretary, Frank Knox, continued, "As far as I know the whole raid was a false alarm and could be attributed to jittery nerves."

"False alarm?" Mrs. O repeated. "But Los Angeles was under attack, the newspapers claimed . . ."

The broadcaster rounded up the announcements, "All enemy aliens must be removed from military sites, airports and major utilities. Yesterday, the first 250 aliens were shipped from San Francisco inland, to Fort Lincoln in Bismarck North Dakota, as the exclusion of enemy aliens from these war zone areas is paramount to the safety of the United States."

Billi reached forward than snapped the radio off as a dark silence fell over the room.

"What will they do with us?" Eileen's voice sounded small in response to the magnitude of the pending 'exclusion.'

"It's utter nonsense." Billi rose beginning to pace.

One of Pepper's eyes opened enough to watch that his master did not leave the room before he closed it again.

"You are no threat. You are no traitor. You are . . ."

"We are Japanese by descent, by coloring, and the slant of our eyes. We are now seen as different in this world." Eileen's pragmatic approach a tribute to her father's training.

"Jack will know what to do," Mrs. O put in hopefully.

"Ha." Billi's rage now geared toward her husband she had not seen in over one month. "He's useless."

Mrs. O shifted, her finger beginning to tap the solid wood of the arm rest, as her shoulders raised and lowered in silent indignation.

"I had better go home." Eileen stood forcing a smile in the direction of her friend. "Kenny and father will be wanting their supper. Besides, it's getting dark and I do not want to be out after the curfew."

The two young women hugged at the door then Billi watched as Eileen carefully walked down the steps leaving her footprints in the layer of fresh snow. Suddenly, everything felt cold, the house, the world, her heart. Above all else, she missed her husband.

DANNY SAT ON THE CHATTAHOOCHEE Choo Choo in the blazing Georgia sun. The Dinky Line, just one of the many nick names for the light rail servicing Fort Benning, had not budged. He wiped a drip of sweat trickling down the back of his neck as he tugged at his new stiff woolen collar waiting to be shipped overseas.

Sanchez, one of his newformed friends, leaned closer. "What do you think they are up today? We pullin' out?"

Danny regarded his dark Hispanic eyes and profile. "Who knows. But I liked yesterday's uniforms better. Those lightweight khakis made me think we were heading for the Pacific. My best friend, Eddy, is a pilot over there. I sure would love to run into him."

"How do you know where he is?"

Danny spoke with pride, "Eddy was at Kane'ohe during the attack."

Sanchez nodded with respect. "Maybe that's why they're doing this. Don't want us writing home, letting everyone know where they're sending us."

Another infantryman, the overbearing Tex, joined the conversation. "You can bet these damn wool duds mean we're headed to someplace cold. Guessin' Europe to fight Hitler."

"Guessing." Danny smiled. "That's what they want to keep us doing."

Whatever the Army was up to didn't make much sense. Yesterday, his unit sat completely outfitted with light uniforms for three hours in this very spot anxious for the engine to chug to life then rattle them toward Fort Lawson Airport, or at least that is where they assumed they were headed. Now again today, they waited for over two hours, dressed in heavy wool uniforms, packed and ready for what lie before them.

"Well, I just hope the war ain't over before we get there." Tex, restless, sat back, focusing out the dusty window at the new recruits marching toward the firing range.

"Not to worry. From what the papers are saying, there will be plenty for us to do." Danny took out the journal he kept in his breast pocket next to the rosary Mrs. O handed him before he left Seattle.

"You plan on filling that book with war stories?"

Danny realized Sanchez's question presented a way to pass the time. He pinched together one-fourth of his small booklet. "I hope we're back home by the time I've written this much."

Tex jumped back into the conversation. "You want to kill Japs or Krauts?"

Danny paused, the vision of Kenny Nakamura, his classmate and best buddy, floated before him. "You ever meet any Japanese?"

"Hell, no." Tex almost spit the words. "Any of 'em showed up in my town, they'd be lynched. What they did at Pearl Harbor and all. We need to . . ."

"I met some in Los Angeles." Sanchez broke in. "The Japanese had a large community there as well San Francisco. But, they're both our enemy right now. And our duty is to America."

Danny remained silent as he studied the two men. Tex, big and burly, had a hot temper as quick as his gun. Sanchez, slim with the roasted skin of his heritage, a whiz with the large anti-tank guns, preferred to strum his guitar in the evening. Aside from the trio performing in the top of their classes for their specialty, the other thing they all had in common was their age. All had been members of their local Army National Guard. Then after Pearl, enlisted at age seventeen, before graduating from High School. He watched their faces, serious with memories of back home mixed with the anticipation of surviving the one thing they had all discussed, their first kill.

As they reached three hours of confinement in the heated train to nowhere, their sergeant swung up the steps. His grim face told the story before he gave the command.

"Come on, Daisies. You're to report to exchange to pick up your new supplies. Then back to barracks. Sanchez, they want you pronto at headquarters."

Sanchez blinked, then stood. Grabbing his duffel, he followed the Sergeant off the train.

Danny struggled his duffel past Tex into the open air. Unbuttoning his heavy jacket, he lingered, allowing the slight breeze to cool him as he wondered what the Army had in store for him tomorrow.

Overhearing Tex's loud proclamation, he spun in his direction. "What did you just say?"

"Sanchez ain't American. He's Mexican. Bet they won't let him fight." Tex hovered daringly over Danny.

"Well, he's one of the best shots we have." Danny felt his cheeks go as red as his hair in defense of his friend. "Besides, he's been in L.A. since he was a baby." Danny glared at the towering Texan. Prejudice knew no boundaries.

By the time they made their way back to their barracks Sanchez came through the door.

"What's up?" Danny almost whispered, not wanting to solicit any comments from the overbearing Tex.

"My paperwork got delayed. Somehow my citizenship papers haven't cleared yet." He put his duffel on his bunk. "So, they're keeping me back until I can join you later."

"Any idea how long?" Danny couldn't help his concern. Trusting the guy next to you was drilled into every maneuver, every hour, every day. Of all the men in his unit, Sanchez proved the one he would depend on the most.

"The paperwork's been in for six months, so it shouldn't be long. Besides, the Major reviewed my records and said he'd personally try to rush it through."

Danny slapped his back. "Great. You'll be right behind us." Yet, as he spoke the words he wondered at the concept. Not an American by law, but a willing soldier for this country nonetheless. The common goal, the overwhelming urgency to destroy the enemy in both theaters overseas, made it possible to slowly knock down barriers of the heart and mind back home. At least that is the way Danny intended to see this new world.

JACK SMILED AS HE STOOD just inside the broken wooden door of the house on Laguna, just inside San Francisco's boundaries of Japantown. This raid, performed brilliantly, netted several illegal aliens from the highly trained and secret Military Virtue Society with deep ties to the Nippon military and Emperor. The defiant men who stood before Jack emitted hatred. In the past two days his agents had also gathered 139 members of the infamous Black Dragon Society, adding to the nearly 800 men already arrested in the Bay area. As San Francisco remained the largest population of Japanese outside of Japan, he elected to stay in this vicinity until the mandatory evacuation of all Japanese was scheduled to begin the next week, on April 6th, a process expected to take at least one month.

Jack thought of the Japanese map created in 1934 with the small red dotted lines representing their intent for expansion. He breathed heavy at how the dashes lead directly to San Francisco. Eight years later, the City by the Bay remained a key point of influence for the Japanese.

Not surprising, some of the men standing before him did not possess the correct paperwork to even be in America. He eyed them for hidden answers. He suspected they'd been funneled illegally through Mexico, or come across the waters to pose as fishermen in Alaska, only to drift down the coast to the Bay area.

Jack looked into the men's unemotional dark eyes, remembering his brief encounter years before in Seattle. He had stepped inside the Toyo Club at 614 Maynard Street to question the gangster boss, the masterful Kanekichi Yamamoto. A staunch supporter of the Emperor, the native of Yatsuo, Japan, arrived in Seattle in 1918, only to be escorted by the FBI and the Office of Naval Intelligence off McNeil Island penitentiary, through the Puget Sound, the Strait of Juan de Fuca and out into the vast Pacific Ocean in 1939. The FBI referred to Kanekichi as the "Yellow Al Capone." They had never been able to pin him for any of the murders he had committed, for his expansive drug dealing, gambling, running whore houses, involvement with the fishing industry in Alaska, or his efforts supporting espionage. They finally imprisoned him on tax evasion. However, during his years as head of the Toyo Club, Kanekichi sent immense fortunes back to Japan to supplement their armed forces.

The irony that these ill gained US dollars helped build the Japanese war ships and planes used to attack Pearl Harbor igniting this expanding war did not escape Jack. It only amplified the thoroughness of the Empire to prepare for battle. He focused back on the men before him, an attack from within the soft boundaries of the United States must be prevented at all costs.

He let out a sigh at the enormity of the task. He needed sleep before heading to Seattle to oversee that evacuation and to face his wife. The chill of their recent conversation continued to widen their unresolved divide. The brewing orders, created by the newly founded War Relocation Authority to meet the demands of DeWitt's mandatory relocation of all persons of Japanese ancestry, created the discord. Yet, no other solution presented itself. While time kept ticking the enemy spread across the Pacific.

Purposely he called Billi as he hurried out the door, busy, making their talks brief. When it came to his wife, his cowardice darkened their relationship. If the men lined up before him knew his weakness they would laugh. In response to his own shortcomings he approached the man closest, the one all eyes seemed to fall on.

"Name?" Jack stood a good foot taller than the man to whom he spoke.

"Ishihara."

Jack pulled the photo of Akio from his pocket. "Tell me all you know about this man."

The man's gaze lingered on the picture of Lieutenant Sumiyoshi. Showing no recognition, the suspect looked straight ahead.

Jack's frustration grew, it had been the same for months. Outside of Terminal Island, no one recognized Akio. Each time he inquired the response ended up the same, dead silence. Hatred scorched Jack's nerves. As each day passed, his search became more futile, he would not unearth Akio in America. Yet, he had to keep looking.

Billi strolled past a few boarded-up businesses in Japantown, declaring the family's early departure from the war zone. Heeding the advice of the President for voluntarily evacuation, some Japanese families moved over the mountains to Spokane, or Yakima, or further inland. While this area still bustled with daily activity, a sense of doom hovered like the darkest of clouds on this beautiful spring day of March 30th.

She saw Eileen pull her coat closer as she waited before her father's grocery store. His new sign, *We Are American,* hanging in the window creating no impact on those strolling by.

"Come on, the ferry should be in soon." She took Eileen's elbow and they continued in matching stride toward the waterfront.

As they rounded the corner of 2nd and Main, a bracing breeze greeted them. She shivered as she regarded the thick chain binding the tall elegant front doors of the Bank of Tokyo. The detailed relief of the bank's emblem, the strong pillars, every inch of the architecture claiming success in the new world, now dark and lifeless inside. She bent her head in shame, focusing on the purple glass imbedded in the sidewalk above the catacombs of the remains of the Seattle fire, where, out of the embers, new life had taken shape. In an area which the city planners designated for immigrants from Asia after the fire, Nihonmachi had proudly emerged carved in solid stone, brick and love.

"My friend said they have already taken her father. They live on Bainbridge Island with the others."

Billi feared the answer. "Do you know why?"

"Her father rode the ferry every day into Seattle and worked at Friedlander's Jewelers. He sold jewelry to visiting Japanese onboard their ships." Eileen's words fell flat.

Billi remained speechless. She knew firsthand some of the intricacies of the Nippon espionage web and how their tentacles spread to unsuspecting occupations. How easy it would be to bring on board maps of naval bases, designs for new planes from Boeing, or models of important bridges.

As they waited for the ferry to bring the Japanese who lived on Bainbridge Island into Elliott Bay, she considered why the inhabitants of this island were among the first in the nation chosen by government for evacuation. Observing ship traffic at the major Port of Seattle from the shores or hilltops of Bainbridge posed no difficult task. Along the south side, many spots offered a grand view of any vessel coming or going from Bremerton Naval Base. The Army recently expanded up "Swede Hill" requisitioning the Swedish and Norwegians to sell their homes and farms built next to Fort Ward, with its highly secretive Station S. Across from Bainbridge on the west side, a small peninsula extended into Liberty Bay, where the Pacific Torpedo Station prepared their weapons. She wondered if the location of the Japanese Consulate's summer home, the one that Jack searched, overlooking the waterways to the naval bases, had impacted the decision to move these Japanese residents so swiftly. It certainly did not help when the FBI searched homes on the island in January, finding contraband, and arresting 35.

"Hurry." Billi found a place at the railing on the overpass that loomed above the railroad yard leading to the ferry terminal.

When Eileen stepped next to Billi at the rail, someone from behind spoke loudly from the crowd. "Why aren't you going with them? We need to get all Japs out of here."

Billi pulled her heavy coat closer against the cool wind of the chilling words.

"Here they come." Someone else shouted.

"It's about time." Another voice answered.

A hush fell over the watching masses who had packed themselves onto the overpass in anticipation. Below a long, orderly line of 227 Japanese, men, women, old and young, started from the ferry terminal toward the waiting train. They carried their suitcases, walking with dignity and determination. The papers had reported the Japanese were "wistful and willing" to register their families as requested. Furthermore, if this evacuation would help the country they were "proud to obey the order."

As the train pulled away down the tracks, Billi hurried Eileen up the street, uncertain of the crowd surrounding them. Some might be itching to take matters into their own hands. While some shook their heads in disbelief, some had tears in their eyes, others appeared electrically charged with the excitement of watching the enemy ride off into the distance.

As she regarded the faces around her, she remembered Jack quoting one of the military officials, "How do you tell the goat from the sheep?"

JACK STOOD AT THE CORNER of Sutter and Stockton Streets regarding the newspaper stand where others gathered in silence. Three headlines for April 9th, 1942 boldly told the story. The *Oakland Tribune Extra* rested on the top wire rack claiming "*36,000 US MEN FEARED LOST IN FALL OF BATAAN.*" Just below, *The Post Enquirer* corrected the number with "*JAPS TRAP 36,800 AS BATAAN FALLS.*" While the *San Francisco Examiner*, occupying the lowest rack supported the other with headlines "*BATAAN COLLAPSES Japs Crush American Defenders.*"

A woman hurried up behind him then he heard her muffled cry. Jack turned in time to see her begin to sink toward the pavement. He caught her, and together with another woman helped the sobbing woman upright.

"My husband's there somewhere." She choked out.

It was the "somewhere" that encouraged others to chime in as they gathered around her with soothing words.

Jack stepped back, watching, listening, as the disheartened men and women, young and old, cursed the Japanese and the Nazis. It was just last week that the Allies rejoiced with the sensational bombing from the British Royal Air Force of the town of Lubeck. The German city suffered catastrophic damage, enraging Hitler but bolstering the spirits of Americans, British, Canadians and Australians around the globe. While the battle in the European Theater relentlessly raged since 1939, the sting of the Greater East-Asia Co-Prosperity Sphere just recently became agonizing for the Allies.

The US botched their attempt to defend the ill-prepared Philippines, leaving a few troops along with some of the British forces and the Filipino scouts to shoulder the battle. But, in just four short months, the entire country had fallen. General MacArthur, relocating to South Australia in March claimed, "I came out of Bataan and I shall return." Jack bit his lip upon reading the words of that audacious man with his singular statement. The man did not think to include his fighting soldiers in his callous statement, "I shall return." Not without your fiercely courageous men.

However, that pronouncement seemed improbable as of today's headlines. This news of Bataan only increased Jack's anxiety. The removal of the Japanese along the coast had just begun and if they didn't hurry, mobs would do their job for them.

Suddenly, nothing mattered more than talking with Billi. He hurried down the block stepping through the door to the Sir Francis Drake hotel. Impatiently he waited for an empty elevator. He fingered the edges of the special key as he rode the elevator past the mezzanine with the couple who entered at the last minute. Finally, alone, he arrived back at the mezzanine level to slip through the curtains to the locked door and his sanctuary.

He lit a cigar, breathing deeply it's intoxicating aroma. The world spun too fast and he couldn't keep up. Pulling the phone across the desk he sat in his accustomed wooden chair to dial.

The phone rang seven times when at last he heard an unfamiliar voice.

"Fort Knox," the male voice announced.

"Who is this?" Jack demanded.

"Who is this?" The stranger bellowed back.

Jack took a deep breath. "Is Billi there?"

"And who wants to know?"

"FBI Agent Huntington. And if you know what's best for you, you'd step on it."

When no response followed, Jack attempted to regain some calm. He listened intently until he heard Pepper's bark draw nearer, somehow that glorious sound made his pulse relax.

"Hello," Mrs. O'Shaughnessy's voice sounded sweet as he felt his pulse increase again.

"Hello, Mrs. O. Is Billi there?"

"Oh, hello, Jack." He heard a different tone in her voice upon recognition. "No, Billi, is down at the Elks Club. We baked dozens of cookies for a USO dance tonight. I don't expect her back until later."

He chided himself for his negligence realizing he didn't even know the daily routines of his wife. He didn't dream she danced with other men, furthermore, now that "Fort Knox" had launched into active duty, she shared her home with soldiers. He snorted, last week she stood at the waterfront watching the removal of the Japanese, tonight she danced in someone else's arms.

"I'll call back." He hung up the phone before he realized the impact his abruptness would have on the household.

He stormed out of the room, finding no peace in the stark gray walls. Jack chomped on his cigar as he propelled his car past the slowly moving Army cargo caravan. The soldiers, khaki clad and baby faced, rocked with the motion of the vehicle as one. The poor bastards.

His tires screeched as he pulled into the driveway of his mother's home. The garage door stood open, empty, the old La Salle gone. Good, he wouldn't have to say goodbye to Lilly, he had said too many already.

He started down the path to the kitchen door. Bursting inside, he paused. Howard sat with his arm around his mother, her tears dripping on her white apron.

He hesitated a moment. "Has something happened?" His immediate thoughts went to his mother and Lilly's unborn child.

Bella shook her head "no," then "yes," with renewed tears.

Jack stood above the mother and son, their resemblance unmistakable, and waited.

"It's Howard." Bella's big brown eyes looked up at Jack.

"I'm right here, Mama." He patted her hand.

She ignored him. "He's shippin' out."

Jack sank into the chair on the opposite side of the table, then stood again and put three cups on the shining wood surface. Snatching the coffee pot from the stove he poured a small amount in each cup. As he sat, he reached inside his overcoat, shaking his flask into the open he topped each mug off with strong whiskey.

Bella clutched the cup, then nodded, drinking deeply.

Howard blinked at his mother's behavior then followed her lead.

Jack swished his drink before sipping. "You remember when you were really little how your mother chased us when we got caught throwing rocks at the bird in that pine tree?"

Howard's contagious laughter filled the room. "We had rocks all over your tennis court."

Bella eyed them both. "That's nothin' like the time you decided to build yourselves a swimmin' hole." She stood, heading toward her stove only to return with a pie.

Jack caught sight of his younger sister, Lilly, as she pushed through the door. She stood, her usually tidily coiffed hair at odds with conformity. The light blond whisks stood out at differing angles reminding Jack of their childhood. Her chiffon robe trimmed with feathers bulged over her expanding belly.

"The prodigal prince has bestowed us with a visit." She scowled at her brother.

Bella pushed the remainder of the pie to an open chair at the table and announced, "Don't get between a pregnant woman and her pie. Come on now, Lilly. Have a piece so you get some sleep."

Before Lilly could sit, the door swung wide again as Mrs. Huntington entered, assessing the group.

"Howard's shipping out." Jack spoke with the sorrow of claiming someone dead.

Lilly's head bent, hiding her fear, as his mother lowered in a seat next to her.

"Howard," the matriarch began. "We will expect daily letters. Where will they send you for training?"

"In a few days I head to Fort Huachuca, Arizona. I've never been anywhere."

Mrs. Huntington extended her hand toward the child raised with hers.

Howard stood, his black skin now covered with the glow of anticipation and alcohol. He leaned in to gingerly accept her handshake.

"Thank you." Mrs. Huntington grasped his hand fiercely the act carrying unspoken words.

Jack marveled at the change the war had brought to his mother. She no longer sat in her room, behind the closed curtains excluding light and life. Instead, her limited strength focused on helping others, especially those within the vast walls of her home.

"And when I return," Howard announced. "I'm going to medical school."

"We're counting on that." Mrs. Huntington smiled.

Bella wiped away a new tear. "You better come home. Dr. Gill."

Jack felt Lilly pull at his arm and looked down at her growing stomach.

"What have you heard from your wife? I miss her." Lilly asked.

"So, do I, Frilly. So do I."

"So?" her voice grew louder.

This drew the attention of those at the table.

"Where is your wife, Jack." Lilly, crossed her arms over her belly pouting.

His mother raised her eyebrow, waiting.

"You better not let her slip away." Bella, the one whose opinion he regarded the most, leveled her gaze at him.

He stood now, somehow the center of the attention, and could not find the words to explain his own cowardice.

"We'll be fine." His mother's graying head nodded. "Go to Billi."

It was a command. He felt sweat begin at his temples. His fear must be obvious. He wondered how long they had known he was stalling. A new concern chilled him to the bone. What if she didn't want him anymore?

# NINETEEN

BILLI SMELLED THE LIGHT SCENT OF cigar as she entered the foyer at 304 30th Ave. South. She stood for a moment, listening, only to have all sound obliterated by the welcoming bark of Pepper.

His short brown legs ran toward her, then spun around to run back into the living room. He repeated this action, his excitement making her laugh. She hung up her coat then followed the prance of her guard dog through the tall archway, noticing that the wooden doors to the dining room were pulled shut. Odd, the closed door usually signaled guests, a warning her mother used since childhood. The very warning she ignored the first time she met Jack, as he waited on the other side of the solid wood doors to speak with her.

She hesitated listening, hearing nothing, she pulled at the brass door openers, then halted.

"Come in," Jack finally spoke over Pepper's bark.

Billi remained at the door evaluating those who sat at the table. Three of her mother's new renters, sat bolt upright, hands folded on the tablecloth, with perspiration forming around expressions of anxiety.

She stepped through the arch as all four men stood. At her hesitancy, she watched her husband round the table to stand before her.

"Hello," she whispered, searching his good eye for any hint of warmth.

In the awkward silence she heard one of the young men's nervous voice. "We sure are glad to see you, ma'am."

"Yess'um, we sure are," another joined in.

"This here FBI agent has been asking us questions, but we didn't tell him nothin'," the third voice claimed.

"Well, I hope I passed the test." Billi felt her anger begin to mix with the excitement of Jack's presence.

Suddenly she was in his embrace, his lips were against hers. Pepper seeming to understand the moment, whined then sought his spot under the table.

"Hey, listen here fella." The young soldier came to her defense.

Billi merely waved her hand at the approaching man laughing. "Jack. You rascal." Her blush as red hot as her blood.

"We'll, I'll be," the comment came somewhat muffled.

One of the men stepped forward and straightened. "Can we go now, sir?"

She watched Jack turn back toward the startled young men. "Yes. How much longer before you ship out?"

The shortest quickly replied. "Three days."

"Keep watch and keep me informed."

"Yes, sir," they answered in unison.

Billi stifled a laugh as all three soldiers attempted to push through the door as one solid mass.

"Well, you sure made an impression on them." She started for the kitchen. "I'm starving. Have you eaten?"

When he didn't answer she turned to face him. "What is it Jack? How many bodyguards do I need?"

She saw him relax. "As many as it takes."

"So, we don't know if Akio's alive?"

"No."

She walked to him, running her hand over his light scar running down his cheek. "Then let's enjoy what we have."

He answered with a kiss as she willingly gave into his passion.

Pepper's bark broke them apart as the front door slammed.

"Billi." Mrs. O's excited voice rose above Pepper's fuss. "Billi, turn on the radio. Tokyo has been bombed."

"Did you know about this? Is that why you came?" Billi briefly studied her husband then hurried past him into the living room to snap on the dial to the tall mahogany radio.

. . . reporting damage to all three major cities of Tokyo, Kobe, Yokohama. This is a major blow to our Nippon enemy. That's one heck of a response for Pearl Harbor from our brave Yankee pilots. We are still waiting to hear how many of our planes were lost . . .

Billi snapped the radio off. "Eddy doesn't fly a bomber Mother. There is no need to worry."

Jack stood in the archway of the door. "Mrs. O, those brave young pilots were originally from the Pendleton, Oregon base and have been preparing for this attack since early February. Eddy was not involved in this mission."

"Oh, good heavens." She slumped into her large rocker, signaling Pepper to her lap. But as soon as the pup landed, he was ejected as Mrs. O leapt to her feet. "Jack, when did you arrive?"

Billi bit her lip as she watched her mother's expression go from startled to accusation.

"Did you know he was coming up?" she sputtered. "I don't have any rooms available."

Sensing her husband needed some encouragement, she stood beside him. "Well?"

"Not to worry, we'll make do."

Billi felt her heart lighten. He planned on staying, even if briefly, her husband would be by her side. Turning she watched her mother's shoulders raise and lower in her usual nonverbal response of confusion.

"Jack," Mrs. O's eyes filled with tears as she posed the question. "Are we going to lose this war?"

His answer was strong and forceful with his conviction. "Never."

"Good." Her plump cheeks creased with the joy of her smile. "I'm counting on your word."

AKIO STRUTTED FROM THE TRAIN clutching the paper with instructions to report to headquarters in Tokyo. He stepped lightly with spirits high. The summons meant an opportunity to present his plan. As of yet, his design remained his secret. He thanked the Gods his fan with the hidden design, the fan the whore with the blue eyes kept in her possession, had not fallen into anyone else's hands. This knowledge did not dampen his desire for Billi, it only enhanced his need to hear her scream with submission.

Inside the large building, the commotion made his heart race with the palpable sense of urgency. Led to a small room he waited, anxious to be acknowledged for his talents. When the door opened, he was surprised by the young man who stood in his navy uniform.

"Warrant flying officer Nobuo Fujita." The newcomer announced.

They bowed in greeting. Akio assessed the man with the long nose and full lips to be just a few years older. They waited, eyeing each other, with a hint of mistrust.

"It is an honor." Akio took the lead, not wanting to offend the pilot in such proximity to higher ranking officials.

"The honor is mine."

The silence once again deepened around them.

"Are others joining us?" Akio's impatience grew.

"No. You are to transfer to the crew of the I-25. We leave in two days." Fujita bowed and was gone before Akio digested his words.

Akio could feel his blood rising. What happened to his meeting with Yamamoto? Had no one recognized his family seal and delivered his letter to the Commander in Chief of the combined fleet?

He approached the desk down the hallway from Yamamoto's office requesting an interview. The clerk withdrew in silence waving to a chair against the wall.

Akio sat, letting the steam from his anger drift into the hall. He would wait. Determined, he did not leave his post as daylight began to dwindle. Footsteps from down the hall announced yet another visitor leaving Admiral Yamamoto's busy office adding to his frustration.

Suddenly, a man halted before him. Akio stood to follow him down the length of the passageway, matching the heavy pounding of his heart with each step. As he walked into the office, the light of the setting sun streaming into the tall windows struck him. Red shards of light streaked through the heavens, the blood of the enemy, the red ball of the flag, an omen for victory.

He bowed deeply, waiting.

When Yamamoto spoke, Akio stood tall. "The resemblance is strong. Your grandfather, Count Sumiyoshi, would be proud of your achievements." Yamamoto came from behind his desk. "Your arrival is timely."

Akio followed the short, stout man to a long table. A large map of the Pacific Ocean covered the entire surface with replicas of ships at various points across the vast blue seas.

"We have shifted our forces. We will not invade India. We are going to expand south. We will establish an airbase at Tulagi and Port Moresby crippling Australia and New Zealand, as we rule the Coral Sea. Then we will attack Midway. And when we have Hawaii, President Roosevelt will make a deal." Yamamoto put his left hand, the one missing the two fingers, on the edge of the map then stretched using an ornate stick to point at a chain of islands just southwest of Hawaii.

Akio hovered over the map with deep interest, ready to explain the benefits his fighting machine would bring to an attack on the coasts of America.

Yamamoto began again, tapping the small atoll of Midway. "It has been a struggle just to convince the Naval General Staff of my plan. Due to the recent raid by Doolittle's men on our homeland, my concepts are once again of importance. From this dust will rise our glory. We must destroy all American aircraft carriers, especially those we missed at Pearl Harbor. You studied at Stanford University. I attended Harvard and served twice as naval Attaché in Washington D.C. We know the power of our enemy. Their great capacity to build new ships and aircraft has already been set into motion. If we can claim Hawaii, we might be able to negotiate the end of the war."

Akio swallowed hard, stunned. Yamamoto just announced he planned to negotiate the end of the war. He looked down on the man still focusing on the map.

"Your knowledge of the West Coast is needed up here. You will make the perfect decoy for my plans."

Akio looked back at the map. The stick moved away from what would be the main battle to a string of small islands at the end of the Aleutian chain leading to Alaska. He felt the heat of his anger climb to his collar wanting to scream, this was all wrong. He should be in the main skirmishes that way he could prove himself.

He breathed deeply, finding the words took time. "Your . . .

"Come," Yamamoto commanded. "I am late."

Frustrated, Akio fell in behind. He must speak with Yamamoto about his creation. They hurried to the waiting car then were whisked over the bridge, past the railway station then the Shimbashi Embujo Theater to a small street in the heart of the Shimbashi district. The geisha house sat below a cherry blossom tree dripping with over-laden blooms.

"I must write another poem about the beauty of the blossoms." Yamamoto sounded wistful in his declaration.

Waving to Akio, he hurried from the car passing through the main gate. A lovely geisha bowed in greeting.

"Ume." The Commander in Chief bowed in response speaking softly, "Your beauty makes the cherry blossoms tremble with envy."

"Your praise is the beat of my heart." Her eyes sparkled with the truth of her statement.

"Is this someone who will lose his money at your card table?" She teased, as she bent in welcome to Yamamoto's young accomplice.

The flow of her traditional gown made the slightest rustling as she led them inside, past the luring scents carried on the steam from the kitchen to the back room. Akio felt a tinge of envy at the sight of Ume's well-bred upbringing, apparent with even the slightest gesture. He noted her artistry with makeup did not conceal the fact that she was in her mid-thirties, which merely enhanced her allure. In awe he watched her, the famous Kawai Chiyoko, better known as the gei-sha Umeryu, or to some, Plum Dragon, Yamamoto's lover and friend since 1933.

Shoes removed, they sat on the tatami mats at a table where other high-ranking officers waited. Geishas fluttered around, bringing sake accompanied by platters of food, while Ume sat beside her lover.

"This is Lieutenant Akio Sumiyoshi." The minute Yamamoto spoke all turned to appraise the tall man beside their leader. "He guided the 1-17 submarine to the honor of being the first to fire on the American mainland to destroy their oil field."

Akio slipped into the spotlight at Yamamoto's announcement. "It was but a pin prick against the giant. But many such inflictions will bleed the weak country to its death."

His confidence did not convince the others of his abilities. Glasses raised, while some eyes spoke of a different feeling. Among the murmurs of approval, the brashness of the newcomer reflected in blank stares.

Ignoring their glares, he turned to the Commander in Chief addressing him bluntly. "I take it you were pleased with my proposal for . . ."

"I am considering your words. That is why you will go with Fujita." Yamamoto watched a graceful hand pour more hot sake into his glass. "He does not trust you, your techniques in battle."

Akio barked a laugh, leaning back. "War is for the samurai, not the shellfish."

"But the large clam has a shell even the hand of a man cannot break alone. We will talk when you return." Yamamoto turned back to Ume.

Akio peered over the head of the great man to where Ume sat watching him. Taken aback he blinked at her.

It was then that he heard Yamamoto ask his lover, "How should I win this young man's money? Mahjong or poker?"

She had not looked away from Akio. "You would win too easily at cards as his poker face is not hidden. Possibly mahjong or hitting billiards would satisfy his impulsiveness."

The Commander in Chief laughed at her wit, obviously respecting her intelligence and quick ability to summarize a person's character.

Akio realized he had been dismissed, not only by his commander but by a woman. The feeling in his gut burned rancid with terror. He looked around the table as the high-ranking officers mumbled comfortably among themselves of their hatred of Doolittle, the inferiority of the United States and the growing need for retaliation to save face. He bit his tongue; he felt the outsider who must take daring steps toward success to be heard. He would prove himself a man capable of cracking any shell with his bare hands.

BILLI STOOD NEXT TO EILEEN as the police posted the long sheets of paper on the thick wood of the telephone poles. A small crowd hovered, waiting to read the declaration of the Japanese Exclusion Order. Her head ached, as did her heart. Some Germans and Italians were also to be swept away in the tide of relocation.

She stepped back to watch as members from families, those who read English, move closer to the towering pole to read, then translate. As they spoke their faces reflected a mix of concern and determination.

Eileen kept her head bent as she spoke, "The evacuation is to begin next week. There will be three groups leaving, one on Tuesday, then Thursday and Friday."

"I will visit you." Billi reached for her friend's delicate hand. "After all, being married to my husband must have some benefits."

"They fear him here."

Billi looked around. No one had overtly shunned her making her wonder if they fear her as well.

It was all happening so fast. The tally of those Allied forces lost to the Imperial fighting forces, mixed with the tensions of the tangible apprehension of another attack on the West Coast, only added salt to a bloody wound. A sudden wave of nausea swept over her.

"I have to go and pack more things." Eileen's voice held no bitterness. "The church will keep most of our belongings, we can take what we can carry, some will be shipped later."

They began to walk back toward the Nakamura's store as once again Billi approached the mounting situation. "Why don't you head inland with the others? What about heading to another state? Back East? Just move away from the war zone?"

"I have never been over the mountains to Yakima or Spokane, or out of this state. I will try again to encourage father to make the move. I would like to go to New York." Briefly her eyes twinkled mischievously, before the shadow or reason took hold. "But I do not want to leave father. He says we must do what our new government tells us."

They continued in silence. Billi, fully aware the disappearance of her brother Tak threw suspicion over the entire family, understood Mr. Nakamura's reasoning.

"I'll give you my new suitcase." Billi announced.

"No." Eileen smiled. "I have one. You'll need yours. Who knows where you'll end up."

"Okay." Billi matched her friend's smile. "I'll keep it to so I can visit you in New York."

# TWENTY

IT WAS ONLY 7 A.M. ON Tuesday, April 28th, 1942 and the rain outside reflected Billi's emotions. She pulled Mrs. O's new blue car just below the steps leading up to the Nakamura apartment. As Billi rounded the front of the car she grimaced at her white lie to her mother. But she would have the car back before long. She opened the large glass door leading to the steps then paused, inhaling the lingering scents of the distinctive dishes from Japan. Quietly, not wanting to disturb any of the memories she had built behind these walls, she slipped up the stairs. The kanji claiming peace still hung next to the door. She realized Mr. Nakamura would leave it there to protect the spirit of his deceased wife, who had passed away just last year.

She felt exhausted and hoped it didn't show. The week of waiting had numbed her senses. She stopped arguing with Jack as security intensified as did the threat of Tokyo's retaliation for Doolittle's raid. The element of the unknown still lurked in the shadows of Japantown. If there were an invasion, it was believed the Imperial forces would invoke the demands of Hirohito on the residents of these distant shores. It remained speculation whom among those with Nippon lineage living in the US would obey their god Emperor, a ruler demanding death before surrender. These uncertainties lay deep in the minds of all Americans as Japan's forces might quickly spread through Thailand, into Burma, down through Sumatra, Java, and into Timor. With the Philippines totally lost, the enemy captured all of Borneo then part of New Guinea. The Caroline Islands and New England now flew under the rising sun flag. This left Australia, a strong ally, within striking distance from several fronts.

As Billi stepped inside she wondered how long it would be before her friends could return. She stood awkwardly facing Eileen's family, at a loss for words. Kenny stood looking down at his suitcase that sat next to his father's, each displaying dangling slips of paper. As the Western Defense Command and Fourth Army Wartime Civil Control Administration poster hung on the telephone pole advised, the Nakamuras had registered at the Civil Control Station over the weekend. The tags they had been issued now hung from their coats, suitcases and bags of belongings. Number 10612084 was assigned to the family. Not their name, but their number would be how they would be known in Camp Harmony, the fairgrounds in Puyallup providing a temporary assembly center.

Billi noticed Kenny's bachi sticks, the wooden sticks for his taiko drum, crammed into the straps of his baggage in defiance.

"Where is your drum?" Billi regretted the words the moment she spoke them.

"It'll be brought later on one of the trucks." Kenny's eyes brightened. "I won't stop playing. They say there is a master taiko drummer who will teach us while we're in camp. So, when I get back, I'll be even better at my drum."

She nodded at him, smiling. "I believe that with every beat of my heart."

"Billi, I must entrust this to you."

Billi turned toward Mr. Nakano's voice. He held out a box, neatly tied with silk ribbon.

"Our tea set. Keep it safe so we can all drink together again." His smile appeared halfhearted, his eyes dull, as Billi reverently accepted the box. "Oh, and most importantly, this." He lifted the orchid in its new flowerpot.

Billi caught her breath. Against the dark blue of the new container, dragons swirled toward the brim, reminding her of the Professor's gift of the fan. "It is a masterful container. Where did you find it?"

"When I told my friend I must ask to impose on your kindness to care for my orchid, he insisted I give you this. He said it will be acceptable if by chance it breaks."

"Please tell your friend I will dutifully care for both. When you come home the buds will be in bloom." She held the pot with trembling hands.

"That would be a gift from Kono-Hana-Sakuya-Hime."

"Lady who makes the trees bloom," Billi whispered.

His low bow toward her a sign of respect. He straightened then looked around at the bare walls of the home he had known for years.

"We will be back, father," Eileen encouraged.

"The bus comes in one hour. We need to go now and get in line," Mr. Nakamura calmly announced.

"I have mother's car. Can I drive you?" Billi's voice attempted a sense of normalcy.

"We must say our goodbyes here." His gray head bent to pick up the box that held his shrine and photo of his wife.

Their shoes hitting the wooden stairs for the last time sounded hollow as they reverberated down the hallway.

"I'll write when we get settled." Eileen held her friend close.

Billi squeezed her closer. "I'll come and visit soon."

"I'm counting on it."

Billi slumped against her car, watching the three Nakamuras join other families as they headed toward the corner in the gray rain. She clutched the orchid closer, the shiny green leaves fanned out in opposing directions, creating the appearance of arms spreading toward the sky in prayer.

"Keep them safe." She spoke the words the plant could not.

EDDY WATCHED THE FROTH on the waves pass under his PBY as the last tip of the Hawaiian Islands disappeared. His mind traveled back across the green blue waters to Lani. The thought of leaving her so suddenly with hordes of service men filling the streets as they shipped in and out on their assignments made his skin crawl. Uncertainty nagged at his heart. Lani had remained distant with his orders arriving before he could penetrate her guard.

They soared through the cloudless sky as his thoughts turned to Ray. Eddy felt his deceased friend's presence riding through the clouds. Silently, he pledged he would fight for the two of them as he headed out on his first overseas mission.

"Have you heard where we're headed yet?" Scooter asked, adjusting his goggles.

Eddy thought of the night he delivered the top-secret package from the brilliant Rochefort, breaking codes in the "dungeon." How, before he handed off to the package to the powerful Admiral Nimitz, Rochefort insinuated all pilots would be needed and wished him "Good luck, kid." Wherever they were heading must be a clash of titans, a battle America desperately needed to win.

"No. We aren't far enough out to sea. They probably think we could shout it back to the shore."

Scooter laughed at his friend. "Well, they might think that about you. All that secret work you were doing at Pearl for a while."

He glanced over at his co-pilot. "Scooter, my boy, it's who you know."

"Well, you must know someone to get us off the base and into action. I just hope we fly between Jap bullets, not into them."

"A cake walk. We'll knock those bastards from the sky like shooting stars." He cringed at his own bravado. Their inexperience in battle he brushed aside as the least of their worries. The fact their big, slow machine made an easy target created an alertness he knew he shared with his co-pilot and crew. However, if rhetoric could kill, the war would be over very soon.

"Admiral Fletcher didn't fare too well in the Coral Sea." Scooter sounded pessimistic.

Eddy had memorized the details. "Yes, the *Lexington* and the *Yorktown* were severely damaged, and it was a standoff on who won."

"It's hard to believe the Blue Ghost is gone. They say two hundred and sixteen were lost on her. Damn fine ship the *Lexington*."

"New tactics," Eddy continued. "That's why they're tightening our strike coordination and adding more torpedo bombers. It was the first time any battle was fought strictly by air. No shots fired between ships." He paused a moment. "I just wish our PBYs had more firepower."

"Are you kidding. With as slow as we go. We can't out maneuver those Zeros. That's for our fighters."

"Yeah, well I think our old birds have more to offer than scouting, rescue and a few bombs. I'm working on it."

Scooter gave out a low whistle. "You afraid to kill a man?"

"Nope. The harder we hit 'em, the sooner we're home." Eddy looked again at the diminishing green specks of the islands.

They continued in silence ticking away the moments before they could hear their assignment. Finally, the radio crackled as their lead, Lieutenant Taff's voice penetrated their anticipation.

"Men, we'll be up a while. As the crow flies our destination is 1,072.98 miles, bearing 196.89 SSW. Let's get there, make a difference and come home safe. Stay sharp." The lieutenant's voice held the confidence everyone needed.

Each aircraft responded in order.

"Number 3," Taff addressed Eddy's PBY. "O'Shaughnessy, did I hear you packed a snorkel for this trip?"

Eddy laughed as he pressed his mic on. "Yes, sir. I figured I'd start a shell collection from every island we stop at."

"Let's hope that is a small collection and this war is over soon."

"Yes, sir." Eddy enjoyed the banter. He forced his mind on the endless horizon where the blues blended as the water met the sky. "I brought you one too, you know."

"One what?" Scooter sounded edgy.

"A snorkel. I figure we'll get some extra socks and keep the shells in the socks. That way, when we're headed home, they'll already be wrapped and easy to pack."

Scooter leaned back. "You never fail to amaze me. That's why I'm with you."

Eddy cleared his throat. "I thought you were with me for my looks."

"Depends on the situation." Scooter smiled before his forehead gathered in a frown. "Eddy, will you do me a favor?"

"Depends." He turned to observe his friend.

"If anything happens to me will you write my mother and tell her I love her. Hell, I know we filled out those form letters issued to us. They've thought of everything." His voice held the sarcasm many felt. "A form letter going home if you die where you have already filled in the blanks. Yes, I love you mom, take care of everyone little brother. They just seemed so damn impersonal. I mean a real letter. You're good with words."

"Won't have to, Scooter. Because nothing is going to happen to you that won't happen to me. And if I die out here, my mother will kill me."

Scooter laughed at the absurd statement.

"Obviously, you have never met my mother." Eddy sounded defensive. He understood they needed each other to stay alive, as they headed toward their first fight against the enemy over unfamiliar seas.

"Stay sharp," Scooter repeated.

Their navigator's voice broke into their conversation, "The lieutenant's coordinates lead us to Midway."

"Thanks, Fletch," Eddy nodded. "Midway Atoll." He knew his charts. He understood they were headed to the one small speck of land at the tip of the Hawaiian Archipelago now held by the Americans that the Japanese needed to secure in order to attack Hawaii and then the mainland. Midway. He now understood Taff's comments about returning safe.

Fletch spoke again, "It's literally midway between Asia and North America. The Atoll has two islands: Sand and Eastern. The air strip we're heading for is on Eastern. But the PBYs will have nothing but blue waters to take off in."

"Does Tōjō know we're coming?" Scooter posed a reasonable question.

"He will when he sees us. But by that time, it'll be too late." Eddy's confidence spread down the entire plane as the crew grasped their fate.

AKIO STOOD ON THE DECK of the I-25 submarine watching the men assembling the Yokosuka reconnaissance floatplane for takeoff. The crew had moved the plane from the watertight hanger at the front of the sub onto the steel track from whence it would be catapulted after assembly. He closely observed the time it took to correctly add and adjust the twelve components for flight, especially the wings. Twenty-three minutes. Ridiculous. He could feel his blood rushing through his veins at the concept of his drawings. The superiority of his airplane's wings and the precious time it would save. It was dangerous sitting on the surface, open and exposed, as the men scurried about. His aircraft was far superior, larger engine, swifter, more maneuverable, not as sluggish in the air as this green and gray painted craft. He smiled at the large red rising sun painted on the side. His invention would make him accepted at any gathering.

Nobuo Fujita, the pilot he met weeks back at headquarters, stepped up for closer examination. Akio watched him put his foot on the pontoon, then his weight. The seas were a bit rough which would make landing and recovery tricky. He realized the pilot must also be considering his return.

They had spoken very little, Akio closely guarding his improvements of the design to further the superiority of the Japanese. He watched now with anticipation as Fujita approached.

"Not bad wind for flight," Fujita sounded positive.

"The base on Kodiak Island is situated between mountains, according to the maps we have."

"And that is why I am going to give it a visit. To be certain we have the correct information."

"The other ships and soldiers are to arrive in less than two weeks." Akio could not help demonstrating his knowledge of the situation. "America will be shocked by the attack on their own soil. It will be a great victory for the Emperor."

"You lived among them, am I correct?"

"Yes." Akio was wary of the direction of this conversation.

"A prodigious school?"

"Of course. You have not heard of Stanford University?" He could not help himself.

"Your insight must be greatly valued." Fujita smiled.

"My training has brought me much fortune." Akio looked out to the small dots of islands that made up the Aleutians Island off the large land mass of Alaska in the distance.

"So, I have heard."

Akio did not like the tone of Fujita's statement, it held a tinge of an edgy undercurrent. He wondered if this pilot had also heard of the stolen fan with the embed drawings that somehow appeared in Billi's grasp.

"It is time." Fujita adjusted his flight jacket, then pulled his gloves tighter.

"We will be waiting just below the surface. Do not be seen."

Fujita looked up at the white puffs that floated on the breeze this chilled day of May 21ˢᵗ. "There is enough cloud coverage. I will be invisible to the enemy."

"But your photos will be priceless."

Fujita paused looking over his shoulder at Akio. "Yes, most favorable for our troops. And then we head down along the coast. I have always wanted to see Mount Rainier."

"Ah," Akio licked his lips. "That region holds many spectacular sites and promises."

Fujita waved disappearing into his floatplane while Akio counted the days before they would be cruising off the coast of Washington State. He smiled at the concept of reaching out to his contacts regarding Billi.

As the reconnaissance plane catapulted into the sky, Akio felt his spirits soar with the aircraft. His dreams for greatness expanded into the fabric of the sky, his prospects for revenge drawing near. Satisfied with the path of his life, he hurried below before the submarine slid under the icy waters to periscope depth.

JACK CLENCHED HIS CIGAR between his teeth, braving the cold wind to face the sea once more. His vigilance over the shoreline his new obsession. He strolled closer to the massive boulders that created the breakwater just under the Golden Gate Bridge at Fort Point. Behind him the old Fort dating back to 1861, built of brick with sod added to the roof to absorb cannon fire, once again prepared for battle. Its strategic positioning now housed the 6th US Coast Artillery Regiment, charged with manning the searchlights and rapid-fire cannons guarding the bridge and the 7,000-ton metal submarine net stretching seven-miles from Sausalito to San Francisco.

The end of May had only brought deepening uncertainties around the globe. The Royal Air Force sent one thousand bombers streaming into the skies over Cologne issuing destruction and a trail of blazing fires in the rubble. The China, Burma, India fighting, CBI campaign, had all but collapsed to the Japanese. With the strategic Burma Road blocked, Allied troops scurried back to regroup in India. Rommel commanding his Afrika Korps continued fighting in North Africa for control of the vast supply of oil, so greatly needed to win the war. Even though it looked like the Imperial Japanese Navy had the upper hand, Jack sensed that was about to change. According to his informants, the Nippon fleet sailed into a trap. He had not told his wife that her brother was part of that trap at the Midway Atoll.

Jack kept pace with the giant ships as he watched the *USS Colorado* and *Maryland* chug out of the San Francisco Bay to form a line of defense for the city. Rumors swirled as gas masks were issued to air raid wardens in preparation for retaliation after Doolittle's raid.

He tossed the stub of his cigar into the waves smashing against the rocks then headed for his car. Just over one week ago, six busses loaded the last remaining Japanese from this coastal city to be driven about twelve miles south to the Tanforan assembly center. The old racetrack, used as an assembly and training camp during World War I, the government pressed back in use. And, once the Japanese were moved to the new relocation camp being built, the racetrack would be maintained by the Army. Perhaps, like the Santa Anita racetrack, the plans were to become barracks for US soldiers.

He pulled his hat further down in frustration remembering his futile search of the Japanese reporting to the collection point at Raphael Weill School. He had not recognized any of Akio's accomplices. This only emphasized his suspicions, either they had already escaped back to Japan or slipped into Mexico to wait further orders. He smiled at the fact Mexico declared war on the Axis on May 22. The net closing around those traitors.

Large military busses, shuffling men from training to ships for departure, hampered Jack's trek across town, through the Presidio, to the Sir Francis Drake. He parked below the hotel then hurried up to his private room. He snatched at the phone, dialing Seattle.

"Duckworth." Jack tried not to take his frustration out on the man in Seattle steadfastly protecting his wife. "Give me some good news?"

"I wish I could, Jack," Duckworth reflected Jack's mood. "There has been no recognition of any of the photos we handed over to the guards at Camp Harmony. Oh, trucks delivered bundles of belongings to the camp. They must have been glad to get their things, living out of a suitcase is not easy."

The comment made Jack laugh. He didn't know where the hell his home was anymore.

"Is my wife behaving?"

"So far, but she is your wife." Duckworth attempted a joke.

"Well, she's not going to like the next announcement. The Western Defense Command is issuing a warning to the public to be watching for any Japanese in military uniform." Jack picked up the notice he had been handed at the Presidio to read aloud. "All Japanese who are members of the Army of the United States have been removed from the Western Defense Command and Fourth Army, except three on the post at Fort Ord who are on a special assignment."

Jack let the paper drift back to his desk. His chances of finding Akio alive on American soil diminished with the new laws. However, the chances of his wife remaining in danger also diminished. He let out a long sigh.

"I regard that as good news." Duckworth interjected.

"Let's hope so. Thanks."

Jack hung up the phone and stood. He told himself there was no time to contact his wife. He had no answers for her questions on the topic of the relocation camps and used that as an excuse to keep his distance. He needed time to work though his pending choices.

# TWENTY ONE

EDDY LOOKED AT THE COORDINATES HE had been given to scout for enemy ships this early morning of June 3rd, 1942. As his lumbering PBY ascended high into the haze, he prayed Pacific Fleet Commander Admiral Chester Nimitz's calculated risk would pay off. Below all three of the US carriers were ready for battle, an incredible loss if the tide of this skirmish went in the other direction.

All the preparations had gone smoothly, so far. On the advice of his intelligence Nimitz ordered fake information to be sent over the open radio saying the main water pump at Midway had broken. Yamamoto immediately told his ships to carry extra water, confirming the location of their next attack to be Midway. The morning news of the Japanese attacking Dutch Harbor in Alaska turned out to be a strategic decoy for the expected major conflict at Midway.

"What are you thinking?" Scooter spoke into his mic, tugging at his gloves.

"Today's the day we show those Japs who's boss." Eddy smirked with confidence.

"Roger that."

It didn't take long before they sighted a line of four Imperial battleships. The large ship's wake of white froth sailing only five degrees off the original speculation of the Japanese path of attack. Silently he thanked those intelligence men and women sequestered away, privately making certain American troops had the upper hand.

"Send back their coordinates, direction, speed and distance. Be sure they hear clearly that PBY #3 is reporting this find. And send it to the Yorktown as well. I'm taking us higher." Eddy spoke with a mixture of confidence and misgivings at their discovery.

The approaching enemy ships plowed through the waters about 170 miles offshore, when PBY #3's message reached the US command. Eddy continued to circle in the clouds before heading back to their new base at Midway. Upon approaching, they skimmed across the water toward their buoy through frenzied activity. Eddy smiled, proud their message put the base on heightened alert.

With growing anticipation, the entire crew silently crawled into the launch bound for the shore. Excitement and fear vibrating on the crystal blue waves as those who had never encountered battle gazed out to sea wondering what the dawn would bring. America, he concluded, would be more than ready for this battle.

Eddy followed Scooter down the path that led below the sand and rock, where the offices and sleeping quarters had been dug into the hard earth. Like ant hills, the many openings blended with the contours of the island, hard to discern from above, providing greater protection from bombs.

The assignment board for the next day stood before them. The directive clear; all PBYs to be airborne at 0400. It looked so simple in black and white.

"Let's grab some chow and some sleep," Scooter suggested.

"I'm heading for a swim. I saw some beautiful shells along the shore."

"Well, don't bring those damn shells inside. The last ones you put in your socks for safe keeping, stink worse than your feet."

"Yeah." Eddy had to laugh at himself. The shells he'd already collected harbored living creatures. Once out of the water, as they began to die, the smell permeated their sleeping quarters. "But those shells will be great gifts for the ladies back home."

"If it doesn't kill us first."

Eddy slapped his co-pilot on the back. "After I collect more gems, I think we have time for a game of cards. I haven't won all of your money yet."

"Oh, yeah. Well, I think it's my turn to scalp you."

The banter began, the idle chatter calming their nerves, keeping their spirits high as they started for the mess area. Tomorrow, a day of reckoning with their first battle would hopefully be one that brought the promise of more sunrises.

In the hours of morning, a cool wind greeted them as they pressed toward their PBY in the dark. Eddy scanned the wake spilling from the sides of their launch into the darkness. He couldn't make out the well disguised base and wondered if it would be there when they returned. Midway resembled the golden ring that both nations vied to possess in a war America appeared to be losing.

They hoisted the extra bologna sandwiches and coffee aboard PBY #3 in anticipation of their lengthy journey. The engine roared to life as they taxied away from their buoy and base. The sun wouldn't rise for over an hour but, by then, they would be over what they believed would be the path of the nearing enemy.

It felt surreal, flying in the blackness before daylight, toward battle. When the sun broke over the horizon, they spotted the Imperial Japanese Navy at 5:30. Once again calling in the coordinates. It didn't take long for the American bomber pilots, following their M.O. signals, to swarm the Japanese ships like mad hornets.

Eddy wiped the sweat from his forehead as they hung high over the ensuing battle. Most of the US strikes fell short, creating skyrocketing volcanos of water flanking the invading ships. Then the attack squadron retreated, having inflicted little damage. Eddy drummed his fingers in frustration.

Hank's voice came across their system with discouraging news. "They just radioed us. At 6:30 a.m. Japanese planes swept across Midway. They set the oil tanks on fire and hit the airstrip." He paused as the reality there might not be a Midway to return to sunk in. "Hopefully, better news is coming."

Eddy's reply did not reflect his sinking heart. "Count on it. Besides, we're just getting warmed up."

Calculating the time for the enemy pilots to rejoin their carriers Eddy whistled.

"Do they see us?" Scooter shouted, pointing at the enemy planes approaching their PBY from the direction of Midway.

Eddy banked into the clouds, climbing higher. The white fluff provided protection but restricted observation. When he punched back out just a few aircraft lingered over their ships, but the entire fleet had changed course.

"Holy mother of God," Scooter leaned further into the expansive glass of the cockpit.

"Yep, they're heading right for our ships. Get those new coordinates out, Fletch." He instructed his navigator.

They watched helplessly as Japanese aircraft took off from the decks of the carriers heading directly toward the *USS Enterprise*, *Hornet* and *Yorktown*.

Squinting into the horizon Eddy felt the sweat soak his shirt. Almost one hour passed yet still nothing. He gripped the controls as the tension climbed up his back reverberating down his arms.

"Here comes the cavalry." Scooter's announcement met with cheers of encouragement from the crew.

In the distance swarms of US B-17's headed directly toward their mark.

"Hang on boys, it's our turn at bat." Eddy called out the battle below to the rest of his crew as if they watched a rout at Yankee Stadium. In under ten minutes fires blazed from direct hits on three prize Japanese aircraft carriers. An exhilarating sense of relief swept through the PBY.

The dark smoke drifted on the wind as the entire Japanese fleet veered toward the three blazing carriers, then, just as abruptly, returned to their original course. Eddy watched the black puffs of flak from the anti-aircraft guns below subside. Our boys, targets hit, headed back toward their aircraft carriers.

"Take that Tōjō. Nothing like a few less Japs to fight." Scooter clap his hands with excitement.

Scooter pointed at one boat remaining in the wake of the retreating Imperial Navy fleet. "That what I think it is?"

Eddy didn't hesitate. "We're goin' in."

They started their descent, but no guns blazed in their direction from the ship below.

"All at ready, Beau." Eddy spoke calmly to his flight captain, as if asking the man to prepare for church, not drop a bomb. He brought their plane low, approaching them from behind.

"Ready." Beau's one word reflected the anxiety streaming through the crew.

"Drop 1." Eddy pulled back on the stick, lifting the nose of the aircraft higher into the sky.

Charlie, the waist gunner had the clearest view. "Nipped them on the starboard, sir. But they got a good bathing with that blast."

"Not done yet." Eddy waited for Fletch to recalculate the coordinates as he circled back around. His determination driving the big bird low above the waves.

"Drop 2."

The crew felt the shattering blast as the next bomb landed on the helpless ship's conning tower. For a moment all remained silent in the newness of their first kill. With the reality of their safety, rumblings of jubilation began to spread down the PBY.

Scooter bellowed at the sinking ship, "Sayonara."

The toll of the dead from their efforts would remain a mystery. Somehow, that didn't seem to matter. What did matter, the fact they had sunk an enemy ship. Hopefully the first of many.

Eddy checked the gauges. Knowing his big winged bird could tolerate hours of abuse he continued to escort the dwindling, sea foamed line of the enemy. Minutes turned to uneventful hours, when, once again, the direction of the enemy altered drastically.

"Mark it." Eddy watched with growing delight.

"Are they . . ."

"The bastards are heading home." Eddy's yell did not need the amplification of his mic.

While the Nippon ships retreated the battle continued, far from over. Just before 5 p.m. Eddy's crew cheered on the fighter pilots from the USS *Yorktown* and *Enterprise* as they demolished the retreating aircraft carrier, *Hiryu*. Four Japanese carriers destroyed in one day. Time to go home. The storm of the battle, fought in clear skies, now behind them.

Their joy turned sour when the smoldering hulk of the *Yorktown* appeared below. Damaged during the Battle of the Coral Sea, then refurbished and sent into this battle, the *Yorktown* lifelessly smoldered on the waves that would soon claim her. Her injured frame a tempting target for any Japanese submarine. Her inability to accept those pilots left in the sky after their brave raids drove home the point that no one wins completely in a war.

"Hey, Hank. Any news from base yet?"

Hank's, response sent chills through him. "No, sir, it's been silent for hours."

Eddy checked his gauges. They would need fuel. Yet, without radio contact they had no inkling who had won the Atoll of Midway. He watched the sun in the distance, brilliant with its last rays reaching into the twilight, as if it didn't want to slip over the edge. "We'd better just put her down here."

Scooter nodded. "No place like home in the middle of the ocean. Who the hell knows if there is even a base left to go back to. Besides, I'm not in the mood to be shot at by our own guys."

"Ditto, too easy for friendly fire in the dark."

With ease Eddy settled the large craft on the rolling waves of the Pacific Ocean, leaving a small wake aft. He put his goggles above him, then stretched. As he started down the passageway, Scooter followed.

"You have a look that means trouble. What's up?"

Eddy ignored him, reaching for a sleeping bag and rope. Next, he grabbed a sandwich continuing further toward the ladder that led to the hatch.

"You guys can fight over the hammock. I'm sleeping on the wing." Eddy raised one eyebrow, daring Scooter to join him topside.

"Well don't fall in. Because I'm not going swimming to save you, you crazy bastard."

"I thought so." Eddy started up the rungs. "Besides the peace and quiet will be a nice change."

Eddy stepped onto the wing to settle in. He strapped the rope around the antenna, then tightened it around his middle before chewing on his dry bologna sandwich. Night came like a blanket studded with the shimmering lights that arched into eternity. The brilliant constellations floated peacefully above him as he reflected on what he had witnessed. He closed his eyes suppressing the visions of bombs spraying lethal fountains of water, oil fires spilling over the sides of ships continuing to blaze on the ocean's surface while specks of men scrambled for lifeboats. He did not want to even attempt to calculate the thousands of lives now consumed by this very stretch of the Pacific Ocean.

He opened his eyes then laid back. "You see that Ray? Today was for you too, Sam. Thanks for riding with me. Keep a watch now, don't let any damn Japanese sub find us out here." His next words caught in his throat. "Thanks, God. I'm sorry."

Feeling he'd settle things with the Almighty for killing other humans, he tightened the knot establishing his lifeline, snuggling into his sleeping bag. Beneath him the PBY bobbed with the rhythm of the waves. He felt his tension melt into the cool aluminum of the wing as he familiarized himself with the subtle sounds that surrounded him; the waves hitting the pontoons, the wind nudging their craft along the surface, the silence.

His nerves kicked in again as something splashed near the aircraft. Holding his breath his listened intently, but no other disturbing sound followed. He let out the anxiety of the moment with a brief laugh. If he jumped at every bump in the coal blackness around him, it would make for a very long night. Focusing his gaze on the twinkling stars he breathed deeply of the cool sea air and visions of Dahlia.

BILLI FOLDED THE PAPER to stack it next to the fireplace. Again, the ominous headlines foretold of the world exploding on so many fronts. This week's coverage spanned the Japanese bombing of Dutch Harbor, the days long battle at Midway and the evacuation of Dunkirk.

The news of Midway twisted her gut with the suspicion of Eddy's involvement. She wasn't certain where Danny fought, but prayed he wasn't anywhere near the shores of the evacuation of Northern France. However, it was the news of Japanese planes bombing Dutch Harbor, Alaska that sent chills down her back. The first strikes on the US continent rolled across the country instilling overwhelming apprehension. If the Japanese established a base in Alaska, the West Coast became easy prey. Furthermore, she would be within Akio's reach.

Her mind turned to Eileen and her family now living at Camp Harmony in the Puyallup Assembly Center and felt a sense of relief.

206 | Denise Frisino

At least they were safe. Instead of the tall fences keeping the Nippon community inside the camp, the same structure acted as their guardian, keeping them safe from those wishing retaliation if the Japanese landed on the West Coast.

"May I?" A voice from behind her inquired.

She turned to see this week's addition to their ever-changing household. The tall thin man pushed his spectacles further up on his nose nodding at the paper she had just folded.

"Help yourself." She stepped back allowing his thin hand to scoop up his treasure. "When do you ship out?"

"Uncertain." He dropped onto the couch then raised the paper, shielding his face.

Shrugging, sensing his dismissal, she turned for the kitchen.

"There you are," her mother chided as she entered. Pepper, however, lavished her with his sharp barking, followed by the whines signaling his need for food.

"I fed you." She petted his expanding sides. "Time for a diet, like the rest of us."

"Yes, food rationing is going to be interesting." Her mother stirred the pot of oatmeal she prepared for the young men.

Billi slumped into the chair.

"What do you hear from Jack?" Her mother smiled cunningly.

"Why?"

"Well. I was wondering if he has any connections along the lines of rations booklets."

"Mother, please." Billi brooded, watching her mother pout at the scolding. Changing her mind, she decided to press her mother. It was better to know her train of thought as opposed to the surprise of the results. "I'll ask him, but what is it you want?"

"I was just thinking with a bit more sugar we could make more cakes for the dances. Oh, and coffee." She batted her eyes innocently.

Everything told Billi her mother was up to no good which usually resulted in trouble. "When he calls, I'll ask."

"Oh, that's a dear." Mrs. O disappeared through the door carrying the steaming pot of porridge with Pepper at her feet.

She sat in the silence, watching the birds in the big walnut tree next door when Susie and Dahlia bust in.

"Sorry we're here so early . . .

. . . but we got a letter from Danny," They spoke over each other in their excitement.

"What does he say?" Billi waited as the two sat.

"He can't say much, in fact look." Dahlia held up the letter.

Billi looked through the slashes into Dahlias disturbed eyes. Someone had painstakingly cut out all references pertaining to his whereabouts.

"The sky's here are so blue and the . . ." She stopped reading to explain, "They cut out the kind of trees he was talking about."

"Trees tell a lot about a place. We have cedar." Billi smiled encouragingly, reminded of her favorite tree out back.

"I bet it was palm." Susie whispered conspiratorially. "He's in the South Pacific."

"It could be fig trees, or what was that place in Germany? Some forest?" Dahlia played along.

"You have to write him and have him devise another way to let you know where he is." Billi suggested.

"How?" Susie looked determined.

Dahlia refolded the letter, following the exactness of the creases. "It's just so maddening. Why can't we know where he is?"

"Are there really spies here, around us?" Susie sounded breathless with the concept.

"You'll never know until it's too late." Billi's somber reasoning cast a brief shadow. "We must remain vigilant and keep the troops' location a mystery."

Mrs. O entered to the silence which had fallen over the three young women. They explained their predicament as Mrs. O took up the last seat at the kitchen table.

"What's your middle name?" The older woman directed her question to the youngest.

Her nose wrinkled as she spoke, "Bernice. Suzann Bernice Lattice. My mother's two sisters' names."

Mrs. O's shoulder went up and down as she spoke. "Have him spell out his location by changing the letter of your middle name each time he writes."

Billi looked at her mother in astonishment. She possessed a treasure chest filled with unexpected tricks.

"I get it," Dahlia squealed. "Susie H. Lattice. Susie A. Lattice. Susie W. Lattice . . ."

"Hawaii." The high schooler bobbed up and down in her chair. "That's it. I can't wait to tell the other girls."

"Remember," Billi cautioned, aware how quickly word spread. "Like the poster says, loose lips . . ."

"Sink ships," all at the table chanted in unison.

Mrs. O patted Susie's knee. "When is school out so you can come and help me?"

"Next week, and I can't wait. The halls are so empty. Garfield High is so big with no one there. First, like Danny, some of the reserve left. Then it was the Japanese students. The classes are so small now. And the recruiters are there all the time, everyone is signing up for something. I'm not looking forward to next year."

"Coffee?" Mrs. O stood then moved toward the stove. "We are all doing something. And having you here helping will be a joy."

"I'm signing up too." Dahlia announced. "I just have three more quarters then I'm a nurse and I'm signing up."

"Which branch?" Billi looked at her friend with admiration.

Dahlia pulled her skirt up past her knees, exposing the inviting curves of her legs. "I think the Army. They have natural colored stockings, not the white ones of the Navy, and that will show off my legs better."

The room burst into laughter.

Suddenly, they all stopped at the sight of the thin soldier standing in the doorway. He pushed his glasses further up his nose, gawking at Dahlia's hiked up skirt line. His blush deepened as he backed out of the room, tripping over the yelping Pepper.

Billi waited until the young man retreated safely out of ear shot. "Definitely Army."

This brought another round of hoots from the women.

It felt good to laugh. Her eyes swept around the room. Her mother, a born survivor, the block captain organizing events and packages, poured hot black coffee into the waiting cups. Dahlia would soon wear an Army uniform, making an excellent nurse. Susie would continue in school, diligently writing letters to her love, Danny. A hollow feeling pulled at her gut. There had to be more she could do for the cause, now that her freedom had been restored. How ironic, the loss of the Japanese in the city, her best friend among them, made the streets safer for her. The long reach of Akio could not touch her. At least that is what she chose to believe.

# TWENTY TWO

Jack kicked at the pebbles on Rodeo Beach just below the Marin Headlands tucked across the bay from San Francisco. The rocks brilliant multi colors gave him a much-needed distraction and sense of calm, even if for just a brief moment. Peace sparkled across the water as a cool breeze swept over him. Breathing deeply of the refreshing scent, uniquely born of deep saltwater, he scanned the horizon devoid of any large ships.

Turning away from the blue seas, he let the wind push him up the slight embankment toward Fort Cronkite cantonment. Where rock met grass he paused, focusing further north toward the Marin Headlands which concealed the fort's secret big guns. He spotted Townsley, one of two such batteries sequestered under dozens of feet of concrete and earth. The massive armory ready and poised to protect not only San Francisco Harbor but the men gathering there to board ships bound for the Pacific, those pouring into the city for work at the numerous plants building war machines and ships, and the families who bustled about their now overcrowded home town. He considered the range of those big guns stretching twenty-five miles out to sea at the approaching enemy. Yet a thick fog would render these mighty guns useless. For that, the city counted on the submarine nets and mine fields arching around the entrance to the bustling San Francisco Bay.

Heading toward the newly constructed barracks, he stopped at the first building, set apart from the others. This structure housed the 54th Coast Artillery Regiment, one of the few all colored regiments. Nodding at the black soldier waiting on the small steps, he continued.

As the soldier caught up, Jack attempted to put him at ease. "I heard you're good with note taking and can be trusted."

"Yes, sir." The soldier sounded confident at his task.

Jack, aware of the answer, asked his question anyway. "Where were you in school?"

"Fisk University, Nashville. Science and journalism."

When he stopped, so did the soldier beside him. Jack liked the young man's demeanor immediately. He looked directly into his dark eyes. "You can keep your mouth shut?"

The young face grew more intent with his conviction. "With my life."

Jack nodded then proceeded down the line of barracks. At the far end they halted just outside the last low building. A soldier, his gun and bayonet at ready, stood guard.

"Sir." The guard clicked his heels, his slightly quivering hands showing the nerves of his assignment.

"This is W. James Melonson." Pulling out his identification, Jack stepped up to the door. He watched as the two men from the same base with different colored skin exchanged a nonverbal recognition. The guard looked quickly from James to Jack with a questioning look. Aware that those sporting dark skin were, as yet, to be given any substantial duties Jack added, "James is going to be a professor and publish science books. But for now, I need him inside."

The guard's head snapped back toward James, who smiled at his new title. He lifted his pen and notepad as his ammunition following Jack through the door.

The long two room barracks held several empty cots, neatly made and waiting. Occupying beds near the center support beam, three soldiers lay across from each other. The trio of emancipated bodies sported layers of bandages covering their wounds. Their feet, swathed in white cotton, stuck out from underneath the wool blanket. But it was their eyes that drew Jacks attention. As he moved closer, their eyes reflected the terror and death these American soldiers had witnessed.

He stood a moment smelling their fear mixing with the antiseptic applied to their sores. For once, his eye patch appeared to have the opposite impact on those hollow cheeked men gazing up at him. His scar implying the comradery formed in the ravages of conflict.

Motioning for James to pull up a chair he observed the young soldier adjusted to the sight of these three miserable men, then sat, head bent over his writing pad.

"I hear you're the lucky ones." Jack watched as their eyes focused on him. "I just need some information. Take your time. You're safe here and will be allowed to go home once you've recovered a bit." He stretched the truth.

"Lucky? They're animals. They killed for no reason but the pleasure of seein' us die."

Jack nodded. "Are you Toniella?"

"Yes, sir. Corporal Mario Toniella." The spokesman nodded toward the soldier on his right with one eye bandaged.

"I'm Private Silvan Howard." The man with the bandaged eye announced, his speech slurred on his "S" as he spoke to Jack. "The doc thinks my eye will work again." His smile revealed several teeth missing.

"Bastards took Silvan's teeth. The Japs wanted his gold fillings."

At Mario's words, Silvan shyly closed his mouth.

"Water." The third whispered, appearing on the brink of death. He laid with his arm confined to a sling, his legs covered with gauze while his skin still recovered from the deep scathing sunburns.

"Ralph, it's okay." Mario strained to look over his bandages at his friend. "We're state side and safe, remember?" He looked back at Jack. "They stripped Ralph an' left him in the hottest damn sun ya ever felt, with nothin' to drink, but facing a pond of beautiful fresh water. If he moved, they would a killed him. Called it the 'sun treatment.'"

"There wasn't water to drink. If you tried to get water, like those poor guys when we were just outside of Limay—God in heaven, they just beat the shit out of them or shot them on the spot." A tear escaped down Ralph's cheek. "They got such joy out of killin' and torture. It was terrible . . ."

Ignoring his toothlessness, Silvan added, "If you didn't keep up, the squint-eyed Nips put their bayonets through you, then laughed. Didn't give us enough food to keep up our strength for the long walk. Hell, they didn't feed us the first day, or was that two?"

Jack determined Mario lead the miraculous escape from the prison camp at Bataan.

Jack waited. "How many dead?"

"Hundreds."

"Thousands," Mario corrected. "It started on April 9th with our surrender. We were out of ammunition and low on food. The damn Jap liars said they would treat us proper. Like hell. They don't believe anyone should surrender, they're trained not to, it's an insult to their Emperor. We were less than dogs to them. We marched for hours. If someone fell, we quickly learned to leave 'em behind or feel the butt of a gun or those sticks the Japs liked to use on us. Then what, you die too? Those filthy bastards are animals."

"We didn't have it as bad as those local boys from the Philippines." Silvan slurred. "They just up and killed hundreds of 'em at a time. If they found any Japanese money or souvenirs on you, they shot you on the spot."

"We walked the first day without food. If you had water, they took your canteen and gave the water to their horses." Ralph choked up again before continuing. "They put us in these boxcars, it was like an oven in the heat. Many died where they stood. You pissed or shit where you stood, pressed against dead bodies. One Filipino scout was real tall. I watched him pressed up against a hole in the side of the boxcar to breath. Lucky bastard. Yet, he was the only one strong enough to help me when we unloaded and started marching again."

Silvan's one eye teared up. "So many got malaria, dysentery, you name it and died. Hell, they were feeding us monkey meat. After a while we dug graves with Filipino scouts, and when the fuckin' Japs weren't looking, we hightailed it out of there. Shit, I was scared shitless."

"But we made it." Mario's statement lacked the joy of life. "The evil gooks found the flag on Silvan once and they almost killed him. Ya see, one of the guys made a small American flag and we took turns hiding it on us. It was an honor to carry it. We knew we'd die if they found it, but it meant hope. We'd pass it off daily. Oh, they'd burn, torture or kill the fella who had it, but we'd just make another."

"Would do it again." Silvan didn't hold back, his toothless smile evoking the courage of his actions.

When the lengthy interview concluded, Jack shook their hands filled with admiration for their fortitude and strength of spirit. These heroes escaped certain death, hiding and scavenging for food, making the long journey home to tell their stories. Their new challenge, the road to recovery.

Stopping at the door he tipped his hat at the three men before leading a stunned James outside into the cool breeze of the evening. Their hours of listening complied in James stacked pages of notes. The sickening cruelty of the Japanese in Bataan burrowed deep in the soul, beyond comprehension.

Jack let out a sigh at the other injustice. These three soldiers, guarded night and day, their whereabouts kept secret, would not be allowed to contact their worried families and loved ones. These heroes held too many important insights. They would be moved quietly to another hospital back east then guarded from reporters until the President decided when the timing of the story would deliver the most impact. The anger and hatred emerging from their story of the march of death endured over sixty miles at the hands of ruthless enemy at Bataan presented the perfect tool to enlist more volunteers and instill a fierce desire for payback. And this was not just among the American and British troops, but the thousands of Filipino soldiers sent to their graves along this path.

"What do you think?" Jack looked beyond James at the turbulent dark waters.

"Slicing a man's chest open then pushing him into a ditch because he isn't walking fast enough is incomprehensible."

Jack turned toward the soldier. "That's why you can't talk about this to anyone."

"Frankly, sir." James adjusted his stance, shaking his head in one swift movement. "I don't think any normal human being would believe me."

"The Japanese soldiers aren't normal. Remember that when you face them. More importantly, never be taken as a prisoner by these sons of bitches." Jack lit his cigar. "There's a desk and typewriter set up for you in the back of the officer's club. I'll be waiting just outside the door. That typed report goes to me only. After that, you know nothing."

James reached for his pack of cigarettes. "Permission to smoke, sir?"

"Hell, yes." Jack led the way toward a building that James, being of color, was not allowed to enter. He held the door wide for the young man he hoped would live to write a book and become a professor.

Billi drove her mother's car into the thick mud of the nearly empty parking lot just outside of Camp Harmony in Puyallup. She grabbed her camera resting next to her on the seat then sloshed toward the gate.

Her foot caught in the deep mud causing her to slide forward. The guard at the entrance caught her arm before disaster struck, holding her firmly until she made it inside. Another guard followed her to the desk.

"Why are you here?" The person behind the desk quickly sized her up.

"I'm here to visit, Eileen Nakamura. Please." She smiled.

A young Japanese man pushed his glasses up closer to his eyes as he hurried through his list of names. "Yes, family 10612084." He nodded as he spoke. "They are in the exhibition hall." He looked up. "They are lucky."

Billi wondered if it was "luck" or if Jack had indeed been helpful.

"Hey, what are you doing with that camera?" One of the guards sprung from his chair sprinting around the desk. "Hand it over, Babe."

"Billi." Her expression went to that of steel. "My name is Billi."

"Don't care if it's Queenie. Give me the camera or get out."

It was all she could do to restrain herself as she slowly held the camera out. "I want it back in the same condition I'm giving it to you." Billi did not take her eyes off his movements, until he had put her prize inside his desk.

The young Japanese man watched the exchange then sprang into action. He passed the number to another member of the Japanese American Citizens League, those who volunteered to aid the military in organizing the arrivals at Camp Harmony.

Billi moved to the small window to wait. Outside a truck marked "Special" pulled to a stop. The doors opened as soldiers slid in the mud toward the back of the tailgate. Bundles of belongings were carried to high ground as members of various families emerged to claim their things.

At the sound of a door closing Billi turned to see Eileen's smile, a reward well worth the long journey.

"Billi." She half whispered, "I am so happy to see you."

"In here." The young man pushed at his glasses, gesturing slightly with his head.

The two young women entered a small room then sat awkwardly facing each other.

"They took my camera." Billi snorted. When she noticed Eileen looked a little pale, she continued. "How are you?"

"They have been feeding us canned Vienna sausage every day." Eileen twisted at her skirt.

"You're kidding."

"No. That grease is not in our diet. We all got sick and were running for the bathrooms." Eileen's eyes grew wide with her story.

"What are they thinking? You need vegetables, rice, tofu."

"They are working on that. Some of the chefs from the restaurants in Japantown are organizing our food for us. Things are much better."

"Good." Billi felt a sense of relief. "How are your father and Kenny?"

"Father is organizing for the next move. Some are here from Alaska. Can you imagine? Kenny wanted to volunteer to go to a camp called Tule Lake to help with the construction, but father said the family stays together. I'm going to apply to be sponsored to a school back east, but, of course, I haven't told anyone but you yet. You are always the first to hear my dreams."

Billi reached out her hand covering Eileen's. "Always sisters. I'll ask Jack to help."

She looked at her friend's shoes noticing mud covered the short heel and part way up the soft leather, an uncommon sight for Eileen's fastidious nature.

"I'll send you a new pair of shoes when I get a chance."

"Don't trouble. They say there will be a store at the new location, and we can order through Montgomery Ward. They will give us a stipend. And Auntie will get a piano to teach music and dance. The Government will pay her to teach. They want to help us keep our traditions alive."

"That should keep your spirits strong."

"Did you know the Principal from Garfield came down to visit and will let some of the students graduate? Kenny is excited his name is on the list." Her head went down as she whispered. "No, no news from Tak."

"Are you staying busy? Remember? You must stay busy to be positive." The words sounded so hollow and lifeless.

STORMS FROM A CLEAR SKY | 217

"I'm in a choir with some of the others and sewing. It will be all right. We will make it."

"Will you give them my love and let me know what I can bring next time?"

"Father is asking for seeds to start a garden. His plan is to stay involved." She smiled at her friend. "Send me books? Anything."

"Yes," Billi let out a long sigh. "I'm heading south for a while."

"Tell me. Does this have something to do with your husband?"

Like old times their heads almost touched as they giggled once more like young girls.

# TWENTY THREE

As promised, the Imperial Japanese Navy, IJN 1-25, now headed along the Canadian coast toward Washington. Akio did not want to show his disgust that the other submarine, the IJN 1-26, had missed its target of British Columbia's Point Estevan Lighthouse with its prized radio station. All those shells exhausted with nothing to report.

It was just after midnight when he felt the thrill of the chase tingle down his spine. He shifted his weight as the new target, the coal burning Canadian trader SS *Fort Camosun,* steamed into view. The command given, the fish propelled forward, whizzing through the water. When the explosion hit the port side of the Camosun, below the ships bridge, joy surged through the submarine. The cargo aboard would be lost, and hopefully the men as well.

Riding the surface as the batteries recharged, Akio waited impatiently in the early dawn light for the three men put ashore near the Quinault Indian Reservation along the coast of Washington State to return. Their mission was to convince the tribe to side with the Japanese then share in the rewards of conquest. However, with the morning light came the search planes and the three men were abandoned, their fate now of their own making.

The air quickly took on the rancid stench of the unwashed crew as the submarine dove to the safety of deeper waters in search of more prey. The inability of Akio's contacts to reach him set him in a foul mood as he stomped into the galley.

"Maybe we should have sent you to shore," Akio grumbled at Tak.

Tak raised his cup of tea to his mouth, ignoring his superior. Akio slapped the cup from his hand, splashing the hot fluid on the man sitting next to Tak.

Eyes turned to the raging Akio, his nostrils flaring with his uncontrolled anger.

Fujita slid up behind Akio. "If we kill our own men, we have failed the Emperor."

Tak picked up the cup. "My humblest apologies for being so clumsy," he whispered, lowering his eyes at the great pilot's wisdom and intervention.

Ignoring Tak, Fujita pressed Akio. "Our shore maps indicate the safe passageway into the Columbia River is very narrow."

"Yes, the sand bar is famous as the 'Graveyard of the Pacific.' But it will not be our grave." Akio spoke with confidence. When the pilot did not respond he continued. "I have observed the entrance used by many fishing ships. We will simply follow one through. That way if there is a mine, they will let us know."

At this idea, Fujita nodded. "There is a company that builds ships along the river?"

"Correct, the Oregon Shipbuilding Corporation. We should strike those buildings as well as Fort Stevens, then the new submarine base."

"Let us go look at the maps once more. Tonight will bring us even more rewards." Fujita turned, disappearing through the small opening leading further into the sub.

Akio looked down at Tak with disgust. He must bide his time he reasoned. The young sailor held secrets to his goal. Akio could feel his spirits soar at the prospect of his plans as he followed the pilots lead. Yes, tonight under cover of darkness, the United States would once again feel the sting of the enemy's penetration of the mainland.

BILLI WATCHED THE RED CAPPED Filipino man work his way through the crowded train station with her large luggage. Just a few months back these jobs were held by those of Japanese ancestry. She sighed at the ghostly experience of driving down Jackson Street with her parents, past Japantown, to reach the railway station.

"Come, come." He waved with his free hand.

"You heard the man." Billi turned to her parents.

"Oh, dear." Mrs. O shuffled next to her husband. "Will there be room on there for you?"

Billi knew it was her mother's last-ditch effort to delay her departure. Truly, the surprise event exhibited little planning. But how do you plan a life in times like this?

"You'll be writin'?" Her father's words sounded more like a command, not a question.

"And I'll call." She kissed her father on the cheek.

Her mother handed her the orchid plant Mr. Nakamura had left in her care.

"Are you sure you want to take this?"

"Yes, because when the Nakamuras are back, I will have to come home to give it to them?"

"Oh, good idea." Mrs. O'Shaughnessy brightened at her daughters reasoning. They hugged, mother and daughter, in the uncertainty of goodbye.

Billi turned, disappearing deeper into the crowd of those bidding farewell and boarding the Southern Pacific heading down the coast.

The click of the rails beneath the train worked their magic as Billi leaned into the soothing vibrations of the railcar. The mesmerizing motion of coffee in its sturdy cup on the table before her held her attention as her mind drifted to the last time she was on this train heading to San Francisco to surprise Jack for Christmas. When he sent her back to Seattle for protection it created a wedge that expanded with uncertainty.

She eyed the young man in uniform across from her. His head slumped back as he breathed deeply with slumber. It appeared he had never shaved; his smooth skin showed no unkept bristles of manhood that came with days of the journey.

An older, black porter approached with her breakfast. "Here Miss. You want me to wake him?"

"No. This might be the last peace he knows." She smiled. The porter emitted a knowing grunt, shaking his head as he turned back to his duties.

The smell of the coffee must have woken the soldier as he blinked into the daylight. "Ah, sorry." He sat up straight, licking his lips.

"Would you like this?" She pushed the plate in his direction.

He almost fell forward into the food with excitement. "Really?"

"Yes." She pushed it even further across then watched him cut into the eggs with enthusiasm.

"I haven't eaten," he announced between bites. "I—thanks."

"Where are you from?"

"Montana. I got sick, hospitalized overnight, and my sergeant told me to get down to San Francisco pronto."

"I'm glad you're better."

He had obviously seen her wedding ring. "You're husband in the war? Seems like everyone is."

"In his own way, very much so." She sipped her coffee.

"I've only hunted animals." His eyes grew concerned. "But I'm ready to kill any Nazis or Japs."

"Japanese." She nodded. "Thank you. Now, eat up. We're almost there."

"Yes ma'am." His head bent over his task.

Picking up the bloomless orchid plant, she gripped her suitcase. Its weight thudded against the seat. She had crammed in as much as possible hoping it was enough for her new life.

"Let me do that." It was her young hero who stooped to grab her case. They stepped from the rail car onto the platform into a sea of men in uniform. All different shapes and sizes, most with the grim recognition they were shipping out to face the enemy.

"I can get it from here," she insisted.

He tossed his duffel higher onto his shoulder before extending his hand. "Thanks for my first breakfast on a train."

"I'm certain it will not be the last." Impulsively, she kissed his cheek.

He blushed as someone whistled. "Have to go."

The young soldier disappeared into the mass of uniforms without her even learning his name.

A black hat in the distance caught her eye and she started toward it. A hand went to the hat. The black onyx pinky ring secured her destination as she pushed forward toward Jack.

His arms were around her in an embrace that included a light kiss. "Thank you for coming."

"I'm your wife, remember?"

"I'm one hell of a lucky man."

"Why, I think you missed me," she teased.

"Come on. Let's get you home." He kept his arm around her as he guided her through the throngs of men to his waiting car.

The drive to Hillsborough seemed short as they tried to catch up, leaning into an unknown future.

"So, I'll be staying out here?" She was trying to remain calm at the new housing arrangements as she fingered the pot of the plant.

"Yes, Bella has everything arranged."

"What does she think of Ginger coming to live permanently?"

"Mrs. Huntington, both Ginger and Billi, are welcome."

"So, am I to be Billi by day and Ginger at night?"

Jack laughed at the proposal, "That would suit me fine."

"You cad." She hugged the orchid, watching the car climb through the winding roads of wind bent trees toward San Raymundo Road and the stately home of Jack's youth.

As they pulled onto the acreage toward the massive Tudor building, Billi's stomach began to flip.

"We'd better go in the front door or Bella will have my hide." He had her elbow and suitcase as he strode toward the door full of confidence. A confidence Billi did not share.

As she stepped inside, the aroma of Bella's cooking reminded her she had not eaten in hours.

"That you?" The dark wood of the kitchen door flew open as Bella charged them at full steam. "Hummph, Hummph, Hummph," she stopped before them before taking Billi's arm. "Mrs.," Bella leaned in conspiratorially to continue, "you aren't ever going to get yourself with child if you don't eat somethin'. You come right here with me."

"Maybe she doesn't want to have a baby." Lilly appeared in the archway leading to the grand living room. "I won't recommend it to anyone." Her large stomach arched her back while her thin legs stuck out below her skirt like toothpicks.

"Now you hush, and you come and eat somethin' too." Bella hurried to Lilly's side, humming her unique soothing tune as she helped the small woman with the overwhelming belly toward the large dining room table.

Billi looked questioningly up at her husband.

"Any day now." His smile appeared lined with concern.

"I see." She handed him the plant, her coat and left him standing in the hallway. The situation she just willingly walked into surpassed the daily home making chores of husband and wife. Her duties included the needs of a new baby, new mother and two ageing women. However, Jack asking her to be by his side spoke of the promise Akio and his men were nowhere near. A time to build their future.

EDDY LISTENED TO THEIR NAVIGATOR, Fletch, explain the scenario. "If these guys got out safely, if they got into their lifeboat, the winds would have pushed them due north."

"Closer to enemy shores." Scooter interjected.

After Midway, they were assigned to Havannah Harbor on Efate Island. A beautiful port surrounded by the dense green of coconut trees with white sand stretching out to sea under the translucent blue. The Seabees built two ramps for the PBYs, using light colored coral bound with mesh wire. The buoy for their plane anchored safe in the calm waters. The task of rescuing downed pilots and their crews transformed into their PBYs bread and butter when not scouting.

Today, like so many missions, the endless blue with distant dots of green below held the secrets of the fate of those planes. Following the pattern of the fighter pilots' last signal south of the Solomon Islands, they made large arching loops high above. All eyes remained riveted on the surface in the hopes of catching a glimpse of floating scrap or, with the Almighty's blessing, a yellow raft adrift.

They droned on for over one hour working out further with each circle, creating rings like those made when a stone is tossed into the smooth surface of a lake.

"Poor bastards." Scooter lowered his binoculars arching his back in a long overdue stretch.

"We're not done yet." Eddy faced the expansive window in his relentless search. "We have thirty minutes of sunlight."

"What's that?" Charlie's excitement came over the mic.

They all looked to their left, where Charlie manned the gun.

"What do you have?" Eddy echoed his excitement.

"Blue, no more yellow."

Eddy banked in the direction of his gunner's view, dropping lower.

Scooter snapped his binoculars back up then his free hand shot out like a direction marker. "There."

Below, a ring of yellow began to emerge against the blue.

"I'll be damned." Scooter laughed. "They've taken their blue dungarees off to cover the yellow of the life raft."

"Damn ingenious." Eddy snorted. "Anyone else out there?"

"Clear on my side," Allen reported from his position as right-wing gunner.

"We're heading in Beau," Eddy reported to the flight captain. "Let's make room. When we have them aboard, call in their report Hank."

Dipping their wing in recognition, they closed in, approaching upwind. Eddy skimmed the tips of the waves before settling onto the sea far from the vulnerable raft. He watched the inflated survival boat roll with their wake as the men aboard struggled into their blue jeans. Cutting the engine, they drifted closer to the smiling, sunburned men.

One of the men stood, still in his BVDs. Eddy assumed he was the captain. What they couldn't see from above, was one of the men lay in the bottom of the raft, with a pair of the tan trousers covering his face.

Eddy pulled back his window.

"I'm not leaving him here." The man in his underwear announced.

"Okay." Eddy understood the situation. They would take the deceased airman back to base. Without hesitation he gave the command. "Get the sleeping bag, rope and some drinking water down there."

The crews blended as one while they struggled the corpse aboard.

"Thanks for the lift." The pilot's dark shadow of his beard sprouted through the rough red of his sunbaked chin. Accepting a blanket, he sat. "Damn Zero came out of the sun, didn't see him until he was on us."

His men watched him intently while he paused to gulp some coffee. "Eat your sandwiches slowly," he recommended. "We're going to need our strength to get back up there."

The men smiled in response, slowing their consumption of the dry bread and spam.

Eddy waited, giving them a moment as they bobbed gently on the flattening surface.

The downed pilot raised his mug in salute. "To Ralph. Best damn co-pilot ever."

The prickling that shot through Eddy's body reflected on Scooter's face as the newcomers raised their mugs in unison.

Eddy nodded. "We'll get out of here. Don't want that Zero coming back."

"No chance of that." The captain nonchalantly took another sip savoring it as if it were whiskey. "He's burnt to a crisp on the bottom of the ocean."

# TWENTY FOUR

"WHY DIDN'T ANYONE FIRE BACK?" JACK sat at the glass top table in the plotting room on Fire Control Hill at Fort Stevens, Oregon, waiting for the answer.

He had left San Francisco just after 1 a.m. when the call came in. Again, the Japanese attacked on a Sunday. The shells fired by the enemy submarine did little damage the evening of June 21$^{st}$. The commander ordered an immediate black out as the soldiers scurried in the dark to man the large guns at the Columbia River entrance.

"I counted about sixteen, maybe seventeen, shots fired at us from the sub." Corporal Tully pointed to a part of the ocean just off Battery Russell, obviously ignoring the question.

"So, why didn't anyone fire at them?" Jack had already been given the information, but he wanted it repeated.

"Indications were the sub was out of range." Tully's voice wavered a bit.

"We had four 12-inch mortars ready at Battery Clark and others up and down the coast." Captain Davis tapped his finger indicating the positions on the map. "Man, oh man, did we ever want to fire! My men were so excited to shoot at the enemy."

"Where are the men now? Can I talk with them?" Jack leaned back to watch as Davis' mouth twisted.

Abruptly Captain Davis straightened his shoulders. "Twenty–two of my men went over the hill last night, they were so disappointed at not being permitted to fire. They're Jap-Happy and utterly disappointed they couldn't have a go at the bastards."

"Most of us were in our tents, in our underwear, when we heard the first shots. But within minutes everyone was ready. I was asking to be allowed to fire," Captain Wood added. "But we were waiting for Colonel Doney to give his word."

"Last night was a Sunday, just like Pearl. And it was the longest day of the year and the sun set at about 8:50 p.m. We couldn't see the sub very well, except for when he shot at us. He looked like he was beyond our guns." Another captain of the Coast Artillery reported.

Colonel Doney entered the room as the men backed away from the lighted table and Jack.

"I'm Colonel Doney." He stood holding his hard hat upside down. "Two little girls just handed me these, they found the fragments near the base."

Jack stood picking up one of the jagged pieces of metal.

"People are finding parts of Japanese shells all over, sir." Tully added breathlessly. "They just missed the Hitchman's house with their kids inside, about three miles south. We've had calls coming in from all over."

"So why didn't you fire back?" Jack regarded the man who would not let his troops respond when under attack.

"I was in bed at the time and when I got here the sub had departed. They were out of our range. It would have been useless."

Jack did not budge, feeling disgust for the man before him. This was the first attack on an American Fort. A show of gun power along the coast might deter more attacks.

"They shelled the Estevan Lighthouse on Vancouver Island the night before they hit us." Captain Wood announced, obviously agitated by his disappointment. "We extinguished the Lighthouse at Cape Disappointment at the head of the Columbia. We're thinking he followed a fleet of fishing boats who knew the waters."

How like Akio, Jack almost smiled at his enemy's thoroughness. He could see his roommate at Stanford hovered over the old maps of this coast, wishing he had been more alert at the time. He remembered one in particular held Akio's attention. The old 1918 coastal map consisted of proposed submarine bases. He made a mental note to check, but he remained confident he would find a proposal for a submarine base somewhere near the Columbia River. Akio's knowledge of this coast made him dangerous. More importantly, with a sinking heart, Jack realized his nemesis was near.

"I want to see the areas hit." Jack stormed for the door, barging through the arch before the Colonel had time to object.

The jeep rattled toward the base of steep steps. As they reached the top of the ridge the large guns, ready and waiting, loomed to their right. To their left four Army men squatted inside the bowl of a crater, hats pushed back, posing for a picture. The impact of the bombs leaving deep scars on the earth, illustrating the strength of the blast.

Jack climbed up on the battery for a better viewpoint of the Columbia River. The large guns, if pointed into the harbor, might inflect damage to the bustling industry that lined parts of the shore. The dock side building of the all-important liberty ships lay just up the Columbia. Those hard-working men produced about one vessel per week. A misguided blast from the big guns would have devastated that shipyard.

He let the wind pass over him, realizing his report to the one man who secretly depended on his evaluation would not go well. The teletypes were already heating up between newspapers across the country with the powerful headlines of another strike on American soil, this time a base with soldiers. He understood the Japanese, enduring great psychological damage or "loosing face," when attacked by Doolittle in Tokyo, would continue to avenge their disgrace in the name of their Emperor.

Jack moved closer to the group of soldiers conferring among themselves, posing question after question. Jack's frustration mounted as he could not divulge the answer.

Akio knew how to maneuver past the mines protecting the harbor. Akio. He wished he'd killed him in the alley in San Francisco that night he kidnapped Billi. He wished he'd disobeyed orders aiming for Akio's heart, hoping he had not traded his quest to unearth the espionage ring for the mounting bloodshed his nemesis' knowledge of the west coast brought to battle.

As Jack stood looking out to sea, more than likely Akio slithered just below the surface heading south down the Oregon coast to California. Jack wasted no time as he hurried back to his car.

UNABLE TO SLEEP, Billi picked up a flashlight and slipped out the kitchen door. She reasoned a walk around the grounds of her new home might calm her. Jack had disappeared three nights ago, leaving no note or indication of when he might return. She paused, looking up at the stars in the late June sky. How she longed to be at Dyes Inlet at her father's home, swimming in the cool salt water. A star shot across the sky and she took it as a good omen. Continuing past the empty tennis courts, she wandered toward the garage. The large structure had never been of interest before, but tonight she was restless.

She pulled at the side door which opened with a slight squeak. Stepping inside, she snapped on her flashlight, moving it across the large empty room until it hit upon the chrome of the old family car. When Lilly picked her up at the train station, she had not noticed the splendor of the automobile. Fascinated, she moved closer letting her light move past the large spokes on the wheel then across the fender that gracefully sloped down to the running board. She held the light over the circle with the imprint LaS in the mat on the side runner before her lamp moved to the rear of the golden and tan toned auto. A matching storage case, secured to the back, spoke of a different era. She circled the car, past an extra tire strapped to the side, to the massive front where the immense radiator gleamed between two enormous headlights. On top of the radiator a chrome figurine of a man, his coat flowing behind, with scabbard and pistol tucked into his belt, held his large hat upward, as if to catch raindrops.

"Rene-Robert Caliver, Sieur de La Salle," Jack's voice broke through the silence of the darkness.

"You son of a bitch." Billi swung round, her light fixing on her husband's black coat. "You scared me to death."

"What kind of greeting is that for your hus—"

She leapt into his arms, kissing him, pressing her body against his. The frightening anguish of the most recent attack on American soil slipping away with his touch.

She worked her way from his arms and pointed her light back on the stunning vehicle. "Are you going to take me for a drive?"

"Sorry, can't." He took off his hat and coat, draping them over the windowless front door of the car.

"And why not?"

Jack opened the gleaming rear door and held it for his wife. She slid onto the fine leather seat as he crawled in beside her.

"This is Mother's prize 1927 La Salle."

"As in the explorer La Salle, and is that supposed to be him on the hood?"

"But, of course."

Billi laughed at his attempted French accent.

"When did she stop driving it?" She turned to look at her husband.

"Why the hell don't I have you do my interrogating? Father bought it for mother and sent her, and the car, and her driver, over for the opening of the Royal Hawaiian Hotel."

"Where were you and Lilly?"

"We were to stay home with the promise of one day joining them."

"And why didn't you?"

"The stock market dictated our lives." His head leaned against the tall back rest with what she recognized as the weight of the memories.

"Sorry," she whispered, snuggling closer.

"The keys are above the driver's seat. I have it maintained regularly. If you ever need to get out of here quickly. Go. Use this car and go."

Something in his voice brought tears to her eyes. "I'm not going anywhere without you."

He put his arm around her and held her tight. "Don't wait for me. I mean that."

"Jack, what is it? What happened? You know something," her voice quivered. "Where were you?"

"Billi, you know I can't tell you everything."

"It's Akio. He's alive." Jack's warm touch did not stop the twist in her gut.

"Akio had always been very interested in the World War I Forts along the coast. He drove the highway one semester break. Have you ever visited Astoria, Oregon? He did. From there you have a full view of the river, the Fort, and the Columbia River Harbor."

Billi's body went limp. "Oh, my God."

"You need to stay out of the city for some time. Promise me."

She nodded, and he drew her closer snapping off the flashlight allowing darkness to settle around them.

THE CRY OF PAIN ECHOED down the hallway as three doors flew opened in unison. Billi sprinted toward the sound to find Lilly twisting and moaning with sweat pouring down her temples. She squatted next to the delicate blonde's bed, taking her hand.

"You'll be fine." Billy whispered.

Bella charged forward as Jack and Mrs. Huntington stood in the doorway. Both looking paler than Lilly. "Call that ambulance. And get some hot water. Go." She shooed the two into action.

"I can't do this," Lilly's agony resounded off the walls.

"Yes, you can," Billi kept her voice low and firm. "And once that baby has arrived, you are going to love that little one to pieces."

"No. I won't. I hate this baby." She screamed louder.

"You can do this, and you will." Billi felt the small hand tighten around hers, squeezing with inconceivable strength.

Bella checked the dresser where she had stacked blankets, towels and other essentials in the event the ambulance did not make it in time. "Breath, baby breath."

Jack entered the room blanching as white as his baby sister. "I called . . ."

"Get out and get me some of that whiskey," Bella's arms went up with her command.

Between contractions Bella mopped Lilly's brow with a cool compress. "That helps, Bella. When will this be over?" She turned to look at her mother. "You did this?"

Mrs. Huntington's laugh eased the tension for a bit as she lowered near her daughter. "Twice, to be exact."

"Why the hell did you do this a second time?" Another wave of contortions rocked her small body eliciting blood curdling yells.

"So, I could have you." Her mother smiled.

"Well that was just stupid." Lilly scolded. Suddenly, her eyes rolled up and she stopped breathing.

Bella slapped Lilly's face and the young woman's arm went up in mild defense as Jack rounded the corner with a full bottle of Bourbon.

Cupping the blond head in her strong black hands, Bella poured a touch of dark liquid down her throat. Some dripped down her chin while some provided a hint of relief. Her blue eyes opened wider, pleading for more.

"Get that hot water bottle up behind her hips," Bella nodded toward Billi. "Get out and bring that doctor." Bella directed her command toward Jack as he ran out of the room. "Everybody's messin' with me." She grumbled then started humming as she steadily worked her hands along the sides of Lilly's stomach. "That's just fine," she announced. "Just fine. Baby, you're going to be fine."

The spell the large black woman cast fell over the women as they waited.

Outside, tires screeched to a halt followed by the pounding steps below and the urgent call of male voices. As Jack and the doctor burst through the door, the strong wailing of the newborn baby greeted them. Billi watched Jack regain his breath as he stood perfectly still looking down on his sister and the tiny, squirming newborn, the vernix of waxy film still covering his limbs.

The doctor pushed past Jack to examine the infant, eliciting a loud wail from his minutes old, strong lungs.

"The baby's fine but I think we need to take Lilly in for observation." The older doctor's voice held concern at the sound of the ambulance drivers approaching.

"She's not goin' anywhere." Bella handed the doctor another clean towel then placed her large frame at the foot of Lilly's bed.

"She's lost a lot of blood and . . ."

"I know that." She ignored the red blood of birth splattered across the white of her apron. Her arms found her ample hips as her head went higher.

Jack stepped closer to the doctor. "Can we talk outside?"

Billi noticed the men from the ambulance peeked around Bella at the limp and frail mother. Mrs. Huntington, lost to undeniable love, tenderly counted the finger and toes of her grandson.

"That mama needs to be with her son, not in any damn hos-pit-al." Bella's exaggeration of the word emphasizing her hatred for hospitals.

The new arrivals backed out of the door into the hall. Billi moved closer to listen to the doctor.

"I wouldn't cross Bella on this Doc," Jack confided with the man.

"Well, if anyone could handle your sister, I guess it would be Bella. I forgot. Sorry, I should never had mentioned the hospital in front of her."

"How about a drink?"

As the men continued down the stairs Billi snuck into the hall to listen.

"Never seen that before?" The doctor sounded amused.

"Can't say I have. Not sure I want to again."

Billi held her breath at her husband words.

"That will change. Your new wife was helpful. How are you two doing?"

"Considering there is a war on, and we hardly get to spend time together, I'd say we're doing fantastic."

"Well she's here now. So, things will change."

"You have no idea, Doc, what . . ."

The babies cry muffled the rest of her husband's statement.

ONCE AGAIN AKIO WAITED at Imperial Naval Headquarters outside of the office of the great Admiral Yamamoto, the man who in January of 1941 proposed the plan to attack on Pearl Harbor. He would report the success of the mission, attacking the soul of the enemy, a United States base on the mainland, along with sinking valuable ships and their cargo. However, more importantly, he hoped the reason for the meeting was to discuss his design.

He checked himself, brushing an imaginary spec from his uniform. He noticed Yamamoto's secretary walk toward him and stood, catching himself briefly as his sea legs wobbled. At the door of the Commander in Chief of the Combined Fleet, he straightened, breathing deeply before entering.

He recognized most of the men from the dinner at the geisha house with Yamamoto's lover, Ume, his beautiful Plum Blossom. Aware of their rank, he bowed before them, while the perspiration accumulated at his temples. He dared not wipe away the proof of his anxiety.

"Ah, Lieutenant Sumiyoshi you have had more success," Yamamoto complimented him.

"As you have so wisely stated, 'Sensible Americans know the submarine shelling of the Pacific coast was a warning to the nation that the paradise created by George Washington is on the verge of destruction.'"

There was a moment of silence before Yamamoto nodded. "We walked ashore at Kiska and Attu, but our ships suffered greatly at Midway. That is why you are here."

Akio could feel his heart racing as he watched Kurojima, the Admiral's personal staff officer, unroll the draft of his aircraft on the large table. Everyone stepped closer to observe the design.

"Lieutenant Sumiyoshi." He nodded at Akio before continuing, "Your drawing has been studied by the Bureau of Naval Construction." He eyed those in the room. "The Aichi D3A, the Val, is responsible for sinking nine allied destroyers and cruisers. The Aichi Aircraft Company will now expand and build a new plane to attack New York City, Washington D.C. and the Panama Canal. These planes must have speed and range to carry the largest bombs we can build. Please, explain." He waved toward the table.

Akio stepped toward the drawing. His finger moved to the cockpit. "My design requires two crewmen. The pilot will be able to drop the bombs. Riding in the rear, this man will be responsible for radio, navigation, calculation for dropping the bombs, and act as tail-gunner." He tapped the position of the tail-gunner with pride. "This man can swivel 180 degrees to open the cockpit's canopy while his gun will automatically raise into firing position. In addition, there are less removable parts so the seaplane can be assembled quicker once on deck." He paused just long enough to catch his breath. "Most importantly, the wings rotate 90 degrees and lay flat against the fuselage, saving space. The tail stabilizers fold down as does the tip of the vertical stabilizer. With a small propeller there will be clearance inside the narrow hanger of a submarine."

"Do you have a name for such a plane?"

Akio stood back breathing heavy. "Seiran."

"Mist of a fair day, like a storm from a clear sky. How poetic. Excellent." Yamamoto paused before announcing. "We will form the God-Dragon Special Attack Squad."

Akio looked into his superior's dark eyes. He understood that Yamamoto's time at Harvard followed by serving as an Attaché in Washington D.C. gave him a better understanding of the Americans than any other person in the room. "Attacking the West Coast, New York City, Washington D.C. and the Panama Canal will bring the enemy to their knees. It is a wise choice." He bowed in awe of the remarkable plan.

As Akio hurried down the steps of the four-story brick Navy Ministry building to pass through the gate at the tall iron fence, his need to celebrate made his hands tremble.

Suddenly, Kurojima was at his side. "You will join the honorable Commander in Chief for dinner." He held out a small piece of paper.

Akio accepted it, bowing low before the one man he knew Yamamoto trusted more than most of his staff. It was an honor to be treated as one of the inner circle. Tonight would be a night like no other.

# TWENTY FIVE

Eddy looked over at Scooter, the black mixture dripping from his brush. "What do you think?"

"It's a good thing you're a pilot. You'd never make it as a painter."

He squatted next to his PBY at their new base on Espiritu Santo. They had leapfrogged to the newly constructed Luganville Seaplane base, code named Button, closer to Guadalcanal and the Japanese held Henderson Field. He squinted at the plane's new inky coat giving her a drab appearance. He rose, sliding under her massive wing, checking for spots he'd missed. After a few minutes of closer inspection, he put down the brush.

"I like it."

Scooter lit a cigarette. "So, when are we trying this paint job out?"

"As soon as she's dry. There's no moon tonight and now being black, they won't see us coming." He squatted next to his friend in the white sand. "We've been given permission to load her up with bombs and go hunting."

"I bet no one ever thought a Catalina would be used like this?" Scooter blew rings of smoke in the slight breeze.

Eddy watched a small sailing craft in Segond Channel manned by the Ni-Vanuatu natives of the islands glide across the surf. He remembered the night he passed one of the islanders on the path to headquarters. He only spotted the man's tan shorts as the native's smooth dark skin made him almost invisible in the shadows. They had nodded, then smiled, their dependency and mutual goal bringing them together.

"A black cat prowling at night. That's what we will become."

"Jesus. Where the hell do you get these ideas?"

"I just know the PBY can do more than scout and rescue. It can be a killing machine." Eddy stood, his excitement uncontrollable.

"Killer black cats." Scooter hissed.

"Now you're getting it." He started toward the aqua blue waters. "I'm taking a swim, getting a haircut, a nap and planning to take my black mistress out on her first raid."

Scooter tossed his cigarette to the side racing past Eddy toward the beach.

"Oh, no." Eddy broke into a run.

They hit the warm crystal blue water at the same time, matching strokes, venting their anxiety with each pull against the slight drift of the waves. They touched a buoy where one of the PBYs was moored then spun back toward the shore. Danger now their way of life, these fits of play heightened the reality that today, this minute, is all that matters.

Eddy examined his new hair cut in the makeshift mirror inside the Quonset hut shared by the pilots and their crew. The air had cooled with the now setting sun. With one last adjustment to an errant strand of hair, he turned toward Scooter. It was time.

They walked in silence under the palm trees to the dockside apron.

"Damn," Eddy whistled. "She's beautiful."

He walked around the PBY again trying to find spots he had missed. In the moonless night it became impossible to tell where her wings ended. The black cat was perfect.

One of the ground crew patted the side of the black airplane. "We put some coffee and sandwiches inside."

"Thanks," Beau smiled, his white teeth lighting up the dark in the soft light provided by the beach crew.

The PBY crew helped guide the large craft into the water allowing it to float on its pontoons. Like clockwork they assumed their assigned positions to remove the wheels. Beau secured the tail, keeping the boat from drifting on the light chop, as the other six men, three on each side, preformed their task of removing the heavy wheels.

"How many bombs were you able to get aboard?" Eddy began his pre-flight check.

"The regular. Two 1,000 pounders and two 500," Beau responded.

Scooter started up the ladder to the cabin. "Let's hope we find a target."

"We'll find one." Eddy tossed his cigarette into the sand, stomping on it to signify his intentions. "Poor bastards. They'll never see us coming."

Eddy, the last one aboard, readied for their first attempt as black death invisibly riding in the skies. As the propellers began to chug up to speed, a hoot went out from those who stayed behind, hoping and praying for a successful mission. The added weight of the bombs made take off longer as they skimmed the surface of the sea, heading upwind, to help lift the nose. They bumped three times and then were aloft, still riding low with the weight.

"Hey, Fletch," Eddy spoke into his mic, "this weight will always mandate a longer approach. What's the calculated distance?"

The navigator responded quickly, "An additional 30 yards, just as I predicted."

"That's why I love you." Eddy laughed.

It was so black it was hard to tell water from sky as they climbed to a safe altitude. They slowly worked their way up the chain of islands, hugging the coastline watching for enemy supply ships. It was about 1:50 a.m. when they spotted what looked like puffs of smoke and the white tips of the wake from large vessels.

"Look at that line up." Scooter checked control panels for height and speed as they turned toward the enemy below.

"Have the coordinates for me, Fletch?" Eddy leaned further into the glass composing the front of the plane. "Let's have some fun."

Choosing the last ship in the lineup as his first target, he approached the ship from behind at 200 hundred feet.

"Drop."

The first bomb skidded past the enemy vessel into the water on their port side.

"Damn." Scooter kept watching as they banked to the far side of the ships.

"We're too high. I'm going in low." Eddy dropped to just above the water again approaching from behind. As they reached the end of the long deck, they let their bomb drop. With all his might, Eddy pulled back on the stick rocketing the plane skyward as the bomb hit its mark causing the center of the ship to explode below.

The PBY shook from the blast. "Holy mother of God. Thank you." Scooter slapped at Eddy's shoulder.

Eddy swung around heading their PBY for the flank of another vessel as search lights from the enemy ships began to illuminate the moonless sky. They swept across mid-ship, dropping their load in the midst of the ack ack from the large guns. The blast swung their tail with the impact as Eddy struggled to lift them above the flames.

In swift succession three Mitsubishi fighters took to the air for a counterattack. The planes, circling from their launch, guided by the glow of the fire, headed directly at them.

Eddy turned from the sinking ships, blazing against the black waters. He spoke calmly to his side gunners. "Allen, Charlie, heads up, got three Zekes headed our way."

The old black cat presented no match for the Mitsubishi Zeros as the enemy swept into the dark skies. The hunter now the hunted. Eddy started to dive, flattening out just above the waves, heading away from the convoy. He could sense the entire crew praying their camouflage worked. The miracle occurred as the enemy planes, not seeing the big black bird against the inky water, flew directly overhead before disappearing.

A new tactic emerged, bringing death in the colorless night. By the time the planes circled back toward their burning ship, Eddy had slipped his black cat into the night ready to pounce again.

"We'll call her the Phantom." He hissed, emphasizing the plane's feline nature.

"Phantom," echoed through the cabin as each crew member voiced their own rendition of their PBYs new name.

A gentle wind carried the August heat through the second-floor open windows of Jack's father's study. His eye patch rested on the desk, as he leaned back, both eyes closed, in concentration. "Read that again."

Billi shifted the letter she held closer to the lamp. "It's not going to change the meaning," the alarm in Billi's voice apparent.

Jack opened his eyes to regard his wife. "What does Eileen know of your visits to San Francisco before the war?"

"That I came down here to be a secretary. But I hated being away from Mother, Dad and Eddy. That was all. Do you think I would want to endanger my best friend?" Her gaze did not flinch in its truthful statement.

"Read it again." He leaned forward to watch her form the words.

"The most amazing thing has happened. A man named Kito, who is in the small building next to ours, was visiting with father. He saw the photo you sent me of the two of us in front of father's store last summer and began asking about you. I quickly told him you were married. The most interesting part was father. When Kito asked if you spoke Japanese, father assured him you did not. I have no idea what has gotten into father. Maybe it is that he does not want in any way to hinder his favorite 'bright eyes.' He did want to know how his orchid is doing."

Billi stopped and bit her lip. "Is Eileen in trouble?"

"Hardly. It certainly would be helpful to find out who this Kito is and where he had seen you before." Jack's hand massaged his temple and scar. "Have you given Eileen any other photos? Any of us?"

"No. No. I told her you don't like to have your photo taken. Did you think it was someone I met down here when . . ."

"Yes. I do. The only good news is he is secured in the camp."

She folded the letter and held it out toward Jack. "What do you want me to write back to her?"

"Nothing. I'll see if I can get a picture of this man. Maybe he was one of the men with Akio. Billi," he picked up her hand and held it. "You need to be careful. When I lived with Akio at Stanford, I learned two things. His pride never lets him forget if he has been offended and, like that night in the snow at your father's, you won't see him coming."

A shiver ran down her spine. "What else should I know about him?"

"He's one hell of a gambler, cards, anything. But the problem is, he cheats."

"He cheats?" She slid her hand from his, holding back a laugh. "Is it just that you lost some money to him and think he cheats?"

"I lost a lot more to him. And believe me, he has no honor."

She screwed up her lips at the concept of a Japanese person without honor. But as the words sunk in, so did the memory of Jack's assistant, David, and how swiftly Akio's blade severed David's head from his body, without so much of a twitch from the killer's eyes. Eyes that seemed to reflect the joy of the kill.

"Yes, I will remember." Her shoulders slumped forward.

"It's just that he's out there somewhere. I can feel it. There are hundreds of beaches along our shoreline that would make easy landing. The Coast Guard is expanding but his tentacles reach far, and war only gives him license for more atrocities."

"Do you think he knows I'm here?"

"No. It's late. Let's not talk about this now. I'm sorry I didn't mean to frighten you."

"Jack," Billi spoke calmly. "I am not frightened. I know that if Akio ever shows up again, you will kill him. And if you don't, I will."

Her resolve filled the room and left no doubt between them. Jack pulled her close, his tender kiss sending a different kind of shiver through her body.

"I'll tell you one thing, lady." His warm breath brushed against her cheek. "I sure am glad you're on my side in this war."

The battle for Henderson Airfield on Guadalcanal continued from land and sea. Since the seventh of August, thousands of Marines had swept ashore to control this strategic site. If America lost here, it endangered their ability to support Australia.

At first, when they were assigned to Cactus, the code name for Guadalcanal, the crew exhibited the thrill of being closer to the action. Then the downside settled around them in the form of rain and mud. The showers had finally stopped for the day, at least that was the hope. Eddy stood in his tent in mud well past his ankles, frustrated by the depth of the muck they lived in. Flipping back the mosquito net, he stepped outside into the sunshine. To his surprise Major Fowler sloshed in his direction.

"Morning Major. Welcome." Eddy beamed as his plan took shape.

The Major slipped in the deep mud before standing beside Eddy. "You invited me to look at some of your plans for the PBYs."

"Yes, sir. Thank you for taking up my offer. By the way, it was a real delight having you go out on our mission last night." Eddy nodded toward the tent he shared with Scooter. "Step into my office."

The mud oozed around their boots as they crossed the threshold. He watched the Major take in the conditions of their sleeping quarters. Their cots dipped above the sludge, mosquitoes clung to their folded clothes kept high, suspended in makeshift slings. Eddy reached for his flashlight, dropping it. They both watched as it disappeared into the slime.

As if rehearsed, Scooter stepped inside. "Not again." He rolled up his sleeve, reached into the guck, feeling for the fallen object. Finally, he pulled it out with a sucking noise. The slop clung to his forearm as he handed the mud encrusted flashlight to Eddy.

The Major's face twisted with disgust. "You mean to tell me that after our flight last night, what 12 hours, you pilots returned to sleep in this place?"

"Yes, sir." Eddy frowned, attempting to control his glee.

The Major sighed, swatting at a buzzing intruder. "I'll see that all pilots are moved out of this, I don't even know what the hell to call it. We'll put you further up the hill in Quonset huts. You grounded for two days?"

"Yes, sir." Eddy and Scooter nodded in unison.

"Bring your ideas to command tomorrow, 0300, and we'll go over them. That is after you move out of this shit."

"Yes, sir." They stood taller, unable to click their heels in the dense slop.

They watched as the Major found his footing to retreat up the hill.

Scooter slapped Eddy's back. "You, my friend, are a genius."

"Yep. Just remember that." He brushed past his co-pilot, picked a dry shirt off a branch of a tree, then scooped up his helmet and rifle. "If you're coming with me you better wipe that, what did the major call it? Shit, off your arm."

Scooter found a bucket of water and rinsed his arm. "Not sure what you're up to."

"Like the man said, we have two days on the ground. But today I feel lucky."

"Lucky? That sounds dangerous. Thinking you're heading somewhere off limits?" Scooter mimicked his friend's moves.

Eddy beelined for a patch of sand where bandoliers of bullets hung from the low branch of a eucalyptus tree like sunbaked snakeskins. He ran his hand down the ammo selecting one warm to the touch, completely dry.

"Oh, damn." Scooter selected his belt of bullets, draping it over his shoulder. "Do I even want to know what we're up to?"

"You'll love me for the distraction." Eddy headed down the beach to a jeep. Hailing the Seabee, the two pilots jumped in.

"Hey, fellas. Where you headin' on this beautiful day?" The Seabee started up the jeep.

"To the river. We want to see what those Marines are up to." Eddy lit a cigarette.

The Seabee glanced at them. "You pilots come back. We're fixing up that airport for you. Got some great white coral we're going to use as the strip."

The incline of the beach caused the jeep to ride at a tilt. They passed a Japanese Zero with its nose stuck in the sand, wing broken, and all good parts stripped for other uses. Days before the Seabees cleared the dead Japanese soldiers' bodies along this strip, but the ghosts of the men lost in battle still spooked those who walked the shore.

"Hear the Marines captured a Nip ice plant at Laguna Point." The Seabee rolled his jeep to a stop before a river that cut the shore in two.

Scooter jumped from the vehicle. "You SOB. Ice? We're going into the jungle to get shot for ice?"

Eddy patted his friend on the back as he led the way. "I'm not getting shot. And for that matter, neither are you."

"See you later." Their driver hollered before driving off.

They crossed the first river, rifles held high, to the far side where stacks of more ammunition and supplies were gathered at the beginning of a well-worn trail. The jungle, muggy and unforgiving, surrounded them as sweat dampened their shirts, dripping down their necks below their helmets.

They came to a second river with a simple rope strung across the murky water. Hiking their ammo higher on their bodies, they held their guns overhead while one hand worked along the lifeline of the rope. Once they breached the other side, the jungle met them with more intensity. In the distance the sound of gunshots warned them of the impending danger.

They slowed just outside the perimeter of a clearing. US Marines moved swiftly in front of a low shack with a thatched roof porch. Behind the makeshift building, tents claimed this strip of the island as American.

The two pilots sauntered forward.

"Hear you guys captured some ice." Eddy smiled at the sergeant standing by the Japanese building.

"What the hell are you two doing here?" The sergeant eyed them suspiciously.

Scooter rested his gun on his boot. "Thought you might need a hand rounding up something more substantial than frozen water."

"Well, I'll be damned." The Marine's hands found his hips. "Just don't get yourself all shot up. These guys are heading to the front. Some of our men are pinned down in a gully. The more bullets the better."

"Thanks," Eddy started toward the men heading further into the overgrowth.

"Christ don't thank me. Just come back in one piece."

When the group of men neared the skirmish, the shots fired were sporadic. They passed one man, shirtless, his legs dangling from a high branch. His field glasses cast a shadow across his face while his gun rested on his lap.

"Ten on the far side, under that low bush in the center of the ridge." The man up the tree kept his voice calm and low as he pointed to some movement in the distance. A bullet whizzed through the air falling short of its mark.

Like a monkey the lookout shimmied down the thin trunk. "One of our guys is hit in the leg down there. That's what the bastards do. Then they wait for others to come out and help. That way they kill more of us."

A moan was heard through the bushes.

"How long ago?" One of the medics in the arriving group asked.

The lookout regarded the new arrivals. "About an hour."

"He'll bleed out soon."

The drab earth transformed into their map as they developed their plan with x's marking positions for an attack.

Eddy could feel the adrenaline stirring his body. Fighting on the ground, next to the Marines, would result in only two outcomes. He didn't consider the worst of the two as he and Scooter crawled forward to their assigned outcrop of shrubs. They all waited as the heat and bugs mounted their own attack. Another moan filled their ears. The kid was calling for his mother.

Eddy looked over at his co-pilot with a nod that spoke volumes. Someone had to break the stalemate. He rolled to another bush, still no reply from the enemy. Encouraged, he began to slither down the hill toward the base of a teak tree, hoping its large leaves would provide cover. More importantly, that his mother kept her pledge of daily placing fresh flowers at the foot of the Blessed Virgin Mary in their yard back home while she prayed for his safety.

Shots rang out from the far side causing the bushes around the enemy to move rapidly with return fire. A grenade sliced through the stale air, striking the opposite hillside. The unmistakable cry of a man dying whaled in response.

Hearing movement next to him Eddy watched as Marines drew closer to the injured man. Then, out of the corner of his eye he saw motion. He fired at the figure sneaking closer, blowing one of the ferns from his helmet before the Japanese soldier hit the ground and lay motionless.

Eddy's heart beat in his throat, constricting his breathing. He had killed before but nothing like this, man to man. A slug struck the dirt next to him sending rage down his spine. He continued forward determined, watching as one of the Marines cleared the brush grabbing the injured soldier by the shoulders. Bullets rained around the two exposed men. Suddenly Scooter was in the fray, tugging at the fallen man's leg as they tried to drag the body to safety.

A speck of bush moved just beyond Scooter. Eddy took aim, letting it fly. The bush jerked forward as the dead man twisted to the ground. He rushed forward to grab the Marine's other leg, hearing the pop of gunfire accompanied by a grunt.

Like crab scurrying sideways the three men made it up the hill into the dense jungle as the Marines blasted the retreating enemy. The sweat dripped down their bodies as a fourth man joined in carrying the injured man to a stretcher further up the trail.

The rush of the exchange surged through Eddy as he turned to his co-pilot. "Jesus, what were you thinking back there?"

"Hell, I knew you were right behind me."

Eddy blinked the salt from his eyes. "Is that so? And how did you know that?"

"Because who else is going to put up with you for hours in a cramped space?"

One of the Marines snickered. "You two lovers ever want to come back to do more arguing, the jungle is open."

"Great." Eddy and Scooter replied in unison.

EDDY HELD A CHUNK OF ICE in his mouth enjoying the freezing sensation as he leaned back against a tree. He watched Scooter rub a cube across his neck then down his arms as he left the hut which housed the ice machine.

"This is one thing to thank the Japs for." Scooter worked the cooling fluid across his brow.

"Damn right." Eddy's words sounded muffled as he shifted the cube to one side. "Trying to figure out how to take some back."

"Can't, we're in enough hot water." Scooter looked toward the beach.

"Yeah." Eddy pushed himself up. "Better get back to base and see what we've missed."

"At least we didn't get ourselves killed."

Instinctively they both headed back toward the hut for another bit of heaven—ice.

# TWENTY SIX

A KIO WROTE IN HIS JOURNAL, AUGUST 15th, 1942, depart 6:00 a.m. Cargo: six 168 pound incendiary bombs. He smiled. Their straightforward mission held high hopes for spreading immense damage to the vast forest along the Oregon coast of the United States. The concept sprang from the knowledge of the uncontrolled Tillamook fires, one in 1933, destroying 350 acres of prime lumber, then a second blaze scorched an additional 190 acres in 1939. Dropping the incendiary bombs, igniting fires, would unnerve the enemy, while consuming vast amounts of needed resources. Putting down his pen, he leaned back in his small compartment, shifting to find support. Like all submarines, the I-25 did not offer comfort as it stealthily moved toward its target.

He reviewed his notes from their last mission, pausing on the pages showing his June entries. He had not been chided by his superiors when the three men set ashore near the Quinault Indian Reservation were never heard from again. The submarine received their last message reporting their situation. The three had made contact with a Native American man who promised to guide them to their tribal leaders. He snorted at their obvious incompetence.

Securing his notebook, he stepped into the cramped passageway and headed for the control room. He fought his restlessness. While no one had acquired the fan from Billi's clutches with the dragons representing his design, it did not diminish his desire for revenge. Inadvertently, he rotated the shoulder where the deep scar she inflicted remained.

He passed the new crewmember, the one who replaced Tak, and could not help but feel his blood churn at the choice of his superiors. Tak had been sent to the Nakano ward to the special school designated for training spies.

Akio visited the school in 1939 to speak with potential candidates to help with his endeavors in America. He had admired the tactics drilled into the men who studied in secret behind the nondescript, unmarked building. The elite men chosen, spoke several languages, wore suits and their hair long. Their schooling in the arts of defense, such as kendo and judo, accompanied with their education on various cultures and societies, made the graduates of the Nakano school of the shadow warrior invaluable for infiltration. Akio had enlisted some of the graduates from the Nakano school for his secret assignment, creating a successful espionage web from Alaska to Mexico.

He fought back the enormous sense of loss suffered when the lines of communication filtering information back to Tokyo had been cut. The Japanese Consulates in America, a prime conduit back to the homeland, now closed. The flow of monies raised on American soil to be sent back to the Emperor to purchase much needed supplies for the Imperial forces, dried up. His contacts, rounded up by the likes of Jack Huntington, now sat in relocation camps out of reach. But espionage never dies. If the information did not come willingly, it became a matter of finding a weak spot then compromising the target. All was not lost. Furthermore, Operation To, based in Europe, continued to provide information from abroad back to his homeland.

Now Tak would be a part of the select group. Again, he snorted. Yes, the young man had been useful on many occasions, but Akio needed him. He held the key to Billi. But with his recent transfer, even that had slipped away. When he returned to Tokyo, he would pay Tak a visit. With that resolution firmly in mind, he breathed deeper.

The musty smell of men already penetrated the confines of the submarine as he stood over the map illustrating their progress. Failing at Midway cut deep, not only in the number of ships lost or damaged, but strategically. Midway created a stepping stone to Hawaii. Had they taken Hawaii they could have secured a better port for supplies before crossing the Pacific to the mainland. These long journeys back and forth to resupply only illustrated the need for a more powerful submarine. He rocked back on his heels, feeling heady at the secret he held against tight lips.

JACK'S CAR PULLED INTO the Port of Brookings Harbor, on the coast of Oregon. Excited, Billi hopped out to explore her surroundings. While the leaves still bore their shades of summer, the coolness of fall already gripped the air. She gathered her jacket closer as the chill seemed early for September.

"I just need to stretch my legs," she announced.

Turning down toward the dock, she slowed to an imperceptible pace as she approached three shimmering seals at the end of the pier. One overly stout seal lifted his head, barked in her direction, then slid off into the dark blue water. A younger pup rolled on his back before following suit, disappearing below the surface of the cool waters where the Chetco River meets the ocean.

Billi breathed deeply of the salt air. "I could live here." She spun toward her husband only to discover she made her declaration to no one.

Stomping back up the dock, she marched into the boat house. Jack leaned forward over a small desk examining a map of the Siskiyou National Forest.

"MOUNT EMILY IS RIGHT HERE." The man with the close-cropped hair turned toward Billi, "Good Morning ma'am, how can I help you?"

She looked at the map before answering. "Morning. Do you have any boots that are already broken in that would fit him?" Her head tilted toward Jack.

He smiled at her. "I'm Les Covill, Forest Service, I'm not certain we've met."

"I'm Billi, and I don't need a pair." She smiled brightly. "I brought my own boots." She leaned in closer to the map. "Any good lakes for fishing up there?"

"Les, have the Army already sent men in?" Ignoring his wife, Jack faced the supervisor.

"Yes, sir." He answered, his focus remaining on Billi.

"Then I think my wife has the right idea about those boots. Could you help me with a pair before we take off?"

Les bobbed his head in affirmation. "How long you planning on staying up there?"

"At least two nights." Billi gave him one of her biggest smiles.

"Are any of the fires still burning?" Jack's question brought deep furrows to Les' brow.

"Yes, a few. We were darn lucky when that Jap dropped those fire bombs that it was so wet up there."

"How many are ahead of us?"

"Two of my young men who spotted the smoke are taking a few soldiers up to where they found the split trees and phosphorus on fire. But you should be able to catch up with them. I guess most of them didn't consider the condition of their boots before they left. My men radioed back that some of the Army guys have dropped off and are heading back."

They drove up the Winchuck River Road to Wheeler Creek trailhead and parked next to the Army jeeps. True to the Forest Service Supervisor's warning, a few soldiers leaned against the jeeps, boots off, with dust caught in the perspiration of their shirts.

Billi took the backpack Les helped her organize then stood in the mid-morning sunlight, waiting for the men. Nodding at the Army men, Les took the lead for the three-mile uphill hike into the dense forest where fires had ignited from the incendiary bombs dropped by a Japanese airplane. Billi fell in line behind Les who carried an "S" radio and a few rations. Jack kept his hat pulled down as he strode into the shade of the trees along the rock encrusted dirt trail. His large pack and old boots a different image from his usual city clothes.

"You are going to love this adventure," Billi whispered. Her voice reverberating the thrill of their wild surroundings.

"I just wish we weren't heading out with half the US Army and Japanese planes dropping incendiary bombs around us." Jack grumbled.

"Do you think they will drop more?" Billi hadn't considered that aspect of their journey.

He fell silent, an attribute of his job Billi now recognized as off limits information.

Les set a comfortable pace with Billi hot on his heels. Jack, sweating, relaxed into his stride, appearing almost calm in the beautiful surrounding of sun streaked tree limbs scooping down toward them. The three-mile switch back continued up toward the fire site through age old large trees. The freshly blazed trail emerged through the heavy brush to the site, the worn path easier to follow with the number of soldiers and rangers carving notches in the trees as markers. The threesome moved in silence under the canopy of cedars, hemlocks, tanoak, myrtle wood, Douglas firs, shore pine and spruce, the heart and soul of the Siskiyou National Forest. The peacefulness of their surroundings in drastic contradiction to the purpose of their journey.

Voices shouted ahead, breaking the spell of serenity. When they rounded one large cedar, they saw the backs of the men's uniforms huddled around an object. As they neared the site, they noted the crater, not overly large, with the ring of men squatting close.

"Hello, Les." Johnson, the young ranger, stood to address his supervisor.

Les nodded, lowering his radio and small pack. "Johnson."

Billi looked at the youthful face of the boy who stood before them. "Hello, I'm Billi. Is this your summer job?"

"Yes, ma'am. At least it was. I'm eighteen now and going to enlist." Johnson stood taller, proud of his intent.

As her husband helped her off with her pack, she noticed Johnson's expression when he turned to Jack, seeing his eye patch for the first time.

"Did you find this?" She thought of Danny, his youth, his head of red hair, enlisting at age seventeen.

"I got the call from Gardner, the ranger at Mt. Emily, yesterday afternoon. He'd seen smoke so I hiked down. There." He pointed, leading them a few feet from the crater. "Those are the fragments of metal casing and thermite pellets."

Billi and Jack stood side by side looking down on the blue-gray bomb casing with just a few of the pronounced strokes of Japanese kanji. When she looked up at Jack's face, she shook her head slightly. Not enough of the printing remained to make out one word. However, the source of the markings claimed their undisputable origin.

Army Sergeant Zlock came up behind the boy. "Thought it was one of ours at first, but it's defiantly the damn Japs, excuse me ma'am."

Billi folded her arms over her chest in defiance. "Those some of your men down there that couldn't take the hike?"

Jack interrupted. "How big was the ring of fire?"

"About 50 to 75 feet across," Johnson answered.

They walked the ring noting the split, sheared off trees and some of the singeing from the blaze that could not ignite the damp trees and soil.

When completed, Sergeant Zlock gathered his men and turned to Jack. "I'll have the report ready. Never seen so much brass pouring into the base. The newspaper broke the story before anyone told us about it. Everyone is hopping mad. But we've put a stop to all information getting out on this."

"Good." Jack nodded realized the man before him literally walked out of this fire pit into another.

When the small group had gone, Les pulled out lunch, handing out the sandwiches he had packed in. "You two sure you want to stay up here?"

Billi didn't let Jack get a word in, "We wouldn't have it any other way."

"There were a lot of eyes watching me last night," Johnson put in. "You might want to head up to Bear Wallow tower for the night. I can get you started on the trail."

"How far?" Jack did not sound overly enthusiastic.

"About eight miles," Johnson stated flatly.

The challenge hung in the air.

"Sounds good to me. Any fishing lakes along the way?"

"Not if you are going to get there by sunset."

"What a day." Billi slung her pack on the hard wood planks of the makeshift bed in the lookout tower. Her hair was damp from exertion, her cloths streaked with sweat and dust.

Jack stood at the door regarding the view.

"I hope you packed something to sooth my aching bones and feet." Her hands went to the arch of her back where the pack chaffed at her skin the long trek up the steep terrain.

"Only if you drink it."

"Ha. Don't tell me you don't want a nip."

"More than one, my dear." He dug into his pack and pulled out a canteen.

"Is that special FBI issue?" She teased.

"Be nice or I won't share."

Together they lifted the wooden flaps covering the open framed windows, bracing them securely in place. Huddled inside the small eight by ten room they admired the three-hundred-and-sixty-degree vista of the dark green valleys below with mountains beyond. In the west the sun began its quick descent behind Wheeler Ridge, splashing pink and purple hues across the sky.

"Isn't this heaven?" Billi sighed.

"Only because you're here with me to share it."

He took the two tin mugs that hung from his pack, filling them to the brim with the rich liquid.

"Mrs. Huntington." He offered her a mug. "What are you serving your husband for dinner?"

"Our usual, escargot, frog legs and steak." She plopped the can of beans on the shelf next to the sterno burner then pulled out a loaf of bread.

"You're truly amazing." He raised his tin cup drinking deeply as the sounds of the night surrounded them.

BILLI FELT CHILLED THE INSTANT the warmth of Jack's naked body left her side. She sat up to the new day breaking across the tree tops. When she twisted to move off the rock-hard platform of their bed, she felt the intense tightening spasm down her shins and thighs.

"I can't move," she moaned, lying back down. "I ache everywhere."

The smell of the Nescafe coffee encouraged Billi to sit up again.

"Come on, look at that," Jack insisted.

She pulled the bedroll around her as she stood looking out from their perch. Below, a sea of fog, white and crisp, concealed the treetops. The mesmerizing blanket of puff brought with it a silence edged with a sense of isolation. It felt as if they floated on high above an invisible world. She looked around at the drops of morning dew sparkling in the filtered light, decorating the brush and spider webs with magic crystals.

"Gardner, the lookout who saw the fire first from Mount Emily, said there'd been morning fog sweeping down the valley. He heard the airplane that sounded like a back-firing model A Ford. He couldn't make it out but noted it had pontoons, an unknown model. Gardner called it in on September 9th, two days ago, just about now at 6:24 a.m. No one responded or paid any attention to his sighting. They thought it was coast patrol."

The spell broken, Billi sensed Jack's frustration. The enemy so close, yet no one realized the threat. She posed her question a second time. "Do you think he will try again?"

"Yes."

She felt the palpitation of her heart increase. Here they were touching heaven, surrounded by deep, tree topped valleys, where mountain meets sky. Theirs should be a morning of lovemaking and bliss. But duty blurred their sight, like the dense fog below. What lie ahead for them, and for the world, would only be revealed with time.

The sound of an airplane drifting on the breeze, became stronger. Jack lifted his field glasses then spotted the craft as it twinkled in the sunlight.

"One of ours." He breathed a bit deeper. "Where the hell was he two days ago?"

They watched a few minutes more as the sun rose, causing the mist to disperse. More of the terrain became visible as the plane headed back toward the coast.

"Jack." She let the blanket slide to the ground. "Come back to bed."

He turned toward his wife, her naked body glowing in the morning light as she stretched like a wanton cat. "Christ woman." Was all he could mumble as he moved toward her.

"DID YOU GET IT?" Jack shouted.

"Try it now." Billi called down from the branch where she adjusted the antenna.

Jack stepped from the trunk of the cedar tree, stubbed his cigar out and clenched the unlit butt between his teeth. He flipped the switch on the "S" radio as it crackled to life.

"Calling Gold Beach Ranger Station, over," Jack spoke low and clear. He listened for the voice on the other end then responded. "Any reports of sightings?"

"Nothing, sir. Over."

Disappointed Jack barked into the radio. "We'll be there by three tomorrow. Over."

"Okay." He returned to the base of the cedar. "You can come down now."

Billi lowered the antenna in her husband's direction, then let the wire fall for him to catch. She felt her heart tighten at the reality their paradise would end far too soon. "Not just yet."

She sat a moment on the thick branch thinking of her cedar tree in her mother's back yard. The tree with its reddish bark where, as children, she, Eddy and Raymond carved their initials. A tear slid down her cheek, landing on her woolen plaid shirt. So much change to endure in one year: Ray dead, Eddy flying against the Japanese, Danny fighting somewhere in Europe, and Eileen in a relocation camp in the remote high desert of Idaho. Home. She felt it calling her again. Her home. Not the one where Jack visited on an irregular basis when his duty would allow him brief moments or reprieve. Not in her new surroundings among the other women she had grown to love and the baby that gave them hope. But her home, with her mother making lists as she conspired to regain her place in society. Billi could almost smell her mother's cooking as she sat high among the trees, unable to stop her tears.

Suddenly, it came to her, like a voice on the wind through the branches. She could no longer sit idle in the big house in Hillsborough. In confirmation, the breeze twirled the limbs around. She vowed to do more to end this war shredding everything she loved into fragments of compartmentalized existence. A vast world unfolded before her as she considered the various war fronts. She became determined to discover a way for greater involvement.

She heard the snap of a limb as her husband stepped from under the tree into the sunshine below. She could only see his right shoulder, the unlit cigar he held in his teeth, and the patch over his bad eye. Yet, he looked relaxed in these surroundings. Maybe they should not go back. They could spend the winter in the one room high on the mountaintop where lovemaking blended with the basics of nature.

Jack moved from sight when a sudden fear gripped her. She did not want to be without him by her side. How to juggle her pledge for involvement and the duties of a wife ripped at her gut.

Distracted by a huffing sound she looked in its direction. A five-point bull elk sniffed the air from the other side of the tree where Jack stood.

Billi picked a cone from the tree and threw it in Jack's direction. The buck froze, he lifted his head slightly again, exposing the white marking across his cheek. The beast's black nose twitched, then with horns lowered, he started in Jack's direction. She whistled then rattled the branch. The large animal's hooves hit the hard ground at a run followed by a thud and a moan. Then there was silence.

Billi slid down the tree, dangling her legs from the lowest branch. "Jack?"

"Shh."

She shifted on the branch, seeing the elks head inches from Jack. Without warning, the animals head pressed against Jacks face. Then the buck snorted and leapt over Jack's prone body.

Landing at the base of the tree, she raced toward her husband.

"What the hell happened?" She examined him.

"He took my damn cigar. Right out of my damn mouth." He wiped the side of his face, spitting.

"You're so lucky he didn't gore you."

"Jesus." Jack looked stunned.

She couldn't help herself as her laughter filled the silent woods that surrounded them.

JACK SAT ON A LARGE ROCK above the creek where Billi worked the riverbed sand into the cooking pan, scrubbing away any debris.

"Better build me a fire, husband." She stood, gathering their cleaned metal plates and pan.

"Yes, ma'am. I have enough wood for us to watch the stars by."

"Good, because I'm planning on bathing."

"In that case, I'll get it going immediately." His wry smile a treasure.

Jack moved to help her carry the few things up to the top of the ridge as the sun began to dip on the horizon. Gathering more wood, he paused as Billi started back down the trail, whistling, towel in hand.

Jack dropped the wood to follow. "Need help?"

"Not a bad idea as being near water, at sunset, in the woods can be dangerous."

"Madam." He caught up to her. "Keeping you safe from peril has become my lifelong endeavor."

In the filtered sunlight, as it angled through the trees, Billi stripped. Jack, taking her lead, followed suit. They ventured into the ice cold water, careful of the slippery rocks, to the center pool of the creek.

"You first," she teased.

"Oh no, no, this was your idea." His speech a bit breathless from the chilling water. "Ladies first," he added quickly.

She dropped with a yelp shooting back out just as quickly. Then lowered again with a deep breath. "This is delicious."

"You're not a good liar." He began to shake with cold.

"Better hurry." She raised her hand to splash at him when he dunked to his waist.

His yell ricocheted off the rocks and trees surrounding them.

"Well, at least you are keeping the bears away." She stood causing the water to drip from her white skin in gleaming rivulets. Her long legs moved swiftly toward the bank.

There was a thunderous splash behind her as Jack slipped going under. Again, he roared as he surfaced, then dripping, with the chill propelling him, he dashed past her. He scooped up his clothes scrambling up the trail.

The fire, having blazed for hours, burned red hot coals emitting leaping blue flames. They sat pressed together with stars glimmering above in an endless blue night.

"Doesn't it feel like we could just reach out and touch them?" Billi spoke softly, afraid to disturb the celestial heavens.

"O look at all the fire-folk sitting in the air! The bright boroughs, the circle-citadels there." Jacks voice rose as he chanted the words.

"Go on," she encouraged.

"Those were the only two lines that stuck with me. Hopkins was not just a poet but a Jesuit priest."

"I see, too much religion?"

"This is religion, above us." He put his arm around her as they silently beheld the beauty surrounding them.

Billi leaned back praying their newly formed bond would never end. She thanked God for giving them these brief moments. It had been heaven indeed to be perched on the mountain top where worries slid down the hillside, were buried in the morning fog, chased away by the afternoon sun, and as darkness fell, forgotten as they snuggled under the show of brilliant stars.

IT WAS EXACTLY 3 P.M. when they stepped from the bottom of the trail onto the old dirt road. Billi felt her heart sink as she observed her husband, his quiet, intense FBI persona covering him in the impenetrable shell of his occupation.

Young Johnson, leaning against the Forest Service car, smiled at them. "Howdy, glad to see you. Any problems?" He hurried toward Billi to help her with her pack.

"No, we did fine," Billi reassured him. "Even though it's damp, we spread the coals of our fire then soaked them with creek water."

Johnson nodded his appreciation for protecting his precious Siskiyou Forest.

"They're waiting for you in town." He hurried around to the driver's seat to start the engine.

The "they," and the young man's quick motions, foretold of what lay ahead. Billi felt the muscles in her back tense as she leaned against the back seat. The car rumbled down the old road as the three were caught in their own thoughts, leaving nothing but the sound of the engine between them.

As they drove down into the town of Brookings, Oregon, Billi let out a deep sigh. It was over. Their bit of a honeymoon on a lonely mountain top, a memory of stolen time from the realities of their lives.

"Can you find us a room for the night? One with a hot bath." Jack added as he stood, adjusting his shoulders. He guided Billi into the small office where men of different ranks and services waited.

"Glad to see you made it." Army Sergeant Zlock smiled.

Jack looked around the room at the men and nodded. "Any updates?"

"Not really." The disappointment showed on every face.

They looked from Jack to Billi then shuffled away from the desk where a map spread before them of the shoreline and mountain range. Jack moved forward to inspect the map.

"Is this a lighthouse?" He pointed to a small spit of land that jutted out into the ocean just off Port Orford.

"Yes, sir, Cape Blanco," a captain from the Navy interjected.

"Is it still lit at night?"

"I'm afraid so. It is a very dangerous part of the coast, windy, rocky, several boats were lost there before . . ."

"The submarine used the light to stand off from shore, launched the sea plane, which was probably carrying very little fuel due to the weight of the bomb, and then surfaced to fish the plane back out of the water and store it below. Now why is that light still helping the enemy?"

A Coast Guard Commander with the newly formed shore patrol looked directly at Jack, "We have men all up and down the shore in shacks, with radios and dogs. By foot it's hard going to cover so much coast."

"Horses." Billi suggested. "Use horses."

The men turned to her as if she were a boil on the backside.

She met their stares full on. "We rode on the beach as children."

Jack cleared his throat, then continued. "The news of the submarine is not to leave this room. If you can't turn the damn light off, have your men watch that lighthouse like a hawk, because the Japanese are. If they intend to drop more fire bombs to destroy our forests and our resources, let's not light their way."

He took Billi's elbow and escorted her out of the door.

# TWENTY SEVEN

Eddy's legs wobbled a bit as he carried his duffel toward the barracks. The weight of the duffel felt like nothing compared to that of his conscience. He was one of the lucky ones. While so many pilots did not return, here he stood on terra firma, in one piece. He had left this island innocent, eager for battle. Now, he felt the sobering weight of his long list of completed missions. He dropped the bag in the dust of the knoll and stood breathing the familiar scents of Oahu. Adjusting his sunglasses, he attempted to wipe away the image of his beloved PBY, a large gash slashing the Phantom's side wide open. He hadn't seen the rock waiting just below the surface in the dark. They called it heroism when he fought the rising water inside the cabin to pull Hank free, pushing him toward the arms of the rest of the crew and a life raft. He could still taste the salt water as it slid down his throat, choking him.

They'd been lucky when his favorite mechanic, Gus, promised he'd pieced her back together. Besides, his first reports of the success with the PBYs camouflaged in black, had just gotten higher up approval for expansion. So, when he got back, after marrying Lani, he would be ready to hit the night skies with the blessing of the brass.

Luck, he mused, rode with him.

He strode further into the sunlight, praying his luck would hold with Lani during his brief R & R. His unanswered letters bore holes in his heart. And tonight, after a quick shower with water from the base, not something rigged from a tree, he would seek the answer to the question that had haunted him for the last six months.

"Come on." Scooter slapped his back. "Let's get this over with so you can sleep without calling out her name."

Eddy adjusted his bag, following his co-pilot. "I don't call out her name, you SOB."

"No." Scooter gave him one of his devilish smiles. "You call out someone else's name."

"Well not yours, I hope."

The base at Kane'ohe held no surprises except for the influx of recruits. As had become his custom for good luck, he pressed his hand over the hole in the wall where the enemy bullet whizzed close to his head during the attack on December 7th. It seemed like a lifetime ago as he passed into the coolness of the mess hall.

Scooter approached with two juices in hand, extending one toward Eddy. "You want company?"

Eddy gulped down the chilled liquid. "No. Thanks."

"If you need me. I'll be the one dancing on the bar, somewhere in town."

"That narrows it." He put down his empty glass heading for the door.

"Hey, Eddy."

He turned back toward the man he had faced death with on so many occasions. "Yeah?"

"Good luck."

The invigorating trip back over the Pali, the winding road up the side of the mountain with its lush vegetation and flowers, floated by like an apparition in comparison to the bombed-out air strips and scorched shores of the islands where battle raged. Eddy's stomach tightened as he turned up the hill toward Aiea and Lani's home. No one had answered his many phone calls and the apprehension he felt gnawed at him more than when entering battle.

He hesitated at the base of the driveway. The shattered windows had long been replaced while the garden appeared even more lush and inviting. As he rang the doorbell, he shifted the flowers he had brought to his other hand, removed his white uniform cap, then felt his knees go weak. He rang again. When there was still no answer, he rounded the long house to the back yard. No one was in sight.

He ventured to the small chapel then stepped into the coolness of the afternoon light as the colorful designs from the windows streaked across the polished floors.

"Please let her be well and . . .," he whispered the prayer, which today he could not finish, fearful the spoken words would curse his dreams. He left the flowers by the small statue of the Blessed Virgin Mary then hurried to his car.

The grade school where Lani taught was locked up tight, everyone had gone home. He searched the beach where she might have taken the children to swim but beyond the barbed wire only a few soldiers splashed in the waves. He had to find her.

At loose ends, he drove to the Royal Hawaiian Hotel then parked down the street. Grabbing his flashlight for the blackout he knew would be mandatory soon, he strode past the palm trees to the main entrance on the side of the building. As he approached the desk, a sailor, reeking of rum, teetered toward the ocean where the sun prepared to set in the glory of reds and oranges. Eddy could not help but observe the change in his surroundings. The once impeccable interior showed definite signs of wear and misuse, as this majestic seaside hotel had been appropriated to house the men who fought below the waters in their submarines. The beautiful Pink Lady now a raucous playground for the sailors returning from months of living in the dark.

"May I help?" The young woman's voice caught him off guard and he stared at her blankly.

"There is a show tonight at Fort DeRussy." She pointed to the flyer on her desk. When he didn't answer she continued, "There are church services every day, and . . ."

"Do you know Lani Daniels?" He sounded so lost.

"No, but try the show. So many sailors say it's wonderful. A great cast, and local hula girls." She put a flyer in his hand then smiled promisingly at him.

"Thanks," he heard himself say before drifting off toward the hotel bar for a strong drink.

As the second whiskey arrived a sailor plopped down beside him. "I see they gave you a flyer to the show as well." The dark-haired man laughed. "I hear the babes are worth it. You goin'? I'm Tino Rosetti. The bastards call me Rosie."

"What will I be if I call you Tino?" Eddy didn't mind the distraction.

"One in a million." His smile showed cigarette stained teeth. "You just get here, flyboy?"

"On leave."

"You look lost?" Rosie downed his drink then waved his glass in the air for a refill.

"No, just can't find my girl."

"Hell, that's lost buddy. Come with us tonight and forget her for a while. I think we're headed to Chinatown after the show and it ain't for no damn tattoo." His smile gave the distinct impression of his eagerness for the wanton women of that district.

Eddy's third drink concluded the conversation with the acceptance of tailing along with Rosie and his buddies to the show.

The Theater was packed with service men of all shapes and sizes, sporting a variety of uniforms, overflowing the seats, floor and sides of the cramped room. The MP's had missed the bottle Rosie stashed in his pants and he handed it over to Eddy as the lights dimmed.

"Just don't start singin'." He laughed, his breath as strong with liquor as the bottle he had just passed along.

"How did you know I can sing?" Eddy kidded as he took a long sip.

Rosie snatched the bottle back. "You look the type."

The third routine sashayed onto the stage. One of the girls brought Eddy to his feet. "Lani! Hi baby, I'm home." He shouted toward the slender figure standing at the microphone. "That's her . . ."

Rosie grabbed his belt pulling him down. "Sure, bud. We all love that one."

"No, that's my girl, the one I was talking about."

"Shut up." A voice from behind gave a warning.

For a moment, he questioned if it was really his gal as he waited for the song to begin. Her long glorious hair now cut in the shoulder length rage of Hollywood, her dress no longer of the island, but of mainland America.

Eddy listened as Lani's voice took hold of his heart. Yes, it was his love. The imploring lyrics of *I Wonder When My Baby's Coming Home*, took his breath away. He was home. He was sitting right here at her feet.

She started the second verse when, without warning, the lights went out in the theater. Yet, she did not stop. Lani's voice rang out, unfaltering, pure and strong. The words floated over the men like a dream, eliciting visions of their loved ones and hope even in the uncertainty of darkness.

Eddy pulled out his flashlight, flicking the beam on her face. A gasp ran through the room while others followed suit as the soft single glow evolved into one strong stream of light. As she swayed to the rhythm, illuminated by the many golden torchlights, the men watched riveted in utter silence. When the last chord of the music drifted into silence, the room erupted with thunderous cheers. Eddy could barely contain his beating heart. Lani, more than ever, cast her spell over him.

"Thank you for sharing your light." Lani bowed, all pau, all finished.

The crowd cheered again. No one could subdue American ingenuity. Their ticket to the future depended on that genius. Tonight became a prime example, as long as there was a song and a simple beam of light, by God, there was hope.

When the lights blinked back to life, the men continued clapping. While the cast came back on for their final curtain call, Eddy headed out of the theater then ran around to the stage door to wait. Minutes passed as he tipped his hat at the exciting singers, dancers, actors and musicians, yet Lani never emerged. He caught the stage door as one of the actors exited then dashed inside. Just as he passed a group of young women starting for the exit, he caught sight of Lani.

She stopped, catching her breath, clutching her purse closer to her chest, her face a mix of alarm and joy.

"You're here. I meant to write . . ."

Eddy had her in his arms. He kissed her and she responded, melting the months of anxiety away as he pressed her body to his.

"Oh, you don't know how much I have thought of this moment." He whispered into her hair.

"Hey Lani," one of the other performers kidded as they passed. "I wouldn't let your husband see you doin' that."

Eddy's heart stopped. He held her at arm's length watching the tears of truth streaming down her cheeks.

"She's kidding right? I'm going to be your husband. Right?"

"Come with me." Her head bent toward the floor, as if to inspect her shoes, then she walked out under the starlight. A stunned Eddy followed in a trance of disbelief up the slope behind the building.

"I didn't write you because I didn't know how to put it into words," she began tentatively.

"I hope you can find those words now." Eddy tried to hold back the anger he felt surging through his veins.

"I could not marry you."

"What? Why? Your father gave us his permission. Remember?"

She looked at him now, whispering through her tears, "I could never give you the sons we spoke of."

"What?"

"The bombs. The blast. When it shattered the window and I was—I am no longer a woman who can bear children. I will never have a child of my own. I could not do that to you." She reached her hand up to gently touch his face. "I love you, Eddy. I always will."

"I don't care about that, Lani. I only want to be with you." As he spoke the words, he knew they were lies. The image of their children had been part of the dream they had built together. "We can adopt."

"I already have, in a way." Her hand floated back to her side and he saw the simple gold ring that bound her to another.

"What do you mean? I love you. I . . .'" He stepped back to look up at the heavens for strength. The same heavens he had filled with dreams of their life together. "Who?"

"Please forgive me. This is my fault. I should have answered your letters." Her new tears reflecting the hardship of her decision.

"Who?" his voice was louder this time.

"Mr. Kani, the one with the three small children, whose wife died last year. You remember them? The little ones who danced hula with you before the war did this to us. They needed me. And I needed them. I am a mother to children I did not bring into this world. It was my choice."

Eddy slumped to the ground his legs no longer able to support his frame.

"You can still have your sons, Eddy. I did this for you too." She sat beside him.

"That's rich. You got married to that man for me? Jesus Christ, why didn't you write me? I wouldn't have let you do this."

"And that is just why I didn't write you. I had to make up my own mind. Believe me. It is better for both of us."

"How the hell can you say that?" His voice echoed off the back of the building.

An MP rounded the corner then slowly strolled further down the walkway.

"I had better go. They will be waiting." She rose looking down at the man she professed held her heart.

"Can I see you again?" He knew her answer before she said it.

"No. Unless it is here, in the theater, where I come to forget what I have done to you."

She kissed his forehead, "Aloha No Au Ia 'Oe."

He watched her gracefully stride as she passed the MP, nodding in the guard's direction before disappearing into the shadows.

THE MOON WAS HIGH above Kane'ohe over the Koolau Mountains. Eddy sat in the white sand leaning against the simple white cross that bore the name of his friend.

"Son of a bitch, Sam," he cried to his friend's ghost. "She's married. What the hell do I do now?" He took another sip of his whiskey feeling the warm breeze sweep over him. "I just can't, I just can't let that happen. What's it like being dead? Huh? Because that's how I feel right now. Goddamn dead."

He stood then staggered toward the water. Through the haze of booze, he watched the surf catching the moonlight as it rippled down the beach, the mist of white spray floating into the air. Eddy stooped to pick up a piece of the incandescence that he and Lani had used to paint each other's body. The memory of that magical night pulling him, unsteadily into the surf. How gently they had spread the tiny dots over each other in the erotic steam of love. He could feel her pulse under his fingers racing as he had smeared the magic organism down her neck and over her breasts.

Rage took hold as he fell into the surf, kicking at it and the visions it stirred.

"Goddamn you." He flung the bottle high, watching it plummet into the ocean with the sucking sound of lost dreams. A wave knocked him forward again and he struggled, the weight of his clothing adding to his fight. "I hate you." His fist pounded the water. "I hate you."

"Hey, Eddy," a voice came at him from the dark. "You want to be shark bait?"

"Who's that?" Eddy stood dripping, facing the moonlight. "What the hell do you care about me?"

"I have to fly with you again, you son of a bitch."

"That you, Scooter?" He headed for shore when a wave caught him, tumbling him into the glistening sand.

His friend started toward the water's edge. "Yeah, come on."

"She's married." Eddy lay in the surf, letting the foam of the waves roll over him.

Scooter leaned down, hooking his arm around his drunken friend, he pulled him up with the next wave. "Yep, I heard. But you still have me," He added lightly.

"Shit." Eddy spit sand from his mouth. "Thanks for the offer, but I'm taken."

"Yeah, well you were almost taken by those mating hammerheads out there." Scooter helped Eddy to his feet, the weight of his friend as heavy as his darkened soul. They faced the ocean together, where the large sharks shimmered just below the surface in the dance of nature.

"Well, maybe that's where I belong. Dead in the sea."

"Not while I'm your co-pilot, my boy. Come on. Tomorrow is a new day." Scooter shifted Eddy's weight then, arm in arm, they staggered up the sand toward the bachelor's barracks.

# TWENTY EIGHT

JACK HAD DISAPPEARED AGAIN SETTING BILLI's blood on fire. They had returned to the isolated Hillsborough house when, in less than two days, he did not come home. Billi stormed into the kitchen to find Bella feeding the baby.

"I never seen no mama not take to her baby like Miss Lilly be doin'." She smiled down on the small infant almost lost in the folds of her arms.

"Hello sweetheart." Billi leaned over the baby as his small fists flew into the air, waving at the new image before him. "She will come around. How is she today?"

"Refusin' to get dressed." Bella's voice resounded with the anguish she felt, a reaction to the child she had raised behaving so badly. "But, I got you, lil man." She rocked and hummed to the baby who sucked at the bottle contentedly.

Billi slumped across from Bella, pouring herself a cup of coffee from the steaming, polished silver service.

"Jack'll be fine. Don't go botherin' your pretty head over him. Nothin' is goin' to get that stubborn man. Here." She stood. "Hold this child. I'm fixin' you breakfast. You need to keep up your strength too."

The child nestled into Billi's arms then looked at her with his large brown eyes, a reflection of his father's eyes, as Bella draped a burping towel over her shoulder. Without warning, the baby began to fuss, puckering up his face like an angry little man.

"Burp him, he has gas from that bottle. This lil man needs his mama's milk the right way." Bella continued scolding over the eggs she swirled in a bowl.

Billi lifted the baby over her shoulder then gently patted from his small backside up his spine to the nap of his delicate, unstable neck. He calmed down before letting out a loud burp emitting a bit of spittle which dripped down Billi's back past the towel. She hummed while bouncing the baby as he responded with the delightful cooing sounds of a happy infant.

"You're goin' to be a fine mama. I just need to get some fat on your bones." Bella's chuckle an acknowledgment of her approval.

The door swung open as Lilly marched in with her flowing robe trailing a bit. "Bella, I have been ringing. Oh, my lord, look at what that baby has done to the back of your dress." She flew around the table unable to look at her child or the natural part of burping a baby.

"Lilly, you hold your son for a while, I have to check on the mail." Billi stood, adjusted the child in her arms, before extending him toward his mother.

"No. Bella can hold him. I'm just here for some coffee and then I'm going back to bed." Her hand shook as she poured the coffee.

Billi took the baby to Bella. "Would you leave us alone for a moment please." The other women's eyes grew large as she accepted the baby, clamping her mouth shut. Billi held the door as the older woman carried the newborn into the front hall.

When the kitchen door swung shut Billi rounded the table to stand in front of Lilly. The two young women glared at each other in silence.

"He is your child, made with love and pride from the man you married. A fine man, who wanted children and would be appalled by your behavior."

"How do you know? He's dead. And I'll never love another man again." She plopped into the chair turning her back to Billi.

Billi pulled the chair around toward her. "You spoiled brat. You have hope in that beautiful baby. Your son. Do you know how many women don't have what you do? A child. Something of the man that has gone. Something worth living for."

"Just because you seduced my brother, doesn't mean you can talk to me like that. What, did you tell him you were pregnant? Is that why he married you, Ginger?"

The hand that slapped Lilly's face left a mark, red and hot, like the person who delivered the blow. Billi stomped to the door, took the baby from Bella returning to stand over Lilly. She gently lowered the baby into his mother's arms.

"Say hi to your mother, darling," Billi's voice was trembling with rage. "Shhh. It's okay."

Bella stood behind Billi, her arms on her hips, defying Lilly to speak.

Lilly looked down at the small being in her arms, the unmistakable resemblance to his father. Tears splashed on his bare arm and blue night-shirt. "I'm scared," Lilly whispered.

"We all are. But this baby needs you." Billi knelt beside her. "The more you hold your son, the stronger you will be."

No one had noticed the door open and close behind Mrs. Huntington until she spoke. "The biggest mistake I ever made was not holding my children."

Without saying a word Bella held a chair for her long-time employer. As the matriarch sat, she looked up at Bella with the acknowledgment of who had reared her children.

"Hummph. I better put more eggs on. This lil man is goin' to need all of us women to be strong to care for him." She moved toward her stove.

"Have you decided on a name?" Mrs. Huntington inched closer for a better view of her grandson.

Lilly looked around the room as if naming a child was a brand-new concept.

Billi touched the soft fuzz of golden hair. "We can't keep calling you baby. You need a fine name."

"Timothy?" Lilly bobbed her head with her decision.

"Timothy Archer sounds wonderful." Billi smiled aware the name mimicked that of his father Todd Archer.

"Timothy Huntington Archer." Lilly firmly announced as she drew her child closer to her chest.

The room seemed to heave a sigh of relief as mother bent over child, kissing away her own tears as they splashed on the soft newborn skin.

"HEY, EDDY."

Eddy turned to see his favorite mechanic, Gus, emerge form under the palms. It felt good to return to battle and to be back at the base at Cactus, the code name for Guadalcanal. His failure with Lani would only push his wings further into the fracas inching across these islands. He waited for Gus under the overhanging fronds at the edge of the water near Henderson Airfield hiding his PBY, the Phantom. So far today, the blue sky over this portion of the Solomon Islands held no enemy aircraft buzzing at the field, destroying the surroundings and their nerves.

"Lookie what I found for you." Gus held the black cat up in the air, the animal's long legs dangling over his meaty, tanned forearm. "What do ya think? Good luck, huh?"

Eddy smiled at Gus. "No bad. Put him aboard."

Gus studied the cat. "Ah, it's a girl."

"Even better," Eddy stroked the head of their new mascot.

Where Gus found most of the items he always seemed to have on hand remained a mystery. The mechanic's ingenuity morphed into a legend as big as his style of dress. While not standard issue, the look defined Gus. His white sailor's hat, smudged with the grease from his duties as a mechanic for the big Catalinas, also sported several large holes cut around the crown for ventilation. He'd cut his sleeves to the top of his shoulders and made shorts of his trousers. However, his appearance cemented the truth, if something needed fixing, you called Gus.

"What's this?" Scooter adjusted his sunglasses.

Eddy laughed. "Our new mascot."

Scooter didn't respond, so Eddy continued. "We'll call her Midnight. Our very own Midnight Marauder."

The two watched their crew greet their new member as they entered. Fletch, tucked his latest map under his arm to pet her head. The two side gunners, Charlie and Allen, silently stroked her back. At first, Hank stood back, eyeing the black beast. Then he tickled her under her chin, whispering something inaudible. Beau stopped to scratch behind her ears.

"Beauregard, you believe in mascots?" Eddy eyed him seriously.

Beau continued to scratch when suddenly the cat's paw stretched playfully his direction. "This one likes us and will bring us back alive. Right?"

Her paw batted through the air.

"That's the ticket." Gus stepped up the ladder then gently put the cat inside the PBY. "She'll bring you back safe."

"Well, that settles it." Scooter smacked Eddy on the back. "Ready?"

Eddy understood his co-pilot's statement. It was their first flight after their brief respite in Hawaii. A trip that still reverberated with the shock of Lani's marriage to someone else. Yet, "ready" held another meaning. Was he ready to go on living and fighting? Or had the cut been so deep he intended to draw them into danger by taking unnecessary chances in response to his broken heart by putting an end to his agony to die a hero's death?

Eddy stood firm. "Our new mascot won't be the only one bringing us home alive."

"Good. Then let's go find the Tokyo Express and give 'em hell."

As the sun set, they skipped with their heavy load of bombs across the small chop before lifting into the darkening sky. Their path would take them high over "The Slot," a strip of the Solomon Sea whose waters ran between several islands in the New Georgia Sound. Each nook and cranny along these shores presented possible danger as the Allies patrolled between Bougainville and Guadalcanal. While under the cover of night, the Japanese cargo ships slipped their troops much needed food and ammunition.

Controlling this vital span of islands in the South Pacific area of the ocean began in February 1942 when the Japanese captured the exiting base of Rabaul, at the tip of New Britain, in the Australian Territory of New Guinea. The enemy quickly established the area as their major jumping off point for the rest of the islands leading to Australia, just over one thousand miles away. By August, the Imperial forces pushed dangerously close, having spread from Burma down to Java while capturing the upper half of New Guinea. Very little remained between the Japanese forces and the vulnerable island of Australia. Seizing the vast resources of that country would bolster Nippon supplies, skyrocketing their morale. Therefore, stopping those fighting night and day at

Guadalcanal for their Emperor, who expected his soldiers to die before surrendering, became imperative not only for Australia, but the world.

American boots hit the ground on August 7th of that same year to take Henderson Airfield. US troops, led by the Marines, continued their assault against the entrenched Japanese, slugging it out in a grueling jungle battle fought through mud, mosquitoes, dengue fever and a relentless enemy. The treacherous Japanese tactics including attacking in the cover of night, created constant skirmishes with little rest. So far, for the first two months, the Allies gained little ground, just lost lives.

It was just before 2:00 a.m. when, through the low cloud cover, they saw barges hugging the shores heading toward Vella Lavelle Island.

"Oh, they are sneaky." Eddy could feel his adrenalin surging at the sight. "Call in their position."

"Those must be flat bottom boats, easier to get men and supplies to shore." Scooter adjusted his safety belts for an ensuing attack.

"Yep. And easier to offload if hit." Eddy tightened his grip on the controls.

"Comin' at them from behind?"

"Like the prowling black beast that we are." Eddy noted the position of the half-moon then swung wide, avoiding casting any recognizable shadow.

Battle built a team, they attacked with precision, side gunners ready. Their dangerous cargo of heavy bombs waiting. Approaching the line of barges low, they prepared to strike on boats carrying troops.

"We're on them." Eddy announced. "Drop." He counted to five. "Drop."

One bomb exploded on the deck of a barge, igniting a blaze which quickly spread across its surface. The second smashed into the next ship, sending water, bodies and bits of the boat high into the night. As the one boat began to sink, the second ship listed to port, out of formation. It took a few minutes for the enemy to register the assault, firing in retaliation at the large swooping black object.

Eddy heard the bullets rip through his right wing as he adjusted his position with the strain of the draft. They were too low. He saw the housing on one barge spike in the air before him then pulled back hard. Bullets ripped through the air around them. Now the boats toward the front of the line, awake to the battle, aimed their deadly guns into the darkness above them.

Eddy circled out of range.

"We have one more bomb?" He watched Scooter.

"Let's not take it back."

Eddy nodded. "Come on Midnight, we're counting on you."

He waited until the clouds took their position over the small light of the moon. Driving at the second boat from the lead, he flew just above the dark waters toward the long side flank of the barge, his black camouflage blending in with the surroundings. The release of the last bomb hit its mark with brilliant success.

"Trees. Shit trees." Scooter shouted.

Again, the strain of the pull against the controls ran though his entire body. A thud bounced the plane once as they climbed higher into the sky.

"Report," Eddy demanded into his microphone.

"I'll check, but a pontoon might be dented."

He waited, still climbing, then noticed one of his side gunners had not responded. "What's up with Allen? Hey Allen?"

Fletch's voice responded. "Allen's hit and out, but breathing."

"How bad?" Eddy held his breath.

"Losing blood."

Eddy heard another voice in the small area of the gunner and knew his crew would do the best they could for their injured member. It was his job to get them back as swiftly as possible.

"Enemy at three-hundred coming in fast." Scooters voice caught everyone's attention.

"Hang on. Beau, take Allen's gun. Everyone hold fire until needed." He heard his flight captain scramble toward the side gunner's position.

Instead of continuing his climb, right into the path of the much quicker Zeke, Eddy started a descent, leveling off just above the water. He could not outrun the Japanese fighter, or outmaneuver him, but he could outwit him. Hovering close to shore where there was no light, he flattened out and prayed.

Just as swiftly as the Zero approached, it disappeared, flying right over the slower PBY.

It seemed everyone exhaled in unison as Eddy pulled up higher from the murky sea below.

"His bleeding's slowed, but he's having trouble breathing."

Eddy began to sweat. He had never lost a man before and did not plan on starting that trend now.

"Hang on Allen. Hang on."

THE RISING SUN WARMED his back as Eddy sat on the steps outside the infirmary. Their new mascot, Midnight Marauder, fulfilled her duties, paying for her keep. The bullet hit Allen, piercing his stomach then embedding in a rib. Yet, he was going to make it. As the sun rose higher, the rest of the crew slept while Gus patched the holes in the wings.

Eddy stood when Scooter headed his way. "He's okay." He turned to enter the infirmary with his co-pilot on his heels.

The stench of rancid flesh and blood assaulted his nostrils and he unconsciously held his breath. They passed beds where those near dying looked to the sky with blank eyes. Some called for their mothers, while others sought the help from a god who did not appear to have a heart.

Allen's bed sat pressed up against the half wall, lined with mosquito netting. He lay still, his eyes shut tight against the sun beating through the tent, with his head drooped to one side. A spot of red seeped through his white bandage wrapped around his chest. His breathing, even and regular, brought a sense of relief to Eddy.

Eddy squatted next to the bed, he felt the lump in his throat tighten at the sight of his side gunner, his responsibility. "Hey, Allen. The good news is you're going to be fine. We'll all be waiting for you to recover."

"You bet," Scooter punctuated Eddy's claim.

The wounded gunner did not move, his eyes remaining shut.

"He was awake a while ago," a voice from behind them offered.

They turned to see another soldier in the bed next to Allen. His leg in a cast up to his hip, and his right arm bandaged.

Without being questioned the Marine started in, "You fly boys need to get those bastards. I was in the battle at Matanikau River last week. They put us ashore to get the Japs making their way toward our airfield, only to find out our damn commanders picked the wrong landing site.

Japs everywhere. So, they had one of our ships point its big guns at the shore. Blew the hell out of some of them. It was grizzly."

"How did you get out?" Scooter always liked the details.

"The Coast Guard rushed back in with their landing crafts to get us out. This one guy, a real hero, positioned his boat between the last Marine getting off the island and enemy fire. He just kept shooting his machine gun, until he was hit. His last four words were, 'Did they get off?'"

Eddy hesitated, "Did he make it?"

"No." The Marine blew out a long breath of air. "His name was Douglas Munro, he deserves a damn medal. God bless the Coasties for saving my life, such as it is."

Eddy stood, extending his hand to shake the one good limb of the Marine. "You'll be fine. Shipping home soon?"

"Yeah." The injured man grabbed Eddy's hand, squeezing it hard, as tears formed in his eyes. "But I'll be back. In the meantime, do me a favor."

"Anything," Scooter and Eddy assured him in unison.

"Stay alive and keep killing those bastards. They're ruthless. They sneak up on you in the night, come crawling out of the dark with their bayonets and knives right into your fox hole. Who the hell attacks at night? They're crazy and don't care about life, especially their own. It's an honor to die for their Emperor. Jesus. That's what makes them so dangerous."

"Will do." Eddy looked straight into the man's bloodshot eyes as he made the vow.

"When he wakes up," Scooter interjected nodding toward Allen, "will you tell him we were here and will be back?"

"You got it."

"Don't let those bedpan commandos get to you." Eddy shot back as he headed out the door.

Eddy took a long drag on his cigarette before turning to face Scooter. They sat in silence under the brilliant sunshine, watching the puff of a cloud drift in the blue horizon. He shook his head then tossed the butt of his cigarette into the crushed-up coral creating the pathway to the infirmary. "Our three hits don't seem like enough."

"They add up." Scooter sounded encouraging. "Look, when we take out a transport boat, we kill hundreds."

"If they don't swim to shore. That's why those barges hug the shoreline."

"That and to hide against the trees. Hopefully the sharks get them."

"The Tokyo Express." Eddy kicked at a piece of coral. "Let's go check on Gus and see how soon we can get back up there."

When they rounded the corner of the beach where the Phantom sat just off a small inlet, hidden by the overhang, they spotted Gus. He held a brush dripping white paint while he stood back admiring his work.

Eddy laughed. As most things in war, customs are born to boast and boost morale. The new contingent of the expanded use of the black cats wing of the Navy had developed its own markings for strikes on enemy ships. The first symbol—the head of the cat. As the aircraft met with more success, the image of the painted cat acquired more detail. The image on their PBY, the Phantom, had expanded to included eyes and now two paws.

"Don't run out of paint," Eddy teased. "You'll be adding the entire body soon enough."

"As long as you return her in one piece," Gus shot back. "How's Allen?"

"He'll make it. I'm heading up to command to see who they can give us until he's back on his feet." Eddy walked closer to his plane to inspect the repairs. "How long?"

Gus lifted his hole-filled hat to wipe his brow. "A few days. I have to tear off some parts from some junked planes over there then tack on some patches and straighten out that pontoon. But the Phantom will fly again."

Eddy felt the rush those few words sent through his body. Another chance to keep his promise.

Scooter smacked his friend's back. "That means we have time for me to win back some of my money."

"Fat chance," Eddy scoffed.

"Yeah, when I've won all your money, I'm going after your shell collection."

"Uw-wee." Gus shook his head. "Now that's really going for the meat."

"Here they come." Eddy shaded his eyes at the sight of the incoming Zeros. He watched with disgust as an enemy plane screeched low over the airstrip, firing into a palm tree, cutting it in half, casting shards in various directions.

Several times a day and into the night, the Japanese bombed Henderson Air Field. The US would protect their base with anti-aircraft guns, fighter planes and prayers. Then the Seabees would dig up more coral to fill in the holes from the blasts. The enemy attempted to destroy not only the airstrip but the Allies' nerves as sleep became a dream with the booming of guns the norm.

# TWENTY NINE

BILLI FELT THE MATTRESS BOW A little as Jack slipped into their bed. She rolled over leaning on her elbow, eyeing her husband still in his suit and shoes. Her feet hit the cold floor and as she rounded the bed to help him, listening to his unintelligent mumblings. By the time she removed his second shoe, his snoring filled the room.

Knowing sleep would not find her again due to the racket he emitted in fitful slumber, she took his shoes downstairs. A thick mud covered them, and she could only wonder at the source. The shoes needed a good polishing, she reasoned, looking forward to the simple task.

Several days had slowly rambled by between Jack's promise of, 'I'll be home tomorrow morning' and his actual arrival. Time and time again, days stretched into weeks, as she questioned her place in this grand house.

Remembering the wallpaper in her bedroom back in Seattle, she shook her head. Odd, she mused, when she first met Jack, he watched her every move, making her feel like one of the caged birds in the design that covered her walls. Their cage doors sat open, but the small creatures remained inside seemingly observing the cherry blossoms flowering around them, unaware they could flee. She did not know how much longer she could simply look through the gilded surroundings without becoming more involved supporting those fighting for the existence of America.

The sun hid behind the morning mist casting a subtle light on the bright fall colored bushes outside the kitchen windows. She found the shoeshine box and spread old newspaper on the table. Working the thick black paste into the leather soothed her nerves while keeping her sense of uselessness at bay. With each stroke of the cloth the gloss of the leather brightened with the reflection of the hanging light fixture. The movement affirmed her decision. She would speak with Jack. Waiting, not knowing if Jack would return, or if she attracted danger to this house, left her sleepless and edgy.

"Hummph."

Billi jumped at the sound.

"If this ain't a changin' world," Bella declared as she pushed through the door. Still in her long, pink, chenille robe, she stood at the sink. She waited until she had the pot on the stove for coffee before sitting across from Billi. "Yous remindin' me of my son Howard."

Billi paused briefly. "I'm certain your son would do this much better than I can. What have you heard from him lately?"

"He ain't sayin'. I don't care, I just want him to come home in one piece."

"Same here." Billi held the shoe out for Bella to inspect. "How did I do?"

"Hummph. It's a good thing you're married to Mr. Jack." Her large bosoms heaved as she chuckled at her own joke.

Billi laughed too as she stood. "I'm pouring you coffee this morning."

Bella didn't resist but just kept staring at the one shined shoe on the table before her. "He just has to come home alive. He's all I have."

"You have us Bella. And that baby will need you for years to come." She changed the subject. "Jack's upstairs snoring away."

Bella raised her large brown eyes to watch Billi. "He sure do love you. Hummph. You come in here acting all Ginger-like, puttin' us in a tailspin and all. I thought the good Lord had gone crazy. But, it's just fine. Just fine."

As the coffee perked over the heat of the stove it sent the enticing aroma into the room. Billi waited until the brew bubbling in the see-through cap on the top of the pot churned a dark rich color.

"You know, I don't even know if you take cream." Billi poured a cup then handed it to the gray-haired woman.

"I like it black. But if I'm feelin' sassy, I put in cream."

Billi went to the refrigerator then pulled out the glass bottle of cream. "Today is a sassy day."

Bella chuckled. "All right then."

"You know, my mother had a suggestion on how to find out where the men are stationed." Billi picked up Jack's other shoe as she explained the concept of changing the middle initial of a name as a code that would eventually spell out the town or continent.

"You're missin' your mama, aren't you?"

Billi's smile appeared lifeless as she picked up a clean cloth to work the final shine on the leather.

"Like I said, he sure does love you."

"I know," Billi whispered. She felt Bella could see right through her. Her eyes began to water at the mere thought of leaving this family.

"And you sure do love him . . ."

The sound of the baby fussing made them both turn toward the door. Lilly entered cradling her son, hair flat on one side and old robe draped over her at angles with her frame. Yet the smile on her face lit up the room.

"He slept through the night." She offered the bundle to Bella who opened her arms with joy. "Furthermore, I changed him. Just look."

Bella peeked under the nightgown exposing the white cotton diaper with lopsided safety pins, yet the twisted cloth still covered the essentials.

"Wonderful." Billi kidded. "I knew you had a domestic side."

"Well, I see you do too. Or is that yet another occupation of yours?"

Billi picked up the shoeshine brush then went at the leather as if it were the enemy. "Just keeping busy."

The silence filling the room felt claustrophobic, as Billi realized all eyes measured her frenetic movement. Finally satisfied with the sheen of the leather, she stood.

"It's fine. Jack's home now." She ignored Bella's and Lilly's looks of concern as she swooshed out the door with Jack's shining shoes.

As Billi entered the bedroom Jack's head popped up, he snorted, then rolled over.

"Let me help you out of your clothes." She went to him, gently tugging at his arm.

"They dropped more firebombs on Oregon on September 29$^{th}$."

Billi went motionless. "Where? Was anyone hurt? Did they get him?"

Jack rolled back over, looking up at his wife. "Near Port Orford again. So far they haven't found anything in the forest. It was extremely damp so if there was a fire, it probably just went out after impact. No one was hurt."

"Did they find the sub?" She held her breath.

"No." He took her hand. "The last attack we leaked after a few days to boost morale and confidence in our fire patrols. Also, to alert the citizens of the reality that America could be bombed. It seemed to have gotten through to some of the civilians of the danger, even on our shores. But, this one we're keeping under wraps for a while."

"Are we headed back to the mountains?" She felt her heart flutter with the memories of their nights spent under the stars where the world at war drifted so very far away.

He pulled her onto the bed next to him. "I would give anything to be back there with you."

She snuggled closer, listening as his breathing deepened, once again, into the rhythm of sleep.

BILLI WIGGLED UNDER THE COVERS searching for the warmth of her husband. When her efforts were not rewarded, she sat up, scanning the dark room. His shoes were still by the dresser, so he couldn't be far. Cinching her bathrobe tight against the cold, she ventured down the hall to the study. Again, there was no sign of Jack in the dark, still room.

Of course, he had slept most of the day and would be in the kitchen with a pile of food before him. She started back down the hall toward the back staircase when a sound from the other direction caught her attention. Hugging the wall, she tiptoed toward the small balcony that overlooked the grand living room, just off the wooden steps leading down to the foyer.

Jack had told her of the many times during her parent's large parties, he and Lilly had taken up their secretive stations to spy on the activities below. The concept made Billi feel a bit childish but none the less inquisitive.

She heard Jack grunt then saw the flickering of the fire cast frenzied shadows on the long dark curtain covering the expansion of stain glass. She dropped to her knees, then her belly to slide forward.

Below Jack crouched with his long sword suspended before him. He shifted from one shoeless foot to the other, his bare back glistening with sweat. When he spun toward her, she froze. He was not wearing his eye patch. He continued, not acknowledging her presence. His swift movements like a dance, sideways, lunging, recoiling to a low crouch, up on the very tips of his toes, his sword constantly slashing an invisible enemy.

Billi watched breathlessly. His fierceness, agility and concentration commanded her undivided attention. There was no mistaking his message, he would be ready when trouble crept into this household.

The significance of his training sent a chill down her spine. Jack practiced below, preparing to kill his nemesis in the manner Akio would choose, with the blade. A cut that would not heal, like the scar on Jack's face.

She thought she heard the baby cry from the bedroom down the hall and slipped backwards further into the shadows. She sat a moment in the dark watching Jack's shadow on the curtain, larger than life as the blade sliced through the air. However, it was the soft cooing of the baby that dug the deepest into her heart. She could not be the reason danger crept into this home. Her heart raced, pumping her decision through every vein and into her pounding head. She would have to find a way to tell Jack.

As she made her way back to their room, she heard his feet heavy on the wooden steps and hurried to shut the door behind her. Once back in their bed, she pretended sleep as he strolled across their room in the dark.

"Did you get something to eat?" She attempted innocence.

"Sorry if I woke you." He climbed across the bed toward her.

"It's okay, I . . ."

Not given a chance to finish her lie, he slipped on top of her and she tasted the salt of his perspiration. The sensation mixed with the image of his muscles flexing before the fire created a response as primitive and wild as the flames.

Akio controlled his frustration. Their submarine still had two incendiary bombs aboard, yet they headed home. He steadfastly argued with the captain of the I-25 sub, the bomb must be dropped on the enemy. However, the captain held fast, not wanting to risk surfacing to launch the Glen seaplane again, fearing the US Navy air patrol who waited above the waters.

He snorted then smiled at their other successes, concluding their mission not a complete loss. Luck rode the seas with them. As they scoured the West Coast for targets, they torpedoed the merchant marine ship the SS *Camden* on October 4th then watched the men abandon ship. On the evening of the 5th, Akio thanked the gods for their next gift. The *Larry Doheny*, the same vessel he had fired on unsuccessfully while aboard the I-17, sailed into view. A second opportunity to kill plied through the water above them carrying a full cargo of oil. The submarine crew sent two deadly torpedoes at the large oil tanker then waited. The strike resounded through the water while flames burst through the sky. The *Larry Doheny* buckled on the starboard side before sinking, leaving her men scurrying for their lives.

Oh, he had wanted to surface to spray the retreating sailors with their deck guns, but the sinking ship lay just off the Oregon coast where the heightened American shore patrols responded quickly. They remained below the waters slithering back into the night.

Thoughts of home occupied his mind on this long journey. His restlessness, coupled with his desire to learn of his proposal, often brought him topside in the black of night as the submarine's batteries recharged. Under the stars he contemplated his future. Two things had burrowed into his mind, bending his will. He would insist on seeing Yamamoto regarding his drawings, and he would take a wife. While his career flourished, his seed would grow with strong sons.

The thought of bedding a woman brought the vision of Billi. It seemed so unfair that the submarine cruised just off the Washington coast as it made its way back to their homeport in Japan. His breathing intensified with his desire to slice, first her clothes, then her soft skin, all done slowly, ideally with Jack watching.

The vision disappeared when the attack siren whistled through the compartments of the sub as the sweaty men rushed to their battle stations. Akio hurried to stand beside the captain, feeling the heat intensify. They had shut down the engines in the event the enemy utilized sonar. Unfortunately, no engine also meant no circulation of air.

"Which one?" The captain stepped back from the periscope.

Akio adjusted the periscope for his height to look through the scope at the telltale bubbles from two submarines heading south, toward them. Listening to the coordinates, he considered his decision. The lead sub presented her starboard flank, an easy target.

"The lead." He licked his lips in anticipation of the kill.

"My choice as well." The captain nodded then gave the command. The crew silently waited for the results.

The perspiration worked though Akio's shirt, trickling down his neck and back as the seconds ticked by.

The blast shook their submarine and momentarily, their nose lifted on the turbulent wave that followed. Within twenty seconds the US submarine with all of its crew, began to sink toward the black depths of the ocean floor.

Akio wiped the sweat from his brow. The I-25 engines churned to life as the Japanese submarine dove for safety. His remarkable luck held, marking a powerful sign for his future. His vision of Billi returned with the assurance the gods would make certain they met again.

"NOVEMBER 8th, 1942," Danny's voice shook as he whispered the date while, with trembling hand, he entered it in his journal. "Eisenhower is sending us with Lieutenant General Patton into a place called Fedala. Operation Torch. I will not die today. I promise."

He carefully put the string back around his small book then stuffed it inside his jacket pocket, fingering the rosary beads Mrs. O had folded into his hand before he left. He touched the crucifix, reciting the prayers as his constant mantra. While he repeated the words, he stroked the rifle he'd cleaned meticulously in preparation for today's landing. He was ready.

He waited among the other soldiers looking out at the Atlantic Ocean just off of French Morocco. Given the signal, he adjusted his rifle and pack to crawl down the rope webbing to the landing craft below. Once aboard he faced the shore where alabaster sand rose to the earthen structures of homes and businesses. The Vichy French were on the other side, waiting, their rifles pointed at the American ships. Soldiers on both sides would die. French soldiers who had families in America and US troops whose families had visited France, were about to kill each other. The world made no sense.

The hum of nervous chatter filled the landing craft as boys, crammed against each other, prepared to become men. The high walls prevented their view in all directions except one, the beach.

"Mama, pray for me." One soldier spoke above the others.

Danny stayed focused, blocking out the increasing fears of those about to shoot their first man. The thud of the ramp dropping into the water reverberated between the frightened soldiers. He pushed forward, jumping into the murky water up to his thighs. Head down, he splashed for the shore. Bullets whizzed through the air above as he dove onto the coarse sand. Catching his breath, he heard someone beside him but didn't dare look away from the source of the enemy fire. Crawling up to a low embankment drew a new barrage of bullets exploding overhead. The sweat of fear dripped into his eyes, sand clung to his face and the blasts from larger artillery sent geysers of mud spraying skyward.

An object hit the ground in front of him. Horrified, he blinked at the remains of a hand, scorched from the explosion. The brutal image made something inside him click. He took a moment to regard the man beside him. With unspoken commitment, they nodded at each other, then, as one, stood to rush toward the deadly red flame spewing from the tank's turret.

Again, they hit the sand in unison behind a small mound of rock. Checking their rifles, both paused to watch the shells of the big guns from their ships arch overhead, blasting the wall of one building. In the deafening explosion they ran forward again, diving into a crater where a shell had missed its mark. The grinding of moving metal gears of the tank drew nearer.

Danny took out his hand grenade, his actions mimicked by his new best friend.

"If they catch us in this hole, we're dog meat." Danny shouted. He had heard horror stories of German tanks running over fox holes only to spin on top of them, making certain their vicious tracks left the occupants unrecognizable.

His mate peeked over the top at the underbelly of the tank as it raised over a pile of debris. He pulled the pin then threw his grenade like a professional pitcher, right over home base. The green ball exploded against the bottom of the tank.

"Now," he yelled at Danny. "Throw the damn thing now."

Danny popped his head over the ridge. The tank, its tracks not moving, remained suspended on the rocks. He threw his grenade only to watch it bounce off the exposed area.

The man across from him looked incredulous. "Shit, you forgot to pull the pin."

Danny placed his rifle over the edge resting his arm on the sand as a soldier dressed in the tan of the Vichy French rounded the side of the tank. He sighted down his barrel firing three shots, the last one hit the grenade, ripping into the side of the tank, flinging the enemy skyward. His body landing at unimaginable angles only the dead can achieve.

Crouching, they worked their way toward the tank. Suddenly, the turret turned toward them. Danny hit the ground as the bullets ripped at his pack. He flipped onto his back, aiming his rifle at the top hatch. A figure appeared from the far side followed by an eruption that tore at his eardrums. Smoke streamed from the tank while flames leapt from the open hatch.

He hurried around to the far side. In the dark haze he saw the prone body of his friend. Bending over him, Danny gently rolled him over. His eyes fluttered open, startling white against dark ash. They settled on Danny and he smiled briefly. "One hell of a morning."

A bullet came from the direction of the town, pinging as it hit the mangled tank.

"It's not over yet. Let's get out of here." Danny grabbed at the other soldier's uniform, helping him up.

They struggled back to the crater sliding below its protective rim.

"I'm Danny." He leaned against the sand.

"Roger." His hand moved the smudge of black from his eyes like war paint across his cheekbones. "From South Carolina."

Danny nodded, checking his ammo. "Seattle, Washington."

"Don't really make much difference. We're both one hell of a long way from home." Roger's head went back as he sucked in one long deep breath before looking at Danny again. "You ready?"

"Where to?"

"Heaven or hell, they're both right over that ridge. Today, I'm going for hell."

Roger slithered over the top of the crater with Danny following. Inching toward another bombed out hole closer to the wall and enemy fire, they slid down the sides, only to land a few feet from another soldier. His young eyes met theirs as he gasped for air, the khaki of his uniform a rakish brown where his blood gushed from his chest, across his abdomen and down his right leg.

Danny took his bloody hand squeezing it tight. "You'll be fine. Where you from?"

"Nan . . . Nancy . . . love." His cough prevented more words. His head turned towards the merciless sky as his breathing stopped.

"Damn." Danny slowly let go of the dead soldier's hand. The battle, less than twenty minutes in the making, and already he'd killed one man and sat with another as he passed.

Roger leaned across Danny and closed the kid's eyes. "Let's keep moving."

The day continued as it started, with only one goal for success—take a bullet or hit your mark. By evening the Allied troops claimed their victory, maneuvering freely along the beach in anticipation of another day of fighting.

Danny sat in the cool sand under the stars shining gloriously above. He could only imagine how many new souls rested among those twinkling prisms. He looked over at Roger, his head propped on his helmet as he emitted puffs of smoke. Extracting his book, he opened it to the words he wrote just that morning, before his first kill, before he had walked through death to live. 'Eisenhower is sending us with Lieutenant General Patton into a place called Fedala. Operation Torch. I will not die today. I promise.'

His head went back to emit his laugh. Leaning over his entry he added, "Promise kept."

He slammed the book closed, securing it tight, as if to hold his vow from escaping. Tomorrow would be another battle as they made their way to Casablanca. Another day and another oath to stay alive.

# THIRTY

BILLI, RESTLESS AS A CAGED CAT, picked up Mr. Nakamura's orchid from above the steaming kitchen sink where it had thrived in the hot summer months. She carried it to the large windowed living room in the dimming winter light. The household had grown accustomed to Billi's plant popping up in a new location to encourage its bloom. Bella had simply dusted around the plant wherever it appeared.

However, the sight of the plant today in the sprawling room only made Billi think of Eileen, now in Minidoka Relocation Camp. The last letter from her dear friend revealed a mix of the various activities now filling Eileen's days: afternoons spent helping Auntie Katsuko teach dance to the young children after school, setting up a beauty parlor for a friend, how at the first dance she met a young man from Tacoma, Washington she found interesting. She also included tidbits about her father, involved with the camp's food supplies, proposing they build a space to make tofu. Kenny, along with his new friends, started some sports teams as he continued his studies and drumming. She shared Kenny's desire to join the service as soon as allowed. Adjustment equated to survival.

Billi paced before the large fireplace as shadows began to fall across the room. She would remind Jack to find a sponsor for Eileen. If cleared, the WRA, War Relocation Authority, allowed Japanese men and women to leave the camps and relocate to the Midwest or back east to continue education or seek employment.

She found herself racing up the stairs to the library, knowing Jack's habit of returning to this office first. Stepping inside, she felt her heart sink. The dark room, empty, except for the light scent of embers and Jack's cologne, felt cold. She scolded herself for not telling him her desire to be more involved. Yet, he had left as quickly as he arrived.

Bored and frustrated she plucked a Stanford University yearbook from the neatly arranged bookshelf. Plopping onto the leather couch, she snapped on the light to thumb through the oversized annual.

She stopped at the photo of the Japanese Student Association. The young group, mostly men, sat five rows deep. Billi pulled the picture closer to the lamp. In the bottom center, sat one older Caucasian man, more than likely their professor, and another gray-haired Japanese man. The stoic students surrounding them reflecting the culture of their homeland. Their suits neatly pressed, with hair combed back, few smiled below rimless eyewear. However, one held her interest above all the others. He stood off to the side, almost in the bushes, his sneer emitting pure confidence. Akio, the killer.

Something about the photo bothered her. She examined every face again, which only left the same nagging feeling. She flipped to other pages, searching the drama club photos, speech, debate, and then found the lineup of athletics, golf, football and fencing. She paused again. Jack, smiling, both eyes focused on the camera, posed with his metal fencing mask in one hand and his thin fencing blade in the other.

She couldn't help but smile back at his handsome face. The face of his youth, before the scarring that penetrated to his heart. His smile so carefree, an alarming contrast to the man now her husband. The small writing below the picture claimed Jack as captain of the fencing team. Her finger moved across the page, as if attempting to touch his lost youth.

Slumping against the couch, she closed the yearbook. Flipping it over, a corner of a piece of paper slid into view. Carefully, she opened to the marked page, revealing the women's athletic section. The young females wore white short sleeved shirts with white shorts that came well up their thighs. She picked up the thick stocked paper, a note card, flattened open with time.

> Darling, you were fantastic last night. Meet me at the lake for a swim? Mother is insisting that we have dinner with them this weekend. More wedding plans I fear.
> Love you always Mary Beth.

Billi felt her stomach tighten as she gasped for air. Jack had never mentioned a Mary Beth, in fact he mentioned very little of his past. She pulled the book closer to read the names. Sure enough, the names coinciding with the images claimed the tall girl perched on the crest of a small mound of green as one Mary Elizabeth Montgomery. Her arms were spread wide, her long legs in the revealing shorts bent just so to demonstrate her abilities on the pair of snow skis strapped to her feet.

Billi couldn't help but laugh. The ladies were learning to ski in shorts in the warm sun on the grass.

"Darling," she mimicked the voice she had never heard. "Meet me for a swim."

"I'd love to." Jack's voice came from behind her.

The book slammed shut and fell to the floor as Billi scrambled from the couch. "How did you get in here?"

"What kind of greeting is that?" He pulled off his long woolen, rain-soaked coat. "Here I thought you wanted to go swimming with me?"

"Looks like you've already been." She brushed a kiss on his lips, taking his coat to drape it over a chair. Realizing the path of his entry, she fixed her gaze on the wall behind him. "Oh, the secret panel. I bet that came in handy when you brought your lovers upstairs."

"I've obviously left you alone far too long, your imagination has strayed." Jack stood at the desk pouring two glasses of scotch.

She moved to the other side of the couch to kick the yearbook underneath, out of sight. She smiled then, pushing aside the image of Mary Beth, the one who skis on grass. "You're home early and I'm glad."

"That's more like it." He kissed her again then pulled her down with him onto the couch.

"Any news?" She leaned her head back against his shoulder.

"Not that's printable."

"Has Akio ever been to this house?"

"Yes."

Billi sat up to face her husband. "Jack, I just can't sit here and wait. I need to be doing something."

"You are doing something. You're helping with the baby, my mother, Lilly."

"You didn't mention Bella." She crossed her arms. "Because Bella can take care of everyone. I need to be active, to feel I'm helping with the war effort."

Jack didn't answer, but she understood the look he gave her. His good eye showed a combination of dread and need.

She bit her lip. She couldn't just leave him. Yet, she felt trapped in this large house, isolated. She knew no one in San Francisco. Maybe if she went home, she could work with her mother, she could feel a sense of accomplishment.

"I will find you." Jack's comment reverberated his matter of fact promise.

She fell back into the security and warmth he provided. The thought of leaving Jack ripped her in two. He would find her, of that she was certain.

"Lilly has become a doting mother. Well, somewhat."

He smiled, thankful for the change of subject. "Here. Here. Now that is something to celebrate." He raised his glass.

"What if I brought us dinner up here and no one else knows you are home until the morning."

"You are devious. You do know that?"

"I'll use the real door." With that she stood and disappeared. How devious she was, her husband had yet to learn.

LILLY SAT ALONE LOOKING out the large windows in the living room as Billi approached.

"You know, I don't really like going outside of this house anymore." Lilly spoke softly.

Billi stepped closer. "With all those men out there to dance with? They need you."

"Every time I see a uniform, I see Todd." Her head went down.

"He would not want you to stay home." Billi moved toward Mr. Nakamura's orchid on a side table by the French doors then spun the larger leaves toward the filtered sun.

"What are those wild things growing out from the roots?"

She regarded her sister-in-law. "They seek new soil to expand in." She cleared her throat. "And that's what you need to do."

"Look for new soil?" Lilly cocked her head.

"Your son needs a father."

"I need a drink." Lilly swept to the sideboard, picking up the vodka and pouring a healthy amount before adding a twist of lemon from their tree in the garden.

Her approach failed. Deciding to try a different tact, she lowered onto the couch, waiting for Lilly to join her.

"You have to help me . . ." Billi confided.

"Really?" Lilly barked a laugh.

"Who is Mary Beth?"

Stunned, Lilly lowered her drink mid sip. "Didn't Jack tell you?"

Billi blushed, the image of the women who snow skied in shorts on grass a constant reminder of how little she knew of her husband. She lied. "Oh, just that they had been engaged and it didn't work out."

"I'll say it didn't." Lilly took another gulp of booze.

The two eyed each other for a few moments as Billi suddenly understood the exchange of information would cut deep.

"That's why we were glad to see Jack with any woman, even Ginger." Lilly drank again.

"That bad?" Billi slumped back.

"They were the perfect couple." She twirled the twist through the clear liquid then drank again. "And I hated them. I was so jealous. That woman seemed to walk on water in this house."

Billi stood, taking the empty glass from Lilly. She poured a second for her and one for herself before returning to her place.

Lilly reached for her drink, eyes wide with the memories of Jack and his fiancée. "Her wardrobe came from Paris, his pedigree from Washington D.C., and her heart from hell."

Touching her sister-in-law's glass in a salute of conspiracy, she coaxed her on. "Do tell."

"Darling Mary Beth," Lilly's voice twittered, high-pitched with exaggeration. She sipped again, then giggled. "Oh, Mary Beth, who knew everything about everybody, could not be depended upon. When father—" her arm went through the air as if it carried her father's spirit. "When he left us, penniless, I might add." She sipped again, then leaned forward toward Billi. "Then Jack had his accident.

Well, his scar and all, ended it and all dreams of their perfect marriage disappeared."

Instantly, Billi hated the woman for hurting Jack. "What happened to her?"

Lilly looked startled, her large eyes examining Billi as if for the first time. Then she raised her glass. "She left. Went back home to Daddy and quickly married a Harvard man. She was a bitch." The alcohol clearly having an impact on the story telling. "And, rumor has it, she wasn't a virgin on her wedding night."

This news caught Billi off guard as she gulped a deep sip.

"Oh, sorry." Lilly swayed forward, attempting to land her drink upright on the coffee table. "I should not have told you that part."

"No, that's okay. I expected Jack had—well you know."

"No." Her blonde hair shook from side to side. "I didn't know anything my first time with Todd. But I bet Ginger knew something."

"Actually, no. Ginger and I were clueless."

"Noooo." Lilly's eyes went wide again as she began laughing.

She watched the young mother's laughter turn to tears. "I just want Todd back."

"You will find someone to love again, Lilly. Jack did." Billi's statement sounded flat, uncertain. That uncertainty crept through her. She understood, even if the bitch deserted him, there had to be a deep reason Jack hadn't mentioned Mary Beth.

"What in the name of the Lord is goin' on?" Bella growled, standing before them.

"Oh," Lilly sat up right. "We, we have been dis . . . dis . . . discussing my brother."

"Hummph." Bella crossed her arms, glaring at them. "And that takes booze?"

"You bet." Lilly attempted to tidy her skirt. "Especially if we also talk about Miss M.B."

Bella seemed to blanch at the mention of the code name. Her gaze fell on Billi while her face attempted to control her anger. "She ain't anythin' around here. Don't you go listenin' to that gossip."

Billi felt her heart tighten. If Bella still harbored such strong feeling about Miss M.B., then she had only heard a portion of the story. She fought the question rattling around her brain. Did Jack still love this other woman?

"How do I look?" Lilly examined her peach dress in the mirror.

"Like a new person, but even more beautiful." Billi watched the transformation, her encouraging words the balm the young widowed mother needed.

"I want to feel totally free tonight. I'm not even taking a purse. Will you carry my lipstick and driver's license?"

"Don't forget your USO identity card. We worked hard proving ourselves worthy to be hostesses."

Teasing, she looked at Billi. "One of us worked harder than others."

"One widow, one bride." Billi imitated the high-pitched voice of the elderly spinster in charge of their indoctrination. "Don't dance too close. Serve tea, do not encourage any type of alcoholic drinking. Never go home with any of the men you meet. Make certain they eat all of the cookies."

"It sounds like church, not men going off to war." Lilly shook her head.

"That's why we'll break a few rules, except for the cookies."

"Here." Lilly organized her driver's license, USO identity card and lipstick on the table. "Put these in your purse. That way I have nothing to worry about."

"Nothing." Doing as told, Billi stuffed the identification cards in her handbag.

They hurried down the wooden stairs to the living room where Mrs. Huntington sat by a small fire. "You are certain Jack said this would be all right?" The elder woman eyed the two suspiciously.

Billi put on her coat, all smiles. "It was his idea. He thought that with Thanksgiving and the Holidays around the corner the men would enjoy something to remind them what they are fighting for. Besides it's the opening of a new canteen, they need us."

"It can't hurt anything. It's just dancing." Lilly brightened and bent over the bassinet next to her mother, kissing her son's cheek.

"Hummph." Bella entered with hot tea on the silver tray. "Ya'll just keep dancin'." The rest of the sentence did not need verbalizing.

"You both look marvelous. The canteen of my day was operated by the Red Cross on the wharf by the Ferry Terminal. We served hot food and a feeling of home." Mrs. Huntington raised her head ever so slightly with pride.

Billi's enthusiasm spread encouragement for Lilly. "Well, I'm glad to help. And thanks for the use of the car."

"This war has changed many things," Bella mumbled as she placed the steaming cup before her mistress.

Billi bent to kiss baby Timothy goodnight. She lingered a moment to whisper in his small ear, "Stay well, little man."

His little face scrunched up as he omitted coos of baby chatter, forming slight bubbles around his beautiful full lips.

She fought back tears. Plastering a smile on her face she turned to regard the living room. She looked back at the scene lit by the soft amber light of the fire when her gaze caught Bella's. She gulped. Bella appeared to know her plan. She looked deep into the brown eyes of the woman this household depended on, as if pleading for forgiveness. It was not her intent to hurt anyone under this roof. Especially the man she loved. Hopefully they would come to understand her actions.

"Well." Lilly adjusted her overcoat. "Let's get there before the war is over." She started up the two steps to the foyer.

Bella had not looked away, but her face had almost gone pale with concern as tears welled in large eyes.

"Just don't go breakin' any hearts tonight." She shook her head slowly.

Lilly's laughter came from the hallway. "Oh, Bella, how boring you can be."

Billi stood torn between her choices. "I won't," she pledged. Then tightening the grip on her handbag, she rushed out of the room.

THE LINE OF VARIOUS UNIFORMS continuing out the door indicated they had arrived. This space utilized by the USO looked smaller in comparison to some of the photos of other canteens across the country, especially the Stage Door in New York and the Hollywood Canteen, where movie stars boosted moral dancing with soldiers.

Billi squeezed Lilly past the men then hurried to hang up their coats. Inside, the lead hostess nodded toward Billi as they set to work, trays of cookies and food in hand. The band blared, while on the small dance floor men and women of all shapes and sizes, jitterbugged at a heart thumping pace.

Before long, Lilly swayed on the dance floor, swinging and gyrating at a frenetic pace, as if this represented her last dance, not that of the soldier across from her.

Stanley Haas, the manager of a local theater, now in charge of this USO Canteen, signaled to Billi. She stepped backstage where Hass stood with a strikingly handsome sergeant.

"This is sergeant Nells. He has agreed to help."

"Thank you." Billi eyed him a moment before continuing. "Do you see that woman in the peach dress?"

"The blonde?" He showed no reaction to her beauty, simply a soldier about to undertake an assignment.

"Her car is parked down the street. An older, golden and tan La Salle. Just follow her home. Please, make certain she's safe."

The nod of his commitment, strong and determined, made Billi smile. "Thank you. Oh, Lilly is a widow. Her husband, Lieutenant Todd Archer was killed on the *USS Reuben James*. He never met his son."

The sergeant's eyes hardened, followed by a slower nod of understanding.

Satisfied that Hass had chosen the right person to be entrusted with Lilly's safety, Billi headed deeper into the darkness behind the stage.

# THIRTY ONE

Eddy tucked the letter from his mother, written in her bold hand, into the neat stack he tied with a string. His mind traveled the thousands of miles across the sea that separated them. What he wouldn't give for just one bite of her beef stroganoff or her famous cinnamon rolls. If he saw one more meal of Australian lamb, he was going to claim jungle fever and ask to be shipped state side. He missed everything about 304 30th Avenue South yet dared not let his mind linger in the dreams of home.

He pulled out his pocketknife to start whittling. When he realized his endeavor took the shape of a woman, he let out a deep sigh. Obviously, his loneliness etched its way into every undertaking. He'd been stupid to think a marriage with Lani would be accepted when the battle over racism, even among the troops, still raged on. With each swipe of his knife he recounted the changes to the invisible cultural divide he'd witnessed before leaving Hawaii.

The One-Puka-Puka, the 100th Infantry Battalion, mostly Japanese American soldiers from the Hawaiian National Guard, left in the dark of night for training on the mainland. Japanese from Hawaii would become soldiers for America. At Tuskegee University they trained black pilots, a giant leap from the duties of cooks, the previous limit of a colored man's rank. The war became a common denominator that did not care about the shade of the outer skin, as long as your blood ran true to the United States and their Allies. He shook his head, how long after the war would this last?

His knife slipped, nicking his finger. He watched the small drop of blood from the tiny cut, so round and exact, form on the tip of his finger. Too bad he wasn't somewhere he could run to find a nurse asking for a kiss to make it better. The image of Dahlia, with her sweet smile and contagious giggle, floated before him. He felt his heart race with desire as the drop of blood landed in the hot sand. He would not let the bastards win. He would live to go home, stuff himself on his mother's cooking then kiss the girl of his dreams.

Standing, he brushed the lingering speck of blood on his pants heading for his hut with a renewed spring in his step. Now clear, his intentions formed before him. He found pen and paper then sat to write the letter he had been putting off for almost one year. He waited, no thoughts came, no words formulated. He'd left her with nothing more than an "I'm sorry. I'm in love, with someone else." The cruelty of it seemed more poignant with the turn of events as he forced Lani's image out of his mind.

He tried again. "Dear Dahlia."

In the passing hour, he composed several pages of words, this time recounting the truth. He could only hope Dahlia could tell the difference.

"Hey, did you hear the news?" Scooter slid onto the seat across from him.

Eddy folded his letter before his friend had time to read anything he might call mushy.

"Your favorite battleship just sank two Jap battleships."

"The *Washington*?" Eddy smiled.

"Yep. Sank the *Kirishima* and the *Ayanami*. That's what they get for sinking the *Hornet*."

Suddenly Eddy felt tired. "Are they sending us out on patrol soon?"

"Probably." Scooter eyed his friend suspiciously. "Tell me that's not a letter to Lani."

"Nope."

"Good." When Eddy kept his lips sealed Scooter continued. "Okay, who's the babe?"

"An old flame. Thought I'd wish her Happy Thanksgiving."

"Better make that Christmas, by the time she gets it." Scooter brightened. "I like your taste. She got a sister?"

"Nope."

Scooter pulled out a deck of cards. "I win, I get her address."

"You win, I'll swim home and you can keep my shells."

"WHAT DO YOU MEAN SHE'S GONE?" Jack stood over the three silent women in the grand living room.

They sat motionless, aware of his anger not only at them but at the situation. No one budged with a reply. Even the baby seemed quiet in his bassinet as Jack paced in front of the large fireplace, fuming.

"Okay, Lilly tell me again about that night." Jack bit on his cigar to fight his trembling jaw.

"We went to the canteen, like you suggested." She waited but her brother did not add his consent or opinion. "That was three . . ."

"Four," Bella corrected her.

"Yes." She fiddled with the sleeve on her dress. "Four nights ago. We called your office, but they said you were away, and we didn't want to just tell you this over the phone." Again, her pause brought no reaction from his interrogation. "Well, I was out dancing, and she was there and then she wasn't. I didn't see her go or anything. She didn't even say goodbye." She pouted.

"So how did you get home?"

"When I realized she was gone, then this nice sergeant noticed I looked worried and he helped me. I asked around, and no one had seen her. The hostess said Billi become ill and got a ride home. The sergeant offered to follow me home to be certain I made it safely. Which he did." She straightened her skirt as if the added movement brought the subject to a close.

He moved before his sister. "What was this sergeant's name?"

"Nells." She brightened at the mention of the handsome young man's name. "Signal Corps. But he shipped out and I don't know..."

"Christ." Jack ran his hands through his hair. His wife had gone, and he didn't know where.

"Did you check your room for a note of some kind?" His mother's concern very real.

"No, I haven't been upstairs yet." With that he flew up the stairs. They all sat quietly listening to his feet pound down the hall then stopped.

Bella was the first one to stand. She slowly followed in Jack's footsteps. When she reached the door to the room he had shared with his wife, she silently watched the frantic movements of his search.

"She didn't take anythin' from here. Means she's comin' back. I checked an everythin's here. Even that plant she fusses over so much is in the livin' room."

"Thanks Bella." Jack slumped onto the bed. Then he shot back up and ran past Bella into the office. Eileen's pillow was gone. The pillow that hid the fan was nowhere to be found. He pulled open the top drawer and the three-large diamond ring still sat in the box.

Bella stepped inside. "She's comin' back. That girl loves you. She promised."

"Christ Bella. Have you seen the pillow Billi brought with her? The hand made one, she kept it in here."

The sudden realization that she hadn't noticed the object disappeared reflected in her wide eyes as she shook her head "no."

"I need to find her. To know she's okay."

"Sure you do. I didn't touch nothin'. Didn't even make the bed up with clean . . ."

Jack stomped past her again. He pulled the heavy bedspread back and there it was. A note in her handwriting, tucked under his pillow.

> Dear Jack,
>
> This is not about us. It is about the safety of those in this home we both love. I cannot sit idle. I realize you are trying to protect me with every breath you take. You need to stay focused, not be torn between your duty to me and to our beloved country. I'll let you know where I am when I arrive.
>
> I will always remain your loving wife.

Bella's face started to quiver with emotion. "Has she left for good?"

"She's gone to visit her mother. Mrs. O's ill and she had to leave quickly." Jack sank onto the unmade bed holding his head in his hands.

"I'll fix you a plate of somethin'." Bella turned to begin her journey back to her domain of the kitchen.

Jack fell back onto his bed. He had seen this coming but ignored the signs, taking no steps to prevent her from leaving.

He re-read her first line, "This is not about us. It is about the safety of those in this home we both love."

He thought back to their many conversations then zeroed in on her question, "Has Akio been to this house?"

The old sensation gnawed at his heart, had he kept her close out of love or duty? It made no difference now. He had frightened her away. Now, he would have to explain her departure.

BILLI TRIED TO CALM her excited puppy, his barking and whining echoing though the high ceiling of the kitchen straight up through the heat vent to the second story hallway. She remembered how she and Eddy had sat upstairs next to the grate for hours listening to their parents' parties or discussing their divorce. She noted the kitchen clock read 3:13 a.m. She heard her mother's feet hit the ground and could only wait for her arrival. It did not take long before the kitchen door swung wide. Her mother nearly tripping on Pepper as the small dog charged at her with enthusiasm, only to spin around to dash back to Billi.

"What?" Her mother looked shocked. "Why didn't you tell me you were coming home?"

"I wanted it to be a surprise. It's okay, shhh." She knelt beside her dog whose tail vigorously swept a small patch of floor.

"Where's Jack?" Mrs. O moved into the kitchen to hug her daughter.

Billi waited for the long bear hug from her mother to subside before answering. "He's so busy working and gone most of the time, I thought I would spend Christmas and New Year's up here. I'm exhausted, the train was full."

"Oh." Her mother backed away. "Oh." The second "oh" held more than the simple word. "I thought you were one of my paying guests depleting my larder."

"That's right." Billi in her determination not to let anyone in on her plan, had forgotten about her mother's prospering business. The Fort Knox of Seattle, her wily mother had entitled her housing of soldiers en route to the horrors of war.

"Oh," her mother repeated.

"What's the matter?" Billi folded her arms, watching her mother. "Can this wait until morning? I'm too tired to talk. I thought I would head straight to bed."

She turned to go when her mother caught her arm motioning her toward the table.

Billi sat across from her when Pepper promptly jumped into her lap. "My, you've been trained well in my absence. So, what is it?"

"You remember your room—" She coughed a bit. "Your room is still rented and there are three men in there now."

Billi just stared dumbfounded at her mother. In response, her mother's shoulders rose and fell in her wordless fashion of communication.

"I see. So, I'll sleep on the sofa."

"Oh, no." Her mother's strong German back arched. "We can't have you sleeping down here with strange men in the house."

"Mom, I'm so tired I can barely stand. Where can I sleep?"

"Back with me?" She clapped her hands together at her own brilliance sending Pepper to the floor in excitement.

BILLI TURNED AWAY from her snoring mother cursing her impulsive action. Unable to sleep her mind traveled the distance to her husband and all who lived under that sprawling roof on San Raymundo Road. Exhausted, she dragged herself from bed pulling one of her mother's old bathrobes tight against her slim body.

She half expected Jack to be sitting downstairs in her mother's overstuffed rocking chair, waiting for her. She carefully skipped the fifth step from the bottom, the one that creaked, so as not to wake her mother as she passed into the dining room with Pepper on her heels.

"Shhh," she commanded her dog as she pushed the door to the kitchen open.

"I didn't realize I was makin' that much noise." The young man who sat at the table smiled at her.

"Oh, hello." She headed for the coffee pot and the tall tin of canned coffee grinds. "I'm—-I'm Mrs. Huntington. I'm just visiting my mother. Briefly visiting."

"You can stay as long as you like, cookie." He folded the newspaper that sat before him. "I'm the one shovin' off."

"Oh, when?" She carefully measured the grinds due to the coffee rationing.

"Today, have to be at the station by 10:00. So, I thought I'd get up early and listen to the birds. You have beau-te-ful trees and birds around here."

"Yes, thanks. And you are?"

"Giovanni Bertelli. Jersey. I ain't never been in such a big house before."

"Do you know where you're headed?"

"To war, cookie. To war. That's all they tell us. I don't care if I'm killin' Japs or Krauts. As long as I see some action I'm fine."

"What did you do before this?" She focused on the rhythm of the perking coffee steadily increasing.

"Nothin' really. I guess I worked on cars from time to time."

Billi smiled at the young dark-haired man with prominent nose as she got down two cups.

The door swung wide again as another man in uniform joined Giovani. "Good morning." He nodded politely toward Billi then looked questioningly at the Italian.

"The dame's her daughter." He swatted at the new arrival with the newspaper. "And she's married, so sit down."

Doing as told, he plopped down into the empty chair. "I'm John Lungren. Wisconsin is my home, ma'am." He nodded again.

"And are you leaving today too?" She reached for a third cup.

"Oh no, I'm here for longer. We don't have our orders yet." His sweet baby face wrinkled into a smile.

"You got any friends?" The Italian asked her. "This guy needs a gal to write to when he's over there. I have my Theresa, an six sisters, an the best mamma in the world." He smiled charmingly.

John from Wisconsin blushed as his head drooped.

She poured coffee into the three cups, smiling at the boys in uniform. "Giovani, you have given me an idea."

"Swell." The Italian leaned back in his chair, once again directing his concentration to the peaceful scene of the birds swooping in and out of the branches of the walnut trees.

THE EIGHT FRESH FACES of the young men renting from Mrs. O sat lined up in the living room.

"It's easy." Billi insisted. "Just answer a few of the questions on the list about the type of women you would like to meet, and I'll see what I can do."

John from Missouri immediately put pen to paper.

Billi took up her post behind her mother, who sat overseeing the situation from her rocking chair. Sweat beaded up on one of the young boy's faces. Such youth, such exuberance, such a shame. She fought back the tears that wanted to work their way down her cheeks. She was glad that these fine young men had landed in their home. Somewhere, across the vast United States, mothers looked only at pictures, while she beheld their very essence.

When the young men finished, they looked at Billi with renewed hope.

"So, we'll have a Christmas party tomorrow night and I'll see if I can find lucky ladies that you might find interesting. Don't worry, no one else will see these."

"That sure is nice of you." With Giovani gone to an unknown destination of the war, John had become the group's spokesman. "What should we bring?"

"Just your smiles," Mrs. O answered. "And your good manners."

"You bet. Come on fellows. The ladies have work to do."

"Yeah, especially if they're going to find a gal for you, knot head." The tallest of the group rustled the shortest man's hair. Like the young puppies that they were, they half wrestled, half ran out the door in one big mass of moving parts.

"Well, this should be interesting." Mrs. O rose from her throne, shuffling to the dining room table where Billi spread out the papers for them to review.

"Have you spoken with Jack today?" Mrs. O did not look up from the page she held.

"Yes, he's fine. Said hello." Billi lied easily.

"I see." Mrs. O slapped the page down on the table. "What about Dahlia for this one?"

Relieved her mother did not pry further, Billi began in earnest with the new project, planning a party.

# THIRTY TWO

DAHLIA BURST THROUGH THE FRONT DOOR at 304 without knocking, rushing past the yapping Pepper, to the kitchen.

"I have a letter from Danny," she announced, waving the envelope high in the air with excitement.

Mrs. O sat in a chair with a sigh. "Thank God."

"That's wonderful." Billi dried her hands on the towel, moving closer to see the handwritten note for herself.

"And look." Dahlia unfolded the paper. "No holes."

The solid mass of paper spoke for itself. The sensors, who carefully combed intimate letters for any details that might give away the position of the servicemen, were quick to cut out—or put black lines through—any incriminating words or sentences. Yet, they had not altered the content of Danny's message.

"He's very clever." Mrs. O laughed.

Dahlia continued. "He said he's fine and the stars are so bright he could touch them."

"He's in the Pacific." Billi blurted.

"I don't think so." She snapped the paper, straightening the creases, to read. "How is the new sand box? Do the kids love playing in it? Tell Mrs. O I have developed a new love of spicy food and I can't wait to be home for one of her meals, especially her deserts."

There was a moment of silence as the three women regarded each other attempting to solve the puzzle. Pepper, sensing the tension, plopped down at Mrs. O feet.

"Sand, stars and spices." Billi looked over Dahlia's shoulder at the squiggles of Danny's script.

"It is just so hot here during the day. I'm trying not to get sun burned and wish there was a place to swim. When you go to see the new movie, think of me."

A tear ran down Dahlia's cheek at the bravery of her brother who just turned eighteen.

Billi eased the letter from Dahlia's shaking hand, continuing to read for her. "We are winning the battles for our country. I am not afraid. I love you all very much and can't wait to see you again. Please write often. Love and kisses, your Danny."

Her eyes scanned the page again: the burning sun, sand, no water to swim.

"The desert?" She looked at Dahlia. "How did I miss that?" She pointed to a portion of his letter. "'Especially her deserts, not desserts.'"

"Oh, God pray for him," Mrs. O quickly made the sign of the cross, finishing with her hands clutched tightly together.

Putting the precious piece of correspondence on the table, Billi retrieved the coffee pot from the stove. The three women, cups in hand, huddled over the sheets of paper as if it would suddenly speak out loud.

"What movie?" Dahlia looked forlorn.

"New movie," Mrs. O corrected her.

"Wait." Billi shot through the door only to return moments later gripping a section of the newspaper. Respectfully moving Danny's letter aside, she opened the section to *Entertainment*. Splashed across the page was the image of a man and women cheek to cheek. His slicked back hair and her youthful beauty creating the allure for both sexes.

"I just love Humphry Bogart." Mrs. O leaned closer. "And Ingrid Bergman is so lovely. I want to see that movie."

Dahlia looked startled as the newly released Warner Brothers film pinpointed her brother's whereabouts.

"Oh," Billi tapped the title with understanding. "We'll all be going to see Casablanca."

"The globe." Dahlia dashed out then quickly return gripping the world globe. She put it on top of the newspaper, spinning it to find Africa.

"Danny's in Africa fighting with General Eisenhower." Dahlia sat with the implication of the news.

"Then he's in good hands and the war will be over with soon." Mrs. O reached for the young woman's arm, patting it comfortingly.

"Yes. Imagine Danny in Morocco! But for now, ladies, we have a party to prepare for."

Billi's stomach lurched with anxiety. Danny, with his freckles and fair skin, struggled somewhere under the burning sun fighting the enemy. Again, her sense of uselessness chaffed her nerves. She prayed the right opportunity would present itself for greater involvement.

JACK SAT IN HIS OFFICE listening to Duckworth in utter amazement.

"At least eight service men and eight young women are now inside. I haven't seen Billi leave or go in. And with those black out shades, I can't even see shapes and sizes. Do you want me to go back and knock on the door?"

"No, no. Just keep an eye out. Sorry to ask you to do overtime like this."

"It's okay. Billi will be fine." Duckworth put down the phone, heading back to his car. He would return to his watch over the O'Shaughnessy home. As he turned down 30th Avenue toward the house, in the subdued light of his vehicle's partially covered head lights, he saw a figure dash into the bushes. He slowed the car to a stop, shut off his lights, then slipped from the car. Familiar with the surroundings, he quietly made his way down the long circular driveway of the house next door. He climbed into the lower branches of the sprawling walnut tree then waited.

The rain began in earnest with its cold and biting wind. After twenty minutes Duckworth decided his prey had already disappeared into the darkness. Adjusting his position to drop from the tree, he discovered a bent figure, silently moving through the yard under him.

Duckworth gauged his leap only to land on the back of the figure as they rolled to the ground. He could feel the slight frame, wiry and muscular, work free of his grasp. His hands slid down the slick material of the slim body and, as swiftly as it had begun, the skirmish ended. The intruder broke through the bushes, running at full speed. Duckworth stood, catching his breath when his eye caught a slight reflection. Partially stuck in the wet grass was a button. Extracting it from the mud, he held it to the light, recognizing it instantly. It was the yellow button claiming the bearer to be of Chinese descent.

He put the evidence in his coat pocket before strolling around to the back of the O'Shaughnessy house. Finding no one else lurking in the shadows, he waited, listening. The night stalker worked alone. Soaked through to the bone, he went back to his car to continue his vigil. He fingered the button trying to fit it into this new puzzle. There were only two options; someone of Chinese descent was following Billi or he disguised himself to walk freely in the shadows.

BILLI FUSSED WITH THE FLOWERS in her mother's cut crystal vase, smiling at their beauty. How like Jack. They arrived on the porch that morning without a card. Just a large bouquet of bright flowers. His signal he knew her whereabouts. She carried the arrangement to the table where a young couple sat in deep conversation.

"This has been the best evening ever." John from Wisconsin whispered to Betty sitting across from him.

"Mrs. O knows how to entertain." Betty blushed as her hand tightened on the remainder of the one drink allowed for the celebration.

"It seems that way." John leaned in to whisper, "does she do this often?"

"Well, if she does, I've never been invited." Betty met his eyes.

"Will you see me again?" The young man's words sounded urgent.

"Sure, after my classes. I'm at Seattle University studying and I know Dahlia. But I want to be a teacher. I just couldn't go into nursing. I just couldn't . . ."

"That's okay. We need good teachers too. And hopefully this war will end soon, and all those nurses won't be needed."

"I like your optimism. It shows great strength of character."

It was John's turn to blush as he reached for her hand.

Dahlia appeared at Billi's elbow. "What a wonderful idea this has been. We should do this more often."

"Thank you for helping select the girls."

"Are you kidding me? There's more where they came from."

"How is Gilbert?"

They both looked in Gilbert's direction sitting across from the small Christmas tree. His Adams apple protruded below his thin face as his knee pumped with anxiety.

Dahlia turned back toward her friend. "I don't think he's ever spoken to a girl."

"He was mother's choice for you." Billi stifled a laugh.

They nodded in unison. Mrs. O's intentions evident. While Dahlia would be included in this evening's exchange, she would not be allowed to meet anyone who would compete with Eddy.

"Oh, well," Dahlia sighed. "Gilbert needs some attention too."

Billi put more festive cookies on the table then looked around the room. Eight soldiers, eight young women, all couples leaning toward each other in conversation. Six of the ladies smiled broadly, but Ruth Ann rolled her eyes in boredom. Billi walked closer to the couple stifling a laugh. Frank, from New York, slide rule in hand, feverishly showed the extremely uninterested young filly next to him how to use the ruler to compute equations.

"Frank," Billi interjected, "have you heard about Ruth Ann's family, and their wonderful . . ."

"Oh yes." Frank briefly looked away from his fixation with his ruler then his fingers nervously went back to his self-imposed task.

Ruth Ann crossed her arms and legs then sat facing the fire. "Do you need any help in the kitchen?"

"Not really." Billi felt sorry for the young woman.

Dahlia came to her rescue. "Let's put on some music and dance."

Fifteen sets of shoes hit the floor. The large radio cranked out the latest songs as the young couples danced with Mrs. O tapping her foot from her chair. However, Frank just kept his hands moving his slide rule solving an unknown problem.

BILLI UNPLUGGED THE LIGHT on the tree before quietly moving up the spiral stairs to the long windows in the turret. Pulling back the black shade, she checked the street. Spotting Duckworth's car her emotions railed between concern and defiance. She wondered if Jack had discovered some information he could not share. Suddenly, she regretted bringing Eileen's pillow and fan home. Duckworth's appearance signaled danger, making her parents' home no longer a safe harbor, possibly putting those inside at risk. She had spent three nights in her mother's home but realized she could not stay.

# THIRTY THREE

CAREFULLY, BILLI SET OUT FROM HER mother's house early in the morning. The presence of Duckworth, while a comfort at night, made moving about in the daytime a challenge.

Her shadow's nightly presence only drove home the message, she must stay clear of those she loved to avoid drawing danger toward them. No concept on where to head emerged but she prayed some miracle would present the solution.

Things must be intensifying. Betty, one of the young women attending the party, had been approached at school and asked if she had seen Billi when she visited the O'Shaughnessy house.

Billi smiled at Duckworth's uncertainty of her whereabouts as she skipped across the neighbor's back yard. She hurried down Jackson with her hat pulled down against the gusty wind and rain. She passed the boarded-up windows of her friend's store and the other Japanese merchants who hoped their stores and homes would be intact when the war ended. She wondered at the story Jack told her about Los Angeles. After the evacuation of the Japanese in Nihonmachi or Little Tokyo, the owners rented to those coming from the south seeking work. African American and Hispanics found themselves crammed into what was now referred to as "Bronzville."

She brushed the image aside, allowing herself to enjoy stretching her legs at a swift pace. The stress of the last few days as she dogged the daylight only to feel trapped at night slipped past with each block. Today her outlook brightened. The name of a family back east, willing to sponsor a young Japanese woman while she attended secretarial classes, had mysteriously appeared in the mailbox at 304. Jack had sent the help he had promised. His back east friends would sponsor Eileen. Once the paperwork was in and approved, Eileen would be free to leave the relocation camp.

Billi relaxed at bit once inside the warmth of the post office. She stood in line behind women with packages going to faraway places where their lovers, husbands, or family fought the brutal war. Subconsciously, she pressed her letter containing the information needed by the War Relocation Center closer to her chest, not wanting to draw any attention to the destination of her packages. While sending a letter to the numerous German or Italians restrained in camps on American soil might not receive a reaction, it did not bode well in the hail of hatred aimed at the country who attacked the United States, to flaunt sympathy for the innocent members of that culture.

As she waited, she noticed a new poster. A striking brunette, blue uniform and cap, held the arm of the iconic image of the white haired, fatherly figure adopted by the country. "Make A Date With Uncle Sam" the poster advised. "Enlist With Coast Guard SPARS." The word SPARS appeared in red. Just below that one bright word, printed in blue, she read, "Apply Nearest Coast Guard Office." After paying for her packages, she studied the confident face of the proud woman in her crisp blue uniform as a new idea formed.

Inspiration sent Billi hustling into the rain. Heading further down Jackson to the waterfront she turned north. Before entering, she removed her gloves, took off her wedding ring placing it safely in her purse. Adopting the determination of the poster girl, she entered the headquarters for the 13th District of the United States Coast Guard.

"May I help you?" A guard asked as she stepped into what appeared to be the main office.

"Apply at nearest Coast Guard Office, is what the poster said. And that is what I am doing." Billi smiled, holding her head as high as possible. "I want to be a SPAR?"

The man eyed Billi. "A SPAR. I see. Can you come this way please?"

In the small office Billi sat before an older woman whose obvious military training left little time for the imagination.

"Name?"

"Lillian." Billi swallowed. "Lilly Huntington."

"Married?"

"Widowed. My husband was a casualty of war."

"I'm sorry." The woman briefly made eye contact with Billi.

"Why the Coast Guard?"

"I've met some Coast Guardsmen and admire their responsibility. That is the vast shorelines they are entrusted to protect." Billi's confidence left no room for any doubts as to her goal. "I was raised on the water and am very comfortable on boats."

"Do you have your identification with you?"

"I have my card I was issued when I was working at the Canteen in San Francisco on me and a driver's license." Billi opened her handbag extracting her sister-in-law's identification cards she neglected to give back to Lilly the night she left for Seattle. Those two small pieces of paper now represented Billi's freedom, a new identity, a definite sign from above.

The women looked at it briefly. "You from the Bay area?"

"Yes." She started to sweat.

"I have family down there. Love that city."

"How nice. I heard there was on the job training in some areas? I hope this is one of them."

"We'll see after you take your tests. Where are you residing now?"

"A nice old lady is taking in soldiers and had an extra room. Next to hers," she added quickly.

"So, will you be staying there, or will you need us to provide housing?"

"Well, no offense or anything, but she snores so loudly, I just can't sleep. So, if you have something, I certainly would like to hear about it."

"After the test." The woman pursed her lips, studying Billi.

"You aren't running from anything are you?"

"Heavens no." Billi's back shot up straighter as she held her face from twitching.

THE COOL BREEZE on the Black Ball Ferry to Bremerton acted like a salve healing all wounds as the salt air brushed over her, covering her in a light mist. She didn't see anyone follow her from the Coast Guard office to the terminal. She had looked at some of the Coast Guard Stations praying for one far away, up north near the Canada border. Besides, no one would bother her if she lived on a base. "Hide in plain sight," as Jack would say.

When she stepped onto the dock, she saw her father waiting. His bowed legs began moving in her direction with the unmistakable smile of a man with renewed confidence.

"So good to see my darlin'." His hug engulfed her. "Wait 'til ya see what I have for ya."

She kissed his cheek letting him hug her all the way to his newer Ford truck. She stood a moment eyeing the canopy that covered the truck bed. There was no sign on it claiming the truck to be Bremerton Meats, his former employer. Nothing told of his new enterprise, the canopy reflected the same black as the rest of the vehicle.

"Where did you get this?" She shifted, afraid of the answer.

"Yur, father has been very busy lately. I'm the new supplier to the Army." He held the door open allowing the stench of butchered meat to drift toward her.

He slid in behind the wheel as she cranked down the window for a bit for air. "What are you supplying the Army with, Dad?"

"Lard." His pride was undeniable.

"Lard?" She could not put the two together.

"Don't be tellin' on me now. But I get the lard for pennies from the butchers and then sell it to the Army for a hefty price."

"Lard?" She could find no other word to express her confusion.

"They use it to make ammunition. Last month alone I made a fine fortune." He began to whistle, his indicator the conversation on that subject was over.

FROM WHERE BILLI STOOD, Dyes Inlet felt like a safe harbor, even though the white tips of the waves, swept by the strong wind from the south, beat against the shore. On the far side of the water, the limbs of the green trees swayed constantly with the gusts. Yet, somehow, she found peace in the storm.

She marveled at her father's surprise. The cabin appeared neat, orderly with a few new furnishings replacing the hand-me-downs acquired when her Mother left him years ago. The biggest surprise, her parents were courting, explaining the tidiness of Mr. O's cabin. She shook her head in wonder, their rocky road together exemplified love, strength, and hope. A lesson she would tuck into her prayers for her future with Jack.

"So why did ya leave him?" Her father sat in his new rocker, watching the flames of his fire dance to life.

"Who said I left him?" She snapped, not in the mood for interrogation.

"Well, you're not here fur your health, or are ya?" He faced her.

"I'm just taking a break. Jack is gone most of the time and I wanted to be near my family for the holidays."

"So, you're headin' back for the New Year?"

"Yes, I will be gone soon." Not entirely a lie she reasoned. Suddenly tired, she sank into a chair. "I just want life back the way it was."

"Darlin' we all do. If the damn Japs hadn't gotten us into this mess." He bit his lip. "Just remember, if you don't know the way, walk slowly."

Her father's wisdom brought the tears. She couldn't explain her behavior, even she didn't know the answers.

"I miss Eddy, Dad. I want him home safe. Now."

"I do too. But there's a war, and that changes everything. Do ya miss Jack?"

"With every breath."

"There now, that's the answer yur old father was hopin' for. He's a good man."

"WHAT IS SHE SAYING?" Mrs. O stood above Billi looking at the letter she held before her.

"Eileen is a marvel." Her excitement uncontrollable. "She is helping Auntie Katsuko teach Japanese dance. In fact, some of the families from other relocation camps have asked to be transferred to Minidoka so they can study traditional dance with the famous Katsuko."

Billi read from the letter, "Father has been very busy. He is on the council and they are ordering seeds to start a garden for next spring. With my monthly stipend from the Government I have placed an order for heavy socks from Monkey Wards." Billi paused to look up at her mother, "That's what she calls Montgomery Ward."

"Monkey Wards?" Mrs. O shooed Pepper onto the floor to sit next to her daughter on the couch. The pup promptly jumped back up into Mrs. O's lap and settled down. "At least she hasn't lost her sense of humor in all of this."

"Not Eileen." Billi began to read aloud again. "It has been cold, very cold. The wind seems to rush right through the walls. So, we have become very creative. Every scrap of wood that is left over from the construction of these long buildings is being used. One man is making getas for us. They are better than our regular shoes in this climate and keep us out of the mud. They have built pens for pigs and chickens. Kenny has joined one of the bands they're organizing and we're going to have a dance for New Year's Eve. The rec room is always busy and we've decorated it for Christmas. Oh, I have signed up for piano classes. Some of the girls have been working in the hospital but I am hoping for a job at the small store they are finishing. Father keeps saying a busy mind is a healthy mind."

"That is good sound advice." Mrs. O nodded her approval.

"And, as for the young man..." Billi began to fold the letter.

"Well," Mrs. O demanded, "don't stop now. Who did she meet?"

Rising, Billi tucked the letter back into the envelope heading for the foyer. "We're going to be late for Mass. We can finish the letter later."

Mrs. O set the sleeping puppy on the couch then pushed herself up. "Don't forget."

Billi watched her mother gather her warm wool coat and gloves. A sense of pleasure shot through her as Mrs. O fingered the "Remember Pearl Harbor" pin on her lapel with the opalescence real pearl set between the two words, a gift from Jack. Just over one year had passed since Eddy survived that horrific day. She would light as many candles as the church had to offer for the end of the war on this Christmas Day.

A sense of quiet filled the house, most of the last group of men just shipped off, but not without carrying with them the hearts of the young women they had met under the roof of 304 30th South. She would light more candles for the young soldier's safe return, including a special one for Freddy, in the hopes he would put down his slide rule and embrace a girl instead of his math.

Mr. O, sporting his going-to-church suit, stepped from the living room with a beaming smile for his ex-wife. "Aren't ya the most beautiful woman alive."

"Thank you." Her shoulders raised then lowered with his attention. He kissed her cheek making her giggle like a young schoolgirl.

Billi smiled broadly at her parents as she stepped back into the room. "Shall we go? We have a lot to pray for."

The three filed out of the front door, each tapping Eddy's blue star hanging in the window before stepping into the cold. The O'Shaughnessys, like so many other "blue star" families, had adopted the small act of tapping the cut-out cardboard as a reminder of the sorrow that accompanied a "gold star." A tap for luck, for life, for Eddy.

THE SUN NEVER REALLY MADE IT through the clouds delivering a dismal Christmas day. By eight that evening, Billi sat watching her father flirt with her mother over a game of cards. When the phone rang, Billi did not jump to get it, but let her mother be the first to respond.

"If it's your husband, are you going to talk to him today of all days?" Mrs. O's crankiness apparent in her disapproval of her daughters situation.

"Hello." In the pause that followed she turned to glare at Billi. "Jack, how nice of you to call. Yes, please send our best to your family as well. Yes, all is well here. We are all fine."

Billi did not budge. She sat as still as a mouse facing a cat. Her stomach and nerves tight as hard leather, her breathing shallow.

Finally, her mother turned away from her to speak into the phone again, "Yes, I will pass that along if I see her. And Jack, all will be well. Merry Christmas."

Her mother stomped back to the table without saying a word. Billi ran up the spiral stairs, stopping at the top to look down the hallway at the closed doors. She slowly opened the door to the bedroom of her youth. The wallpaper, with the caged birds, looked bleak. The room held three more beds, squeezed up against the wall for more soldiers as they traveled through Seattle on their way to the war. All beds, neatly made, waited in anticipation of their next occupants.

Billi ran back down the stairs, picked up the phone, then turned and fixed her stare on her mother.

Mrs. O, taking the hint, stood then walked into the kitchen. Her father, whistling, followed.

"Jack," Billi's voice sounded weak. "Yes, I'm fine. No. I can't come back just yet." She heard his deep breathing. "I just wanted you to know how very much I love you."

She listened intently to her husband's vow, "The minute I know he's dead I will come for you."

"I know." He understood. Tears rushed from her eyes. "I'm leaving soon."

"Good. Will you let your husband know where to?"

Hearing the concern behind his attempt at a joke, she responded with the same tone. "I think my husband always knows where I am."

"You surprise me sometimes."

There was a long pause between them that filled both with hope.

"I'll be taking your advice."

"That will be a first," he snorted.

"Hiding in plain sight."

"As long as I can see you. Be careful."

"Yes. And that goes for you too."

# THIRTY FOUR

J ACK SAT IN HIS DEN LISTENING to the laughter from the living room bounce down the hallway. He stood to close the door. As he returned, he picked up his drink where the one ice cube now bobbed like a small frozen dot on the surface.

Billi's voice rang in his mind. He missed every inch of her. Yet their reality, driven by the constantly changing events of the war, presented unexpected challenges. He had made peace with her decision until Duckworth informed him of the Chinese man watching 304 30th Ave.

He gulped more scotch with the decision he would pay a visit to the dragon queen, Shirley Chow, in Chinatown. Her long greedy fingers, with nails of glossy red, spread far and wide. Like the consummate spy, she held valuable information. He only hoped she didn't require much in return and certainly not from Billi.

Spies, Jack mused as he sat behind his desk to rehash the stack of information before him. Nothing presented a clearer picture than the valuable decoding machine Magic. Without reading the enemy's mail, the world would be tilting in another direction.

The agents sent from Japan to South America to control the spy net along the West Coast before Pearl, had, for the most part, retreated to their homeland when Mexico declared war on the Axis. When the US and Canada removed all persons of Japanese descent from their coasts, very little support for any subversive activity within the continent emerged. Undeterred, the Japanese enlisted the Spanish Government to establish spies in America, only to use the consulates of Spain to relay the information. Spies still collected pertinent information on the maneuvers and whereabouts of fleets, training facilities and other valuable intelligence. However, Japan's exchange with Spain had its flaws. American decrypting teams were able to read the exchanges sent from the Japanese Consulates in Europe to Tokyo. These communiques divulged much of the Axis movements and plans. The circular game of the intricacies of espionage.

He leaned back in his chair with thoughts of Billi. The war simply must end soon. In a few days hopeful families would ring in 1943. He scoffed at the concept of New Year's resolutions. He wanted his wife safely back by his side, but in order to do so, he had to make certain Akio died. He poured more scotch into his glass. His one resolution, kill Akio.

Pulling photos of the fan given to Billi by the Professor from his desk drawer, Jack reconsidered the purpose of the gift. The Professor expected Billi to win the competition then travel to Japan, carrying this fan with her. Once there, who knows what would have happened to her as the fan, displaying the hidden design, obviously held great value. Discovering who besides Akio is aware of the fan's existence could hold the clue to the spy's next move.

He thought again of the Japanese airplane that dropped the fire-bombs over Oregon's Siskiyou Mountains. A submarine, deftly moving into range, carrying in its bowels a small plane able to catapult from its deck, presented untold danger.

The importance of Akio's drawing nagged at Jack. The wings of the new American built Grumman "Hellcat" fighter plane bent and rotated for storage on an aircraft carrier. The wings did not hug the body as Akio's design appeared to indicate. Jack finished the last swallow of his drink; it burned into his throat and spun his brain awake. A plane whose wings could be pressed close to the body allowed more room for other deadly aircraft. Very Japanese. Very dangerous.

He would make calls in the morning. If spies still sought the secrets of the fan, they continued their search for Billi. A valuable new design would be welcome in any war chest.

HER NEW COAST GUARD Spar uniform looked smart, the wool softened over her curves, transforming Billi. They let the hem out a bit on the skirt but the jacket, with its silky lining, fit comfortable. She fingered the blue braid that ran around the bottom of her sleeves. Standing erect she examined her image in the mirror. The whistle on the ferry sounded as she hurried back to the group of new trainees. Hoisting her newly issued seabag over one shoulder she followed the line of squawking women, their excitement growing with every step.

The bus rattled into Port Townsend, marking the destination of their training. As it bumped past the Palace Hotel, she slid down in her seat. From the partially steam covered window, she regarded the hotel where, before the war, Jack delivered her for a different type of training. She thought of Marie, the proprietor and madam of the "Palace of Pleasure" with her wayward women inside the old brick front building. It seemed so long ago. Now, ironically, once again, she came to the shores of this small town to prepare to defend her country.

At the end of Water Street, the bus rounded the corner onto Monroe then swung right on Jefferson. The young women spilled out onto the rain soaked mud that led to the small white building at Fort Worden, their headquarters.

Adjusting her seabag and cap, she fell into the line mushing toward the barracks they would call home. She inhaled the salt air on the cold wind moving rapidly down Admiralty Inlet. The air tasted of life. Attempting to force away the image of Jack, she wondered how long it would take him to find her. She wondered if he would see the humor of her circumstance, being back in Port Townsend, as she stomped her feet harder with her commitment.

"Lilly," a voice beside her kept repeating. "Lilly, what is the matter?"

Billi turned suddenly, bumping into a table in the hallway. "Oh." She looked in the direction of the voice. "Yes?"

"Heavens, Lilly." Karen, the short red head, looked at her concerned. "You are the most absentminded person I know. Here's our room."

"Sorry." She blushed, scolding herself for not staying alert. Posing as Lilly Huntington provided her with two avenues of protection she could not afford to lose. One from spies, like the Silver Shirts, the anti-Semitic Silver Legion of America, whom the Japanese approached to continue their reconnaissance when the war broke out. The other, a safe haven from which to work for the country.

The shorter women eyed her. "So, which bunk do you want?"

"No offense, but I have the legs for the top one." Billi smiled at her new roommate.

"Golly, thanks." Karen slumped on the lower bed.

She opened her seabag, stuffed Eileen's pillow out of sight under her covers, then swung her bag up on her bed. Two more women entered going through the same routine of choosing bunks at the other end of the cramped room.

"I'm Ruth," The big boned brunette with the booming voice announced.

"Trudy, here." The other woman extended her hand in greeting. Her angular teeth somehow fit her round faced and wide set eyes.

"Are you all from around here?" Billi asked.

"Los Angeles," the loud voice answered.

"Montana." Trudy's smiled unabashedly exposing more of her crooked teeth.

"Springfield, Oregon." Karen's short legs tapped the floor from her bunk.

"What about you?" Ruth's large hands found her ample hips to emphasis the question.

"San Francisco, well just outside."

"Well, looks like we have the West Coast covered." Ruth's large hand waved commandingly through the air. "Come on. Can't be late for our first assembly."

Billi fell in behind the others. Letting the strong voiced Ruth take the lead seemed appropriate. They assembled in the large room with the other new arrivals, filling the classroom at the learning center for their introduction into their new roles as SPARS. Taking the piece of paper with the assignments for Lilly Huntington she perused her new life. The day began with drilling, followed by classes on identifying boats and planes, more drilling, then off to the firing range, more drilling, then a course on Morse Code, radio equipment and maps. Every minute accounted for, preparation and marching toward her new life. After all, Semper Paratus, meaning "Always Ready," is how the name SPAR originated. Like the spar on a boat, which acts to support the yard or rigging, a SPAR is trained to support the men in action.

She let her long legs keep pace as they marched back toward their barracks. She reminded herself of her goal: to be just another piece of the cog, following orders, unobtrusively working for her country.

"HERE YOU GO, MISS RAYE." Danny held up a sheet for the famous actress. "I'm going to string this across this wire." He reached for the newly installed wire that now ran from one outcrop of the trench across the sand to the other.

"Thanks. You're a resourceful one." Her large mouth twisted into a smile. "You can call me Martha."

Danny peeked from around the new barrier as a waterfall of dust cascaded onto his shoulders. "I'm Danny. You feeling better?"

"That yellow fever can get a girl down. But the best news is, I dumped 22 pounds."

"You look beautiful. I just want to say . . ."

At the unmistakable sound of a German fighter swooping toward them, Danny tossed Martha Raye her helmet then grabbed his gun. "Get down, I'm going up."

"Well hurry back, you were in the middle of telling me how beautiful I am." She crouched against the hard earth.

Danny watched the sand spray as the line of bullets from the Nazi plane made their deadly path across the desert floor toward his trench. Day three of this assault and the Germans didn't appear to comprehend they were losing ground. The Vichy French had quickly abandoned their alliance with Hitler's Wehrmacht when the Americans' Operation Torch hit the African shores. Bloody battles raged for days in Oran and Morocco while the Allies basically walked into Algiers establishing a coup d'état with the French last November 11th, 1942. Yet, Rommel and his Afrika troops continued their barrages of the cat and mouse game along the Sahara Desert.

The camouflage hanging over their small dugout whipped against the wind and turbulence form the aircraft. Danny pressed his gun sight against his dry sky, pulling the trigger on his tommy gun. Remembering his first kill, and the beachfront with so many young US soldiers dying, he prayed this was not the day he joined them. Besides, he had Martha Raye to protect. The troops, forced to postpone her show, were anxious to get the stage ready for her soul soothing entertainment. A bit of home in this hell hole.

The kraut swastika roared overhead as Danny kept his bullets aimed at the belly of the aircraft. He felt the sand splash against his cheek as a body slid down the trench next to him.

"Can't let you have all the fun," Roger shouted, training his gun on the target. In unison they defended their position.

The blast from the explosion as the aircraft erupted spewing parts, fire and smoke, sent them both back down the incline of the manmade trench. Danny saw the flames spread haphazardly across the netting of their camouflage. Roger spun into action, grabbing the netting before it dripped fire and death into the trench. By the time Danny joined him, Roger's cuffs were singed leaving his hands burnt and bloody.

"Shit, Rog." Eddy stomped out the remaining fire. "You could've gotten yourself killed."

The irony of the statement made them both laugh. They stood shoulder to shoulder in the heat of the roaring fire consuming the enemy plane. The sun added to the intensity as the sand drifted against them on the wind. Yet, for now, no raiders in the sky threatened their position.

A voice rang out from below, "You okay up there?"

"Yes." Danny puffed with pride before saying her name. "It's clear to come up, Martha."

Roger nudged his friend. "You on first name bases with that dame?"

Danny slid down to help her over the rim of the dugout.

"This is Private First Class Roger Doore." Danny turned to his battle-hardened friend. "Don't forget to salute, Miss Raye was just made an honorary captain."

Roger snapped his heals as his burnt and bloody hand saluted all five-foot four-inches of the Hollywood star. Over the last four months, she risked coming under fire while flying through enemy territory with their tail gunner dying from gunshot wounds, suffered the ravages of yellow fever, and now three days stuck in the trenches with intense air raids. All of this to bring brief moments of joy to the troops. She was more than an honorary captain. She was an angel.

"Bloody hell." She saluted back. "You better see about those hands."

He shook his head "no." "And leave you alone with Danny?"

She kissed his cheek. "You get cleaned up. When that stage gets rigged up and they drag my piano out, you two will have front row seats."

Roger started to swoon then caught himself as he bumbled into his friend. "She kissed me," he whispered.

Martha roared with laughter. "Was it my smooch or your injuries that went to your head?"

He grinned before leaning into Danny. As one, the two soldiers, high on hope, struggled toward the medic's tent tucked between two large rocks.

EDDY SAT IN THE SAND under the few remaining palms looking out over what had become known as Iron Bottom Sound. Since the 7ᵗʰ of August 1942, seven grueling months ago, men had spilled their blood at this place called Guadalcanal. He ruefully considered how the code name Cactus became more apropos daily.

The marines had taken a heavy toll here. They had slogged it out between mud, crocodiles, a savage enemy, and mosquitos. All those lives lost to protect Henderson Field, named for the first Marine pilot to be killed in this war as he led his squadron in the Battle of Midway. The deceased Major Henderson would be proud of his men and their efforts. Operation Watchtower had steadily kept the Japanese from establishing more territory. More importantly, keeping communication and supplies between America, Australia, New Guinea, and New Zealand open.

Finally, their night raids on the Tokyo Express, as the enemy attempted to land more men and supplies down the slot, had dwindled. The sight from the sky of Iron Bottom Sound alone provided a grim reminder of the many lives lost aboard ships or falling aircraft to gain this section of the South Pacific. The sparkling crystal waters appeared cool and inviting, telling none of its secrets of the numbers of dead soldiers that had come to rest on its sandy bottom.

He flicked his cigarette butt into the sand watching a crab scurry sideways to hide under a browned palm. The withered palm a casualty of one of the many airstrikes by the enemy along this strip of the beach.

Eddy stood to get back to work. The tropical storm that swept over Milne Bay the last few days brought some unwanted debris which now covered his aircraft. As he had pulled the palm from his propeller the only damage was a scratch on the paw of his cat. The caricature had grown to a full-sized cat with each successful raid in the dark of night. He tapped his smiling black feline then swatted at the buzzing mosquitos.

"Damn, this place is getting to me," he spit in the sand.

"Not for long." Scooter slapped his friend's back. "Come on they want us."

The two walked silently down No. 1 Airstrip toward the make-shift command post. The airfield held an assortment of aircraft ready to strike in anticipation of the large Japanese convoy carrying thousands of troops expected to head down Vitiaz Straight between New Guinea and New Britain. Once again, the codebreakers had set the stage for the Allies to have the upper hand. The hot sun beat against their sweat soaked shirts as they finally made it past the part of the jungle to the large line of tents. They stepped inside the post where the ceiling fan created a warm breeze.

Pilots and crewmen from the Royal Australian Air Force mingled and laughed with their US counterparts. But once Brigadier General Ennis Whitehead entered, the silence of respect fell over the room.

"He flew with Billy Mitchell's demonstration on how an aircraft carrier could work way back before we had them," Eddy whispered.

The comment made Scooter sit taller for a better look at their commander.

"I know you have been training for this mission. Pappy Gunn assures me his new modifications will make the B-25's advantage to strafe ships at a closer range something the Japs will regret. I also hear you have had some success with skip bombing. And that the poor wreckage of the S.S. Pruth over at Port Moresby was giving up her last for your target practice. Well done." Whitehead waited, looking over the group of men before him.

Mumbles of pride drifted through the heat of the room.

"Well done, men." He repeated. "Our target is eight Jap destroy-ers, eight troop carriers and more enemy aircraft than should be in the sky at once."

The plan for the battle of the Bismarck Sea sat before them, layers of aircraft from different directions followed by PT Boats. The excitement and fear, palpable in the stifling air, mingled with the cigarette smoke hanging like haze over the pilots. No breeze penetrated the mosquito netting, just the old fan swirling the heat. The stillness of approaching death clung to them like their own sweat as all present silently prayed for continued luck. Like machines trained to kill they filed from the meeting to drift toward their barracks. All canteens remained closed as night came quickly in the jungle where fear would fill dreams. Before dawn on the morning of March 3rd, 1942, their skills and desire for survival would be tested once again.

Eddy lit a cigarette, more to ward off the bugs than for the smoke. "Look at those stars, Scooter."

"How can a place be so beautiful and so mean at the same time?"

"Just life, I guess. You writing home tonight?"

"You bet. Any news from Dahlia lately?"

"Nope, she's being shipped off somewhere soon with her nursing unit. Don't imagine there will be much corresponding between us now."

"Hey, let's go see Charlie." Scooter started toward sick bay. "He's so pissed off he won't be with us tomorrow."

Eddy stood silently for a moment, listening to the nocturnal sounds of life on the island. More importantly, for the slight sound of any enemy that might be crawling toward them. The several stories the marines told, haunted him. One in particular of a man, hunkered in his foxhole, hearing a slight scraping sound. Not certain, he fired into the night. In the morning, a Japanese soldier, knife in hand, lay dead a mere three feet in front of him. The Empire of Japan's forces on this island worked their best at night, instilling jitters while stripping the Americans of much needed sleep.

With a heavy sigh Eddy followed his co-pilot into the Red Cross Quonset hut where the sick and dying lay surrounded by the gauze of mosquito nets.

"Goddamn malaria. Goddamn jungle. Goddamn war," Charlie's words came from the corner bed.

"That's the attitude. You keep that up and you'll be back in the skies with us in no time." Eddy pulled the mosquito net back around his side-gunner's bed.

"Well, he didn't make it." Charlie pointed to an empty bed. "After all of that. He was a damn medic. Told the other doc to look after us first."

"Haven't you heard?" Scooter sat on the edge of the bed. "The Japs are on the run and we're chasing them all the way back to Tokyo."

"So, don't get too comfortable in that bed." Eddy patted the covers. "Or you'll miss out on all the fun."

Charlie smiled, then began to shiver with perspiration forming around his temple. "I'll . . . I'll be back with you soon. Kill the bastards for m...me."

"Done. Get some rest." Eddy patted the covers again. "We'll be back with the details soon."

Eddy watched Scooter disappear into the night toward their Quonset hut. Suddenly, he began to tremble, his hands shaking, knees buckling, and he teetered toward the dirt. He lay a moment in his own sweat, unable to speak, blinded by the memories of past battles. From seemingly nowhere, boots loomed before his blurred vision.

"You okay, son?"

He recognized the voice but couldn't respond when a strong hand helped him sit upright.

"How many sorties have you made?"

"I was at Kane'ohe on December 7th." He added a "sir," when Whitehead's face came into view.

"They haven't sent you back for R&R yet?"

"We went back for a brief R&R but that was a disaster," Eddy muttered, attempting to hide his waves of fear.

"I'll tell you what." The Brigadier General helped him stand, the two men now face to face. "When you get back from this campaign, you come and see me. We need you son. You're making a big difference for all of us."

"Yes, sir." Eddy saluted, his surge of energy refueling his soul and spirit.

"You been taking your Atabrine pills, son?"

"Yes, sir. One of my crew is already down with malaria and I sure can't afford to lose any more."

"Good job, Lieutenant. See me when you return."

"Yes, sir." He put out his hand. "I'm Edward O'Shaughnessy. See you when we land."

With that, Whitehead disappeared. Eddy watched him go before heading to his Quonset hut for much needed sleep before battle.

# THIRTY FIVE

BILLI QUIETLY LIFTED THE OAR BACK inside the boat. The drips of cold saltwater splashing onto her grey and white striped uniform as she ducked below the rim of the rowboat. She peered over the edge again, forcing herself to breath slowly and not panic.

According to her assignment, she put in at dawn, just beyond Battery Kinzie on the Strait of Juan de Fuca side of Fort Worden. Having rounded Point Wilson and the lighthouse, she continued briskly moving her oars toward the inner workings of Puget Sound. Then, to her horror, she spotted a periscope riding just above the waters.

She hoped the others on lookout on the dock saw what slithered through the water toward her. She dared not yell, or signal them, only hope the fact her boat now drifted on the current would draw their attention. She stole another look. The periscope had not changed course but remained at the same distance, traveling with her on the wind-swept tide.

The concept of how the hell the submarine made it all the way inside this passageway became dwarfed by its intent. If the enemy submarine surfaced now, they would rock her small rowboat over. She gauged the distance of the swim in the frigid water. She could probably make it. But duty compelled her to warn the others. Struggling with her knowledge of the recent sub activity she could not decide which evil this one presented. If Akio were aboard the sub it could surface and take her. It could be planning on launching one of his planes to attack the forts on either side of this waterway protecting the cities and naval yards downstream.

She turned to glance toward shore, nothing moved. Hopefully, someone watched her from somewhere. She thought of Jack and her parents, she didn't want to die. Her boat swept sideways, caught on the wind, pushing her further out into open water. She had to make a move.

Taking a deep breath, Billi positioned herself at the center of the craft, ready to begin her flight. Dipping her oars into the slate blue water, with one swift move she spun her boat toward shore pulling with all her might. Sweat dripped down her back and sides where her uniform clung to her in the cold wind as she furiously fought the thick chop. The waves formed small white tips preventing any headway. Her concentration remained on the periscope. Suddenly, her boat hit something hard, shaking the oars from her grasp.

Spinning toward the loud thud, one of her oars worked out of its oarlock. She secured it just before the large log ramming the side of her boat knocked it free. The deadhead kept battering her skiff, dragging her along with its massive weight. Moving aft, she worked the log away from her boat, setting it adrift on its own course of chance with these unforgiving waves. Luckily, nothing appeared damaged, just a deep gouge of brown from the water-soaked wood.

She moved back to her seat, staying low as the unmanned boat rocked on the building waves. Reclaiming her position, she adjusted her oars preparing her escape. Suddenly, she held her oars deep in the water to watch. The periscope and the log bobbed across the moody surface at the same pace. Furthermore, the periscope had not altered the angle of its scope, it remained facing the southwest having never turned.

Something was amiss. Clearly this was not Akio, and for some reason it made her angry.

Billi spun her boat in behind the scope. With the help of the wind and current, she easily gained on the object. If it did turn now to scan the 360-degree horizon spotting her, she would be killed.

Stealthily, setting a steady comfortable pace, she moved closer. Rage overtook her as she drew nearer. Those bastards. She boated one oar, and as she had done so many times when crabbing, she reached over the lip of the boat grabbing onto the periscope as if it were a buoy.

With all her strength she pulled the mock scope from the water. Bamboo cleverly bound together formed the resemblance of the enemy's periscope. With one last heave she boated her trophy. The decoy reached from bow to stern with a floating device attached to keep it upright just above the surface.

She recognized the kanji claiming this spoof as part of the IJN, Imperial Japanese Navy, and it rocked her senses. They were out there. Someone had set this adrift. There were no Japanese living along these shores or across the waterways to Canada. They had all been moved inland, some say for their protection, others for America's. Yet, what she held provided further evidence of the enemy's penetration into US waterways. She realized the new founded panic this bamboo object would spread.

Hearing an engine in the distance she strained to see which side of those at war were bearing down on her. Keeping her prize safely from view she hurried her stroke toward shore. Glancing over her shoulder, relief swept over her at the sight of a few SPARS on the beach waving at her to hurry. Then, the white hull of the motorboat bounced on the waves toward her as she felt her nerves relax. How ironic, the Coast Guard, some of her own, to the rescue.

Still damp and disheveled, Billi stood inside a room she had never ventured into before.

"So." Lieutenant Nyberg squinted as she spoke. "This was drifting just offshore?"

"Yes, ma'am." Billi watched the naval officer called in to examine the object. "Are you going to contact the FBI along with ONI?"

He looked at her quizzically, as the photographer took another snapshot of the decoy periscope stretching down the long conference table.

"The markings sir. Not totally legible but surely must be from the Imperial Japanese Navy." She smiled blandly.

"Can you read them, Huntington?" His gaze did not leave hers.

"We were trained with a few of the symbols."

Out of the corner of her unflinching eyes she noticed Nyberg slightly shift with her lie.

"Well, done." He gripped the latticed together bamboo to hold it upright. "Has anyone seen anything else along these lines?"

"We'll be on the alert for more and report accordingly." Lieutenant Nyberg moved closer.

All eyes focused on the fake periscope and its meaning.

"Can I get a photo of it with the SPAR who pulled it aboard?" The photographer moved to acquire the perfect angle for his shot.

"No." Billi stepped out of frame before the flash could catch her image. Then quickly continued with a poor excuse. "I'm still wet and a mess. And I . . ."

". . . perhaps another time." Her superior broke the awkwardness. Moving to stand beside the naval officer, the older woman rested one hand on the Japanese artifact just below the officers then smiled for the camera.

Before reaching the door, the naval officer turned back toward the two women.

"Great job." He nodded. "Lilly Huntington, isn't it?"

Billi stood tall. "Yes, sir."

As the door shut Nyberg motioned for her to sit.

"Well, is it?"

Billi felt her stomach tightened. Doing as requested, she sat.

"Is it what, Lieutenant Nyberg?"

"Lilly? Lilly Huntington?"

Billi didn't answer at first, pretending not to comprehend her superiors meaning.

"Where in the Bay Area did you learn to row like that?" She tapped her pencil against a stack of papers on her desk.

The realization this intense, formidable woman read her personal file brought small beads of perspiration to Billi's temples.

"My aunt," she almost choked on the tale she spun. "My aunt, Mrs. Gladys Richardson, they have a home up here and I learned on her beach."

Now the sweat began along her forehead at her continued fib. If they contacted the Richardsons, her deceased fiancée's family, she would be exposed. But the fib wasn't all lie, they were related to the Huntingtons.

"There's a group of trainees being shipped to Northampton for further education." The steely woman dragged out the last word giving it a different meaning. "I will be certain your unit is among them."

Billi leaned forward. "Have I done something wrong?"

"I don't know what you are running from or why. But a change of scenery might help with your situation."

Billi controlled her sense of relief. She smothered her concern of where this "change of scenery" might take her and stood. "Thank you."

"No, thank you for finding that priceless piece of weaponry. I'm certain it will provide much needed information. Hopefully they can find the submarine that set the decoy adrift. Such trickery."

"Yes," Billi mumbled.

Just before she opened the door, she turned to face the lieutenant's dark, humorless eyes.

"It's just too bad, there is no photo of the brave SPAR who landed such a catch."

Realizing her mistake, Billi nodded. Yet, if the photo appeared in the local newspapers, exposing her false identity and whereabouts, the results would have attracted only one thing, danger. Once again, she lived in a different world. With a deep sigh Billi, Ginger, Lilly, opened the door preparing to ship off to be "educated."

THE CROSS-COUNTRY TRAIN RIDE, bumpy and crowded, finally ended in Springfield, Massachusetts. From there the SPARS loaded onto a bus to head north.

Billi pulled her dark blue coat closer against the biting Northampton wind. The stately Smith College, home to the United States Naval Reserve Midshipmen's School, a welcome sight.

One of the many men in uniform, a young pilot, had told her they had been on the train for days. His positive attitude remarkable after all the shenanigans the Air Corps had put them through in preparation to depart from their training base.

His story unfolded in his calm, easy manner. His squad had, at first, been issued light uniforms, indicating his assignment would be the Pacific Theater. The next day, they were issued heavy wool uniforms, marking Europe as their destination. Day three, they shuffled aboard with both uniforms riding the train through Canada then back into the US. The kid still had no idea where he was being shipped. He had laughed, his eyes sparkling, at the apparent message that spies waited, watched and listened everywhere. Any tip to the enemy resulted in the death of soldiers.

"Bet you never thought the war would bring out so many spies." She remembered his flirtatious grin seemed well-rehearsed. "I suppose they must know a lot we don't if they're going to all this trouble to confuse the Jerries and the Japs." She had merely nodded while wishing him the best, in whichever uniform he finally ended up wearing against the enemy.

"Hurry up, Lilly. We can't be late for our orientation." Ruth hustled her past old brick buildings then up the massive steps to the entrance of Smith College's Greene Hall. So like Ruth, still in charge, still concerned with the timetable imposed by the call of duty.

They stepped inside the grandeur of the John N. Greene Hall then took their seats for the assembly. The large cream proscenium arching over the stage and massive organ pipes spoke of the wealth which built this elite college for women. She watched her three friends as they took in their surroundings and couldn't help but grin.

With some fanfare, the graduating SPARS marched onto the stage in formation, performed a few drills then stopped in somber silence. Next, Captain Dorothy Stratton, Director of the SPARS, strode to the mic for a welcome.

Billi heard her stomach growl, attempting to keep her focus on the lengthy welcome. By the time the meeting commenced, including room assignments, she could hardly stand.

Ruth lead the charge across Elm Street to their new residence, the Gilbert House. They climbed to the 4th floor then stood outside the door which adjoined two single rooms.

"I don't care where I sleep, I just need something to eat." Billi groaned lowering her seabag to catch her breath.

At the end of the hallway Billi opened the door to their assigned room. Eight bunk beds filled the space which once housed only one student. At one end, four beds were clearly assigned and at the other, four empty beds would become their home.

In her direct fashion, Ruth assigned the bunks to reflect their previous arrangements. Billi threw her bag on the top bunk waiting for Karen to settle in below.

When the door flew open, the newcomers all turned in unison. The four young officers in training entering, instantly establishing propriety over their end of the quarters.

Hazel, obviously Ruth's counterpart, took the lead. "I'm Hazel, this is Barbara, Anne and Connie. We have the bathroom first in the morning and hopefully there will be time and hot water left. Where did you ship in from?"

"Fort Worden," Ruth barked back, sternly eyeing Hazel. "Bathroom goes to whomever gets there first."

The line had been drawn.

Finally, Hazel snorted. "Well at least you come from a place that has water, not like some of these new gals who have never seen the ocean."

"That's right," Ruth excelled at the banter. "We all have salt in our blood."

Just before lights out, Billi noticed Hazel's team put their bathrobes and coats at the end of their beds above their boots. They had all crawled in under the covers with their warm socks on. She was far too tired to give the behavior much thought. Exhausted, she patted Eileen's pillow safely stashed under her covers, then rolled over to face the dull wall and her misgivings. Orders had arrived for their departure for Smith College the day after she had refused to be in the photo with the mock Japanese periscope. They had been on the train the next day without time to go to her mother's house for a proper good-bye.

She pulled her blanket closer, warding off the feeling of loneliness overshadowed by the bone chilling realization of her behavior. She could only imagine what the Coast Guard, now officially part of the Navy, would do to her when they discovered her true identify. The fact she had lied, taking on another's identity, would surely be basis for a court martial. She imagined the look on Jack's face as he confronted her. Fitfully, she tossed the blanket away then quietly slid from her bunk to stand by the large leaded glass windows. Outside held the promise of a cold storm as the thick clouds began to drop snow blocking any view of the expansive lawn. Suddenly, she noticed flashlights bobbing toward the side of their building followed by a loud blaring siren ringing the alarm.

"Knew it." Hazel jumped from her bed. Slipping into her boots She wrapped her warm coat over her bathrobe, tightening both around her. "Let's hustle."

The four old timers were out the door and down the stairs before the rookies realized the situation.

Shuffling into the lineup in the drifts of snow, Billi understood the situation. A greeting from her new post. A fire drill in the dark of night.

"Not bad, but room for improvement." The lieutenant bellowed.

The women stood in formation, gathering mantels of snow on their curlers or pinned up hair. Those who had just arrived evident by their footwear and lack of warm coats. They shuffled their feet, stomping at the hard earth as they waited the half hour it took to complete the drill while the fire crew checked the entire building.

As they finally marched back inside Ruth caught up to Hazel. "Any more surprises we should know about?"

Hazel flashed a smile as she snapped the snow from the scarf she had over her curlers. "Just count on a fire drill every time we have new recruits. It's part of the training officer's welcoming routine."

Billi, the last into the room, joined her friends by the tall steam heaters below the windows. Pink, numb hands worked together to increase heat and circulation. In an offering of peace, Hazel led her women back to their side of the room not attempting to crowd the one source of heat in the high-ceilinged room.

If looks alone could set someone a blaze, Ruth's glare at Hazel would have set off another, well warranted fire alarm.

She stifled a laugh. Being "educated" had many facets. While their classroom training had not begun, their survival techniques were clearly being well honed.

# THIRTY SIX

AKIO SAT AT A LONG TABLE with several officers at Imperial General Headquarters. Each man displayed his anger and disappointment at the outcome of Operation 81. The plan to deliver nearly seven thousand troops to New Guinea had failed. Conquering the rest of this strategic island would have set the stage for easy access to Australia and the many resources that country offered.

"The enemy aircraft have developed new techniques. Whispering death attacked at sea level and strafed our men at their guns while others dropped bombs from the skies," Imamura, Chief of Staff, continued his report. "Propaganda spreads in the US about the battle, we did not lose twenty-two ships. Their lies are outrageous. We only sent sixteen, eight transport ships and eight destroyers."

"Of which, four destroyers survived to fight again." Admiral Yamamoto pointed out. "The death of nearly three thousand men, along with shiploads of supplies, has cut deeply into our fortifications. Very few made it to their destination at Lae. We must consider our next moves carefully. Our Emperor has endured great loss of face."

"Our enemy was masterful in the Bismarck Sea." Akio leaned forward. "Yes, their tactics changed, many types of planes from different bases and directions. The manner in which they skipped the bombs across the surface at the flank of our ships is a tool we need to employ. Yet, perhaps we need to consider how we can hurt them the most. Cut at their heart."

All attention now anchored on Akio. Some, aware of his bold plans, admired his reputation for ruthlessness.

Yamamoto gave a slight nod.

Akio breathed deeply before beginning. "Attack the Panama Canal and Washington D.C. simultaneously. In this manner we stop their ship traffic through the canal forcing them to round Cape Horn, which is time consuming and dangerous. More importantly, we also strike the nerve center of their crippled President Roosevelt."

Akio looked into astonished eyes as the air seemed to be sucked out of the room.

Yamamoto let the idea settle around his men before responding. "I have commissioned 18 of Akio's design. We have already begun construction on both the submarine and the aircraft. As our supplies for rebuilding are shortening with every battle where we suffer heavy losses, it is time to take bold action."

No one dared challenge this announcement. Previous heated discussions regarding the expense of Akio's invention fell on the deaf ears of Yamamoto. Obviously, some still held a grudge as they refused to acknowledge Akio's new plan.

"For now, we will not attempt to land any more troops in New Guinea. I have personally promised the Emperor retaliation for the disaster we suffered at Bismarck. We will meet again tomorrow."

With the others, Akio stood to comply with the dismissal.

"Akio, stay." Yamamoto did not look up with his second command.

Akio could feel his heart racing. He eased back down to wait.

When the room cleared, Yamamoto looked directly at him. "We are moving our headquarters to Rabual. If I am to fulfill my promise of revenge on Allied troops, a promise to Emperor Hirohito I intend to honor, I must be closer to my men."

"I understand." Akio waited.

"You should be relieved to know that Ume has found you a trusted matchmaker. The honorable Daikai has chosen well for you. If it is agreed, you will marry in two days and plant your seed well before the next battle. Children are important for the continuation of our great nation."

Akio shot up to bow. "I am extremely pleased that your gracious Ume has devoted herself to my lineage. When can I thank her in person?"

"You will meet your bride at dinner tonight and hopefully, the ceremonies will begin." Yamamoto regarded him with hardened eyes. "Harue is the daughter of a friend. She is to be treated gently, like the beautiful flower she has become."

His superior made his threat plain. He would have to be careful with this woman for she was but a means to the continuation of his family bloodline. Silently, he vowed to save his brutality for Billi. He bowed his head again, solidifying the agreement.

THE HEAT FROM HIS BATH continued to relax the muscles that twisted across the wound from Billi's knife. As had become his custom, he stood on his right foot with the damaged toe, checking his balance before stepping over the puddle into the courtyard of the tea house in the Shimbashi district where he was to meet his bride. On two other occasions he had the honor of visiting this tea house with Admiral Yamamoto and his beloved Umeryu. He embraced this third meeting as very auspicious. Pausing to adjust his white naval jacket he huffed, admonishing himself for the act. He did not need to worry about his appearance for this Harue. Soon she would be his wife to perform for him at his command.

Ume swayed in his direction then bowed. "Thank you for your presence this evening." She rose, watching him intently.

"Only a fool would miss his own engagement party." Akio felt ill at ease under her gaze.

"Time has brought you much favor. A cherished blossom will soon be yours. If held too tight it will shrivel and perish. If treated with respect, it will bloom for eternity."

Yet another warning. But this time from one of the most powerful women in all of Tokyo, the one who held the ear of the Commander in Chief of the Combined Fleet.

He quickly bowed before her. "I thank you for your esteemed opinion in selecting my bride. One who will honor me with many sons, who will fight for our Emperor."

He waited a moment, when there was no reply, he straightened. She was gone.

Alone he started down the hallway past the kitchen to the back, favored room, where the shogi screen remained open. Removing his shoes, he stepped inside to find the Admiral reciting to his muse, Ume.

"If that has brought you favor, I will write another." The Admiral slid the neatly penned poem across the low table to Ume.

"I will add this to the others that I keep under my pillow, so you are always with me in my dreams." Her eyes spoke further of their bond.

Without looking, the Admiral waved Akio toward his left. Obeying the command, Akio lowered onto the zabuton, the massive pillow, and remained silent with his uncertainty.

A grunt came from the door as an elderly man, leaning on an intricately carved walking stick, entered. He huffed toward them as two of the younger geishas helped the gray-haired man lower to the head of the table.

The Admiral spoke first. "Daiki. I am glad to see you. You are still as strong as the pine tree."

The older man laughed. "But my branches are twisted with the winds of time."

"Are you saying you will not challenge me at mahjong?" Yamamoto leaned toward his guest.

"I said my branches were twisted, not my brain."

Ume joined the two bantering men in laughter.

Daiki turned his attention to the silent Akio. "Does he have a sense of humor? Or is it he fears you at mahjong?"

"Both." Yamamoto retorted, again finding humor with his statement.

Akio regarded the newcomer, the nakado, the honored go between, who must approve of the swift marriage.

"I have brought Kinpo-zutsumi." Akio's statement fell flat before the others.

Ume sought to sooth the situation. "Akio is a great warrior, where time is precious. He is perhaps overly excited to meet his bride."

"What else?" Daiki countered, accepting that the negotiations had begun.

"For additional luck, I have brought a suehiro." Akio reached inside his jacket retrieving two packets, one held the kinpo-zutsumi, ceremonial money, and the other a fan.

Daiki reached for the fan then snapped it open, revealing silver tones with orange leaves denoting love and happiness next to the revered chrysanthemum. He held the fan, considering it. He slowly closed the black lacquer frame sliding the good luck offering back across the table

Akio felt the perspiration start at his brow as the old eyes watched him, uncertain if this old goat was refusing his offer.

Finally, the old man turned to Yamamoto. "In times of war, strength is needed along with the understanding of timing. Harue will see he embodies both." Without turning, his age spotted hand reached for the packet of money before Akio. He considered its weight then swiftly tucked the packet inside his kimono. Seemingly satisfied, he sat back clapping his hands.

Both sides of the shoji screen opened, revealing Harue. She bowed before gliding into the room. Her head remained lowered as first she acknowledged the Admiral, then Daiki. Ume stood to take her hand, leading her around the table to Akio.

"Akio, this is Harue, who has consented to this meeting." Ume's soothing voice resounded like thunder in his ears as he realized this meeting was a trial.

In his haste to rise, he bumped the fan, sending it to the floor. Without hesitation, Harue swept it up then held it out toward Akio.

When she looked up, Akio caught his breath. She had two different colored eyes. One darker while the other, lighter, appeared to have a mist over the retina. Her foggy eye reminded him of Jack as he fought the urge to leave the room ending the negotiations.

She did not blink or show the slightest recognition of fear. She simply regarded him with such ferocity that Akio faltered, suddenly conscious that everyone waited for his response.

"That is meant for you." He indicated the fan she held toward him.

"Thank you." She bowed again. "I will cherish it always."

She turned to trail Ume to the far side of the table, then gracefully lowered across from Akio.

"I am sure in battle but not before such beauty." Akio bowed slightly hoping his reaction when first seeing her would be overlooked. He comforted himself, reasoning the duty of their consummation would be performed in the cover of darkness. His sudden urgency for this marriage to proceed rattled his nerves. He would make certain his seed grew inside her, then find pleasures elsewhere.

"Let us enjoy some sake to ease the uncertainty of young lovers." Ume poured sake for her lover first, a signal to the geishas waiting to fill the other cups.

Akio began to breath comfortably once he had consumed his second bottle of sake. He turned his attention to the two men exchanging old stories, needing time to think. In the hour that passed, the brazen woman he intended to wed, said nothing to him but chatted quietly with Ume. He waited for more sake to be poured as he eyed her more closely.

Without warning, the thud of Daiki's walking stick struck the wooden floor. "I am an old man, Harue. Take pity." He pouted, watching the young woman.

She lifted the fan Akio offered her as a sign of good luck in their marriage then flicked it open. Masterfully, she spun the silver and orange toned sensu through the air as all fell under its spell.

A flash of swirling fans danced in Akio's memory. He held his breath remembering the one dancer at the club in San Francisco, dressed like a geisha with jet black wig and startling blue eyes. Unconsciously, he licked his lips envisioning his meeting with Billi.

Laughter broke his spell as he looked around at the others at the table.

"One should wait for the feast to be brought to the table before devouring it." The Admiral chided.

Akio bristled with embarrassment, choosing not to respond.

Harue hid her face behind the fan, turning toward Daiki, with one swift nod the table relaxed. The marriage would proceed. Tomorrow they would each take three sips from three different cups binding them together as man and wife.

Her small hands moved toward Akio with her offerings of good luck. She unfolded the embroidered cloth revealing two objects. She touched the konbu first, emphasizing its importance. The offering of the two dried pieces of kelp signified the blessing of healthy children.

Akio nodded with relief. She consented to having his children, not destroying his seed before it came to full term. Watching her touch the white linen threads of the tomo-shiraga, he hid his reaction behind another nod, doubting they would grow old together, their hair turning as white as the threads.

He regarded those unsettling eyes of hers wondering at the matchmaker meaning, "Harue will see he embodies both strength and an understanding of timing."

Confounded, his mind battled to understand the choice of this woman who would become his wife.

JACK SAT ACROSS FROM SHIRLEY CHOW who rested in her usual dragon carved chair inside the back room of the Forbidden City Nightclub. She drew on a cigarette attached to a long holder, emitting smoke through her nostrils like the mythical creature she embodied.

"We have sent millions to Chiang Kai-shek to defend our country."

Jack merely nodded, well aware of her connection to Soong Mei-ling, Madame Chiang. He tapped the March cover of Time Magazine. The image of the daunting Madame Chiang Kai-shek on the cover of the esteemed publication represented her third appearance since 1931.

His finger lingered on the bird perched on a branch of bamboo near the left ear of the formidable wife of the leader of China. "Is this you?"

Shirley snorted a laugh as her head turned to the side, imitating the profile of the bird.

They watched each other intently before Jack spoke. "Madame Chiang was brilliant last month in her speech before both Houses of Congress."

Shirley lifted one eyebrow in challenge.

Jack smiled slyly before his recital. "And I quote, 'Devotion to common principles eliminates differences in race and that identity of ideals is the strongest possible solvent of racial dissimilarities.'"

She waited unemotionally.

"Ah, the part where the US has the opportunity to bring about the liberation of men, I believe she said serving, in every part of the world."

Shirley's mouth twisted into a wry smile. "Soong is very proud of her Engrish."

It was Jacks turn to snort, as Shirley's pronunciation of the word English remained difficult to understand. "Yes, thank the gods it wasn't you talking into the microphones."

Her long nails tapped the head of the dragon on the arm of her chair. "Today you speak the truth."

Her unusual playful mood made Jack cautious. He considered what the wife of the leader of the country, at war for five and one-half years with Japan, might have revealed to Shirley Chow in private. More importantly, he wondered what Shirley wanted from him. He had no information of Akio and she claimed her connections had not provided any further reports. He would try again.

"The China, Burma, India campaign has been slowed again by monsoons and mud. Not to mention malaria and cholera. The Burma Road will continue to be built, and supplies will be routed to the Chinese, British and US forces fighting to keep the Japanese out of China." Jack leaned closer. "But you have done well by sending the funds you have raised. General Chennault has acquired new planes for the 14th Airforce. The Flying Tigers are now better equipped to fight the Japanese, your enemy and ours."

"Yes, the sharks that still roam the skies will fear the tiger." She took another drag causing the red embers to consume more of her cigarette. "How is Ginger?"

There it was. Jack breathed better recognizing the direction of their meeting. He took a sip of his drink, calculating the dragon lady's interest.

"She is safe and well." He rolled the amber liquid around in his glass before putting it back on the table.

"Her mother must miss her." Her eyes had not softened.

So, the wiry person Duckworth wrestled with outside of 304 30th Ave a few months back was one of Shirley's informants. The button claiming his Chinese descent accurate, not a cloak for a Japanese spy.

"We all miss someone." Jack mused. He suppressed the image of his wife as the intoxicating Ginger, clad in her revealing hula skirt, in this very room.

"Perhaps some more than others." She brushed the long ember into the ornate brass ashtray. "You should go to her, Jack."

He could not calculate if her suggestion derived from her heart or from her need to follow him to find Billi. Once more, he sought the reason for Shirley's interest in his wife. Of course, this dragon lady of Chinatown knew about the fan and the possibility of its hidden message, but that seem inconsequential, far too obvious. There had to be more.

"It is too late." He downed the last of his drink.

"For you or for her?"

When Jack did not answer Shirley whispered. "There must be many secrets."

Jack felt his stomach lurch. Shirley would not be beyond using Billi to lure Akio into the open.

"What did Akio do to you that you would brave finding him at all costs?"

"Many secrets." She repeated, exhaling the last of the smoke from her now extinguished cigarette.

Jack stood to leave. He had not mentioned the other part of Madame Chiang's speech before the US congress.

"Know thyself and know thy enemy."

# THIRTY SEVEN

Billi's feet ached as if they had traveled thousands of miles, and perhaps they had. But not in the gentle stroll of one enjoying the evening sunset, or the long stride of hurrying to catch a bus. No. She marched everywhere. The daily drills of marching back and forth for hours on the track, marching to classes at Faunce hall, to the firing range, marching back to Gillett House, and up the four flights of stairs to her room, made her march in her dreams.

Unable to sleep, she sat up exhausted, tossing the covers from her throbbing feet to massage them. Sliding from her top bunk, she quietly made her way to the window where the slip of the moon barely lit the grounds. The deep shadows of the buildings filled the area between the large ornate brick buildings with blankets of inky black. Anyone could move about unseen.

The thought ran a chill through her. Today the news announced that under the cover of darkness, the Japanese attempted to reinforce their holding on Kiska in the Aleutian Islands but were driven back by the US Navy. The report made her think of Akio.

For the first time, she felt calmed by the luck of her situation. Northampton provided security and she intended to keep it that way. Rocking the boat could get her expelled from service, put in prison or sent back to—she stumbled as to where she considered home. She did not know if Jack would accept her with open arms after her sudden disappearance. For that matter, she doubted her mother would make room for her. Suppressing her worries, she headed back to her bunk.

When the floor creaked, Ruth sat up.

"That you, Lilly?" She whispered.

"Shhh." Billi hissed.

Ruth's feet hit the floor as she snatched up her bathrobe. "Grab your robe and follow me."

One to never questioned Ruth's commands, she slung her chenille robe over her shoulders, following Ruth out into the hallway.

They crept down the hall toward the staircase then sat on the top step, the spot where Ruth held nightly court if she had noticed anything out of line with the four women she protected like a mother hen. The range of emotions those polished wooden stairs silently witnessed, the quiet laughter, the tears, the promises to persevere and do better, could fill a novel.

Ruth wasted no time with gentle introductions into the topic. "I've noticed how the instructors watch you."

Billi let out a sigh. "I thought I was the only one."

"Your file has a red dot."

Her spine straightened while her stomach tightened. "Is that bad?"

She felt Ruth's eyes on her as her friend continued, "I don't know, but it must mean something. And you have accumulated quite a few demerits."

"I know. But at least I haven't bilged out like that red head from Texas. She just couldn't quite follow the rules."

"Or made a bed. She only joined to be closer to men," Ruth pointed out.

"You're training in the main office, is that where you saw this?"

"You can't breathe a word of this, or I'll be gone, or arrested. I heard your name, something about Stanford. Holy hell, you didn't tell me you went to Stanford."

"Briefly." She began to sweat.

"Something about the graduating class is going to have a speaker. A senator's wife, and she attended Stanford."

"What does that have to do with me?" She twisted the belt of her robe to keep her hands from shaking.

"I don't know. Maybe they want you to meet this lady and make her feel welcome."

"When?" She heard her voice crack. "When is the graduation for that class?"

"Next week." Ruth turned to lean her back against the wall, facing Billi. "There's something you need to tell me?"

"No."

Ruth saw right through her whispered lie. "I can't help you, Lilly, if I don't know what you're hiding."

"I failed." Her words come with the strength of truth. Those two little words summed it up.

"Your failure at Stanford should not hold you back. You're extremely bright." Ruth spoke in her maternal, reasoning voice.

"It got me a red dot." Billi replied flatly.

They stood simultaneously at the sound of footsteps from down the hall. Hand in hand they crept to the far side of the landing, where the shadows provided shelter. The beam from the night watch's flashlight moved across the closed doors then pointed toward the far stairwell.

Billi felt her racing heart begin to slow as Ruth sighed next to her. When the light disappeared, they hurried toward their dorm room door.

"I'll keep my ears open and see what else I can find out."

"Thanks." Impulsively Billi hugged her. She needed friends she could trust in her web of lies.

Back under the covers of her top bunk, Billi wrestled with a new uncertainty. She needed to figure out a way to avoid the senator's wife who attended Stanford. If not, the walls of her safe haven at Northampton might crumble in one week's time.

"IS THAT WHAT I THINK IT IS?" Eddy whistled with delight.

"Yep." Scooter leaned further into the plexiglass bay of their PBY adjusting his binoculars. His smile resembled a wolf watching sheep graze in a pasture. "There's one hell of a lot of ships and planes down there. Bets are they're up to something."

They had been drifting high in the protection of the clouds for hours; circling, watching, waiting. Below, Kahili Airfield, constructed by the Japanese in 1942 on the southern tip of Bougainville Island, suddenly became a stream of movement. Enemy aircraft launched in four large groups.

"Holy shit. Looks like a hornet's nest of Zeros and Vals. I wish we could have a go at those Nips."

"Not today." Eddy mirrored Scooter's reaction, they had orders. Watch and report. "Fletch, check their coordinates but looks like they're heading toward Guadalcanal. Hank, radio ahead and let base know they're on the move."

"Yes sir." Hank's voice crackled with excitement.

Beau, the plane's captain chimed in. "Set course for Henderson. We'll miss the fun but hopefully our guys can scramble into action and take out a few of those bastards."

Eddy felt the disappointment of his crew. "Sorry, Charlie. All that time you spent just lying around, dreaming of killing more Japs will have to wait. How's it going?"

Charlie's reply reflected a strength he didn't yet possess, his malaria still ravaging his body from time to time. "It's great to be back in the air with you guys."

"The Coastwatchers have verified our report, sir." Hank piped up. "Enemy aircraft approaching from various bases. Coastwatchers, now there's a job I wouldn't want."

"Naw. You'd go crazy if you couldn't lose all your money at cards." Eddy hoped his jest calmed his radio man's jitters. Being alone in a radio shack in hostile territory, in Eddy's eyes, proved ultimate bravery. The Coastwatchers were a unique crew saving thousands of lives.

The Phantom trailed at her slow pace high above as the fast fighter planes screeched through the air toward the Allied forces. At times like this Eddy felt helpless and frustrated. Well aware the vital information they forwarded to base would save lives, it did not lighten his thirst for the blood of the enemy.

As they approached Iron Bottom Sound, drifts of smoke filled the sky before them. The battle was over, debris of downed planes and sinking ships dotted the water.

"Is that the *Aaron Ward*?" Scooter's voice held the edginess of a boxer sitting on the outside of the ring. "She's hit bad. Damn bastards. I want another chance at them."

Eddy could only nod. They all wanted another crack at Tōjō's men. But tonight, they had helped save lives by being the sentinel forwarding enemy movements to their base. Their cat would rise again to kill the rats. That was a promise he intended to keep.

IT WAS JUST AFTER 2 A.M. on April 12$^{th}$, 1943 when Eddy and his crew set their sights on the Japanese airfield at Wewak on the coast of Papa New Guinea. They had flown high above "the slot" that ran through the center of the Solomon Islands with nothing to report, then decided to press forward.

They skirted the major Japanese stronghold of Rabaul. Rumors claimed Admiral Yamamoto had arrived at Rabaul on the 3$^{rd}$ of April to oversee the success of the attacks on the Allied strongholds. That sting had already been felt at Guadalcanal where every soldier stood at ready for the last four days anticipating another strike. However, the Japanese sent their forces to other Allied bases, mounting the largest air attacks in the Southwest Pacific since Pearl Harbor.

Eddy leaned into the dark with pure concentration. Scooter bobbed his head, brandishing his eager smile when Eddy gripped the wheel of their PBY and pulled with all his might, heading their craft closer to the enemy airfield.

"You say your prayers this morning?" Scooter's question not all jest.

"Yep. And I know my mother has placed flowers at the statue of The Blessed Virgin Mary for me, so we're covered." Eddy glanced at his co-pilot with an assured smile. "Besides, there will be plenty of targets for us to choose from there."

"In for a penny, in for a pound."

The night held the promise of a perfect time to be on the prowl. Soft moonlight filtered through the few clouds leaving the shoreline and waters dark as hell. Below in the bay off the airstrip, ships at anchor, large and small, made dark dots across the surface.

"We'll come at them from over the land." Eddy informed his crew.

The silence of anticipation filled their cabin vibrating down the ranks, past the plane captain, navigator, radioman, and side gunners, as they approached their destination. The reason for their mission had arrived, a chance to drop the bombs they carried on the enemy. Tensions increased as they focused on their duties.

As they skimmed low above the trees Eddy suddenly realized they were not alone.

"Shit." Scooter's reaction reflected the situation.

"I'm hangin' with him." Eddy remained calm as he fell in behind a smaller enemy aircraft. "Don't fire yet. They might not know we're here."

"Got one coming at us from behind." Beau's voice came over the headphones.

"Not yet." Eddy commanded.

"What the hell." Charlie shouted. "He's blinking his lights at us!"

"Holy shit." Scooter's voice was filled with awe. "We're fuckin' heading for their airstrip."

"Stay calm. Open the bay. Ready to drop." Eddy's soothing voice resounded his intent in the tenuous situation as they soared between two Japanese Zeros approaching the enemy airstrip.

Eddy rode the tail of the first plane until it began its descent. He pushed forward with the other Zero on his tail still blinking his lights. As the black cat shot past the end of the airfield it approached a large munitions ship anchored in the bay just beyond.

"500 feet to target." Fletch recited the calculations.

"What's the one on our tail doing?"

The gunner's reply came quickly. "Starting to land."

"Fire one." Eddy watched Scooter pull the lever and counted to five. "Fire two. Now let's get the hell out of here."

Pulling hard, cursing the manual steering, Eddy swung the Phantom back above the treetops. They began to climb as the explosion rocketed behind them. In the blaze of the burning vessel, searchlights cut through the night. Tracers streaked into the night from surrounding boats, followed by the rat a tat of guns as those below scrambled to see the ghost in the night that just destroyed a vital ship in their harbor.

"Holy mother of God, they thought we were one of them." Scooter yelled with excitement.

"They're launching aircraft, sir." Beau's sobering announcement seemed to suck the air out of the PBY.

"Direction?" Eddy kept the black cat climbing though the dark sky.

"Heading east over the water."

"Come on baby." Scooter coaxed the massive spread of wings that bore them past the puffs of cloud.

They could not outrun the fighter planes. If they climbed high enough, they would be lost against the stars, leaving no telltale shadow on dark waters as they crossed the crescent moon.

"Report?" Eddy kept his eyes forward.

"They're circling back toward base."

A collective holler of relief spread through the black cat. Eddy took a deep breath as he loosened his grip on the wheel.

"Well done. And that was one that we'll be telling our grandkids. Let's head back."

"We might need to glide a bit, sir." Beau piped in. "Check your fuel gage. Something's wrong."

"Were we hit?" Eddy's heart began to pound, they were hours away from base.

A brief silence followed before Beau came back on the radio. "We found the son of a bitch, sir. A leak. Getting on it. Will report back."

Eddy watched the dark sky and his gauge, the only two things that mattered right now as he struggled the Phantom toward safe shores.

Finally, the radio crackled with the report. "The leak is fixed."

"How much did we lose?"

"Enough to know we'll limp in on the winds."

Scooter looked at Eddy. "Damn. I didn't bring my bathing suit."

"How's our tail wind?" Eddy ignored his co-pilot's attempt at a joke.

Fletch responded in the middle of his calculations. "Fair, as long as we don't hit any unexpected turbulence or head winds, we'll be about six miles shy of base."

"Won't need that bathing suit." Eddy kidded back, dwarfing the uncertainty of their situation.

Riding high above the sea and clusters of islands below, the hours passed filled with the light chatter of distraction. The low fuel demanded an altered course, directing their black cat close to possibly five enemy airstrips before they reached the safety of Henderson.

The first rays of sun glistened on the blue waters with the massive patch of green just beyond. Guadalcanal, the graveyard of thousands of American Marines, Navy, Army and Coast Guard never looked so beautiful.

Eddy looked at his fuel gauge. It registered empty.

"Wind reading?" He knew everyone held their breath for the answer.

"A bit of a nose wind." Beau sounded confident.

"They know we're coming in short, sir." Hank added. "I'll let them know where we land."

"Not a problem."

With a sputter the propellers spun to a stop, pressed in place by the wind. An eerie swooshing of the air blowing past the wings with their new gunshot holes filled the void of the engine.

Eddy felt the heartbeat of his crew as they glided, their broad wings now their life support.

Luck rode with them as the surface of the water remained smooth in the morning light. They glided lower, confident, when suddenly they saw it.

"Tell them to get that damn thing out of our way." Eddy barked into the mike.

The LST-449 slowly plowed through the waters toward base, right smack dab in their path.

Scooter opened his side window to yell at the boat. "Get your ass out of the way."

"Shitttt," Eddy and Scooter pulled back on the flaps, but the large boat of an aircraft did not respond. He could not tilt the wings hard this low to the water without the engine to pull him out. He slowly pulled to the right knowing it would not be enough.

"They can't hear us without our engine." Scooter pronounced the obvious.

"They will now." Eddy yelled.

They all heard it. The screeching of metal on metal as the bottom of their right pontoon scraped across the top of the ship's antenna. The men on the ship below scurrying out of the way.

"Hope that's not deep." Scooter looked at Eddy.

"They're sending a boat out to tow us in." Hank's voice held the essence of relief they all felt.

"Hang on." Eddy didn't allow doubt to overwhelm him. If the pontoon was punctured, it could take on water, causing them to spin. He put her down as softly as possible as they glided across the surface toward shore. Eddy cranked the wheel into the wind attempting to slow them down when they all felt their beloved black cat jerk to the right.

"Get that life raft out. Let's go, grab the oars. Move it. We're home." Eddy unbuckled his seat belt then removed his headphones.

Charlie appeared with their faithful mascot under his arm. "Come on, Midnight Marauder, time for some fresh fish for you."

Eddy watched as the crew slipped out the door, down the side and into the inflated raft with Midnight being shuffled reverently toward the bow of the boat. He stood on the pontoon looking toward the shore.

"You've got that look." Scooter stood beside him.

Eddy started to unbutton his shirt. "I need a stretch."

"Are you kidding me?" Scooter looked toward shore.

"I know, you didn't bring your bathing suit."

"I don't like to swim with sharks." Scooter pointed toward a fin working its way toward their raft.

"Good point. Bastards have gotten brazen with so much to feed on out here." He left his shirt unbuttoned then lowered into the raft behind Scooter.

They rowed toward shore with the shark keeping pace in the distance. The fin disappeared completely as another craft skipped across the water toward them. The ripples from the wake of the approaching boat passed under the raft as it pulled alongside.

"You okay?" Gus, the mechanic, leaned over the side.

"Yeah." Eddy answered for his crew. "Just get the Phantom to shore and get her fixed up."

"Will do." He replied, adjusting his infamous hole filled sailor's cap.

The solid ground provided comfort as they dragged their raft further up the shore.

Charlie lowered Midnight to the sand. The wily cat raced into the thick underbrush toward the Quonset hut she claimed as her home.

"Damn luckiest black cat around." Beau laughed as he hurried off following the four-legged creature.

"You coming with me?" Eddy stepped onto the worn path that led up past the huts and tents to the central command post of the base.

Scooter fell in behind. "You pickin' a bone?"

"Maybe. Just wondering what the hell is up with that LST we shaved this morning."

As they approached the shack that represented headquarters, Eddy noticed a group of young officers, duffel bags over shoulders, starting up the stairs.

"You fellas just arrive?" Eddy led Scooter up the few steps.

"Yes. Just landed and glad to be here." The one who took the lead to answer had a distinct Boston accent.

Eddy knew he hadn't slept in over 48 hours, he needed a shower, a shave and some food. Yet he wanted to know if anyone had been hurt in the mishap, other than his beloved Phantom. "You come in on that LST-449."

"Yes." Boston with the blue eyes answered.

"Anyone hurt when we tapped you?"

Now the eyes crinkled with a smile. "Heard you ran out of fuel. Fine landing. No, the captain is still aboard checking the instruments." He extended his hand. "Lieutenant John Kennedy, you can call me Jack. I'm here to be assigned to my PT boat."

Eddy shook the young man's hand, gauging him to be about his age. "From back east?"

Before the newcomer could answer a voice came from within command. "O'Shaughnessy, I want that report. Now."

"Sounds like some report." Kennedy remarked.

Scooter put his hand toward the lieutenant. "I'm his co-pilot Scooter. And our reports are always something."

Kennedy smiled. "Well O'Shaughnessy, that's the Irish for you. Best of luck."

"And best back at you, Jack, with your new PT boat." Eddy nodded and stepped into the coolness of the office. He chuckled, considering it a good omen that another Irishmen wished him luck.

# THIRTY EIGHT

BILLI SAT ON THE SHORELINE OF Paradise Pond. Smith College, with its elaborate grounds and arboretum, brought back vivid memories of the University of Washington. These grounds, seemingly from the same swath of designers as the UW, brought her comfort. The reflection of the sky in the pond reminded her of the hours spent under the tutelage of Professor Fujihara and the day she met Jack.

A duck disappeared creating a ring of gentle waves that spread across the placid surface. Her impulse was to dive under the chilly waters. She thought of the night, hot and frustrated, she stripped down then dove in the cooling waters of Lake Washington only to discover Jack, having done the same, following her lead with his even stroke. She missed him.

She laughed at the inevitable ripples of reaction from her superiors her impulsive dip would cause. The simple act would crown her ever growing list of demerits and send her packing.

Checking her watch, she jumped to her feet and began running. Ruth promised to meet her in Neilson Library. Hopefully, her main office informant had scoured up more information on the mysterious Senator's wife who graduated from Stanford. She dashed across Burton Lawn to the Neilson Library only stopping to catch her breath before entering the serene building.

Ruth waited at a back table, far removed. Billi sat next to her then conspiratorially leaned across the newspapers clipping her friend had brought.

"Recognize her?" Ruth put her finger near the tall brunette's head. The woman in the photo wore a hat with a partial vail that dipped over her eyes, a mink coat barely revealed her fitted suit and her high heels brought her head to head with the man whose arm she held.

"Never laid eyes on her before." She felt her heart race. If the woman matched her suspicion, Billi's identity stood to be exposed with the wave of the brunette's gloved hand.

"Well that's funny. She stopped by the office just now to acquaint herself with the surroundings before her speech tomorrow. Seems she arrived early and is the kind of bossy woman who has to have her fingerprints on everything."

Billi feared the fingerprints of this tall elegant woman, dreading what they held for her. She looked blankly at Ruth.

Ruth rolled her eyes and continued. "They were looking for you. Mrs. Alfred Adams was thrilled to hear you attended Stanford and even more surprised when she heard your name."

"Why?" Billi gulped.

"She said she was very familiar with your family. She dated your brother, Jack, at Stanford."

"Did you catch her first name?" Billi bent closer to the picture to hide the tears forming in her eyes.

"Mary Beth." Ruth sat back watching Billi. "Ring a bell now, Lilly?"

"Oh, we called her MB. And there is no way I can meet with her." Billi looked straight at Ruth. "I hate that woman."

Ruth folded the article. "I'm not certain that will do. She spoke very highly of you. The captain was impressed with the image MB painted of you. Blonde, petite, lively and always dressed to the hilt."

"I've changed a bit." Billi almost laughed at her own words.

"I'll say." Ruth handed her the folded paper.

"What did the captain say?"

"She promised the Senator's wife that you would be by her side on the lawn in front of the Wilson House, tomorrow. You are to introduce her to the graduating SPARS. Oh, furthermore, MB asked if she could have tea with you beforehand."

"After what she did to Jack? That bitch. Do you know why they stopped dating? They were engaged and he had an accident which left a startling scar. That scar blemished her visions of the perfect life in high society and suddenly Jack was not good enough for miss fingers in everyone's business. She left him." Billi's heart pounded as the words of anger and defense easily slipped into the quiet surroundings of the library. "What do I do?" She implored.

Ruth tapped the table, eyeing her. "Dye your hair blond, cut a few inches off your legs or tell me who you really are before I expose you."

Billi remained silent.

When Ruth began to rise Billi grabbed her arm. "Wait. Sit down."

She attempted to compose herself and do what Ruth asked. Searching the room for anyone within ear shot, she leaned closer to whisper. "I am a Huntington and related to Jack. Those are facts. Our family is deeply involved with the secrets of our national security. We felt it best that I join the SPARS to be sequestered safely out of harm's way. I cannot be exposed."

Ruth blinked at the unexpected answer. "Are you having me on?"

"No." Billi shook her head and repeated. "No. Not in the least."

"Would this MB do that?"

"Have no doubt about this woman." Billi tapped the newspaper emphasizing her explanation. "This woman would do anything to insult us. In fact, Bella, our maid, will not allow anyone to mention her name in the house."

Billi hoped the bit about Bella would add credibility to the depth of the injury inflicted on her husband. She secretly would love to have tea with MB but realized the scandal she would provoke when she round housed this woman who practiced snow skiing in shorts on the grass of Stanford.

Ruth sighed as she stood. "I think you are beginning to look very ill. Do you have a fever?"

"Not until 2 a.m. I won't." Billi stood, placing her hand on her friends' uniform sleeve. "Thank you. Someday we'll laugh about this."

"I hope so, Lilly. You better stay low. I know the captain is booked all afternoon with a party this evening."

"I can't thank you enough."

"You can thank me by staying out of sight and trouble."

Billi smiled, that statement Jack would concur with one hundred percent. Yet, somehow her fate continued to pull her in the opposite direction.

AT 2 A.M. Billi shook Ruth awake.

"I feel awful." Billi mumbled loud enough for the others to hear.

A few heads popped up then sank back down when Ruth threw her covers back then stood to help the hunched over figure of Billi.

"Here. Let's get you to the nurse." Ruth helped her toward the door.

They stepped outside into the darkened hallway, trudging over the hard wood flooring. Billi stopped long enough to pull a small bottle of ipecac syrup from her robe pocket, taking a big gulp. She took another before handing it to Ruth.

Billi's face scrunched up with her displeasure. "It tastes terrible."

"You deserve it." Ruth coaxed her forward.

"Here." Billi extracted an envelope from her other pocket. "Go on, read it."

Ruth opened the note and strained in the dim light to read aloud. "Dear Mary Beth. It seems a lifetime ago since you were with us at our humble home on San Raymundo."

Billi stifled a laugh.

"Why is that funny?" Ruth kept walking as she waited for the answer.

"Nothing really. Keep going."

"Mother is well, and Bella still keeps us in line. I so wish I could meet with you today but suddenly took ill. Please forgive me. I will send your well wishes to the family, including darling Jack and his wife. Au Revoir, Frilly."

Ruth regarded her. "Frilly?"

"Jack's nickname for me."

Billi included the part about Jack being married in the event MB's personal spies had related the nuptial news and, admittedly, out of spite. Her territorial tendencies had never raised her hackles before, but suddenly having Jack's ex around set her seething.

Ruth stuffed the note back inside the envelope. "Very nice."

"It isn't meant to be."

Billi sullenly stood in the hallway on the main floor. "I don't feel so good."

"Come on before you make a mess out here." Ruth hurried her toward the infirmary door.

The nurse took one look at Billi then opened the door wider. Bill doubled over, gripping her stomach as the effects of the ipecac took hold.

"You better get back to bed," the nurse instructed Ruth. "If this is flu, we can't afford to have it spread."

"I'll check on you tomorrow afternoon. Rest and don't get up too soon." Ruth waved then hurried down the hall.

Billi wanted to hug Ruth but turned and dashed toward the bathroom. It promised to be a long, dreadful night.

JACK SMASHED HIS HAT down further on his head as he strode down Powell street in his beloved San Francisco. The streets were mostly deserted this early, with the mist from the Bay adding its own protective shield. He slipped into the Sir Francis Drake by the side door. A bell boy carried a tray with dirty dishes as he stepped off the elevator. Jack quickly entered, inserted his special key, pressing the mezzanine button.

Inside his private office, he slumped into the stark chair then dialed the secret number on his secured line. He took off his hat, lit his cigar, preparing to wait.

At the sound of the click on the line he sat straight. "Jack Huntington reporting."

"Thank you." A woman responded, placing him on hold.

He checked his watch, he was early. He did not mind the silence, the confines of this room or that extra time which presented a moment to reflect. Almost five months ago Billi disappeared, leaving his logical mind to work against his broken heart. He needed to focus.

"Jack," the familiar voice sounded tired.

"Yes, sir." Jack put his cigar in the ashtray.

"Christ, the world is a mess. Reports say the Japanese just slaughtered thirty thousand in Changjiao. The Nazi bastards are killing Jews like flies in the Warsaw Ghettos and we have two-hundred and fifty thousand prisoners on our hands in Africa. Give me some good news."

"I wish I could, sir. I've been to Tule Lake relocation camp. Among those there are the hard-core rival gangs trying to kill each other. Some of the No No Boys rise every morning, put on their headbands, their hachimaki, face toward Japan, then pray to their god, the

Emperor. They want to be sent back to Japan so they can fight against us, I presume."

"I've been apprised of some of their revolts. What of the Germans and Italians?"

Jack stifled a snort. "Nothing important. In fact, one German relocated to Fort Lewis called it the "golden cage." I guess it's all in perception."

"Hell, it's war." The voice grumbled. "Attu, Jack. What are your thoughts?"

"My sources believe the Imperial Japanese Navy won't risk sending the fleet they have gathered in Tokyo Bay. The banzai attack on our troops on Attu was their last gasp. They can't afford to be stretched that thin, even though Alaska is a strategic holding, as Billy Mitchell warned."

"Do you believe them?"

"The nisei and those translating the codes from Magic are devoted to America. Those I speak with who understand the thinking of the Imperial forces have been accurate all along. Besides," Jack sighed before continuing, "My sources are scared to death. They wouldn't screw with me. Excuse me, sir."

Jack ran his hand through his hair praying his field men provided accurate information, and that he had indeed scared them shitless.

"Did that list of names of the Japanese Army officers help you any?"

"We're tracing any connection with the names of those in the relocation camps." Jack had hoped the complete list entailing the names, positions and locations of every Imperial Japanese Army Officer, found on some dead soldiers after the battle in the Bismarck Sea, would somehow lead him to Akio.

"Damn stroke of luck to find those documents. Wish I'd been there when the Auzzie's opened that tin can. Very valuable information."

"MacArthur sure has been crowing about the success of the Bismarck Sea."

"The newsreel will overstate our accomplishments and will inspire continued support. I have some photos I'm withholding of our dead soldiers on the beaches over there. Just in case I need them later to keep the public's ire revved up and assure their involvement."

"Good idea, sir." Jack shook his head at the cunning plan.

Strategy and timing, essential elements of war, included inspiring those at home to continue to work around the clock providing the needed materials to supply the soldiers fighting the battles.

"How's your wife, Jack?"

From the tone of the question he realized the man on the other end of the line probably knew more than he did about Billi.

"Fine, sir." Jack picked up his cigar, toying with it nervously during the ensuing pause.

"Well," the voice finally continued. "That is good news."

"Congratulations on the floating decoy." Jack could not resist commenting on the brilliant plan to confuse the enemy. An Allied submarine had set a disguised corpse adrift off the shores of Spain carrying fake documents.

"Yes, and I quote, 'Operation Mincemeat swallowed rod, line and sinker.'" The laugh that followed made Jack smile. "Churchill's men were brilliant and the Nazis bought it. That poor bastard they set afloat might not have gotten a proper burial, but when all is said and done, he'll be one hell of a hero."

"When all is said and done." Jack repeated, as if willing the moment forward.

"You still trust her?"

The question, spoken evenly, appeared to hold no judgment. Yet, Jack could feel his stomach flip. "Who, sir?"

"Your wife?"

"Absolutely. There is nothing to worry about from Billi."

"Good. Good. Keep me updated and find those leaks. Tōjō doesn't need any more encouragement."

"Their recent loss will bring them to their knees. Thank God for Magic and figuring out the airplane's coordinates. Shot him right out of the sky." Jack took a long draw of satisfaction on his cigar.

"I thought it only apropos that we named the campaign Operation Vengeance. Makes me smile."

"The Japanese people will know soon of the Admiral Yamamoto's death and that will crush them." The truth of Jack's statement would reverberate around the globe in the coming days.

"Now that's good news. Take care Jack."

When the line went dead, he blew his heavy cigar smoke into the stale air. Jack's heart pounded as he recalled the hidden message of their conversation. His superior subtly demanded an update on Billi. He stomped out his cigar. In order to fulfill that order, he must face his wife.

AKIO FELT HIS KNEES WEAKEN as the winds from the sea swept across his dark dress uniform. The wind tasted bitter, matching the bitterness in his heart. He raised his hand in salute as the procession of men stepped from under the canopy draped across the deck of the *Musashi*, Admiral Yamamoto's flagship. A fitting end to a life shortened far too soon.

He held his grief in check as the ashes of his adored Admiral Isoroku Yamamoto, carried high on gloved hands, passed. The white cloth that covered the box billowing around it, as if waving farewell.

The question of how this tragedy occurred, rattled his brain. The reports from Yamamoto's clever plan, Operation I-Go, broadcast wild success. In fact, the report predicted that so many of the Allied ships and planes were destroyed by the Rising Sun's brave men, that the US would be chased out of the South West Pacific Area very soon.

But then, the unthinkable happened. Somehow, someway, the American devils discovered the exact route Yamamoto planned to take as he traveled to inspect and inspire his troops in the Solomon Islands. The Admiral departed early from the airstrip at the Japanese base at Rabaul, planning to fly in his Mitsubishi "Betty" bomber 315 miles. Yet, from nowhere, sixteen US P-38 Lightenings swarmed the eight Japanese planes then shot the Commander in Chief of the Imperial Japanese Navy from the sky.

Akio overheard the whispers of how they found the Admiral's plane, deep in the jungles of the island of Bougainville. Yamamoto had been thrown from the crash, remaining upright in his chair, gripping his katana, his beloved samurai sword. In death his head slumped forward, one bullet pierced his shoulder, a second his jaw.

All that now remained in the ceremonial box were the cremated ashes of the man who had orchestrated the attack on Pearl Harbor, studied at Harvard, served twice as an Attaché in Washington DC, and, more importantly, believed in Akio's designs.

He breathed deeply, mirroring the crowd's sorrow. A grand funeral for the public was scheduled for later. All would weep openly, hearts and spirits crushed, as the Supreme Order of the Chrysanthemum would be laid on Yamamoto's grave. Rumor spread throughout headquarters that the Germans planned to honor the Admiral with their Nazi Knight's Cross of the Iron Cross medal. A fitting display of mutual respect.

Falling in behind the line of men heading to shore, Akio's thoughts turned to Umeryu, Yamamoto's mistress. He blushed, still unable to face her. The passion, respect and quiet love he had witnessed between the Admiral and Umeryu, could not be matched. His heart felt heavy with the knowledge she would only be allowed to attend the public ceremony where some of his ashes would be placed in the municipal Tama cemetery in Tokyo. By tradition, the remainder would be placed at his ancestral burial grounds in Nagaoka City.

As he stepped on the solid ground of Imperial Japanese Naval base at Kisarazu, he cursed the Americans. They had destroyed him in more ways than one. Vengeance whetted his appetite emboldening his need to kill. He would visit a prison camp, select a few Americans at random, then practice with his sword.

THE WARM SAKE BURNED as it slid down his throat. Akio slumped forward, his mind foggy with drink. His visit to the prison camp had sated his frustration with the butchering of five US soldiers. The vision of the frail prisoners emerging from the dark cells, at first, he found off-putting. He preferred strong, healthy victims to bloody his blade.

He huffed. Everything seemed to bring disappointment of late. Upon Yamamoto's death, he had been called before Admiral Mineichi Koga. This inferior man, Koga, did not deserve to replace Yamamoto. Furthermore, he possessed little understanding of the project Akio developed with Yamamoto's blessing.

Akio clearly remembered the stinging words of the new Commander in Chief. "I plan to draw the Americans into battle in the Aleutians. Here." He had used his own pointer, drawing a line on the raised model of North America, tracing from Alaska down the coast toward the United States. "You know this area. You will be of valuable service in the attack."

Understanding an attack on the Aleutian Islands would deplete Japan's remaining resources, angered him. He poured another cup of sake, vowing to find a way around his new commander's orders.

He watched his new wife, Harue, move toward him. The steam from the food she carried added to his alcohol haze creating a mist which partially shielded the tenacious features of her face along with her one eerie eye.

The joy in bedding her already a passing desire. He sneered at her, mistrusting the fact his seed had taken hold so swiftly. She must have been soiled by another before she vowed to be his.

"Is it mine?" The question slid easily from him.

"All here is yours." She placed the tray before him but did not look directly into his eyes.

"Will my son resemble me?"

"Your strength will be inherent with every child I bear."

Akio noticed she still did not regard him directly as she poured tea into his cup. This angered him beyond words. Yet, for the child's sake, he could not strike her as he wished. He began to tremble, the weakness he felt in this perplexing situation overwhelmed his senses.

The reasoning behind Yamamoto choosing this brazen woman as his wife had gone down with his hero's plane. Her intelligence startled him. His home had never known such order. Harue's grace brought him a sense of peace. Yet, she held secrets, he could sense it, and this unrest drove demons deep into his soul.

Clarity came with his first bite of rice. If the child was a girl, he would kill the infant. If a son was born and the baby did not resemble him, he would kill Harue. The lust for blood strengthened his appetite as he shoveled the comforting food into his mouth.

Then another concept brightened his outlook. If indeed he was sent to the Aleutians, he would be closer to Billi. He grinned at the image of her limp body splattered with the sparkling red of her blood where his sword had ripped open her white skin.

Harue's naivety surfaced as her lips curled into a sweet smile in response to his grin.

# THIRTY NINE

BILLI DIDN'T FLINCH AS SHE STOOD before the desk of Captain Dorothy Stratton, the appointed Director of the SPARS when President Roosevelt first approved the new women's branch of the Coast Guard.

"A cloud seems to follow you, Lilly Huntington." The captain dragged out Billi's assumed name with the recognition that it was not hers.

"Again, I apologize if I my sudden illness created any undo commotion at the ceremony."

"Only a brief disappointment. Senator Adams' wife is determined to meet with you. She will be in the area again next week and has requested a visit."

Billi felt the shot of adrenalin rush from her head to her toes. "That should be . . ."

"You leave tomorrow." Stratton cut her off while picking up a slip of paper from her desk. "I could not envision explaining another 'sudden illness' as you called it."

Attempting to control her relief, Billi reached for the carbon copied sheet containing her new orders. "Thank you."

"I was warned of your unusual—talents, when you arrived. The Coast Guard is opening up a new training station in Florida. That should be far enough away from your friend, Mary Beth Adams. At least for now."

"Some ghosts never leave you alone."

Billi's sincerity reflected in the captain's eyes, as she nodded. "Yes."

"Am I going alone? What about the others?" Billi realized she over-stepped her position with this inquiry.

"You'll pass them as you head out the door. I don't like to break bonds, they can be lifesavers in a tight situation."

"I couldn't agree more. Thank you, Captain Stratton." Billi turned to leave. She paused at the door, looking back at the stern image behind the desk. Billi nodded once, then with a light heart slipped out into the hall.

THE FREEDOM BILLI FELT being on the train made her giggle. The Orange Blossom Special, once the famous orange and green luxury passenger train of the rich, now whisked her down the tracks toward Florida. Her good fortune improved with every click of the rails. There were no known Japanese submarines along the east coast. The German U-boats, driven from these shores, slithered up the Atlantic to lurk off Greenland, where they continued to harass the US cargo fleets bound for Europe. While some U-boats rendezvoused with the Japanese off Mexico in the beginning of the war, the shore patrol, including the Coast Guard, appeared effective in curtailing the enemy submarine activities.

Sleep had come in fits and starts as the Seaboard Railway wound down the Atlantic Coast. Billi checked her watch, they had to be close to their West Palm Beach destination as thirty-five hours had already sped by. The trees outside transforming from thick bushy pines to slim palms.

The heat of the sun beat through the window onto her dark blue uniform increasing the temperature inside the overcrowded cabin. Impatient and bored, she slipped on her shoes then stood.

"What are you up to?" Ruth adjusted her position, eyeing her.

Billi pushed the door open to the passageway. "I just need to stretch. Don't worry, I can't go far."

"Do you think it's always this hot?" Karen moaned, her red hair and freckled completion not a good match for the sun.

Trudy attempted to sound encouraging. "We'll find out soon enough."

Pressing into the sea of men lining the passageway who earlier insisted the women occupy the cushioned seats, she brushed past one whose uniform retained the smoke from a cigar. She paused briefly, quickly checking the youth's appearance, longing for the stranger to be her husband. His wink sent her blushing further up the train.

Unable to go further, she stopped at one of the open windows for a long deep breath of the warm air that carried a hint of the sea. The realization of the distance between Seattle and Florida made her sigh. However, if Jack remained in San Francisco, he would be closer. She wondered if he already knew of her destination. In her heart she longed to believe he did, that his job afforded him unbound connections to the most private of information.

She wiped a tear from her eye. The simple scent of old cigar smoke filled her with such desire. Their separation overwhelmed her, and she ignored the second tear making its way down her flushed cheek.

"Need a smoke?"

Billi turned toward the deep voice. He was tall, like Jack, with the same dark hair under the tan of a captain's cap.

"No thanks. I'm married." She blinked at her own answer, then laughed. "I suppose that doesn't mean I can't smoke. Sure."

With great expertise he flicked the Fleetwood pack sending one cigarette higher than the others. "So am I."

She looked at him quizzically as she eased the cigarette from its brown package.

"Married." He grinned leaning in with his lighter.

"But please don't mention it to my friends." Billi suddenly realized the danger she placed herself in with her announcement.

"Only if you have dinner with me."

"Oh, but I can't. I don't know where I'll be or . . ."

"The Biltmore is easy to find," he assured her.

"How do you know where I'm headed?" Taken aback, she straightened.

"Better take a drag on that if you want it to continue burning."

Billi sucked on the Fleetwood only to emit the smoke in one big puff of a cough.

He snatched the offensive cigarette from her fingers with the assuredness of someone accustomed to being in charge, then flicked it out the window. "You don't smoke and I'm not about to be the one to introduce you to new bad habits."

Billi caught her breath. "You haven't answered my question?"

"You haven't answered mine." He leaned back against the side of the train, waiting.

"What will your wife have to say if I do?"

"Probably the same thing your husband would. There's nothing wrong with a bit of cheerful company over a decent meal."

She chuckled. "I think you have my husband all wrong."

"Not really, I see you miss him as much as I miss Alice."

The whistle blew as the train began to slow in preparation for arrival.

"There you are Lilly." Ruth hurried up beside her. "Better get your bag."

"On my way." Billi extended her hand toward the captain, daring him to speak. "Thank you."

His hand covered hers in a friendly exchange. "My pleasure, Lilly."

She pulled her hand away to usher Ruth back toward their seabags.

"I can't leave you alone for a moment." Ruth hissed, as they wove through the men lining the windows with the anticipation of the unknown.

"Relax, all he talked about was his wife, Alice." Billi jerked her bag down from the rack above the seats.

Ruth continued her rant. "The married ones are the worst."

Trudy's eyes grew wide with excitement. "What happened?"

"Nothing." Billi and Ruth answered at the same instant.

Their friends' shoulders slumped with disappointment.

Karen, dripping with perspiration as the train stood still, brushed past them. "Do you think they'll let us swim? I can't take this heat."

"I bet we have to march first." Ruth's comment brought moans from the others as they struggled with their sea bags to step into the line of exiting soldiers.

RUTH'S PREDICTION PROVED to be the first item of business. The hot bus ride was no match compared to the direct sun above them as they stood in formation. The lines of arriving SPARS spread across the green grass before the imposing, Spanish-influenced Biltmore Hotel.

She felt the sweat dripping down her arms and back of her dark blue uniform. She shot a quick glance over at Karen, her pale face streaming drops of perspiration. Billi watched her blink the salt from her eyes.

Their new training officer continued to drone on about the joy and responsibility of being a SPAR. At the blast of a whistle the formation began to march across the lawn exhibiting their training and grit. Following the lead of their new instructor, they spun around then marched back, once again taking up their stance in the beating sun.

Billi heard a slight moan. Turning in time to see Karen slump to the ground, she reached for her friend.

"Leave her." The command shot through the air from the instructor.

She jerked back to attention.

There was a slight thud as a second SPAR hit the ground.

"We will see to them." The order was clear. "March."

The instructor set the pace across the thick grass toward the elegant entrance of the Biltmore Hotel. Their feet resounded in unison as they marched up the tiled steps only to wait in the reverberating heat, just before the front door, for dismissal.

When the command came, the ladies swept into the shade of the foyer to form another line for their room assignment.

"Would you just look at this?" Trudy squealed. "I sweat so much my bra is blue."

"Well, put it in the sun to bleach it out." Billi regarded her once white blouse and cotton underwear, both smudged with the tint of blue.

"We'll be issued lighter uniforms soon," Ruth added.

Billi leaned over Karen to feel the compress on her friend's forehead. "You'll get used to this heat. Here, drink some more water. Slowly."

She helped her up then sat beside her while the smaller woman sipped the cool liquid.

"Thanks." She bobbed her red hair. "I'll be better tomorrow."

"They're giving us a few hours free. We start classes tomorrow. I'm going to find someplace to swim." Billi stood and headed toward her luggage.

Karen laid back down, closing her eyes in response. "I'm not going anywhere."

"I'll tell you all about it. Rest. Anyone want to join me? It should be cooler by the water."

Ruth shot her a disgusted look before reaching for her luggage. As Billi suspected, Ruth would be following her lead. Her new watch dog's insistence of always being at Billi's side, created suspicions. If she didn't know any better, she'd believe someone in the upper echelon assigned Ruth to report on her activities.

THE HOT TROPICAL SUN didn't thaw Jack's frigid emotions, nor did it sooth the tension of his mission. He adjusted his Panama hat to regard Mamala Bay and the vast Pacific Ocean beyond as if the blue green waters were his enemy. Indeed, here on the shore near the airfield at Ewa, west of Pearl Harbor, put him as far away from Billi as he could possibly stand on American soil. Yet, once again, paradise held a promise.

He dropped his bag then kicked at a red lava rock, watching it climb into the cloudless blue sky before bouncing toward the surf. At the sound of shoes crunching on rocks, he turned to regard the Navy officer who might hold some answers. He was tall, blond, young and reputed to be one of the best interrogators to recently graduate from Japanese language school in Boulder, Colorado.

"Mr. Huntington." The newcomer extended his hand, his deep-set eyes showed no reaction to Jack's black eye patch or scar.

"Cary." Jack shook his hand. "Thank you for contacting me."

"You can call me Otis. I like first names." He smiled with eyes that welcomed, not condemned.

"Jack it is then. Before we head to the base, can you fill me in on what you've discovered?"

"Shall we?" The young officer with the easy manner motioned toward an outcropping of large lava rock as if they were the finest leather chairs in his study.

Jack followed as the two sat with their shoes covered in the warm sand.

"What a sight." Cary regarded the open sea.

"Pity it's the war that's brought us here." Jack waited, letting the other interrogator take the lead.

"I suppose you have already researched my background?"

"You are an American treasure." Jack assured him.

"My parents' missionary work makes my job easy. In fact, when one prisoner that we captured in the Aleutian Islands discovered we were both born on Hokkaido, specifically Otaru, he told me details beyond imagining."

Jack bit his tongue. His appreciation increased for this officer of interrogation who, in a very short time, had convinced so many of the selected Japanese prisoners to talk at length.

"The man you are interested in questioning is very prudent. He rarely spends his allotted eight cents per day in the canteen on cigarettes or beer. He accepted a few phonography records, a flute from the YMCA and has joined others in gardening to fill his time. His biggest fear is that we will tell the Imperial Japanese Navy he is a prisoner. They might retaliate against his family as it was expected he should kill himself before falling into our hands."

Again, Jack waited, yet his spirits improved with every word the young man spoke. Otis was indeed a treasure. He had tapped into the human side of the prisoners, gaining their trust, something Jack's appearance alone rarely accomplished.

"It must be very important to gather information about one Akio Sumiyoshi to bring you all this way."

Jack regarded the profile of the man beside him, his long features and confident bearing. "You would like my wife. She speaks Japanese and finds their culture fascinating and beautiful."

Otis turned toward Jack. "Wives hold our hearts. And we would do anything to protect them."

"I couldn't agree more." Jack felt humbled, grateful that Otis, the missionary's son, appeared able to read the situation without the details.

The Navy officer stood, brushing the sand from his trousers. "Have you been inside our Camp Iroquois?"

"I've read some of your secret reports, but the facility itself I've never stepped foot in."

"Few have." Otis waited for Jack to dust himself off. "You're a bit notorious with credentials that open many secret doors."

Jack smiled at the honesty of the younger man's statement.

Otis smiled back. "Come on. I have a magazine that Gaku, your informant, is interested in reading. He said he is willing to help you, but the magazine will encourage him from the distraction of your eyepatch."

He picked up his bag, praying this prisoner held answers.

Cary maneuvered the jeep the short distance to the top-secret Camp Iroquois. As they passed Ewa field, Jack noted the mounds of aircraft bunkers designed to look like rolling hills from above. He marveled at the many clever disguises mandatory to win in battle.

Camp Iroquois, built specifically for this conflict, maintained high security. The lists of prisoners to interview fluctuated; once they were approved through the interrogation process at the larger Camp Honouliuli, they were moved to this smaller site. Jack understood the process. The navy sifted through the arrivals of men and women, in the hopes they would cooperate, offering up much needed information. The captives were composed of many cultures: Japanese and Korean laborers who themselves had been prisoners of the Japanese, Italians, and Germans.

They paused briefly at the gate where the soldier eyed Jack suspiciously before allowing them to pass.

"We keep the Japanese navy men over there." Cary pointed to a section toward the back of the camp. "We have to separate them from their army soldiers, over there." He pointed in the opposite direction from the navy section. "This discourages fighting, they blamed each other for their demise."

Jack wanted to laugh. The infighting reflected the situation at Pearl Harbor, just a few miles away. In fact, the US Army and Navy continued to slug it out, pointing fingers at each other, casting the blame elsewhere for their unpreparedness that horrific morning. Especially, in light of the "war warning" and the Japanese broadcast of their signal for war, "East, Wind, Rain," on December 4th. Human beings from warring cultures mirroring images of their rage and frustration.

"The Koreans, poor souls." Cary broke into Jack's thoughts. "Most of them arrived needing medical help, with injuries from enslaved brutality by the Japanese. Their section is there." He pointed to the tents closest to what appeared to be a medical building.

Cary stopped the jeep before the main building then hopped out. Jack slid from the other side, grabbing his bag, to follow the officer's youthful stride.

The blasting fans offered some relief as they walked toward the back of the building. Jack felt the eyes of those behind the desks follow him before he entered the small rear office. He sat, removing his hat to wipe the perspiration from his brow.

"I'll get us some water. Oh, here's that magazine."

He handed Jack a used copy of *The Saturday Evening Post*, dated April 3ᵗʰ, 1943. The issue was only months old with a cover by Norman Rockwell entitled "*April Fools.*" The whimsical drawing of the upside-down world of the elderly couple, quickly achieving notoriety, presented a startling contrast to the prominent article, "*LAST MAN OFF WAKE ISLAND.*" He could guess which of these Gaku found interesting and why.

When the door opened again, Cary entered with bottles of Coke followed by a stout man in clean, tan pants and shirt.

Jack stood, towering over the prisoner, waiting for the introductions.

Gaku did not look up until Cary spoke. He blinked at Jack's patch then remained stone faced.

"Please tell him my mother called me long distance just to make certain I had looked at the cover of this magazine." Jack held the magazine out toward Gaku.

Cary smiled with his translation. "He said your mother is wise to make certain her son still holds interest in the challenge of interpreting art."

Jack smiled briefly. "My mother claims to have found 43 incongruities in the painting."

Gaku accepted the magazine as Cary continued to translate. "Your mother sets high standards."

Then with the briefest of bows in recognition, they all sat.

Jack knew the process would take time. He waited until asked by Cary to produce the photos of Akio. The sincerity in the captive's eyes of recognition of the man Jack wanted to kill more than anyone in the world, brought a mix of relief while igniting an urgent sense of fear. Jack listened intently to every word. One thing became clear, the last time Gaku saw Akio they were outside General Headquarters. Rumors floated that Akio, a favored of Yamamoto, continued to rise in rank and work on a top-secret project. But there was a shadow over Akio, his temper. He had witnessed it when they served on the same submarine.

Jack relaxed with the knowledge Gaku spoke the truth, more importantly he appeared willing to provide details. If there was some small inkling of Akio's future movement, his connection to the drawing on the fan or what that might represent, he needed to know. He didn't care how long it took. Jack knew he wasn't just there for his country. He couldn't face his wife without the information this Japanese man hopefully possessed.

# FORTY

FLOATING HIGH ABOVE THE BLUE OF the South Pacific Ocean, Eddy observed a light cloud pass over Segi Point at the southeastern tip of New Georgia Island.

"I sure wouldn't want to be with the 4th Marine Raider Division trying to secure more land down there so we can have another airstrip." Scooter raised his binoculars to scan the numerous dots of small islands surrounding the point.

"I just hope that crazy New Zealander is alive." Eddy shouted into the cockpit as if addressing the coastwatcher directly. "Donald Kennedy, you are my hero. You and your band of coast men are our lifeline."

"Do you think the coastwatchers will offer our landing troops a cup of tea this time?"

The image Scooter painted made them both chuckle.

Scooter sighed heavily. "I can't imagine being left behind on an island swarming with those blood thirsty Nips with only the natives to protect you?"

"Better these natives than some. Besides, they hold the knowledge of the islands," Eddy attempted to cheer up his co-pilot fully aware of his growing fear of being captured. The visions of instant death versus the tales of prolonged and violent torture played daily in every Allied soldier's mind.

In silence they continued to survey the horizon. The enemy had been aggressive the last few days in retaliation for their losses over one month ago in the Blackett Strait. In the cover of darkness on the evening of May 6th, the Americans placed mines in the waters at Kula

Gulf. The next night four of the IJN destroyers attempting to run the Tokyo Express met with the surprise. Only one made its way clear. Retaliation swept in on wings beginning on June 7th, then the 12th, striking the US ships gathering for a new campaign at Guadalcanal. The attack brought little success yet great losses to the Imperial forces. The bet was on the table that today, June 16th, 1943, the very day they had been presented with a new campaign, the Japanese would be back.

"Toenails. Who comes up with these names?" Eddy attempted to lighten the conversation.

Scooter snorted. "Operation Toenails, the first stage of Operation Cartwheels—hell, what about Operation Done and Go Home?"

"Not today, buddy." Eddy leaned into the plexiglass. "Looks like I win that bet."

"Got 'em," Scooter sat up straight, adjusting his field glasses.

"Reading." Eddy's voice remained calm as he spoke into his headset focusing on the waves of approaching Rising Sun aircraft.

Fletch responded. "They're heading due southeast, directly for Guadalcanal."

"We've pissed off somebody." Scooter's voice went up an octave with excitement. "My guess is one hundred planes."

Eddy listened to Hank send the report back to base before climbing higher into the clouds. It was useless to engage the swift enemy aircraft. Today their duty mandated observation and rescue.

They turned back toward Guadalcanal. Their PBY, the famous Phantom, now the most decorated Black Cat, a slow beast moving through the skies. Yet the rush of the impending battle bounced off the cockpit, down the long lines of their flying patrol boat past their navigator, radio man and side gunners whose lives dangled between any incoming bullets and the plexiglass enclosure blister that protruded from the sides of the aircraft. Guns ready and manned, the reality of war remained surreal compared to the filtered light streaming onto the calm blue of the Pacific waters. The fact that no storm clouds gathered on the horizon meant clear visibility for the cyclone of killer Japanese Zeros and Bettys heading straight toward them.

Wave after wave of enemy planes flew beneath them. In the distance, in response, the US pilots scrambled into the skies to protect the various ships at anchor.

"Holy shit. I'm up to 120 Tōjō planes." Scooter announced.

"Well, if this is anything like their last two attempts, their losses will be high."

Eddy's prophecy became reality. In the smoke of burning aircraft screeching toward the jungle or sinking in the depths of the ocean, they watched helplessly as two American warships and one transporter took minor hits.

Excitement of the clash held their attention until the skies were all but empty of the enemy. In the lingering drifts of the black fog of battle a few of the dazed Japanese pilots retreated toward their large base and command post at Rabual.

"Did you get a count?" Eddy nodded with confidence at Scooter.

He smiled back. "I think we lost five, but I saw just over twenty Japs sneaking back. A bad day for the land of the sinking sun."

The radio crackled and Eddy waited for the command. "Phantom report your position. Over."

All listened to the exchange with building tension.

"Six of our planes have not reported in. They were observed going down north and south of Henderson Field. Wish I had more. I'll keep you updated. Report what you find. We have boats out now looking. Over."

"Roger."

"Out"

Eddy regarded his co-pilot. They nodded at each other with the resignation of their assignment. The mop up would now begin. They would start at Savo Island to the north of Guadalcanal then work their way low over the waters looking for clues of survivors. With prayers for those pilots tucked into their wings they started their descent.

The water took on a deep blue while the surface began to chop, with white tipped waves lashing toward the sky. This made any landing rough, especially those in open water when attempting to pick up survivors. At least the wind came down Sealark Channel head on.

Eddy cruised about 200 feet off the surface, letting the wind aid in slowing his pace. All eyes in the PBY scanned the surface for signs of life as they passed bits of aircraft floating on the surface.

"Anything moving around that wing?" Eddy asked into the headset.

"It's one of theirs. I don't see a damn thing." Beau shot back.

They worked along the coast past Henderson Airstrip toward Tanu Point. With one wide sweep they turned upwind to climb a bit while searching the middle of the channel. Below, a PT Boat pulled what looked like two men aboard.

"Hallelujah," Scooter leaned into the plexiglass. "Way to go boys."

Eddy knew it made no difference that Scooter's rejoicing couldn't be heard by the wet and exhausted pilots slumping in the back of the torpedo boat. Yet, the jubilation resounded with hope.

"We're not going back empty handed." Eddy's statement mirrored the attitude spanning their floating ship. "Pour some coffee and keep those eyes sharp."

The sun cast shadows across the water preparing to disappear quickly over the horizon, bringing a thick darkness. The good news reflected off the surface of the calming the water as the waves flattened, with gentle breezes pushing rippling patterns across the surface. Once more they headed toward what looked like a broken wing.

A flash in the water made Eddy's heart race. He prayed it was one of ours. Cutting the engine back to drift just above the dark water, he pointed as another flash appeared.

Eddy removed his sunglasses, waiting while Scooter fixed his field glasses in the direction of what they hoped represented a signal.

Scooter spoke slowly as they approached. "Someone is moving, no. They're on the wing but something is approaching from the water."

"Shit, sharks." Eddy's adrenalin sharpened his focus.

"No." Scooter remained steadfast as he studied the situation. "No. Someone is swimming toward the wing."

Eddy's attention riveted on the drifting wing. "Who's on the wing?"

"Yee haw, one of ours." Scooter's announcement electrified the rescue team.

"Is he moving? Who's in the water?"

Allen answered first. "Looks like a goddamn Jap. What's that flashing."

Scooter shouted, "A knife."

"He'll reach the wing before we do," Beau piped up.

"Then we'll just sit on him." Eddy pulled back the gears. "Get a lifeboat ready. Scooter you taking the shot or am I?"

382 | Denise Frisino

Scooter pulled back his side window then stood, his head protruding above their cockpit. He pulled his handgun, waiting.

Without their engines running, they slipped through the shadows like death. As the belly of the PBY slid across the surface the Japanese man in the water turned toward the sound of the rushing water. Scooter took aim then fired.

The swimmer disappeared into the black waters, but his vest kept his dive shallow. He surfaced spitting water, the white from the turbulence marking his spot.

"Damn it, Scooter. How the hell did you miss?" Eddy shook his head. "I have to do everything around here."

Scooter snorted in disbelief.

Eddy pulled hard to the right, circling their objective. The PBY drifted to a stop a few yards beyond the wing rocking on the ring of small waves from the disturbance.

Without a moment's hesitation, Eddy slipped off his shoes, opened the hatch and slid down the side of the aircraft to the small ledge just below the cockpit. He waited, listening in the darkness. A moan set his course. He dove in the warm waters, setting a strong stroke toward the sound.

Flashlights from the cockpit and gunner's bubble combed the surface. The wing suddenly dipped to one side.

Eddy adjusted his approach toward the listing wing. He paused just beyond when he heard a splash in the waters behind him. He hoped the sound indicated one of his men in a life raft paddling to the rescue, not the stealth of a hunting shark.

The moan sounded more urgent, almost a scream as Eddy beat at the water with all of his might. He grabbed at the side of the wing pulling himself halfway up. There, standing in the beams of the flashlights above the pilot, the Japanese warrior held his knife high in the air ready to strike at the limp frame of the injured American.

Eddy sprang onto the aluminum surface, his weight forcing the wing further into the water.

"Hay, kona kasu sh'ine," Eddy yelled.

It worked, the man spun in Eddy's direction, knife still posed over his head. Eddy crouched low, then sprang forward, striking the enemy in the mid-section while grabbing at the wrist holding the lethal blade. The force of the blow knocked them into the water. Their weight carried them deeper into the water as the two men twisted in a dance for survival. In the blur of bubbles Eddy saw hope, a faint stream of blood swirled around his opponent. Scooters bullet had struck its mark, piercing the man in the right shoulder. Eddy grabbed at the man's wrist with both hands then kicked the wounded shoulder. The Japanese fighter buckled with the blow, but his fingers still gripped the shaft of his blade. Eddy kicked again.

The man's eyes popped open wider with fear. Eddy twisted the knife free then kicked the man with both feet before heading toward the surface. He felt something brush past him as the coarse skin of the tail of a shark slithered downward toward the scent of the blood.

Eddy surfaced, spitting several times, the taste of salty water mingling with the bile of fear. He stuffed the knife in his belt, following the beam of light the short distance to the sinking wing. He reached for the other pilot floating above the once shiny aluminum, turned a dark greenish-black, as it hovered just under the surface.

"I got you buddy." He floated next to the injured man.

A soft moan ripped through Eddy's heart. He was still alive.

"Stay put." Scooter yelled. "We have company."

"No shit. Could you move a little faster?"

The life raft brushed up against Eddy reminding him of the dangers below. Hands reached for the pilot, pulling the stricken man aboard.

"Duck." Scooter shouted at his friend.

The bullet whizzed over his head. Eddy pulled the knife from his belt to slash at the water, striking nothing.

Hands pulled at his shirt as he felt himself being dragged aboard to safety. He slumped, panting, next to Charlie, while Scooter reached for the blade, wrenching it from his grip.

"Don't play with sharp objects in a rubber raft." Scooter's teasing tone a welcome relief. As if surprised by the knife's origin, he added, "Nice prize."

Eddy caught his breath then pressed his fingers against the neck of the rescued man to find a pulse beating fast. "Let's get him back fast. He's going into shock."

The rowers responded with mighty pulls at their oars. The warm air passed over Eddy's wet frame as he pushed aside his brush with death. He watched in silence the slip of a moon glisten on the dark surface, the frothy white where the paddles churned the waters and the slithering fin of the trailing monster. They were not home yet.

Once inside the security of the Phantom, Eddy breathed a sigh of relief. He guided their aircraft just above the dark waters, circling the boats moored off Henderson Field, then plowed across the calm waters right up the beach. Medics and ground crew rushed toward them to help with the injured pilot.

Eddy could sense Scooter right behind him as he climbed up the sandy incline toward the path to their Quonset hut. He headed straight to the cabinet then pulled out two glasses. His hand shook, but he did not spill one drop as he filled both with dark liquor.

"You drinkin' both of those, or is one for me?" Scooter stood next to him.

"I hate it." Eddy handed him a drink.

"What? We rescued a pilot and you killed a Jap in hand to hand."

"No." Eddy downed half of his glass. "No, I hate it when I have to admit I was wrong."

Scooter put the Japanese knife on the table, squinted at his friend, then slowly sipped his drink.

Eddy downed the last of his booze. "Keep the knife."

"Why?"

"You killed that asshole."

Scooter beamed. "I did hit him?"

"Yeah, but don't expect me to apologize." Eddy filled his glass again. "The shark helped."

He tapped his friend's glass in a toast of success. With wry smiles they both drank deeply.

Scooter cleared his throat. "You're bleeding."

For the first time Eddy noticed his torn pants where the shark's teeth-like skin shredded the material, scraping a layer of skin.

"But I'm alive." He clicked his partner's glass. "Better than the alternative."

They watched each other intently. Each flight, each brush with death hardened their resolve to fight another day. The war, far from over, now their only way of life. All they had to do was stay alive.

# FORTY ONE

Billi wiped the sweat from her forehead as she climbed the stairs to her room. She considered those who had walked these very halls before all of the gilt and glamour of the era had been stripped to these bare walls. She imagined the clientele of this elite hotel, originally named the Alba after the Spanish Duke of Alba, claiming its grandeur fit for royalty.

She laughed at her own image. She wasn't feeling very royal at the moment, as perspiration dripped down her back, making her gray and white stripped uniform cling to her damp skin. Her legs ached from the marching and doing calisthenics in the sand, while her back spasmed from sitting for hours in class. Those were tolerable compared to the heat. She paused briefly near the open widow at the landing. The warm breeze brought no relief. Even the Intracoastal Waterway appeared to have steam rising from the salty blue sea waters.

Gathering her thoughts and strength, she headed for the cramped room she now shared with the three other SPARS she arrived with. There seemed to be no time in her day to even think of her husband, let alone her parents, brother, and childhood friends. She burst through the door with the frustration of her overheated body and lonely soul.

"Hey." Ruth bounced from her top bunk landing with a thud. "We're bombing Rome again."

Billi dropped into the nearest chair. Rome. The center of her Catholic faith, the land of some of the greatest architectural achievements known to man, with its Coliseum, the Forum, and the Trevi

Fountain. Such beauty she feared she would never witness. She could only dread what would be left after bombs annihilated the citadel city.

Ruth stood above her. "I'm not certain if it's good or bad news."

"The Eternal City will somehow survive." Billi faced her friend. "Besides, President Roosevelt promised Pope Pius our pilots were well briefed to stay clear of the Vatican and only hit military objectives."

"I hope so. I know the importance of holy ground." Ruth sat on the edge of the lower bunk. "When this is all over, I'm heading straight to Jerusalem to pray at the Western Wall for all of mankind." Suddenly Ruth bounced back onto her feet. "Speaking of praying, I almost forgot, they want you at headquarters. What have you done?"

Billi wasn't sure if her reaction to the heat or the swiftness of her pulse created more perspiration across her forehead. A summons to headquarters held the possibility of many dark edges. She breathed deeply while pushing herself from the chair.

"Nothing I'm aware of. I got high marks on my reading and sending transmission the other night. And my marksmanship is superior, my swimming challenge, excellent. Do you think I'm bilging out?" Billi regarded her friend with of look of the confusion that shattered her nerves.

"No. Maybe you're being assigned a post." Ruth words sounded encouraging. "They're creating more of those secret radio stations along the coast. For the SS Loren . . ."

"We aren't supposed to talk about the new radio system outside of the classroom." Billi scolded.

"Maybe you'll go to Fenwick or Montauk." Ruth continued with her line of conversation.

"As long as it's cooler than here." Billi scurried out the door with a chill running through her. Her feet flew down the stairs, across the mezzanine, stopping in front of Lieutenant Willis' office.

The clerk recognizing Billi picked up the phone to announce her. "Lilly Huntington reporting."

Billi waited, showing no emotion at her false identity.

When the clerk nodded toward the lieutenant's closed door, Billi marched forward.

"Semper Paratus," the clerk mumbled.

"Always ready," Billi responded with a smile. Semper Paratus—Always Ready, the words that formed the acronym for the name SPAR. Billi only hoped she was indeed ready for what greeted her behind the door.

As she stepped inside Lieutenant Willis stopped talking mid-sentence. Billi regarded her superior who offered no hint behind the reason for this interview, and more disturbing, no warm welcome.

At the sight of the back of the gentleman's head over the rise of a tall chair, Billi caught her breath. The stranger was not Jack as she had secretly hoped. He sat tall, his dark hair perfectly cut with just the slightest indent from where he removed his officer's cap.

"Come in, Huntington. Sit there." Willis' voice seemed strained as she pointed to a chair next to the dark-haired man.

Billi swiftly moved at the command. The army officer rose in greeting, extending his hand in her direction. She blinked up at him, quickly hiding the fact she recognized him as the captain who offered her a cigarette on the train. He had never shared his name, only that his wife Alice would not mind if Lilly went out to dinner with him. She held her breath.

"So nice to meet you, I'm Captain McCoy."

They shook hands as strangers would. Then Billi sat on the hard chair focusing on her Lieutenant Willis.

"Captain McCoy requested being here during our conversation as there is some concern regarding your relationships."

Billi's head swirled as her throat went dry. He must have informed her superior that she had provided false information regarding her married status. Not a severe offense, as several of the SPARS were married, but the fact she had lied all this time would not bode well. She faced more demerits and bilging out.

Lieutenant Willis picked up a letter holding it out toward Billi. As she reached for it, she instantly recognized Eileen's handwriting. Before flipping the envelope over, she noted that the return address boldly claimed the letter's origin as Chicago. Despite the situation, this made her happy. The new address represented Eileen's brave move, choosing to leave her father and Kenny behind in Minidoka for training, paid by the United States Government, at a school back east.

For the first time Billi considered just how many Japanese had moved inland or to the East Coast to avoid the relocation camps. She resisted the concept any of those now living freely anywhere outside of the War Zone continued to search for her so they could report her whereabouts back to Akio. Focusing back on the situation, she flipped the letter over, then paused realizing her mail had been opened. She regarded Willis, waiting.

"As you are finishing your training with the highly classified communication system, we need to be certain there is no reason to be concerned with your clearances."

"And after reading this letter, what have you determined?" Billi attempted to control her anger at the implication.

The woman bristled with her response. "How do you know this person?"

"Eileen Nakamura and I have been friends since childhood."

When the lieutenant didn't respond Billi continued.

"I felt sorry for her family having to move and give up their grocery store, so I wrote her a few letters." Billi folded her hands protectively over Eileen's letter on her lap. "Was there another envelope this letter arrived in?"

"Why did Eileen send her letter to a Seattle address?"

Billi's mind scrambled to remember her former lies. "That is probably where she knew I was staying last, in Seattle."

There was a pause in which the only thing moving on her body was the sweat that ran like a river down her back.

"May I?" McCoy nodded in the direction of Lieutenant Willis.

With a huff, accompanied by an unchecked look of disgust directed at Billi, Willis stood to leave her own office.

"Take all the time you need." The older woman spoke before shutting the door behind her.

Once alone, the captain stood to his full height. He strode to the sideboard where a few melting ice cubes floated in the pitcher of water. He didn't look in her direction as he poured two glasses. Then, his quick stride brought him back to the desk. He placed one of the glasses in front of her. Without saying a word, he went around the desk, sitting in the tall chair of her superior.

Raising his glass as if to toast, he downed his drink almost entirely before he began. "She doesn't like you."

"I hadn't noticed." Billi sounded as curt as the statement.

"Drink."

She glared at him before she followed his command. The water helped as her mind seemed to clear with the fortification of the liquid.

"Thank you." Billi placed the half empty glass down.

"You're good. In fact, you're excellent." He leaned forward to whisper conspiratorially. "I've never witnessed such a good . . . can I use the word liar?"

"You can use any word you want, Captain. It doesn't mean it fits." Billi breathed deeply, inhaling the overwhelming stuffiness of the room.

"What is your real name?"

She sat taller. "Huntington."

He didn't blink but Billi could see he registered her answer as being truthfully spoken.

"You're the top in your class."

Billi suspected he attempted a different approach to test her. "So, why am I here?"

He sat back. "I'll pick you up at eighteen hundred. Be on the front steps."

"Where are you taking me?"

"You're dismissed."

Billi rose, then turned to go. She pushed hard into the floor to make certain her legs held as she made it across the room to the door. As she passed through the outside office, there was no sign of Lieutenant Willis.

Checking her wristwatch, she realized she only had thirty minutes to prepare to meet the man who intended to escort her somewhere and who had just called her a liar.

JACK SAT IN THE BORROWED CAR on Sunset next to the Biltmore Hotel. He'd been there for over an hour and the heat rattled his nerves. He just couldn't get over how enticing Billi looked in her uniform. It had been all he could do not to rush up and grab her as she marched in formation with the other SPARS over the greens toward the hotel.

The stride of her long legs brought back urges he'd suppressed through their separation in this time of commitment to the war effort. A man is entitled to basic needs and holding his wife right now would satisfy those needs more than anything. To hell with the country, he could only focus on Billi.

Knowing her whereabouts during training filled him with relief, but her move to this distant shore presented obstacles for them. He hoped the surprise of his appearance would not cause too much friction with her superiors. He admired her desire to serve and had no intention of interfering. However, the bit of information he gathered while in Hawaii might bring her home.

Jack snorted. Where was their home?

As he gripped the handle to open the door, he saw Billi stroll down the length of stairs and gave a sigh of relief. He would not have to enter the building, drawing attention to his arrival. He swung the door wide but then drew it quietly closed.

He watched in amazement as a tall striking man in a captain's uniform hurried around the side of his car, opening the door for her. Without so much as a word, she got into the car.

Before the captain drove off, Jack had the license plate number memorized.

Furious, he stormed out of his car, racing up the steps. Inside the Biltmore he heard the sound of his shoes echoing on the marble as he stomped toward the front desk where a blonde, as pale as her white and grey uniform, eyed his approach uncomfortably.

"May I help you. This is the residence for the SPARS and men are not . . ."

"Who are the roommates of Ms. Huntington?" He removed his hat and could feel the sweat run through his hair then down his neck.

The blonde's jaw dropped then snapped shut. She moved to a large book while looking around for support. She opened the logbook then blinked.

"Who may I say is asking?"

Jack flipped his credentials making her eyes blink faster.

"Oh, I'll call the lieutenant . . ."

"Just give me the names and call the roommates. Now."

"Ruth." The blonde waved frantically at a passing figure. "Ruth, come here please."

The other SPAR stopped, quickly sized up the situation, then stepped forward with a no-nonsense attitude.

"Yes. How may I help."

"This man," the blonde swallowed hard before her next words, "is looking for Lilly's Huntington's roommates."

Jack noted the use of his sister's name and held back a laugh. He had only known Billi's enlisted title as Coast Guard Reservist Huntington. The quagmire deepened.

"And who are you?" Ruth firmly stood her ground, not in the least affected by Jack's black eye patch.

"Let's have a seat over there." He nodded toward a couch in the tall foyer before turning back to the startled blonde. "Thank you."

He escorted Ruth to the couch then waited for her to sit.

"I didn't catch your name." Ruth faced him with a cold stare.

"I'm a relative of Lilly Huntington."

"Are you her famous brother, Jack?"

"The very one. I wanted to surprise her, but she left with an army officer. Do you know who he is?"

"Someone she met on the train on our way down here. But I suppose she doesn't tell her brother much." Ruth's attitude softened to almost flirtatious.

"No. She doesn't tell me anything." Jack suppressed his anger as much as possible. "Do you have any idea where they are heading?"

"She didn't say. I suppose he intended to surprise her too." Ruth chuckled at her own joke.

His blood ran cold. "Does he have a name?"

"Captain McCoy. He has something to do with, well, he teaches a class here from time to time. He had eyes for her from the start. He even had her smoking a cigarette. That Lilly is a wild one." She leaned in conspiratorially. "But you know that."

Flabbergasted, he formed his words slowly. "And you have no idea where they went?"

"Most of the guys take their girls to the ocean side, you know moon light, Lilly loves to swim."

Jack felt his anger rise. Noting Ruth's reaction, he attempted to cover his emotions.

Ruth straightened. "Aren't you happy for her?"

"What else can you tell me about Captain McCoy?"

"I heard he tells girls he's married, but one of them found out the hard way he's . . ."

Jack was on his feet, he'd heard enough. He'd do his own investigating.

"Thank you, Ruth."

"Will I see you again? Lilly will be so upset she missed you."

"Don't mention I was here. I have to hurry back to work. It will only upset her." Jack slammed his hat on his head.

Ruth stood, trailing after him. "Maybe they went to The Hut, the drive in. No, I suppose he wants to impress her, so maybe that nice Italian place on..."

Jack took the large stairs two at a time. He couldn't breathe, not from the smothering heat, but from the pounding of his heart.

He had stayed away too long. Now his wife was smoking and swimming and who the hell knew what else with this McCoy. He stood by his car, not sure what to do next, except he had to find his wife.

# FORTY TWO

STEERING THE CAR DOWN HIGHWAY 1, Captain McCoy whistled which Billi found most annoying. She attempted to count the blocks, the miles, then finally just noted the landmarks. However, this stretch of the road looked like any other American Highway with motels and food joints dotting stretches of the concrete, alongside palm trees and homes.

"Where are you taking me and why?" Billi broke the prevailing silence of the past half hour.

"Just thought you might like to see a bit of what Florida has to offer."

He smiled at her making her shift closer to the door. "Aren't you concerned with gas rationing?"

"Not tonight."

"I thought you were taking me somewhere that had to do with work."

"I am." He picked back up the tune from where he had paused to answer.

Billi could smell the ocean as they turned toward a lighthouse, then turned again toward a sign claiming Hillsboro Beach. Her breath stuck in her chest as memories of Jack and his family's home in Hillsborough, California floated before her. This Hillsboro, with its desolate scrap of the coast, created a stark contrast to the palatial homes that fanned out among the hills below San Francisco.

Her heart felt heavy, adding to her rising fear. More than ever, right now she needed Jack. The hairs rose on the back of her neck when McCoy parked at the end of a street then blinked his dimmed car lights.

He held the door as she stood. She could see the water in front of her then felt his hand take her elbow, guiding her to a short dock. They watched in silence as a rowboat, designed to carry passengers, approached.

"My curfew is 9:00, before sunset," Billi blurted, twitching with the sweat dripping down her back. She tightened her hold on her handbag, ready to use it in defense.

His tone changed to frustration. "This interrogation might take long. Besides it's Friday night."

"There are no weekends for the war," she snapped back.

He gripped her arm tighter as they stepped inside the boat.

"Evenin', Captain." The skipper of the small craft regarded Billi before emitting a calculated, "Evenin' ma'am." He put his oars in the water, setting a steady pace over the smooth surface.

Billi's nerves tightened. The skipper's familiarity with McCoy conveyed the message, she was not the first women McCoy had interrogated at this desolate site. She calculated the distance to the other shore across the darkening intercoastal waters. Softly, the sound of music floated toward them as they approached a lone low building in the distance. She watched McCoy flip a quarter into the air as the skipper snatched it from the sky, a routine they both enjoyed. McCoy was clearly attempting to impress her, as the average income per hour garnered thirty cents. She calculated how much money she had in her purse to bribe the man to row her back.

Picking up his whistling, he guided her across old planks set in the sand that served as a boardwalk to what appeared to be a beached barge, with a structure built on top.

Laughter from within made Billi breathe easier but it did nothing for the knots in her stomach. She stepped under the sign Club Unique then through the door to find a tidy restaurant with gleaming pine walls.

"Hey, Cap." McCoy shook hands with a man in bib overalls. "Have any space in the Yellow Room?"

"Give me twenty. I'll find you in the bar."

Again, Billi became the object of scrutiny before the man called Cap spoke to her. "You're new. Welcome. Try the lobster tonight. Just came in." He held back a fishing net that acted as a curtain to let them pass through.

McCoy pressed close against her back as he steered her toward the crowded bar. The bartender, in his white jacket and black tie, stood surrounded by shiny bamboo behind a glossy wood bar. Suspended above, hung an object of art carved in wood, straight from an ancient ship.

"What do you drink?" McCoy wedged himself between two customers to place the order.

"I don't." Billi's voice carried to a lady seated at the bar who turned in her direction. They exchanged looks before the snoopy woman turned back to her liquor.

"I'll have my usual and a Manhattan with a twist for my friend."

Billi choked back her anger. He knew what she liked to drink. She could only imagine what else he had discovered about her but remained clueless as to his source.

McCoy held the drinks high as he worked his way to a table, putting them down next to two empty chairs. Billi reluctantly followed behind.

He held a chair out for Billi as he addressed the other two occupants nursing their drinks. "Mind if we join you?"

One of the men stood as Billi appeared behind McCoy. The other, his leg in a splint, remain seated but nodded in her direction.

"How are the games tonight?" McCoy addressed the man who sat back down to hover over his drink.

"Not hot for me." The tone of his voice told the story.

"That means you left some for me?"

"Plenty." The man with the crutches added ruefully.

Billi listened to their banter, not touching her drink. He had tricked her into this evening, and she would remain silent. She saw the man with the overalls head their way.

"Got the perfect table for you. Roosevelts." He snatched up Billi's drink, leading the way.

Intrigued, Billi stood then heard the man with the crutches chuckle. "Startin' out lucky with the Yellow Room. You should play a hand. Your date won't mind, she's the quiet type."

The Yellow Room was just that, yellow from top to bottom. In contrast with the wood and red carpets of the other spaces, this room presented a totally different feeling. The empty table had a photograph hanging on the wall and Billi bent closer for a better look. At what appeared to be this very table sat President Franklin Roosevelt and Prime Minister Winston Churchill with Cap in his overalls serving them dinner.

Billi lowered slowly into the chair with a feeling of awe. She looked at McCoy, who beamed back, holding up his almost empty drink.

"To the honor of serving in this miserable war."

For once, she agreed with the man across from her. She raised her glass to tap his. The alcohol slid down, warming her throat and spirit. At least they were away from prying eyes for the questioning.

She nodded at the photograph. "When was this taken?"

"There was a meeting here in January, hosted by Secretary of State Stettinius at his estate up the way. All the big war planners were here, including General Marshall, Lord Beaverbrook, even Bull, Admiral Halsey, and Cap sent up several meals. Then one night they came here. All hush, hush secret of course. You know about secrets don't you."

"I don't know what you're referring to?" Billi stared back at him.

He watched her intensely. "So how is your Japanese?"

Billi realized he had read her file that contained the incident which sent her here, the discovery of the floating bamboo that looked like a periscope. When she suggested to her superiors the kanji and design of the object marked the origin as Japanese, they assumed her knowledge of that culture ran deep. The letters from Eileen did not help matters.

"Because I have someone I write to who happens to be Japanese doesn't mean I speak their language. Why should I?"

"Where's this husband of yours?"

She didn't answer. He was a gambling man, so she put on her poker face.

The food arrived. A large, juicy lobster followed a hearts of palm salad. The excellent local food in high contrast with the stilted conversation. The captain was on his fourth drink and had ordered her a second, even though she hadn't finished her first. When she posed the subject of his wife, the muffled and evasive answer revealed her suspicion. Alice did not exist.

"What do you want from me." Billi repeated her question for the third time.

398 | DENISE FRISINO

"Alright, is that how you want to play this?" McCoy raised his empty glass signaling the need for a fifth scotch. "You are not who you say you are. Lilly Huntington is a widow who lives in California."

Billi glared at him. "Hillsborough, to be specific."

"Jack Huntington is not your brother." He shot back.

"Do you know Jack?" Her heart began to race, and she could not stop the blush she knew crept up her neck.

"Ah, but you know him." His eyes narrowed as he leaned across the table. "He's a bit untouchable if you catch my drift. Were you one of his toys? What else are you? A spy? Did he tell you some of his secrets when he was between your legs? Is that why you're running?"

She was only mad it hadn't been a full drink that she flung at him.

He blinked as the liquor dripped down his face. He wiped it clean and stood. "Wait outside. I'll be there in a few minutes."

When Billi didn't move he bent to whisper in her ear. "That's an order."

Snatching up her purse, she hurried out the door not wanting to draw any more attention to their previous exchange. The night stars offered no consolation as she stood alone on the water's edge watching patrons come and go from Club Unique. She kicked at a rock on the shore frustrated and fearful as she waited for a drunk to drive her home. She searched the skyline for an answer to the riddle; who was this man and what did he know about her and Jack?

A shooting star streaked above the waters, as if connecting bright dots in the sky as the warm wind seemed to carry a message straight to her heart. "Go home to your husband."

She turned, determined, heading straight for the skipper in his rowboat. She would go back to the other Hillsborough, back to Jack.

Climbing into the boat she nodded toward the other shore. "Please take me across."

Before he could put his oars in the water, the boat rocked with the unsettling weight of McCoy. "As the lady said," he slurred, "acc..cross."

The drunk captain attempted to put his arm around Billi, and she shoved him away, causing the boat to rock to the point of almost tipping.

"Easy," McCoy shouted as he struggled to sit upright.

As they hit the other shore the skipper helped the captain over the side. Unsteady, McCoy slipped back into the water only to emerge, spitting water, with a gash across his forehead where he had struck the oar.

Again, the skipper went to the other man's rescue, pulling the soaking sailor up the shore.

"You going to be okay, ma'am?" He leaned the captain against the car then began fishing in his pockets. Wads of wet bills were followed by the car keys.

Billi snatched the keys. Taking the damp money, she peeled away a few to hand back to the skipper, before stuffing the bills in her purse. "How do I get back to Ream General Hospital, The Breakers Hotel?"

McCoy mumbled as she drove slowly in the half light of the painted headlamps required by the blackout. The blood from his cut continued streaming down the side of his face and onto his shirt. He would need stitches. She followed Highway 1 then turned onto Royal Park Bridge toward The Breakers, the grand hotel turned hospital for the war. Heading down the long drive toward the main entrance, she did not notice the car following her.

Pulling up to the curb, she rounded the front of the auto to help McCoy out. As he stood, he grabbed her, pinning her tightly against the car. His hand held her face as she pressed her lips closed. When his mouth found hers, the scent of scotch permeating his breath made her gag. When he finished with his attempted kiss, she put her arm under his shoulder, guiding him toward the door.

Once inside the elaborate entrance, Billi looked down the mezzanine, across the shining floors, to the screened off portion that now served as operating rooms. Replacing the once opulent chandeliers, sterile Army-issue lamps hung from bleak cords down the entire stretch of the seemingly endless hallway.

Two nurses stepped swiftly from behind the counter with concerned looks.

"He hit his head on an oar." Billi announced.

One white capped nurse quickly held a towel against his head.

"Here are his car keys. Thank you for the valuable information, Captain McCoy." Billi stepped back across the glamorous foyer toward the door, then turned back toward the nurses struggling with the weight of their patient. "Oh, his wife, Alice, should be notified that he's alive and well."

Outside, Billi opened the car door to reach for her purse she had left on the seat. It was gone. She stood to look around. There was no one in sight.

Unnerved, Billi headed down Breakers Row. No lights shone from the windows and the pathway remained in the darkness of the blackout. It was only a short distance to the Biltmore, so she set a swift pace. She mulled over how to explain losing her identification, not to mention coming in this late. She ignored the fact this incident would bring many demerits, ruining her chances with the Coast Guard. She would think of something.

The reverberating of a car behind her made her pause. It did not speed up or pass her. She turned to see a black sedan slinking slowly up to her. The black night made any identification impossible. Her heart caught in her throat as she turned toward the ocean. Squeezing between the low bushes and a palm tree that flanked the lawn of the hotel, she sprinted across the grounds sticking to the dense shadows.

The sound of pounding feet behind her drove her forward. She leapt over the short wall, landing in the sand. Crouching low, she scurried down the beach but the waves cresting against the shore smothered any other sound. When she felt a hand catch her wrist, she spun to defend herself. The arm she swung through the air was snatched with brute force and before she could scream lips pressed against her. They tasted of cigar and scotch. They tasted of her husband.

She relaxed into Jack's embrace, tears forming, as she reached for his face. Her finger gently ran down the side of his brow, over the strip of material that held his patch in place. It was Jack. She was not dreaming.

Footsteps crunched on the walkway from somewhere near The Breakers. Jack scooped her up, carrying her further into the dark as they waited for the night watch to continue his rounds.

"How did you find me?" She whispered.

"You never make it easy."

She heard the lust in his voice and responded with a kiss. Passion possessed them as they worked silently at each other's clothing. Soon the warm night air whisked across their naked bodies, the cool sand became their bed, the only light the stars in the dark heavens.

Exhausted and exhilarated, Billi sat up. The fine granules clung to her damp skin like sparkling armor, a testament of their lovemaking. Filled with joy, she ran into the surf, splashing the soothing water over her. She felt Jack's body press against hers, as he ran his hands down her back and arms, cleansing away the rough coating. She floated on the waves before him, letting him remove the last bits of sand. When he pulled her to him, she savored the salt on his body and felt the heat of his desire. She slid her legs around him, holding him close against the weightlessness of the ocean.

Man and woman, husband and wife, bound by love, torn by war. Their brief flashes of passion reflecting the story of so many. She held her eyes wide open searching the sky, fearful if she closed them, she would wake from this dream.

They would make it, together. Eddy would be home soon. The war would end bringing soldiers, such as Danny, home alive. She believed this wholeheartedly. While the stars bore witness to her prayers, Jack held her tenderly preventing her from drifting on the soothing surf. He was her anchor.

Jack watched Billi glide up the stairs of the Biltmore as his heart turned to steel. He had no answer for what had just happened. The image of their lovemaking made it hard to breathe. He could feel every inch of her being as they tossed in the surf and clung to each other on the sand. Yet, he had witnessed her kiss the captain, willingly. He was weak. He had not been truthful and lies break unions. But then again, their world depended on lies to get to the truth.

He had so many questions to ask her but the touch of her skin, the nearness of her body had drained him of reason. Their closeness rekindled his passion and love for her. He would put aside his mistrust then talk with her later.

Remembering he still had her purse, he slid it from under the car seat. Feeling the unusual weight of her handbag, he snapped the clutch open. His hand began to shake with anger. His mind went wild at the sight of the wad of money. Had she turned to gambling? Or worse yet, exchanging favors?

"Shit." He tossed her purse to the floor, punching the steering wheel with his fist. His heart burst with the only choice set before him. He would have his attorney draw up divorce papers to set this wild Ginger free.

His tires squealed beneath him as he pulled out into the first rays of sunlight. He needed time to think. But for now, he needed to be as far away as possible from the stranger that was his wife.

The casualties of this brutal war were not just found on the battlefield. They lingered behind every door where lovers, parents and children waited for guns to be laid down and peace to provide an opportunity for new beginnings. Yet, some casualties cut even deeper with their betrayal. The discovery that the person you cherished, the one you vowed to love into eternity had deserted your dreams, slicing at your heart and soul with the intensity beyond that of a sharpened blade, left an unbearable scar.

Jack reminded himself of his duty to his country, to help end global aggression. Peace must be attained at all costs. Setting his sights on that singular objective, he pledged never to let the distraction and blindness of love sidetrack his path again.

Streaking past the Biltmore, he fought to control his flood of spiraling emotions. He felt bile rise in his throat as his hatred for Akio intensified. Akio was the root of Billi's departure. She would have been by his side if she had not become the target of the ruthless assassins.

Jack's breath came in short gasps as his vow to find Akio took a darker, more desperate direction. Killing Akio would not bring his wife back to him. But it might heal some of the pain from the loss of the woman he loved, the beautiful blue eyed Billi.

Revenge. Once again the ancient proverb came to mind;

*When you set out for revenge, dig two graves.*

Not this time he assured himself. The clarity of his mission set him at ease. He would seek the Japanese spy to the ends of the earth—then dig one grave.

# BOOK THREE

B E ASSURED THAT BOOK THREE OF this trilogy is already in the making. This next novel will continue to follow the same characters through to the end of the Second World War.

In the interim, please follow the author's blogs which incorporate some of her interviews with the men and women from WWII. Frisino has taken these true stories and woven them into her character's actions. Thus, creating a historically accurate, realistic, and detailed account of the heroic struggles on many different fronts during WWII.

www.denisefrisino.com

# ABOUT THE AUTHOR

DENISE FRISINO, A SEATTLE NATIVE, HAS spent over seven years interviewing men and women from the Greatest Generation researching for her WWII trilogy, which includes this book. The stories she collected are entwined with the actions of her characters to maintain a true sense of that era and the impact of this devastating global war.

At the early age of five, Denise stepped into the entertainment world and has spent her career performing on stage and camera, teaching, directing, producing, and writing. Incorporating her lifelong passion for acting into her writing, she creates vivid characters with twisting plots. Frisino has received various awards for her work.

She lives with her husband, Steve, and spends her spare time boating or on trails hiking through the woods.

\* \* \*

THIS TRILOGY IS NOT MEANT to just entertain but to present a deeper understanding of this time in our history, the source of much strife and transformation. While Frisino's imaginative storytelling includes the private accounts of those she interviewed, some names she mentioned, the settings, the spying, and the battles are very real.

# OTHER BOOKS BY THE AUTHOR

## ORCHIDS TRILOGY

BOOK ONE—set pre-WWII
### Orchids Of War
*The Untold Story of Japanese Spies in the US Before World War II*

BOOK TWO—set Pearl Harbor to 1943
### Storms From A Clear Sky
*The Story of Spies, Love & Loyalty In a War-torn World*

WATCH FOR BOOK THREE—set 1943 and continues to the wars end.

* * *

### Whiskey Cove
A novel about Prohibition set in the Northwest